ALSO AVAILABLE FROM BLOOM BOOKS

CANE BROTHERS

A Not So Meet Cute

So Not Meant to Be

A Long Time Coming

BRIDESMAID FOR HIRE

Bridesmaid for Hire

Bridesmaid Undercover

Bridesmaid by Chance

BAY AREA PLAYERS

Just for the Cameras

Just for the Plot

How My Neighbor Stole Christmas

Merry Christmas, You Filthy Animal

Till Summer Do Us Part

Rules for the Summer

JUST FOR THE PLOT

MEGHAN QUINN

Bloom books

The characters and events portrayed in this book are fictitious or are used fictitiously. Any similarity to real persons, living or dead, is purely coincidental and not intended by the author.

Published by Bloom Books, an imprint of Sourcebooks
1935 Brookdale RD, Naperville, IL 60563-2773
(630) 961-3900
sourcebooks.com

Cataloging-in-Publication data is on file with the Library of Congress.

Printed and bound in the United States of America.
WOZ 10 9 8 7 6 5 4 3 2 1

I'm lovingly dedicating this book to my walking pad. I would have been sedentary without you while writing this book. Thank you for helping me get my steps in while writing about Bennett diddling Bower. We got steamy together on so many levels.

PROLOGUE
BENNETT

Bennett—Sixteen years old

"BENNETT, HURRY UP." GABBY, MY big sister, bangs on the bathroom door. "Bower will be here any second and I don't want you in the shower when she arrives."

I open the door, startling her so much that her hand falls to her chest.

"What's the big deal? She's just your friend," I reply, trying not to act like the annoyed sixteen-year-old that I am, because my sister takes care of me. She makes sure there's a roof over our heads—even if it's a one-bedroom apartment that we share—and despite the toll on her, she brought us closer to Almond Bay so I have a better chance of getting scouted for baseball. *Yes, I'm grateful. But she's still annoying me right now.* Hence the rant.

"I know, but this is the first time she's going to be at our place since we've moved, and well, I don't need your scrawny body waltzing out in a towel."

I glance down at my jeans and T-shirt and then back up at my sister. "Not naked."

"I can see that, thank you."

Bower has been friends with Gabby for almost a year now, but because of their schedules, including school, I've never met her, only heard about her.

I know she's funny.

She cares for my sister.

And that her dad is the manager at the Olive Garden they both work at, and if Gabby asks for it, she's always given overtime, because Bower's family understands our situation.

Foster kids growing up until Gabby turned eighteen, when she pulled me out of the system with her, begging our foster parents to let us, even swearing they could keep the government assistance, just not to bother us.

Still don't know how she was able to do that, but now we're out on our own. My job is to train while she works to pay our bills. And there are months when all we eat is leftover soup from Olive Garden that's going to be thrown out along with stale breadsticks, but we make the most of it.

Now that I'm sixteen and she's twenty-four, we have a system that works for us. A system that keeps us out of trouble, that keeps us together, and that will lift me into a position to make the most of our dreams.

Gabby glances around our small, five-hundred-square-foot apartment. "Should I vacuum again?"

"No." I groan as I move past her. "She's your friend. I don't think she's going to care that you vacuumed twice before she arrived."

"I know, you're right, but her family has been so supportive of us. I just want her to know that we're okay."

"She will know," I say as I flop back on the couch, the smell of Gabby's Crock-Pot chicken making my stomach ache. It's rare when she buys chicken because it's so expensive, but when she does, I devour it, especially since it's a far cry from the barely buttered noodles or soup we usually eat.

Knock. Knock.

Gabby's eyes fly to the door and then back to me. Whispering, she says, "That's her. Be nice."

"As if I wouldn't." I roll my eyes while she answers the door. If anything, if it's important to my sister, then it's important to me.

"Gabby," a sweet but excited voice sounds through the apartment. "Oh my God, this place is so cute."

"Thank you. It was a good find after, well, you know..."

After Gabby had to live in a car for a week while I stayed with a friend because her abusive boyfriend hit her in the head with a bottle, but you know, we're not talking about that anymore.

My fingers curl into the cushion of the couch as I attempt to regulate the anger that's still simmering in the pit of my stomach from that situation. I can't think about it or I might just take retribution.

"Oh, you must be Bennett."

I glance up, my eyes focusing on the drop-dead gorgeous girl in front of me.

Holy.

Shit.

Long, golden blond hair, straight and tucked behind her ears, letting the insanely light green of her eyes take center stage, highlighted under thick, black lashes and black eyeliner. Her lips are coated in some sort of gloss, pouty and pink, while a beauty mark rests just above the right of her lip.

Jesus...

"Uh, yeah." I clear my throat and stand, trying not to be awkward as I hold my hand out to her. "Nice to, uh, nice to meet you."

"Ooo, the manners, good job, Gabby." Bower smiles brightly at me. "Nice to meet you too, Bennett. I've heard so much about you."

"Thank you. I mean, you're welcome...wait, no, thank you," I say stupidly. *Fucking smooth, bro.*

She smirks and drops my hand just as Gabby's alarm goes off. "Oh shoot, that's the laundry. I have to go switch it."

"Want me to grab it?" I ask, sticking my hands in my back pockets.

"No, I have some...well, some underwear I don't need my little brother fondling."

"Fondling." My voice cracks awkwardly. "I wouldn't…I'd never do that, Gabby."

She chuckles. "I know, but it's fine. I can handle it. I'll be right back. You good staying here?" she asks Bower.

"Of course," Bower says, waving her off, giving me a chance to take the rest of her in. She's wearing a pair of yoga pants with a waistband that folds over her hips, keeping them low cut and showing off a few inches of her toned and tanned stomach. Her white V-neck shirt clings to her torso while the neckline dips just low enough to give me a view of her ample cleavage.

Shit, she's so hot.

"Great, be right back." Gabby takes off, and Bower turns to me, her eyes so freaking hypnotizing that I immediately get lost in them. Like a, uh…mossy field or something. I don't know, I'm no poet, but if I were one, I could spend hours just staring—

"Bennett?"

"Huh?" I ask.

"I asked if we could chat for a moment before Gabby gets back?"

"Oh, uh, sure." I lead her to the couch where we both take a seat, her sitting comfortably on one end, me having a near panic attack from the scent of her perfume swirling all around me.

"Okay, I'm glad I have a chance to speak with you, because after what happened with Gabby's ex and her need to blow it off as nothing, I felt this very protective instinct fall over me."

"Me too," I say.

"I'm sure. I couldn't imagine what you must have been feeling that day. And since she's my bestie, I want to make sure that she's not only taken care of, but that she's not, well…lying about anything. I love her, but she made it seem like everything was good with her ex, when clearly it wasn't."

"Yeah, he was a dick."

"Exactly. And I was thinking, she does such a wonderful job of making sure you have everything you need and caring for you, it's her top priority, but I don't think she ever pauses for a moment to take care of herself. Nor does she communicate with either of us about what she needs."

"Because she claims she doesn't need anything."

"I think we can both agree that's a lie."

I nod, because it is.

"Then, if it's okay with you, I would be grateful if you give me your phone number so if anything comes up, or if we see anything off about Gabby, we can communicate and help her out, even when she denies the need for help."

Wow...I can guarantee you that never in my life have I heard anyone want to take care of my sister the way that I want to take care of her. She spends countless hours working, paying for our shelter, or food, providing for us so that I can have a future. She has set aside so much of her life so I can chase my dream of becoming a professional baseball player that I've ingrained it in my mind that when it happens, the roles will be reversed and I'll be the one taking care of her. But to have someone else want to do that now, want to keep her safe and protected, it hits different.

Makes me feel like this weight that's sitting on my chest is a little less heavy.

Do I have hearts in my eyes?

Because that's what it feels like.

"Do you mind?" she asks. "If I get your phone number?"

"Oh, uh, sure. That's cool."

"Great." She sighs with relief. "I appreciate it. I know this is so heavy for you, but Gabby told me you've grown up faster than any other kid your age, so I thought you could handle helping out."

"I want to help out. I love my sister and just want the best for her."

"I know." Bower smiles softly. "If you're good with it, hand me your phone and I can text myself with it."

"Oh, it's, uh, it's not one of those fancy phones or anything," I say.

"Doesn't matter." She waves her hand at me. "I couldn't care less and you shouldn't either."

Shit, she's cool.

"Sure." I pull my flip phone from my pocket and hand it to her.

"Perfect." She enters her number into my phone and then hands it back to me. "I texted myself so I have your number too. I really appreciate this, Bennett. And feel free to text me if you ever need anything, okay? I love your sister so much. She's helped me through a lot and I want to be there for her just as much as she's there for me, but her stubborn pride tends to get in the way."

"Something I know a lot about."

"And let's make a promise right now to be as transparent as possible. We don't want another situation like she had with her ex." She points at me. "Truth only."

Oddly, I just met this girl and because she's best friends with Gabby, I'm putting all my trust in her. I nod. "Truth only."

Bennett—Seventeen years old

Bennett: Did Gabby go into work today?

Bower: No, why? Did she tell you she was?

Bennett: Fuck, she did. I knew she was lying.

Bower: Okay, no need to panic. I'm assuming she's gone now. Do you have any idea where she is?

Bennett: No idea. She said she was going into work, but she left her work apron and cash.

Bower: Let me casually ask her where she is.

Bennett: Let me know as soon as you can.

A few minutes later…

Bower: I know where she is. She's safe.

Bennett: Where is she?

Bower: Just worry about going to practice and she will be home in a bit.

Bennett: You promised transparency. If I'm not going to lie to you, you can't lie to me.

Bower: Bennett, trust me on this.

Bennett: Bower, tell me.

Bower: Ugh, fine. She was going out to get you a present, found something on the marketplace and had to drive two hours to get it.

Bennett: And she didn't bring you?! That's not fucking safe.

Bower: Trust me, I already yelled at her about it. But she's safe and driving back. For what it's worth, you're going to love the gift.

Bennett: I don't care. I care that she could have gotten hurt.

Bower: Same, but let's just say she's good. Okay?

Bennett: Fine.

Bower: Hey, it's good. Now…how was baseball practice?

Bennett: Don't change the subject when I'm mad.

Bower: Can't be mad forever…especially when she gives you that present.

Bennett—Eighteen years old

Bower: Happy birthday, Mr. Eighteen! Any plans?

Bennett: Gabby has something planned. By the way, did she tell you about the guy she met at the bar? He tipped her two hundred dollars. Do I need to be worried?

Bower: The only thing you need to be worried about is the gift I have for you.

Bennett: Why?

Bower: Gabby might have given me access to some of your teenage pictures.

Bennett: Please...please don't.

Bower: Too late for that. By the way, thanks for the tip on the shoes I got for Gabby. You're right, she never would have taken them.

Bennett: She doesn't like to take anything from you.

Bower: I know, but I told her I got them for me and they were too tight and I couldn't return them. She took them, tried to pay me, so I told her I got them on super discount for fifteen dollars.

Bennett: She bought it?

Bower: Of course, I'm super convincing.

Bennett—Twenty years old

Bennett: Are you planning a party for Gabby?

Bower: I was. I was going to text you to see what your schedule was like. I know she said she didn't want a graduation party, but she got her teaching degree, and we need to celebrate.

Bennett: I agree. I could probably sneak home this weekend, we have an off day.

Bower: Perfect. I'll put things in motion. So excited to see you, it's been a while. How have you been? Met any girls?

Bennett: Things are fine.

Bower: That doesn't answer the question. Did you finally lose that virginity of yours?

Bennett: I lost it when I was seventeen.

Bower: What?? To whom?

Bennett: Someone who was extremely disappointed with my performance.

Bower: LOL!! We can't all be perfect our first time. You'll get better.

Bennett: Already am.

Bower: Ooo, love the confidence, big man.

Bennett—Twenty-two years old

Bennett: Coach Rowley and Gabby? WHAT THE FUCK?? Did you know?

Bower: Of course I knew. I encouraged it. He's so hot.

Bennett: Bower! That's my former coach.

Bower: I know, and he's hot and apparently has an amazing penis from what your sister has told me. Don't blame her. She needed a good boning.

Bennett: Jesus Christ.

Bower: What do you expect from her? To close up shop? No way! You're getting laid every two seconds down there in the minor leagues, and she should get herself some as well.

Bennett: It's not every two seconds.

Bower: Actually, you're right. At least not when it comes to your crush. Whatever happened to that?

Bennett: Nothing. She's not interested.

Bower: Are you sure? Did you even try? You play the shy and innocent, but we both know that's far from the truth. That's how you score the ladies. Maybe she's different.

Bennett: She is different. Different from everyone I've ever met.

Bower: OH MY GOD! Then you need to go for it. What are you doing?

Bennett: Waiting.

Bower: Waiting for what?

Bennett: For the right moment.

CHAPTER 1
BENNETT

Bennett—Twenty-four years old

"BREAKFAST BURRITO. CHORIZO, POTATOES, EGGS, and refried beans," Nolan says as he tosses me a wrapped burrito and then takes a seat next to me in the locker room. "Said to be the finest out of all the ballparks, but I'll be the fucking judge of that."

He kicks back his recliner, propping his legs up, and then starts unwrapping his breakfast burrito.

Nolan joined the team last year, during my first full year with the Bombers. He was traded from the Chicago Rebels after one year in the majors. A fast-as-fuck right fielder, he's fast becoming a fan favorite among the Bombers fans for his gives-no-shits attitude on social media, prominent breakfast burrito reviews, along with his combination of crop tops and dirty mids during warm-ups.

And for those who might not know what a dirty mid is, it's the styling of his baseball pants, tight as fuck, reaching just below his calf muscle, a capri length. There are very few, and I mean very few players who can pull off the look, but Nolan with his burst fade, curly mullet, sleeve tattoo, and friendship bracelets he tends to wear...well, he pulls it off.

With a giant bite in his mouth, he examines the burrito as he says, "Shit, this is pretty damn good."

I chuckle and then start unwrapping mine as well. "Would you say the best?"

"Can't make that kind of assessment just yet." He takes another bite and then moans. "Fuck, this shit is so good, though."

I join him and have to admit it's pretty fucking good.

"So how's the zoo going?"

I sigh and tip my recliner back as well. The rest of the team is milling about. We have hours before the game, so we're all just hanging out, doing our own thing.

"The whole thing is so dumb."

"Yeah, having to do PR for a team that cheated when you weren't around, that shit sucks."

He's right. It does suck.

When I was in the minors, the Bombers were caught cheating, stealing signs from other teams and relaying them. It was a huge fuckup, and the Bombers have paid the price dearly. And because I wasn't on the team at the time, but one of the fresh, young faces of a brand-new era, I was chosen as the player to help the Bombers with their PR image. And can you imagine, the Bombers were not the only ones dealing with a PR problem in San Francisco?

Nope, the Foghorns, which is the football team, and the Rogue, San Francisco's brand-new hockey expansion team, needed a lift in image as well. So they plucked me, Graydon St. John from the Foghorns, and Oden "OC" O'Connor from the Rogue to try to boost morale and improve San Fran's besmirched sports teams' reputations.

So far, not sure it's helping. Although, Graydon started a social media presence with his zookeeper and that has taken off. So maybe it's working for him, but for me, not so much.

"I think the zoo thing is not reaching the way they wanted it to, and I'm thinking about suggesting I do something else, because as much fun as it is hanging out with the lions, I don't see the impact."

"Sounds like a fucking bust." Nolan takes another bite of his burrito and moans. "Fuck me. This is better than the blow job I got last night."

I glance at him and he smirks.

"Nah, that's a lie. The blow job was phenomenal."

Shaking my head, I go to take another bite just as my phone buzzes in my pocket with a text. I wipe my fingers on one of the napkins Nolan gave me with the burrito and then grab my phone, where I see a text from Bower.

My stupid fucking heart trips all over itself from the sight of her name.

I live to see her name pop up on my phone, beg for it every single day because that's how desperate of a motherfucker I am. And I wait for her to text, because if I allowed myself to text her, to start the conversation, then it would be every hour of the goddamn day.

And it would be texts like...

Can I take you out on a date?

Please tell me you're not seeing anyone.

When will you see me as the man I am and not Gabby's little brother?

See? Desperation.

Not hiding my excitement, I set my burrito on the coffee table in front of me and open her text.

Bower: Hey, Benny Boo Boo, what are you up to?

She's the only one allowed to call me that, and it's only because I don't want to tell her not to. OC tried calling me that once and I shut it down really quick.

Bennett: Eating a breakfast burrito in the locker room. How about you?

Bower: Apartment hunting.

Bennett: What's wrong with your apartment now?

"Why are you smiling like that?" Nolan asks while poking my face.

"Like what?" I ask, attempting to hide my smile, but it's no use.

"Like you're about to come in your pants."

I raise a brow. "How do you know what I look like when I'm about to come in my pants?"

"Oh…I know."

Rolling my eyes, I turn back to my phone to see her typing out a response.

"Who are you talking to?" Nolan presses.

"Just a friend."

"Uh-huh." I can feel his eyes burning into me. "You're a fucking liar, dude. I don't smile like that when you text me."

"Clearly you don't love me enough," I answer just as my phone buzzes.

Bower: Well, you see, I might be moving.

Bennett: To where? Almond Bay? Gabby will freak out if you finally move closer to her.

Bower: Funny, I will be moving closer to a Brinkman, just not her.

I can feel all the blood drain from my face and straight to my goddamn dick. My neck heats up and I sit taller in my seat.

Bennett: Wait, are you moving to San Francisco?

Bower: I am.

"Holy fuck," I say, sitting all the way up now.

"What?" Nolan asks, mouth full of burrito.

"My gi—uh, my sister's friend is moving here."

"Uh-huh, and why is that a holy fuck moment?" He wiggles his brows at me, and honestly, what's the use?

If I'm going to spill the beans, might as well be to someone who is not attached to the situation at all. And fuck, to get this off my chest will feel good.

"Because I've had the biggest fucking crush on her ever since I met her and no woman compares to her. Ever. I've tried to shake her from my thoughts, from the way she's branded herself in my fucking soul, but it hasn't worked. She's perfect, everything about her. If she gets a place here, it means I can finally make a move, a move that I've been waiting to make for so goddamn long that it actually hurts."

Nolan blinks, studies me, and then takes a bite of his burrito. "Right on, man."

Right on? That's all he has to say to my confession? To a secret I've been safeguarding for so long?

Probably because that's Nolan.

Now if this was OC I was telling, it would be a completely different reaction.

Chuckling, I go back to my messages with Bower, trying to play it cool even though I'm as giddy as a fucking kid on Christmas morning.

Bennett: That's awesome. When do you get here?

Bower: Well, Adalade—the woman I work for—wants to be in the city by next week. She just bought a Victorian in Pac-Heights and all of her things are being moved there in two days, which means I have to be in San Fran in one day to make sure I'm at the new place for arrival. Which means this girl needs to find a place and soon.

One day.

One fucking day.

My smile stretches from ear to ear.

Bennett: You can always stay with me until you find a place.

Please say yes, please say yes.

Bower: I was actually looking at a unit in your apartment building. Would that be weird?

Fuck no. Is she kidding?

That's the best fucking news I've heard since I was called up to the majors.

If she's in the same apartment building, we could…hell, we could have dinner together, we could bring each other sugar…she can slowly start to realize that I've had a mad crush on her for so fucking long that maybe, just maybe she'd give me a chance.

Bennett: Not weird at all. Might be helpful. I could show you around, introduce you to people.

Bower: People, huh? And who would these people be, Bennett?

Bennett: You know, the people who make the coffee around the corner, the building's security guys, and the one neighbor on floor twelve who has the same meal delivered to them every night.

Bower: Ooo, busybodies, you know I like the gossip. Count me in. I'm headed into the city tomorrow with all my things, and I'm going to check out the apartment. Can I crash on your couch for a night?

My mouth goes dry and I can't type fast enough. Thank FUCK we are in town right now, because if we had away games, I might have cried.

The words of a desperate man.

Bennett: Absolutely. Stay as long as you want.

Bower: You're the absolute best. Thanks, Benny Boo Boo.

"Do you have a boner right now?" Nolan asks as he gingerly pats his face with a napkin.

"No," I answer, even though, hell, my excitement of seeing her tomorrow might possibly get me into boner territory.

"Looks like you have a boner."

I glance down at my lap, only for Nolan to let out a wallop of a laugh.

"Made you look," he says like a dick.

Irritated, I slap his burrito out of his hand, causing it to fall into his lap.

Fire builds in his eyes as he looks up at me. "You motherfucker." I stand from the recliner as he yells, "You better run!"

I take off toward the weight room to get in some reps before he can catch up.

The woman who owns my heart will finally be in my neighborhood… About fucking time I get to make that move.

CHAPTER 2
BENNETT

THIS FUCKING PIECE OF HAIR.

It keeps sticking up in a weird way, and no matter what I do, it won't submit to me.

I pat it down, once, twice…thrice!

And nothing.

So I turn off my bathroom light and go to my closet, where I pick out a Bombers cap and place it on my head. Whatever, I don't want to look like I'm trying too hard, and all she's really known me to wear is a hat, so this would be normal.

Now, the few spritzes of cologne that smells like fresh laundry, that's new, as well as the T-shirt I'm wearing that is loose around my waist but tight around my biceps. Biceps that I've worked so fucking hard to build.

She met me when I was sixteen, scrawny, awkward, and unsure of my body, but I'm not that boney boy anymore. I'm twenty-four now, a major league baseball player with enough muscle on my body to do damage. I also grew into my frame, topping off at six foot three. I know I'm going to tower over her, so much so that her head will meet my chest as her arms wrap around my waist.

I spent last night after the game—that we lost—cleaning up my place, making sure there wasn't a speck of dirt on a baseboard or floor. I vacuumed my couch several times, lint-rollered it, and then sprayed some of that nice-smelling shit on it. I spent too much goddamn time arranging a candle on my coffee table, moving it left, right, and center until I gave up and replaced it with a book about baseball facts. I considered taking down my framed jerseys I have from my high school team and minor league teams, but it felt wrong. So I kept them up, but I did clean them, just in case.

And now that she's going to be here any second, I'm nervous, excited, fucking bursting at the seams to see her.

It's been a while, a few months, since I'm in the middle of my season. I think the last time I saw her was over the holidays when I was visiting Gabby and her husband, Ryland, in Almond Bay. Wait, I know that's the last time I saw her, because she was telling Gabby all about a guy she was dating and how he had some sort of foot fetish and was constantly giving her toe rings to wear.

Hoping that since she's moving, that guy is out of the picture now.

Because with him out of the picture, I'm sure with my track record, I'll just stare at her from afar, never make a move, and then watch her go off with someone else.

I drag my hand over my face.

Christ.

Here I am, pretending like I'm actually going to do something about her being here, but as time ticks by, closer and closer to her arrival, I feel myself grow more and more nervous.

Because, yeah, she might be moving here, but does that mean I'm actually going to do something about it?

I tug on the brim of my hat…

I should.

I really should do something about it.

I've wanted this for so fucking long, and now that there's a chance, a small chance at that—she is eight years older than me, my sister's best friend, and calls me fucking Benny Boo Boo—there still could be an opportunity for me to flip the way she looks at me.

I take a deep breath, thinking about the other women I've been with, how they haven't interested me in the slightest. How they're just my attempt to fill a void, a void that I know only Bower can fill.

But can I really do this?

Can I make a move?

I tug on my bottom lip just as there's a knock at the door.

My stomach bottoms out and my palms break into a sweat.

Fuck, keep it together.

Nerves buzzing through me, I open the door and my heart nearly leaps out of my chest as Bower comes into view, looking so fucking beautiful that it takes everything in me not to cup her cheek, bend down, and kiss her.

"Bennett!" she shouts as she drops her bags and walks right into my chest, wrapping her arms around me.

Fucking fulfilled.

I sink into her hold, my arms encircling her, my chin resting on the top of her head as I breathe in her sweet scent of coconut. As I memorize everything about this moment, like I have with every other hug we've shared, her hands travel up my back as she tightens her hold on me.

I revel in it.

In the feel of her wrapped around me.

In her softness.

In her fucking presence.

"Hey," I say softly, my hand cupping the back of her head for a moment before she pulls away and looks up at me, her hands gripping my forearms.

"Oh my God, you're so…muscular."

I feel my cheeks heat from the compliment.

"That's what happens when you're required to hit up the weight room."

She pats my chest with a smirk. "Required? Please, you know you love it."

She turns around to grab her bags, and I quickly glance at the way her leggings frame her perfectly round ass and how her shirt rides up, showing me an inch of her skin.

"Let me grab those for you," I say, moving to her side and snagging her bags before she can.

"I'd say I got it, but you have to put those muscles to good use."

I pull her bags into the apartment and she shuts the door for us before taking my hand in hers and practically skipping to the couch, where she pulls me down to talk.

Her honey-blond hair fans out around her shoulders in long waves, while her light green eyes shine up at me. Her nose ring is no longer a hoop, but rather a small diamond, and instead of eyeliner on her top and bottom lids, she just has mascara, with a hint of blush caressing her cheeks.

"So tell me everything." That stunning smile of hers fucking gut punches me.

"Everything?" I ask, fidgeting with my hat as I adjust it on my head.

"Yeah, like...do you have any girls in your life?"

Always one of her top questions. She loves asking about my relationship status, and it might seem like I'm a total loser, but I always give her the same answer.

"Nope."

"Seriously?" she asks, pushing at my knee. "No one?"

I shake my head. "No one really catches my attention."

Besides you.

You captured my attention.

"Are you even trying?" she asks, a tease in her voice.

"Not really."

She chuckles. "Typical Bennett. Probably just focused on baseball, right?"

"Pretty much. What about you?" I ask, feeling my throat grow tight with nerves. "Do you have any guys in your life?"

She rolls her eyes dramatically and props her hand against the couch.

"Ugh, no. I was seeing this one guy. We went on three dates, but he just wasn't doing it for me."

"Why not?" I ask, wanting to learn from this fool's mistakes.

Her eyes find mine. "Promise not to judge me?"

"Depends," I say playfully.

She crosses her legs and leans forward, taking my answer as a go-ahead to spill anyway. "He didn't pass the name test."

"What's the name test?" I ask.

"You really don't know?"

I shake my head. "Nope."

"Bennett, the name test is a very important test. It basically tells you if you're compatible or not in bed."

My brows raise. "Oh?"

She nods slowly. "You have to test the person's name on a moan, and if it sounds good, then you can move forward. And let me tell you, he did not pass the test."

"What was his name?"

Her nose crinkles. "Ebenezer."

"It was not fucking Ebenezer," I say on a laugh and a shake of my head. "No fucking way was his name Ebenezer."

"It was." Her eyes widen in sincerity. "I swear. Ebenezer and his friends called him Nezer."

"Jesus, that's not great either."

"Yeah, so tell me how I'm supposed to have this man's dick deep between my legs with 'give it to me hard, Ebenezer' coming off my lips?"

I laugh and tug on the back of my neck, wondering if I pass the name test. Also, hate to admit it, but hearing Bower say *dick deep* might have made me slightly hard.

"Yeah, that doesn't pass the test."

"Exactly." She tosses her hands in the air. "I had to end it. Might be superficial, but anytime I tried to use his name in a sexual way, it just made my nipples invert, and let me tell you something, Bennett"—she gestures to her perfect fucking tits—"these nipples are made to poke against the fabric of my shirt, not hide."

Jesus…

"Can't have inverted nipples," I say, unsure of how to respond to that, especially since my eyes land on her tits for a moment, taking in too much of a fill than I probably should.

"Exactly, so Ebenezer had to go. How I even went on three dates is beyond me. Probably because I'm horny all the time."

Okay, not information I needed to hear when I'm half-hard, but then again, it's Bower. She's never been shy about anything.

"I was reading this book the other day where the female main character came just from nipple play." She grips my forearm. "Nipple play, Bennett. Have you ever come from just nipple play?"

No, but pretty sure I can come just from talking about it right now.

"Can't say that I have."

"Me, either, but I want to have that experience, and let me tell you, Ebenezer was not the guy to do it." She tucks her hair behind her ear. "I love my books, more than anything, but do you think they're setting my standards too high? Is it too much to ask to pass the name test and to make me come from nipple play?"

Christ, I'm so hard right now.

Because, no, I don't think that's too much to ask.

And if she'd give me a chance, I'd love to try.

"I don't think that's too much to ask."

"Really? Because Gabby was saying I should stop reading my books, then I went and told her that was easy for her to say given the dick she has at home and how absolutely satisfied she is every time she mounts it."

"Yeah, maybe we don't talk about my sister and former coach's sex life."

"Oh, we're all adults." She waves her hand at me. "Anyway, I'm hoping this move is a new chapter for me, and I get to have you, Benny Boo Boo, as my wingman in a new town." She takes my hand in hers. "Seriously, thanks for helping me out. I checked out the apartment and I love it. I filled out the application, and if I get it, I think I might just live here. It'll be fun being so close to someone I know. Oh, and when you're away, I can take care of your place for you." She glances around. "Doesn't seem like you have any plants or anything, but you know, I can check up on things for you either way."

Hope springs in my chest because I can't imagine a more perfect scenario.

Actually, I can. It would be Bower moving in here, with me.

"That would be awesome," I say, trying not to sound too excited.

"It's settled then. We're neighbors. Now, don't you have a game tonight you have to get to?"

"I do, but I wanted to make sure you were settled before I took off for the stadium."

"I'm good. You know I can handle myself." She bounces on her butt. "And this couch is going to be incredibly comfortable, so thanks for letting me sleep on it."

"Oh, I was going to let you take my bed and I can take the couch. I just changed my sheets."

"Yeah, that's not happening." She pats my cheek. "Cute of you for thinking that, though, and don't even fight me on it. I don't need you acting all chivalrous. I like a good couch."

"Yeah, but I slept on a couch for almost my entire life." *Well, until Gabby gave up her bed for me every night so I had a solid sleep.* She always sacrificed herself.

"And that's exactly why you deserve the bed." She winks and then gets off the couch, grabbing her phone from her bag. Rather than sitting next to me on the couch, she sits on the armrest and holds the phone up in selfie mode. "We need to send a pic to Gabby. I didn't tell her I was moving, and this would be the perfect way."

B
BOMBERS

She loops her arm around me and rests her head against mine just as she says, “Smile.”

I smile and she snaps the picture, stealing my breath and sanity all at the same time.

She stares at it for a second and then glances at me. “Ooof, you’re so handsome. Still don’t understand how you don’t have girls falling at your feet.”

She stands and texts Gabby while I try to calm the raging heat that’s pulsing through me.

That’s the first time she’s said that to me.

Handsome.

She’s complimented me on my height, my muscles, my build, but handsome…that was the first. She has no clue that she just gave me a fucking truckload of hope.

CHAPTER 3
BOWER

"YOU WERE SUPPOSED TO MOVE closer to me, not Bennett," Gabby whines on the phone.

"I know, but I can't control where Adalade moves," I answer as I throw some popcorn in my mouth.

Once Bennett left for the stadium, I moved my bags off to the side since I'll only be here for a night, maybe two, and then went to the corner store where I picked up some snacks, because after scouring Bennett's kitchen, I realized something important. He does not consume the kind of food I want to consume.

Seaweed wraps?

Blech, what is wrong with him?

I guess that's what happens when you consume buttered noodles for your entire life—you branch out to things you never could have afforded.

But go for a wagyu steak, Bennett, not dried seaweed wraps.

Just something I'll have to teach him now that I'm here.

I have his game on in the background, something I've started doing since reading a sports romance that revolved around a baseball team. Eight books in and I was hooked, needing more baseball in my life, so I started watching the Bombers games.

And if there is one thing I learned, it's that Bennett is by far the best player on the team. Asher Peppers is downright nasty, never smiling, always approaching every situation with a scowl. And Nolan Hart is an absolute menace, but he intrigues me. I know he's friends with Bennett, so perhaps I'll ask for an introduction, if I'm brave enough.

"I know." Gabby sighs. "But I thought she really liked Almond Bay when you brought her here to visit."

"She did," I answer, "but she's a city girl through and through. What can I say? She clearly tried the country thing and it didn't work for her, despite me trying everything in my power to convince her otherwise, but the shops weren't there, and she wanted variety. Be grateful it's not New York City, like she was thinking about for a moment."

"Oh my God, that would have been my nightmare."

"Same. I don't think I could have handled New York."

"I love you, but I don't think you could have either."

"It's nice here, though, and gives you more of a reason to come visit Bennett, since I have an apartment in the same building as him."

"Wait, really?" she asks.

"Yup." Bennett gets up to bat and I watch as the camera scans up his body, showing off his thick thighs, sturdy torso, and biceps I never thought I'd see on him. He fills out that jersey better than I expected, and it's nothing I should be noticing, that's for damn sure. But it's the way his blue eyes shine under the shadow of his helmet that really catches my attention, combined with his five o'clock shadow and the intensity in his expression. I honestly don't understand how he's single. "I'll be one floor above him."

Bennett takes a strike and I can hear Ryland, Gabby's husband, in the background yell about how that was not a strike at all.

Bennett takes a step out of the box, stares at his bat, and then lets out a deep breath before tugging on his helmet and stepping back in the box. It's the same routine, every single time. He's so composed, so calm.

"Now I'm even more jealous," Gabby complains just as Bennett unleashes his hands and swings at a ball, making contact and immediately shooting it over the left field fence, like a bullet straight from a gun.

He's so impressive.

Ryland's clapping in the background while Gabby cheers for a moment and then comes back on the phone. "Sorry, Bennett just hit a home run."

"I know. I'm watching."

"You're watching?" she asks.

"Yeah, I've been watching since reading that baseball series I was telling you about. And have you read it yet?"

"Not so much."

"Ugh." I groan. "You know, it would really help me out if my best friend liked to read like I do."

"Sorry, it's just not my thing."

"Clearly." I sigh.

"Speaking of books, whatever happened to you quitting your job and opening that book truck thing you were talking about? That's a job you could have in Almond Bay."

I twirl a piece of hair with my finger. "Yeah, I still want to do that, but I don't feel like I can leave Adalade right now, with the move and everything. She still needs my help."

"She could find another assistant. You've saved up more than enough. You've built a small following on social media. You could do this."

"I know," I say, nerves blooming in my stomach from the thought of taking the leap into a dream I've had for a little bit. "Just not ready yet."

"Will you ever be ready?" she asks.

"Someday," I answer, even though I don't believe it myself.

I have dreams, I have thoughts, I have ideas, but the reality of the situation is I've never been brave enough to take the leap. I went to school to learn how to start my own small business. I took an internship with Adalade since she runs her own interior design company. She doesn't do much designing herself anymore, but rather employs others to do the job for her. Well, that internship turned into an assistant job, and that assistant job turned into an executive assistant. And now I spend my days running mindless errands for a sixty-six-year-old with a hefty credit card limit and a lot of time on her hands.

Sure, the job doesn't really give me a sense of accomplishment. There are days where I go from store to store to store looking for a pair of camel loafers that she'd like, or fetching a brownie with the perfect gooey consistency, but it does allow for me to have a lot of reading time.

It's also allowed me to dream more—dream of something more than this—but the problem is, when you dream, you must have courage to step out of your comfort zone. And I'll be honest… I'm confident, but I'm not courageous.

I've seen what dreaming can do. My dad was a dreamer, and when I was young, he took a chance on a dream and ended up losing all of our family's money. It's why Mom had to work part-time at my school. It's why he found a job at the Olive Garden. He had to start from scratch and work his way back up. I've seen the stress and the anxiety of it all, and even though the job I have isn't fulfilling in the slightest, it's safe.

Adalade loves me.

She'd never fire me.

I have security, a great paycheck, and it gives me time to do what I love…and that's read books.

"Hopefully someday soon," Gabby says, always pushing me. "But until then, when do you move into the new place?"

"They're finishing up some painting, so probably in the next day or so. Hope Bennett doesn't mind."

"He's pretty chill and he's usually at the stadium most of the time, so he probably won't even notice you there."

"Probably won't. My things are tucked away in a corner, and I haven't touched his food because your brother has some weird shit in here. Seaweed wraps and protein shakes. Gross, Gabby."

She chuckles. "Yeah, unclear where the seaweed wraps came in, but he doesn't keep a lot of food in the apartment because he's always traveling. When he's here, though, he makes sure to eat as many cherry almond cookies from The Almond Store as he can."

"So he does have a sweet tooth. Okay. Maybe I'll force him to indulge with me."

"If it's in the apartment, he will eat it."

"I might just have to test out this theory."

"Once again, I'm jealous, but maybe…maybe this will be a good thing."

"Yeah, I told you, now you can visit us both at the same time."

"No, I mean…you can watch over him a little closer. After what happened when he was in the minor leagues, when his apartment was broken into and he didn't tell me, I just…I worry he hides things from me to protect me so I don't get worried."

"Are you asking me to be a spy?" I joke.

"No, but…you know the promise you made me…"

My voice grows serious. "Gabby, I promised you I would help take care of him and that is a promise I will never break. Ever. I told you, you are not in this alone. I am here for you, helping you any way you need."

"So you'll tell me if you notice something off with him, now that you're living there? Especially with all this PR stuff they're making him do. He worked so hard on his image that I would hate…I would hate for him to take the fall for something his team did prior to him being on it."

"I get it. And you know I would tell you, I promised. You're my number one, always. And he's your brother, therefore he's my number two. Both of you fall under my protection. That's of the utmost importance to me."

"Thank you," she says softly. "I'm so grateful for you, Bower. I don't know what I would have done without you over the years. The reason I was able to raise Bennett is because of you."

"Nah, you did that yourself. I was just there cheering you on."

The lights are off.

The moon is shining through Bennett's floor-to-ceiling living room windows.

And the sheets and blankets Bennett gave me smell so freaking good I'm tempted to raid his laundry room to see what detergent he's using.

I know it takes him a second to wind down after a game. I've seen it firsthand when I've visited him with Gabby, but this is quite long.

I had some Moon Pies delivered to the apartment, hoping to share one with him when he got home, but it's getting pretty late now and I'm wondering if he's not back yet because he decided to hook up with someone.

Which if he did, great for him. I will of course hound him for all the details in the morning, because if anything, I'm invasive and have no filter.

Sighing back into my pillow, which has to be one of the softest pillows I've ever felt, I close my eyes just as the front door unlocks and I hear him walk into the apartment. He quietly shuts the door, shuffling a paper bag, and then locks up. He heads into the kitchen and I sit up on the couch.

He's trying to be quiet and it's super cute, so I slip out from under my blankets and tiptoe over to the kitchen where he's setting a bag on the counter.

Going undetected, I find the light switch and turn it on just as I say, "Welcome back."

"Jesus Christ!" he yells as he plasters himself against the cabinets and counter, hand to chest, a frightened look in his eyes.

A roar of laughter falls past my lips as I rest my hand on his arm. "Oh my God," I say in between giggles. "The look on your face."

"Uh, yeah, because you nearly made me shit myself."

I laugh some more, the fright on his face ingrained in my memory. "I want to say I'm sorry, but I'm not."

"Clearly." He chuckles. "What are you doing awake? It's almost midnight."

Calming myself, I say, "Well, I stayed up because I ordered some Moon Pies and—"

"Moon Pies?" He looks toward the living room. "Where?"

Yup, such a sweet tooth.

"Over here." I pull him toward the living room, but he stops me.

"Hold on, let me put the cold stuff in the fridge really quick."

From his bags, he pulls milk and yogurt and places them in the fridge along with some cheese and chicken.

When he shuts the fridge, he turns back toward me, so I take his hand again and drag him to the small circular dining room table where I set up the box of Moon Pies along with some napkins.

"Ta-da! I know how much you like sweet things, and as a thank-you for letting me stay the night, I bought you—but also me—some treats."

"You didn't have to get me anything," he says as he sits down, opens the box, and snags one right away before taking a bite.

Chuckling, I grab one as well. "I can see you really mean that."

He smiles while chewing. "Seriously, I do. This was really nice. Thank you."

"You're welcome and thanks for letting me stay here for a few nights—that's if a few nights is okay with you."

"Stay as long as you want," he says, his eyes looking directly into mine, causing a weird chill to shoot up my spine. It's the ice blue of his irises, they're, well...chilling.

"Thank you." I set my Moon Pie down and wipe my mouth with my napkin. "Uh...good job on the home run."

His brow lifts, his expression almost comical, because we never talk baseball. Ever. At least not recently. Whenever we text, it's always been about Gabby or stupid things like did you know cronuts existed? But never baseball, because I know nothing about it really and he, well, he doesn't seem to want to talk about it at all.

So it's very smart of me to mention it now.

"You watched the game?"

I casually shrug. "Couldn't find anything else on."

That makes him smirk. "Uh-huh, why don't I believe that?"

"Because it's not true." I break off a piece of my Moon Pie and plop it in my mouth. "I felt obligated to watch you play because I was talking to Gabby and she was watching you play as well."

"You talked to Gabby?" he asks while polishing off his dessert. He gets up from the table and asks, "Drink?"

"Please," I answer and then go back to his previous question. "Yeah, I broke the news to her. She was not happy, tried to convince me to move to Almond Bay instead and leave my job."

"Sounds about right," he says. "Did you tell her you were staying here?"

"Yeah."

"Was she okay with that?"

"Why wouldn't she be?" I ask as he brings us both a glass of water.

He shrugs. "She can be territorial over you. When she found out that we text, she kept asking if you like me better than you like her."

I laugh. "Right, well, I think I've tamped down that paranoia. But she seemed cool with it, no questions about where my loyalty stands."

"With me, right?" he asks, adding a little wink under the brim of his hat.

"Keep dreaming." I roll my eyes. "I'll always fall in line with Gabby. Sorry."

"A guy can try." He stretches his legs out under the table and leans back in his chair. "So, what did you think about the game?"

"I thought it was impressive that you could hit a baseball that far. It kind of boggles my mind knowing that you're not the same boy I first met so many years ago."

He tugs on the back of his neck, his bicep flexing against his shirt. "Yeah, not so much."

My cheeks oddly heat from the sight of it.

Which reminds me…

"So, that guy on your team…"

"What guy? There are quite a few of us."

"I want to say his name is Nolan," I hedge.

"Nolan Hart?" Bennett asks, with a bit of a pull in his brow. "What about him?"

I trace my finger over the glass of his tabletop and ask, "Is he single?"

Bennett's brow grows even tighter. "Nolan? You're interested in Nolan?"

I casually shrug. "I don't know, maybe. Is that weird for you? Me asking about one of your teammates? Even if it's just for one night, I think we could have a good time, and Lord knows I need a good time. Plus, he's hot."

Bennett moves his hand over his jaw. "Yeah, he's dating someone."

"Ugh." I crumple up my napkin and then toss it to the center of the table. "Figures. Might have been weird anyway, dating one of your teammates."

"Yeah…probably."

"Well, if he ever does become available, let me know." I stand and take a sip of my drink. "I'd love to get to know him. This girl is starting a new chapter in her life, and I'm bound and determined to get out there and meet people. Who knows, maybe the right guy is somewhere in the city looking for a slightly bookish type who doesn't have the best filter. Could be a perfect match." I offer him a wink and then take off toward the bathroom to get ready for bed.

CHAPTER 4
BENNETT

"DID YOU SEE THAT? THE giraffe took the lettuce from my hand with its tongue. Simply magnificent," OC says as he marvels at the giraffes in front of him, putting on a show for the camera.

"Cut, that's great. Thank you," the director says. "That should be good for today."

"You don't want to do that one scene I suggested?" OC asks, hope in his eyes.

"Um, that's okay." The director nods at OC. "Maybe next time."

OC winks at the director. "I'm holding you to that." Then he walks over to me and sighs. "Damn it."

"What was the scene you wanted to do?"

OC turns to me and says, "I had a vision. It was supposed to be with me and Graydon, but since he bounced early from these PR promos, I was going to suggest you."

"Yeah, and what did you suggest?" I ask, knowing damn well whatever he's about to say, Graydon never would have participated.

This trio of ours, I'd describe it as eclectic. We have the grumpy, broody asshole football player who's struggling with his feelings for a certain flamingo zookeeper. OC, who plays the fool, can be intensely annoying but also has a huge heart. And then me, who is smack dab in the middle of those two personalities. I can be grumpy, but not like Graydon, who snorts steam when he's angry. And I can get on board with

OC's antics, but not to the extent where I'm poking the bear—that is Graydon—that should never be poked.

"My thought was we reenact the scene from *Ghost* with Demi Moore and Patrick Swayze, where he holds her from behind and teaches her how to work the clay, but instead of clay, it's me helping you feed the giraffes while whispering into your ear."

Given the joy in his expression as he tells me his idea, I almost feel bad telling him he's an idiot, but that doesn't stop me.

"You're an idiot."

His expression falls. "You know, I'd expect that kind of response from Graydon, but not from you."

"I think you should expect that response from anyone you tell that idea to." My phone buzzes in my pocket and I pull it out, seeing two messages, which I must have missed while I was watching OC "delicately" feed a giraffe.

The first one's from Nolan.

Nolan: By the gate when you're ready.

I quickly shoot him a text back, letting him know I'll be right out. I had to take my car in for some new tires today and Nolan said he'd help me out.

The next text is from Bower, which of course makes me smile because I'm a fucking fool and can't help it.

Bower: Okay, don't get mad, but I might have spilled some juice on your carpet. I have spent a lot of time trying to make it seem like it didn't happen. But this V8 juice you got has some powerful staining capabilities and you can still see a faint outline of it. I'm headed to the store to get more products to clean it, but just in case you get home and see it, I didn't want you to think I'd been stabbed and stolen. It was just me being clumsy. Also, I'm sorry and I promise I'll get it out.

Hell, is it too pathetic of me to want her to keep the stain, because then it will remind me of her every time I walk past it?

Probably.

Bennett: Don't worry if you can't get it out. It's fine. No biggie.

"Who are you cheating on me with?" OC asks, arms folded, looking irritated.

"What?" I ask, pocketing my phone and waving to the crew as I take off and head toward the back gate exit.

"I can tell you're cheating on me with someone you're texting."

"Can you not say I'm cheating on you? Jesus, man."

"Is it Graydon? Do you guys have a secret text thread that I'm not included in? Because that would just about kill me. You know I'm already struggling with the trade, this new PR situation, and not being able to fix things with my ex. I'm delicate."

"Trust me, I know. Delicate and…needy."

He follows me toward the gate. "You know, each and every day, you're starting to sound more and more like Graydon."

Knowing he is going through a tough time, I turn to him and say, "I'm not cheating on you, trust me. I can't possibly take on another friend like you."

He places his hand against his chest, relief spilling through his muscles as he relaxes. "Thank Jesus. You know I've been struggling, especially with Grace not answering my messages. I thought she might want to get back together, but I just…I don't think that's going to happen."

I pat him on the shoulder. "Maybe that's the best thing for both of you."

He shakes his head and then grows serious. "I can't get her out of my head."

Fuck if I know that feeling all too well.

"And this trade to the Rogue has made the situation harder."

"I get it, man. Maybe give it a day or two and reach out again."

"Yeah, maybe," he says and then sighs. "You headed to the stadium?"

"Yup. Game tonight."

"Well, good luck. Hit me a home run."

My brow pinches together. "Yeah, don't see that happening."

"You fucking wound me," he says as I move past the gate and spot Nolan in his light blue Porsche Macan.

I open the door and take a seat, buckling up as he speeds off out of the parking lot.

"Jesus," I say, gripping on to the handle, my back flying against the seat.

He chuckles. "Got to love the acceleration capabilities of an electric vehicle. Will blast your dick right off."

"I'd prefer to keep my dick intact."

"Yeah, but what's life without a little wind in your…frenulum."

"Jesus." I cringe. "What is wrong with you?"

"Grew up on a nudist compound."

"Really?" I ask, glancing at him and the fresh burst fade he must have gotten this morning.

"No." He laughs. "But fucking imagine growing up and walking around with your parents fucking nude as the day they were born." He shivers. "That shit is not for me."

"Yeah, me either." I stare out the front window as we come to a stoplight. "Hey, so you know that girl that gave you the blow job the other night, the phenomenal one?"

"Do I know her? She made me see fucking Zeus, dude. I touched pointer fingers with him just as I came down her throat."

Why do I feel like Nolan and OC would be best friends?

"Yeah, well, are you dating her?"

He glances at me, a smile tugging on his lips. "Why? You want to experience the power of Zeus yourself?"

"What? No." I shake my head. "No, that's not..."

He chuckles. "Dude, your face is red."

Yeah, I can feel my cheeks heating.

"That's not why I was asking."

"Why were you asking? Looking for a sister or a best friend with the same technique? I'd ask her but don't have her number. She was a random hookup, but I can tell you where I met her, maybe we can scout out the bar and ask her questions about her blow job techniques."

I did not enter into this topic of conversation correctly, I can see that now.

"No, I was just wondering if you were dating anyone."

"Oh...why? You interested?"

I drag my hand down my face, exasperated with this conversation. "Not for me. I have a friend that was interested in you, but I told her that you were dating someone."

"Interested in me?" He glances at me. "I could see that. I'm fucking hot and women love the crop top. What's her name? I can tell her you were misinformed and take her out tonight after the game."

Over my dead fucking body.

Also, I do think women like the crop top, as it shows off his stupid abs. The number of signs I see for him in the stands every day is fucking stupid. Then again, there are a lot for me as well and I'm not wearing crop tops...

But back to the matter at hand.

"She's not up for grabs."

"Oh?" he asks, glancing over at me. "Wait, is this the girl that makes you come in your pants when she texts you?"

"I do not come in my pants." But my dick might get excited, that's for damn sure. "And yes, it's her."

"The girl you have had a massive crush on, she likes me?" Nolan smirks, mirth all over his face.

"It's not fucking funny," I say.

"I don't know, feels comical to me."

"You're a dick."

"Come on, it's not like I'd make a move on her or anything, especially knowing your reaction to her whenever she texts you. My question to you is: Why are you telling me this?"

Annoyed, I say, "Because she asked if you were single and I told her that you were seeing someone, and I was thinking about asking her to meet me at Maritime after the game for a few drinks and since I know you frequent there, I didn't want it to be...well, awkward."

"Because you want all of the attention on you."

"Pretty much."

He slowly nods. "Let me ask you this, are you going to make a move on her?"

"I don't know," I say, pushing my hand through my thick hair, feeling weird that I'm not wearing a baseball cap. "I mean, I want to, and I feel like the stars are aligned for that to happen."

"So what's the hesitation?"

"For one, she's my sister's best friend. She's known me since I was sixteen, she's eight years older than me, and I think she still sees me as a gangly teenager."

"Eight years older?" Nolan asks, a raise to his brow. "Dude, that's hot. What I wouldn't give for an older woman." He grips the steering wheel tighter. "If it doesn't work out for you, do you think I can give it a go?"

"No," I say through clenched teeth, causing him to laugh.

"I'm just kidding. I won't hit on her. Instead, I'll be your wingman, talk you up, help her see that you're a mature man now, no longer a teenager."

"I don't need you to do that."

He pats my leg. "Trust me, from the way your cheeks redden when you talk about her, you do. Listen, tonight, we'll tag team, watch me work my magic. You'll be going home with her tonight, and not for her to sleep on the couch, but to sleep in your bed."

"Are you sweating?" Nolan asks.

"What? No."

"You're glistening."

"Where?" I ask, panic filling me. Bower will be here any second and the last thing I want is for her to walk up to me while I'm a sweaty mess.

"Nose," Nolan says and hands me a napkin.

I quickly wipe at my nose. "That better?"

"No, you need another swipe."

"Seriously?" I swipe again and he shakes his head. So I swipe again and again until I see a smile tug at the corner of his lips. My worried expression falls as I crumple the napkin and chuck it at his face. "Asshole."

He lets out a laugh and then shoves my shoulder. "Relax, fucker. You're coming off a hell of a win, hitting in the winning run for the team. You're surrounded by people who worship you, you have a beer in hand, and the girl you want to bone is on her way to hang out with you."

"I don't want to just bone her," I say, needing to clarify that, because I want so much more with her.

"Either way, you're in a good spot." He grips my shoulder and squeezes it.

When we arrived at Maritime, we headed straight to the back where the bar holds a sitting area for us. Old worn-leather couches form a large square with an equally sized wooden coffee table in the middle. There are curtains on two sides of the space, offering us a little privacy, but it's open in the front, giving us a view of the general public. Old fishing gear recycled from ocean cleanups hangs from the ceiling and the walls, ranging from broken lobster cages, to sun-soaked buoys, to fishing nets. It's eclectic and reminds me of those bars you see in New York that are decked out in Christmas decorations, but instead of wreaths and baubles, it's thick ropes and nets.

"Just…just be cool, okay?" I ask.

"This is not my first time helping a friend score. I got this in the bag."

He says that just as I catch sight of Bower walking through the bar, glancing around, looking for me.

Her hair is parted down the middle, slightly curled, and draped around her shoulders. She's wearing a pair of jean shorts with frayed hems, a brown belt, and a cropped, off-the-shoulder long-sleeved blouse that's tight around her torso but loose around her chest. Her tanned skin is on full display and my mind short-circuits as she moves closer and closer, almost in slow motion.

She tucks a piece of hair behind her ear.

Her long lashes blink, scanning for me.

Her toned legs move, one step in front of the other, closer and closer to me.

And those pouty full lips glisten from the light bouncing off the gloss she applied.

Fuck.

Me.

"Shit, is that her?" Nolan asks, nodding right toward her.

"Yup." I swallow thickly.

"Fuck, dude," he whispers and then shifts on the couch next to me. "You are so fucked."

Yup.

I am.

Her head turns just as her eyes connect with mine and a huge smile plasters across her face before she heads right toward me and I walk to meet her.

Security walks up to her, ready to turn her away, but before they can, I say, "She's with me."

They nod and step aside, allowing Bower to walk right up, loop her arm around my neck, and give me a huge hug. My arms wrap around her waist, my forearms pressing against her bare skin. Her scent of rich caramel and sweet pistachio, something I can't place, fucking intoxicates me.

Her hand slides across the back of my neck as she pulls away and looks up at me. "Hey there, Mr. Game Winner."

"You watched?" I ask as I keep my arm around her, wanting her close, something it seems she doesn't mind.

"I did! Since I was coming tonight, thought I should probably educate myself." Her fingers dance across the hair at the nape of my neck, sending chills across my skin. "Good job, Benny Boo Boo." She smirks and then pulls away, making me have to let go as well.

"Thank you," I answer and then stick my hands in my pockets. "Can I get you something to drink?"

"What are you drinking?"

"Just beer."

"Then I'll join you." Like she always does, she takes my hand and I guide her to the back of the sitting area, where I hand her my beer and she takes a sip from it before sitting next to me on the couch.

I nod at a waiter who acknowledges me to bring another beer.

"And who do we have here?" Nolan says before I can even introduce him.

"This is my friend, Bower," I say. "Bower, this is Nolan."

Bower's eyes light up as she takes in Nolan, who's wearing a pair of pink ripped jeans, a white T-shirt with the collar torn, and a silver chunky necklace dangling at the base of his neck.

"Nice to meet you, Nolan," she says as she wets her lips.

Yup, this was a bad idea, I can feel it already.

Nolan takes her hand in his and gives it a shake. "Hell, if I wasn't taken, I'd be asking you to sneak back to the bathroom right about now."

Dude, what the actual fuck?

I glance at him and he just smirks before letting go of her hand.

"Jealous that Bennett here has you all to himself." He pats my back just as a beer is placed in front of me.

"Oh, we're just friends," Bower says with a wave of her hand. "Isn't that right, Benny Boo Boo?"

I can feel the fucking wince from Nolan, not even having to look at him. Being friend-zoned right off the bat. Fucking humiliating.

Top that off with her using my nickname. Yup, might as well throw in the towel now.

"Friends," I reply and clink my glass with hers, one of the most painful declarations I've ever made.

"Friends, huh?" Nolan asks. "How could you be just friends with this guy?" Nolan nods toward me. "He's the whole package. Good-looking, killer at the plate, a six-pack that makes every single one of our teammates drool."

Bower glances at me. "You have a six-pack?"

"Uh, I mean—"

"Sure does," Nolan says, lifting my shirt and flashing my stomach, giving Bower a glimpse.

"Oh my God, you do." Bower smirks. "When did that happen?"

I scratch the back of my neck. "Well, you know, I have to work out and—"

"And the dick on this guy," Nolan says, shocking the shit out of me, because what the fuck is he doing? "When I say he's the whole package, I mean the...whole...package."

For the love of God.

Embarrassment eclipses me as Bower takes a sip of her beer and crosses one leg over the other. "Is that right?" She eyes me for a moment.

"Then how come you're hanging out with your older sister's best friend rather than calling over one of the many girls who are clearly frothing to get into this space?"

Nolan chuckles and then an evil glint falls over his face as he starts to say, "Because he has a massive—"

"Donaldson," I say, loud enough for practically the entire bar to hear me. Confused expressions from Bower and Nolan both look in my direction as I clear my throat and repeat, "Donaldson, uh, he's calling you over." I point toward Donaldson, one of our relief pitchers who is at the bar. "He wants you, Nolan." I shove at his shoulder. "Better go see what he wants."

Nolan knows I'm a fucking liar as he glances at me, but thankfully goes with it as he says, "Probably wants to do a shot. I'll be back."

"Take your time," I say, wanting to get the point across that his help is not needed, especially since he was just about to blow up my spot without even a fucking second thought. It was right there on the tip of his tongue, ready to blurt out to Bower that I have a massive crush on her.

Unsure what I'd have done if she found that out. Probably melted into a pile of sweat, never to be seen again.

"So...what was that about?" Bower asks as she leans back on the couch.

"Pretty sure he's already drunk," I say, even though I know he's not.

"He's kind of strange but super fucking hot."

"That's the general consensus."

"Yeah? Your teammates think he's hot?" She playfully smirks at me.

"We have a hard time keeping our hands off him."

"Oh yeah?" Her smile grows even bigger. "Tell me more about that sausage fest."

Ugh, why did I say that?

"What happens in the locker room stays in the locker room."

She sips her beer. "Consider me intrigued." Her eyes travel over the

bar, taking in the decorations. "Interesting place. What's with the fishing gear?"

"The owner is big on ocean cleanup. I spoke to him when I first came here, since I was caught off guard by the decor as well, and he told me that he and some other employees comb the beaches and coasts, pulling debris and washed-up pollution from the shores fairly regularly. They either hang it in the bar as a reminder of their mission, or they recycle it. A portion of their profits cycle back into ocean cleanup as well."

"Huh, now that makes sense." She studies the decor hanging above us. "Kind of crazy that this was all washed up on the shore."

"Yeah, insane to think about."

"Is this where you come after every game?"

"No," I say. "Only on occasion, especially if we have a day off the next day."

"Do you have a day off tomorrow?"

"No," I answer. "Well, technically yes, but it's a travel day."

"Don't you ever get tired?"

"Yeah," I answer. "But this is what I wanted. I'm living the dream. I'll never complain when I get to live out what I worked so hard for."

"Your sister taught you well." She turns more toward me, her scent wafting in my direction, causing my body to ache for her.

If she actually knew how I felt, and if she felt the same way, this scenario would be different. Her legs would be draped over mine, my hand resting on her thigh, claiming her so every other motherfucker in the vicinity knew she was off-limits, and she'd be whispering in my ear what we'd be doing when we got back to my place, rather than saying shit like my sister taught me well.

"So, uh, did you find out about your apartment?" I ask.

"Trying to kick me out already?"

"What? No," I say quickly. "You can stay as long as you want. I'm actually headed out of town soon, and if you want to stay while I'm gone and get yourself situated in your apartment, by all means."

She chuckles. "I'm kidding, Bennett." She strokes my forearm. "Relax."

Christ, if I relax too much and she keeps touching me like that, the results won't be what she's expecting, that's for damn sure.

"They're finishing up some painting and I think I might let the fumes air out before I move in, if you don't mind."

"Not at all."

"My stuff was actually delivered today, though. The movers put it all in the center of the apartment. They were complaining about my books."

"Your books?" I ask.

"Yes, you know I'm an avid reader."

"But you collect them?"

She gasps and sets her drink on the table. "Bennett Brinkman." Hand to chest, she continues, "Of course I collect them. Those are my trophies."

"Trophies?" I ask.

"Yes. My trophies. Every time I finish a book, I can put it on my bookshelf as a trophy that says, look what I did. I read a book. That's more than a lot of people can say."

"You're right about that. Can't remember the last time I read a book."

Her eyes widen and her hand lands on my chest as she grows sincere. "Are you serious?"

"Very serious," I say, wanting her hand to stay right where it is.

"Bennett, we need to change that." Her eyes widen even more. "Oh my God, we can start our very own book club. How do you feel about bloody hand jobs?"

Uh…

"I, uh…what?"

"Sorry, I'm getting ahead of myself. I'm just so excited. I want a buddy to read with me, and Gabby just isn't the one, but if you're willing, I can open your world to romance books, and we can talk about them and analyze all the bloody hand jobs."

I lift my hat and place it back on my head because what the fuck is she talking about?

"Okay, uh, give me a second because I'm trying to understand what you're saying. Are there bloody hand jobs in the books that you're reading? Also, what is a bloody hand job?"

"It's when they use blood as the lubricant rather than spit or lube or cum. I mean, I'd never do it because I'm not really into that kind of mess, but I read it once and never got to really fully discuss it, and it lives in my mind all the time, ever since Ryland and Gabby first started dating. That's how long I've been thinking about it. How is that healthy? It's not! I need someone to talk to about this stuff. Please tell me you will be my person."

Her lashes flutter at me.

She wets her lips.

And I can tell you right now in this moment that if she asked me to walk off a cliff with her, I'd follow her. With one *please* from her gorgeous eyes, I'd follow into the inner depths of hell where bloody hand jobs and whatever the hell it is that she reads exist.

"I'll be your person."

"Really?"

The fucking smile that stretches across her face.

Jesus Christ.

I'm in love.

"Thank you." She throws herself at me, looping her arms around me, hugging me with everything in her.

I put my arms around her as well, holding her tight as my eyes lock with Nolan at the bar.

He smirks and then brings two fingers up to his mouth, splitting them in half and then lapping his tongue between them.

He winks and then turns away.

Fucking inappropriate, man.

Also...if only...

CHAPTER 5
BOWER

SITTING CROSS-LEGGED, RIGHT AGAINST BENNETT'S thigh, I drink my beer and feel excitement race through me as I try to gauge his reading comfort level.

"Okay, so bloody hand jobs are out of the picture."

"I mean, I think for now, yeah."

He finishes his beer in one gulp—which oddly I find hot—and he sets the empty glass on the coffee table.

"Understandable. We need to ease you into romance, I get that. We don't want to scare you off right away with something you're not comfortable with. But just for reference, is that something you would ever do, just so I know the kind of kink you're into?"

"Uh, no. Not that I'm putting down anyone who is into that, because to each their own. If you like a bloody hand job, then I hope you get one every day, but I just think it would terrify me more than anything, seeing my dick covered in blood."

"That's a fast way to deflate the old wiener."

He chuckles. "Yeah, pretty much."

"Good to know. How do you feel about spice in general? What is your chili pepper level?"

"Chili pepper?"

"Ugh, sorry," I say, placing my hand on his forearm. "I'm forgetting that you're all new to this. Chili peppers are what the book world uses to rate the level of spice they're into. Now, this is extremely controversial and many have various levels of spice, but I think in general, I'd say one chili pepper is that there is some hints toward sex and maybe some fondling, but when it gets to the action, it's closed door. Meaning, you don't see anything from there. And then it climbs. Two would be a full sex scene but nothing explicit. Three would be full sex scenes, explicit and creative. Four would be dragging some kink into the picture, and five, well, that's where bloody hand jobs come in."

He drags his hand over his jaw, the sound of his palm against his scruff igniting excitement in me. I love that sound.

"Uh…what do you like?"

"I'm a three–four kind of girl. I like some kink, but the five chili peppers terrifies me sometimes, even though I've dabbled in it and enjoyed."

He slowly nods. "And you're not a one or two kind of girl?"

"Every one or two that I've read I've enjoyed. There is nothing wrong with a one or two, great stories, just the perfect sprinkle of goodness, but I have found that they make me incredibly horny, so I tend to reach for a three or four, not to say that I wouldn't ever go back to a one or a two, though."

His eyes widen, which makes me chuckle. "Uh, really?"

"Yeah, it's like getting edged but never finding completion. I need coming in my books. I need full-on penetration right in front of my eyes. I need to see her feel his dick pounding into her uterus."

He blinks a few times and then chuckles before wiping his hand over his face. "Never, uh…never thought I'd hear those words come out of your mouth."

"What?" I shrug. "We're adults now. It's not like I'm talking to you like this as the sixteen-year-old I first met. You're what…twenty-uh…"

"Twenty-four," he says.

"Ugh." I clutch my chest. "So young."

"Not that young."

"Young enough for me to second-guess the sentence I just said to you."

"You say that as if I've never made a woman feel my dick pound into her uterus."

Uh, pardon me as I pick my jaw up off the ground, because what?

"Bennett," I practically squeal. "Oh my God, I can't believe you just said that."

A waiter brings us both another beer that we take.

"Why not?"

"Maybe because you're my best friend's little brother and you don't ever talk like that."

"I guess you haven't been asking the right questions."

"I guess not." Taking a sip of my drink, I shift in my seat and then ask, "So, do you have a lot of hookups?"

He shrugs. "I wouldn't say a lot, but I'm not a virgin."

"Yeah, I know, Gabby told me when you had your first girlfriend. She was freaking out and we went out and bought condoms together so you didn't get anyone pregnant."

He rolls his eyes. "You bought me a year's worth."

"And you're welcome for that. Shows how much confidence we had in your sexual prowess."

"Too much."

I laugh. "So what are you looking for? Who fits the criteria for you to take someone home?"

He scratches the back of his neck and shrugs as he slouches in the couch next to me, legs slightly spread in that man way, looking all kinds of dark and mysterious under the brim of his hat.

"There isn't much criteria for a one-night stand," he answers. "Have to be attracted to her and she can't be fucking crazy. Prefer if she doesn't know who the hell I am."

"As if people don't know who you are."

"You would be surprised," he says.

"Okay, so what about someone that you would actually date, because I've known you for a good amount of time and you can't tell me that you're the kind of guy that sleeps around. You must be looking to at least date someone."

"Yeah, I am," he says, his eyes straying away from mine.

"And what would that criteria be?"

"Why so curious?" he asks.

"Because I love *love*, and if I can help find someone for you, like be your aunty matchmaker, then I'd feel like I'd fulfilled a duty I was meant to have."

"Please don't call yourself my aunt."

"Practically am," I say. "But seriously. What are you looking for?"

"You really want to know?" he asks.

"I really do."

He nods and sits up. "Okay. If I were to truly put it out there." His eyes travel up and down my body for a moment. "Someone like you."

Immediately my cheeks flush as his eyes bore into mine.

"Someone like me?" I ask incredulously.

"Yeah." He finishes off his third beer since we've been talking and sets the empty glass down. "Gorgeous, funny, charismatic. Couldn't give two shits that I'm a baseball player. Outgoing, gets along with my sister, and knows what she wants."

"Ah, I'm going to stop you right there," I say. "I don't know what I want, so not a good comparison."

He studies me for a moment, a long, stretched-out moment, one that actually makes me squirm in my seat from the intensity of his eyes. After a few seconds, he says, "Yeah, you're probably right, but you get the idea."

"I do. Getting along with Gabby is a must, and she also has to get along with me, too, because we're neighbors and I plan on being in your life a lot more now that we live in the same city. You're my only friend here."

He wets his lips and says, "I hope you are. I expect it."

"So where are we on the whole book thing?" I ask. "We got so caught up in your filthy mouth that we didn't solidify plans. Are you going to be my book buddy?"

He stretches his arm along the back of the couch, all of his attention on me despite the raucous crowd in front of us and the people vying for his attention.

"Romance?" he asks.

"Yeah, romance. Think you can handle it? Some men think romance books are a joke. I personally think it's a fantastic way to educate yourself in female desires."

"I don't think it's a joke," he says. "Just never read one before. Actually not much of a reader at all. Never really put time into it."

"So this is perfect then, because now you can explore and see what you like. Are you a romantic at all?"

He rubs the side of his face. "Never had anyone I wanted to be romantic with."

"You've never had a girlfriend?" I ask, even though I feel like I know the answer to that.

"Not anyone serious."

"Right, I feel like Gabby would have been gushing to me about it. Have you been on a real date?"

He rolls his eyes. "I'm not a complete recluse. Just been focused on baseball so haven't had much time to think about anything else. But yes, I've been on a date. I can be romantic. I know what it takes. Just haven't found the person that deserves that kind of attention from me."

"That makes sense." I finish off the rest of my beer just as a waiter brings us each another as well as a giant soft pretzel to share. Wow, they're on it. Bennett picks up the pretzel and tears a piece off for me before taking a piece for himself. "I haven't found anyone good enough either. Hey, maybe we can set each other up with someone."

"Who do you know in San Francisco that you can set me up with?"

I glance around the room. "I don't know, there are some ladies in here that I could chat with, see if they're interested in you."

He shakes his head. "They're only in here because they know this is where the Bombers hang out. They're certified cleat chasers, and I'm not into that. Plus, I don't have anyone I could set you up with, so that's a no."

"Ugh, fine." I sigh. "But. We're on for the book club?" I point at him and wiggle my eyebrows.

"We're on."

"If he brings over another shot, I won't be able to do it," I say as I lean against Bennett's chest.

We're both slouched on the couch, staring up at the broken-down lobster traps above us, beer swishing around in our stomachs with a shot we just got from Nolan.

"You and me both." He drags his hand down his face. "Fuck, I never drink this much."

"Really?" I ask. "You make it seem like you can handle it so easily."

I feel him shake his head. "Nope, things are getting fuzzy."

"Same."

"Bad things happen when things get fuzzy."

"Am I to hold you accountable from doing bad things?"

"Probably best at this point."

"Your sister wouldn't want it any other way. So what do I need to stop you from doing?"

He sighs. "Well, I get handsy when I'm drunk." He tugs on a strand of my hair. "You can't have me doing that."

"Right, check. I do the same thing. I get cuddly too," I say as I snuggle in closer to Bennett, his arm now draping around me.

"So, no cuddling for you then."

"Nope, none. And no touching for you."

"Correct." His finger twists a lock of my hair.

"Do you tend to hook up when you're drunk?"

"Unfortunately," he says. "It's probably when it happens the most because I'm just trying to get off when I couldn't care less who it's with."

"Trust me, been there done that, regretted it in the morning because it's never a good lay. I do a better job myself."

"You do?" he asks, sounding surprised.

"Uh, yeah, I'm well skilled at providing my own orgasms. I'm assuming you must be the same, because there is no way you're not giving yourself pleasure."

"I don't."

I lift up and look him in the eyes, about to call him a liar when I see his smirk on his face. "You know, it would be best if we don't lie to each other, Bennett. Being that you're my only friend in San Francisco, I can't possibly afford your deceit."

He chuckles. "Sorry, would you like me to tell you just how often I get myself off?"

"We don't have to go that far into detail," I say as I rest back down on his chest. "But I will say, this new book club we have might make you a little hornier. Are you okay with that?"

"Don't think it can get any worse than it already is."

"Great. Then I'll pick our first book and send it to you. We can take a few days to read it—"

"A few days?" he asks. "Not a month?"

"Dear God," I say, lifting up again. "How on earth will it take you a month to read a book?"

"How the fuck does it take you a few days?"

"Uh, I read with my eyes," I say, gesturing to my face.

"So do I, and I can tell you right now there has never been a time in my life when it's taken me a few days to read a book. Isn't that why book clubs have monthly picks? To give people time to read?"

"You will have plenty of time to read."

"Not if I'm doing baseball and this stupid zoo thing."

"What zoo thing?" I ask.

He rolls his eyes. "It's a whole PR thing I have to do. I don't think it's helping at all. Graydon—"

"Who is Graydon? Is he single?"

"Jesus," he grumbles. "No, he's not. He has something going on with his zookeeper actually, and he's on the Foghorns, the football team here. Anyway, he's doing some bullshit that's helping him."

"What bullshit?"

He sighs heavily. "Honestly, my brain is too fuzzy to remember. And then there's OC—"

"Who is he? Is he single?"

"Plays for the hockey team, and he is not single nor is he dating anyone physically, mentally still hung up on his ex. Also, there is no way you would be able to handle him."

"Hey, what does that mean?"

"He's dramatic, needy, and annoying most of the time. You would get annoyed by him before you can share a first kiss."

"Eck, needy, no, thank you."

"Yeah, it wouldn't go over well. We're doing some PR shit together, and well, Graydon is doing well, and I just feel like I need more. Don't like the zoo..." He shuts his eyes and leans his head back. "Get me out of the damn zoo."

"If you get out of the zoo, you'll have more time to read?"

He nods. "Yup."

"Then we must figure out a way."

CHAPTER 6
BOWER

"ARE YOU SURE YOU WANT to sleep on the couch?" Bennett asks, his eyes hazy, a stupid grin on his face.

He's drunk.

Then again, so am I.

We shut down the bar because apparently the boys have a travel day tomorrow and they plan on sleeping on the plane.

Nolan came back at some point and brought us one more round of shots. Bennett and I both took one and that was about our threshold, because I like being drunk, but not unable-to-walk drunk.

Can't remember the last time I felt this way, all wobbly and giggly, but then again, my best friend hasn't lived near me for about two years now and my job consumes a lot of my time, so it makes sense that this is the first time in a long time that I've let myself have some fun outside of my home.

"I like the couch."

"Do you?" he asks as he kicks his shoes off.

"Sure. I don't mind it. Do you like sleeping on a couch?"

"No." He shakes his head. "Reminds me of when a couch was all Gabby and I had."

My parents lost a lot when my dad had to start over, and there were times when food was scarce, but I never lived in poverty like Gabby and Bennett. And I forget about that sometimes, just how far they've come.

"That's why I'm sleeping on it."

He goes to the kitchen and grabs two glasses, filling them up with water for the both of us. "I know, but it makes me feel bad. Do you want my bed? You can have my bed. Take my bed."

"I'm not taking your bed."

"I can change the sheets again." He walks up to me and hands me some water.

"No, you sleep in your bed and I'll sleep on the couch."

He sips from his glass, his eyes staring at me over the rim. "You can always share the bed with me. You can have your side, and I can have my side."

I must be very drunk because the thought of that actually makes me happy.

Thrilled.

Excited.

But sharing a bed with Bennett…yeah, that would be weird, right?

"Sharing the bed seems risky."

"Why?" he asks, a drunk smirk on his face. "Scared of me?"

"Of you?" I scoff. "No." I shake my head. "Not even the slightest."

"Afraid I snore? Because I don't. I'm an excellent sleeper."

"How do you know?"

He tips his glass back to his mouth, drinks down the rest of his water, and then sets his glass down and heads toward his bedroom.

"I've been complimented on my sleeping habits," he says.

I follow him to the threshold of his bedroom as I say, "And who has offered these compliments?"

He takes his hat off his head, showing off his unruly brown hair that he quickly runs his hand through, causing it to cutely stick up on all ends.

"Women," he answers as he reaches behind his neck, grabs his shirt, and yanks it over his head, then drops it into a hamper before turning toward me.

Oh.

My.

God.

My eyes are like a magnet to his rock-hard chest. Well-defined pecs, broad, muscular shoulders with arms to match, but what's taking up all of my interest right now is the six-pack of abs stacked on his stomach, along with the V in his hips. I have only read about those, never seen them.

There's not a single hair on his chest, but there's a small patch of hair just below his belly button that's trimmed. His skin is smooth, carved, so lickable that I actually fear for my life, because given just how drunk I am, how horny I am, and the snack standing right in front of me, I'm afraid this girl will have no self-control.

"You're staring," he says, breaking my thoughts up.

"Because you took your shirt off and shocked the hell out of me."

He glances down at himself and then back up at me. "See something you like?"

Oh my God, Bennett!

Wait, no...oh my God, me. What am I even doing?

I'm staring at him when I shouldn't be staring at him, and yet I can't stop myself. Nor can I stop the words coming out of my mouth.

"I'd be stupid if I said I didn't like a good set of abs. Nolan wasn't kidding."

"He wasn't kidding about a lot of things," Bennett says before winking and then heading into the bathroom, bringing my thoughts to what Nolan said about the whole "package." From the bathroom, he calls out, "Are you going to get ready for bed, or are you just going to stand there, looking for another free show?"

And when did he get so sassy?

"I'm getting ready," I say as I turn away from him and go to my corner of the living room. I snag a pair of shorts and a baggy T-shirt from my suitcase and quickly change into them, excluding underwear, because I can't deal with that shit when I'm sleeping. I tie my hair up into a messy bun on the top of my head, and I remove my makeup with my wipes before heading into the bathroom, where I'll wash my face and brush my teeth.

When I enter his bedroom, he's in his bed, the covers up to his waist, making it look like he's naked under the sheets.

Yup, this girl needs some sleep and fast.

I finish up in the bathroom by washing my face, brushing my teeth, and then lotioning up before I exit and find Bennett lying there still, waiting.

But waiting for what? Does he really think I'm going to share a bed with him?

He's lost his mind if he does think that.

"Okay, well...all ready for bed," I say awkwardly.

"I see that." He pulls down the sheets on the other side of the bed, indicating that I'm to join him.

I chuckle and shake my head. "Not a good idea."

He raises a single brow in that cute way he does. "Why not? Afraid your hands will wander?"

Uh, yeah.

I am.

"Just think you need your space so you get the best rest."

"Trust me, you being beside me in bed is not going to interrupt my sleep."

He says that now until he wakes up to my tongue circling his belly button.

"I just think it might be best—"

"Just get over here," he says with an eye roll that says I'm being ridiculous. And honestly, I feel like that eye roll is justified, because normally this wouldn't be a big deal. Hell, I've borrowed his clothes before, his deodorant... I even used his toothbrush before without him knowing. So why am I being hesitant now?

"You're right," I say, tossing my hands up as if I'm the one being crazy.

Because maybe I am.

He shows me a set of abs and I have a wonderful time with him, and all of a sudden I'm afraid to be around him?

This is Bennett, for crying out loud.

I walk to "my side" of the bed and slip under the covers, immediately sinking into the softness of them.

"Oh my God, Bennett, this bedding is incredible." He switches off his nightstand light and turns toward me, the glow of the moon the only thing shining light down upon us.

"I spent far too long picking out the best bedding."

"Because you never had good bedding growing up?"

"Correct," he says.

"But look at you now. You have money, a home, a comfortable bed. You have it all."

"I don't have it all," he says, his eyes intent on me. "But I intend to have it all."

"And what does 'having it all' mean to you?"

"The girl I want," he says. "The life I've dreamed of."

My eyes drift shut for a moment before I open them again. "Does that include kids?"

"Yeah, at least two."

"Respectable," I say on a sigh. "I want kids too."

"How many?"

I shrug and shut my eyes again. "Don't really care, but I need to make something of myself first."

"What do you mean by that?" he asks as the booze in my body slowly starts to shut me down for slumber. "Bower?"

"Hmmm?"

"What do you mean?"

"I don't know," I say, and then I move in close to him for warmth and rest my head in the crook of his arm and chest and wrap my leg around his, finding so much comfort in his body.

There.

That's perfect.

Just what I need.

And when his arm wraps around me, holding me close, I feel myself finally drift off to sleep.

The smell of coffee is the first thing that wakes me up.

The sound of Bennett cursing to high heaven is the second thing.

I sit up, trying to gather my surroundings.

White walls, light gray curtains, matching light gray blankets, and a comfortable-as-hell bed.

I'm in Bennett's room.

Oh FUCK, I'm in Bennett's bed.

I quickly look down at myself and see that I'm fully clothed, but not just clothed, I'm in a T-shirt and shorts.

Thank God for that.

I do a quick scan of the room for any evidence of misbehavior, but when I don't see a condom wrapper in sight, and nor do I feel the utter satisfaction of being with someone, I know that nothing happened last night.

With that knowledge firmly in place, I slowly get out of bed because, well, hangover, and head toward the kitchen, where I find Bennett on the ground in nothing but a pair of gray sweatpants, holding his foot.

"Uh...are you okay?"

"Stubbed my fucking toe on the fucking dining room fucking table."

"That's a lot of fuckings."

"That's how bad it hurt."

"Can I help you?" I ask, even though the pain of my pounding head is probably going to prevent me from leaning down to help him out.

"Nah, I'm fine," he says before flexing his foot and then hopping up from the ground and walking straight to the kitchen as if he didn't spend the night drinking his body weight in booze. He grabs two mugs and starts pouring us both coffee as my eyes wander over his chest, reminding me of the first time I saw it last night.

Bennett Brinkman is all grown up.

Not just grown up but ripped.

He doesn't just have muscles, no, there isn't an ounce of body fat on him. His muscles seem to pop right underneath his skin, his veins in his forearms flexing as he pours a cup of coffee, and his pecs seem thicker than I even remember from last night. Strong, powerful, can probably spend a good amount of time tossing a woman around in bed...

"I ordered some breakfast tacos," he says as he lifts up to hand me my coffee. I direct my eyes to his face just in time. "Got the kind with crispy bacon that I know you like."

"How do you know I like that?"

He smirks over his mug. "I pay attention to shit." He sets his mug down and allows his eyes to scan over me. "Are you hungover?"

"What the hell do you think?" I ask as I move toward the dining room and take a seat. "And please, don't rub your youth in my face, because from your fresh eyes and clarity, I can already tell that you're not as affected by copious amounts of alcohol consumption as I am, and I can't stomach that thought right now, so please, spare me."

"Do you want me to pretend to be hungover?"

"Please." I sip my coffee, letting the caffeine run through my veins and awaken me.

"Oh fuck," he says, hobbling toward me, hunched over and looking absolutely ridiculous. "What the hell did we do last night? I'm so hungover."

I stare at him.

Blink.

"It's a little dramatic."

"Just mimicking you."

I flip him off, which makes him laugh.

"Other than what seems to be one hell of a hangover, did you sleep okay?" he asks.

"I did, although..." I chuckle. "For a second, when I woke up in your bed, I had a minor heart attack that we might have done something stupid."

"And what would that be?" he asks as there's a knock at his door. He retrieves what I'm assuming is our food before stopping in the kitchen and grabbing a bottle of ibuprofen.

As he dishes out the food, I say, "You know...fuck."

He pauses and glances at me, a question heavy on his breath.

"I know." I roll my eyes. "That would never happen, but for a second I thought it did, and I panicked until I realized that, in fact, we didn't do anything."

"No, we did not," he says, before sitting down and undoing the foil of his breakfast tacos.

"Gabby would have had a heart attack. Probably disown me."

"You think so?" he asks, looking genuinely curious.

Oh yeah, sleeping with her brother would be a huge slap in the face of the promise I made her.

"Of course she would. I don't think she'd be happy at all if her best friend slept with her younger brother of eight years. That's grounds for divorce."

"You two aren't married."

"Spiritually, we are. You weren't invited to the wedding." I wave my hand at him. "It was more of a two-person thing. Either way, glad we kept our clothes on."

"Yeah, good thing," he says and then takes a bite of his taco. He chews for a moment and says, "But when I'm gone, feel free to sleep in my bed."

The temptation is real, because I don't think I've slept that well in quite a long time. I want to say it's the mattress-sheet combination that had me dozing off without a second thought. Not the man I slept on.

Definitely not the man.

But...my place should be ready.

Although, one more night won't kill me.

"I might take you up on that."

He smirks and then says, "Speaking of last night, were you serious about the book club thing?"

"Uh, yeah. More than serious. I want a reading buddy, and if you're up for it, I'd love for it to be you."

He nods. "Okay, because I was thinking of a possible idea that could help me with this zoo business."

"You came up with an idea at this hour? After nearly drinking the night away? Are you made of metal or something?"

"Clearly not if I woke you up from stubbing my toe."

I chuckle. "True, but still, how could you possibly have come up with an idea already and this is your first cup of coffee?"

"Built differently."

"Apparently." I finally take a bite of my taco and moan as the bacon's grease hits me in the right spot. "Oh motherfucker, that's great." I slap the table and stare down at my taco. "Dear God, if you were a human, my tongue would be down your throat right about now."

"Uh...do you two need a room?"

"Quite possibly." I moan again as I continue to chew. "This is marvelous. A-plus. Compliments to the chef. Give me ten more."

"Seriously? Do you want me to order you some more, because I can."

I shake my head, even though it's tempting. "No, this is great. Thank you." I pull my hungry eyes away from my taco for a moment and say, "So, you had an idea."

"Yes," he says while wiping his face with a napkin. "I was thinking that I could work this book thing into the whole PR debacle that we have going on."

"Can you explain the PR thing to me? I feel like it's not making a lot of sense."

"Sure. So San Francisco has three major sporting teams: the Foghorns, which is football, the Rogue, which is hockey, and then there's the Bombers. The Foghorns haven't been able to see a playoff game in I want to say ten years. They're losing the spirit of their fan base and quickly. The Rogue are a new expansion team that's filled with every unlikable player throughout the league and led by owners who just want to win, so they signed problematic but skillful players. The only one who is not problematic is OC. The city doesn't seem to agree with the team right now, giving them a lack of fan base. And then of course, you know about the Bombers' cheating history before I was on the team."

"Naturally." I sip my coffee as he continues.

"The owners of each team came together and decided to help each other out by hiring a PR team led by a woman named Gretchen, who is trying to bring us out into the public in a positive light."

"And the zoo is one of those ways."

"Exactly. Now it's helped with Graydon because he's taken it upon himself to do this whole social media thing with his zookeeper."

"Who he likes, right?"

Bennett nods. "More than likes her. He's working through his feelings, but from what we can see, he's totally into her and it's only a matter of time before he finally figures out that he wants her, at least that's where I think he's at. I honestly can't keep up. Either way, he's doing well, bringing good PR to the team. OC is a hot mess. I'm unsure how he's succeeding. And then there's me. I don't think the zoo has had an impact at all, and I don't know, I was thinking about talking to Gretchen about switching things up, and I thought books might be an effective way to do that."

"Oooo, yes. You could help show that reading romance isn't just for women." I pause for a second and then say, "But you know what? You might need to actually read a romance first before you use it for PR. Because what if you go all in on a book club and then realize you don't like romance?"

He nods. "That's a really good point."

"I tend to make them."

Smirking, he says, "Okay, then what book should I start with?"

"I have a baseball series that's right up your alley. We'll start there."

"Sounds good." He winks, the gesture causing my stomach to lightly flutter.

And I mean *lightly*.

Which only means…I need to start dating, and I need to start dating now.

"Gabby, why is it so hard to find someone compatible?" I ask as I walk around Adalade's stunning Victorian house. Her boxes and furniture have been delivered, and the unpackers are currently at work while I direct them and manage.

"Have you tapped into the dating pool of San Francisco?"

"Uh, yeah. I've been here for five days, on the app for three of those days, and not a single human that I could see myself matching with. Sure, I might be being picky, but I don't want any duds. I can't be wasting my time. I'm twenty-nine, for God's sake."

"You're thirty-two," she deadpans.

I pause in my pacing. "Can't you just go with it every once in a while, indulge in my delusion?"

"No."

"Not helpful. Anyway, the guy is either my type but has nothing in common with me, or there are some things in common, but he still lives with his mother. I'm not going to be fucking mother lovers."

"Umm, want to think about what you just said?"

Groaning, I head over to the kitchen, where silverware is being polished and placed in a hutch. "You know what I mean. It would be great if he has a good relationship with his parents, but not still living with them."

"Yeah, I get that. What about Abel? I know you wondered about him before while you were visiting me."

"Gabby, Abel lives in Almond Bay. I do not live there and I'm not going to have a long-distance relationship. Plus, you and Ryland have both said that he wouldn't be able to handle me. I need someone who understands me, isn't scared of my...idiosyncrasies, and who can foster my insanity."

"Pretty big shoes to fill."

"Yes, and let's hope his feet are just as big as the shoes."

She chuckles. "You have impossible standards. I blame your books."

"Don't you dare," I snarl at her. "My books have shown me exactly what I want and that's not a terrible thing. Not all of us can just bounce on a monstrous dick and fall in love. We are not all lucky like you."

"I'm quite lucky."

Tell me about it. Ryland is not only extremely hot in that father figure, scruffy way that makes your knees shake, but he's a good uncle/dad to his niece and he's phenomenal in bed, from what I've been told. And I know Gabby's telling the truth from the way she lusts after the man.

"I want to find that. How do I find that?"

"Are you really serious? Because you've sort of...how do I say this nicely?"

"Watch it," I warn playfully.

"Well, you've flounced around, you know? Never really serious with anyone."

"I know, but this is a new chapter. Maybe things are different?"

"Maybe?" she asks.

I shrug even though the thought of having a relationship actually feels kind of right at this moment in my life. "Keeping my options open."

"Okay, well, maybe you're trying too hard? Maybe you need to just... let it happen. That's how it went with Ryland. I wasn't looking for it and then—"

"I encouraged you to have a one-night stand with him and the rest is history."

"Yes..." she drags out. "But I still wasn't expecting it and it happened. So maybe just leave it to fate."

"I did ask Bennett if any of his guy friends were available, mainly Nolan Hart, but apparently not."

"Yeah, you don't want to date a baseball player."

"Why not?" I ask. "They're hot, fit, and probably have enough adrenaline after a game to go all night. Sounds like the perfect human to consume the love I have to give."

"That's when they're around. I know Bennett's schedule and he's gone a lot during the season, and it's an exceptionally long season. We're talking six to seven months out of the year."

"Ooof, really? That is long."

"And you're needy."

"I'm very needy."

"Uh, miss, where would you like the Fabergé egg collection?" one of the unpackers asks me.

"In the built-in hutches in the living room. Also, you break it, you buy it, and unless you plan on taking out a mortgage, I'd take great care of those."

"Yes, miss," the guy says before carefully walking them over to the hutches and gently setting them down.

Turning back to my conversation with Gabby, I say, "I'm going to assume any guy in sports is going to be like that."

"Mostly, besides football. They're home most of the time. I only believe they're gone for one or two days a week if they have an away game."

"Really?" I say, interested in that prospect. "You know, Bennett might be able to help me out with that."

"As if he's not helping you out enough."

"Hey, when he gets back into town, I planned on doing something nice for him."

"Oh? And what would that be?"

"Not quite clear on the direction I want to take, but I'll come up with something."

"Is he…is he doing okay?"

"I think so. I would tell you if he wasn't. You don't have to keep asking."

"I know, but now I have boots on the ground, watching over him."

"Is that the real reason, or is it because you're jealous that Bennett and I are friends and we're now in a book club together?"

"Uh…excuse me?"

"Yeah, me and Bennett are in a book club together. He's reading romance, the romances I told you to read that you refuse to partake in."

"Since when?"

"Since the other night."

"Bower," she says in a stern voice. "I swear if you become better friends with my brother, I will scream. You're mine, not his, remember that."

I laugh and rub my finger along the fireplace mantel, pleased to see zero dust.

As if anyone could take Gabby's place. You don't go through the kind of things we have gone through together throughout the years and not hold each other as our number one human.

She's my person.

And I would never do anything or let anyone take that away from me.

"He will never be able to take your place, but if you're looking to join a book club, we'd be willing to take on a third."

"I will not be pressured into a book club just out of fear that my brother is taking my place as your best friend."

"Please, that would never happen. Bennett is cool and all, but you know far too much about my life that I'd never tell him."

"It would be in your best interest if you remember that."

CHAPTER 7
BENNETT

"WHAT ARE YOU READING?"

"What?" I snap my book shut and slide it by my side. "Nothing. What are you reading?"

Nolan stares from the seat in front of me on the plane, not buying my lie one bit. With his arms on the top of his chair, he leans his weight on it. "There's a fabric cover on your book, one of those old lady ones that my grandma used to use to be discreet when reading her Fabio books."

"What are Fabio books?" I ask.

"Romance books with bare-chested men on the front. And given that you're covering up your book and hiding it from me, you must be reading such a book. So, let me ask you again...what are you reading?"

Sighing, because I know he won't let this go, I pull my book out. "It's a baseball romance book that Bower gave me to read, and she gave me this fabric cover so that no one on the team made fun of me for reading it."

"Why would we make fun of you?" he asks, hurtling himself over the seat and landing, not so gracefully, in the seat next to me, knocking his foot against the plane window at the same time. Once settled, he says, "This shit is gold. I've learned some good moves from reading romance."

Uhh...what?

"You read romance?"

"Listen, my man." He points to his ear. "I listen to the books. Nothing gets me pumped up more than a male narrator telling the girl he's spanking to come on demand."

My brow creases. "That's what you listen to before a game?"

"No." He laughs. "But, fuck, the look on your face was great. I listen to them at night, before bed to calm myself down. I also enjoy mysteries, and I'll be honest, I almost never guess right who the killer is. It's a shock for me every goddamn time, and that keeps me coming back for more. But romance, dude, excellent choice. And are you reading it to impress the girl who you couldn't land the other night despite my best efforts?"

"Your best efforts almost had you telling her about my crush and getting us drunk. If that was your best efforts, then remind me never to come to you for help again."

"First of all, if you're going to learn anything from the books you read, it's that communication is vital. So by telling her you like her, you can just get it out there in the open. Second of all, getting drunk is a surefire way for people to get handsy, and that's what I saw when you two were cuddling on the couch."

"Yeah, that's all it was, cuddling, nothing else. And I can't just tell her how I feel. It's not as easy as you say. She doesn't see me like that."

"How does she see you?"

Probably in the most embarrassing way.

"As her best friend's little brother. If I told her I liked her, it would just come off as, I don't know, needy little brother with a childhood crush, and I don't want that."

"Ah, I see. She needs to see you as a man. Easy. Just whip your dick out, put it on a plate, and say dinner is served. That will change her mind."

"What the fuck is wrong with you?"

"Nothing," he says, as if what he just said isn't the stupidest fucking thing he's ever said. "I did that once to a girl, and she sucked my dick to the back of her throat in one breath. Respect the plate, my man."

I drag my hand over my face in frustration, because Nolan is no help at all. "I have a headache. Mind giving me some quiet time?"

"Nah, you don't have a headache, you just want to get rid of me. I get it. I can be a lot, but I'm also telling the truth. You have to tell her how you feel for this to work out."

"And I said, I can't just tell her that. She just moved here, I'm her only friend, and I don't want to make her feel uncomfortable."

"Then build that trust." He shrugs just as my phone buzzes in my pocket with a text, thanks to the plane's Wi-Fi.

I pull out my phone and see that it's a text from Bower.

"Is it from her?" Nolan asks, leaning in to get a look at my phone.

"It is."

"What does it say?"

"None of your business," I say as I read the message to myself.

Bower: Hope the traveling's going well. Staying in my apartment for the first time tonight. If your bed isn't in your room when you get home, it's because I took it. Anyway, I was talking to Gabby and telling her about how it would be great to meet someone…you know, romantically, and she suggested I ask you about the football guy you know and if he knows anyone that might be interested in a five-foot-five girl with green eyes, bendy limbs, and a very adventurous side?

"Ooof, fuck, dude. She's asking you to set her up?"

"Hey," I say, putting my phone away, fucking annoyed. Now I'm really starting to get a headache. "I told you not to read it."

Nolan presses the button on the side of his armrest, reclining his chair. "My dude, that's painful. She has completely friend-zoned you."

"I'm fucking aware."

"Now, the question is…" He takes off his shoes and stretches his legs through the holes of the armrests in front of him. "What are you going to do about it? Are you going to set her up?"

"Why the fuck would I set her up?"

He takes the sweatband he's been wearing this entire time and moves it over his eyes like an eye mask before joining his hands together and resting them on his stomach. That position does not look comfortable in the slightest.

"I love you, dude, but your foresight is lacking." He shifts in his chair, slipping into a state of Zen. "If you set her up with someone, then that gives you the opportunity to show her just how much better you are."

"How the fuck does that work?"

Lifting up one side of his sweatband, he says, "Hey, dumbass, this could not be clearer. You set her up with a real loser, and when she figures out that the man she's seeing is a total dud and the entire time you're catering to her every need, then you have secured yourself as the guy of her dreams. Basic math, brainiac." He taps my head and then covers his eyes again. "You're welcome."

I hate to admit it, but it's not a terrible idea.

If I set her up with someone who's incompatible and am there for her when she figures it out, she might actually see that I'm the one she should give a chance to.

Don't see how I can lose in this situation.

Pulling out my phone while Nolan gets even more comfortable, letting his knees fall to the sides, manspreading into my half of the seat, I text Bower back.

Bennett: Let me see what I can do. I'll ask but not making any promises. Graydon is not the kind of guy who enjoys matchmaking.

She texts back right away.

Bower: Ahh, you're the best! And I'll owe you for sure, even if it's more Moon Pies, I'll repay you.

Bennett: Don't worry about it. Just want you to be happy.

Bower: Ahh, I love you! Thank you.

Those three words nearly burn my retinas as I read them, and sure, I know she doesn't mean it the way I wish she did, but still, seeing her name next to those three words, it drives me to make her mine even more. This idea might be unconventional, possibly risky, but I can see how it might work in my favor. And that's what I need. I need to create a situation with Bower where she's so disheartened by the real loser she's going out with that when she sees me, she recognizes just how good I would be for her.

Simple math.

Now to get Graydon roped in. I have to feel him out first, see if he's having a good day, because if it's a bad day, there is no use.

Freshly unpacked in my hotel room, I take a seat on the bed, kick my feet up, and lean back on my pillow as I pull my phone from my pocket.

Here goes nothing.

Bennett: What are you guys up to?

The moment I send my text to the group chat, I instantly regret it, because if I want to keep Graydon in a good mood, getting OC involved is not the way to do it.

OC is like the thorn in Graydon's side that he can't seem to get rid of, and sure, there are moments when I think Graydon doesn't completely want to plow his fist through OC's face, but those are few and far between.

And why is there so much animosity? Well, it's because Graydon is the grump and OC is the sunshine. Graydon doesn't want to talk to any humans, and OC called our group chat the Gladdy Daddies, because as he puts it, we're "daddies" and we're "glad to be here." We questioned the name because all three of us are childless, and he pointed out that we're not daddies in a literal sense, but daddies in a Pedro Pascal sense.

Can you see why Graydon might not want to communicate with OC?

It's constant with OC, as he's extremely outgoing, dramatic, fun. He has good intentions, but Graydon wants nothing to do with those intentions. And yet, he still hasn't blocked OC, so there's a small piece of me that believes Graydon doesn't hate OC as much as he makes us believe.

My phone buzzes and, of course, OC is the first to respond.

OC: Grabbing dinner. Graydon didn't want to grab dinner with me, the dick. How is a guy supposed to make friends in this city if the ones closest to him aren't willing to share a meal?

See, slightly dramatic. It's why I could see OC and Nolan getting along. Although, whereas OC is more needy, Nolan has the "who gives two shits" attitude.

Graydon: I was busy.

OC: Yeah, busy with Maple.

Bennett: Really? Did you finally make a move?

Graydon: No, and I don't want to talk about it.

OC: Edging us, I see. It's okay, I have a high threshold for being edged. I was once getting blown by a girl when her father called in the middle. She talked to him for ten minutes, naked, breathing over my cock. Kept me hard the entire time.

Graydon: What the fuck is wrong with you?

Bennett: I usually defend you, bud, but…she was on the phone with her dad?

OC: It's called taboo…ever try anything like it?

Graydon: Girls' dads don't turn me on.

Bennett: Same.

OC: It wasn't the dad that was turning me on, even though his voice was exceptionally smooth, it was the thought of—you know what, never mind, you won't get it.

Graydon: You're right, because it's not normal.

Bennett: Not even close to normal.

OC: You both can fuck off.

Bennett: Sorry, dude, wish I could relate.

Graydon: Glad I can't.

OC: Changing subjects. Bennett, are you in Minneapolis?

Bennett: Yeah, just got settled. Three games here and then back home.

OC: Thank God, I could use you at the zoo. The big guy won't work with me on press.

Graydon: You do it to yourself.

OC: I can't work like this. *throws arms in air* I'm going to take a bath.

Thinking this might be a good out, I switch my text messages so it's just between me and Graydon, so OC can cool off and do his own thing, which is not get involved in this ask I have for Graydon.

Bennett: Hey, I have a favor to ask and didn't want to get OC involved. Feel free to tell me no, but thought I'd try.

Graydon: What's up?

Here goes nothing.

Bennett: So I have a friend who's looking to meet someone and I already hate myself for asking, because I know this is not something you would normally do, but is there anyone on your team that might be single and that might border the line of being a complete and utter douche? She likes them like that.

Sure, a lie, but it's all part of the plan.

Graydon: Are you serious right now?

Wincing, I text him back.

Bennett: I know, trust me, you were the last person I wanted to ask, but she's not into baseball players, so my teammates are out, and I just thought you might know of somebody.

Graydon: This is something OC would ask of me. He's rubbing off on you.

Bennett: I feel it every time he texts me. The fear I have of turning into him…

Graydon: You're getting pretty damn close.

Bennett: I know. I swear I'll try to scrub his impression off me, for your sake, but just because I'm slightly desperate here, do you know of someone?

Graydon: Why are you desperate?

Why did I know he was going to ask that? Because Graydon sees things in black and white with nothing in between. He likes to know the facts, and he bases his decisions on said facts. He won't simply help me out. Nope, he's going to question everything.

Bennett: Can I take a rain check on the explanation? I promise I'll tell you, but for now, do you think you could help a guy out? There has to be a douchebag on your team.

Graydon: There are plenty. More than I care for.

Bennett: Are any of them single?

Graydon: What do you think?

Bennett: I'm going to take that as a yes.

Graydon: This really isn't my thing, but I can ask Hutton to help. How much of a douche do you want him to be?

Bennett: If you looked up douchebag in the dictionary, it would be his face.

Graydon: I know exactly who that is.

Bennett: Who?

Graydon: Cougar Vajeen.

CHAPTER 8
BOWER

"THE STAIRS MUST HAVE A carpet runner," Adalade says as she walks through the house, giving me a punch list of things to complete.

She moved in yesterday, and even though every box is gone, her curtains are hung, and her knickknacks are in place, there's still a lengthy list of things she wants completed to feel at home.

"Do you have a specific color in mind you would like for the carpet?"

She waves her hand at me. "I trust your judgment. Just keep in line with the aesthetic of the house."

Which means I'll take a million pictures of the house and have a designer help me because I know nothing about carpet runners.

"And call the painter, because there are some missed spots along the baseboards."

"Already have them coming in on Wednesday. I moved your meetings and booked you a spa day so you're not here while they're touching up."

Adalade smiles. "Thank you."

"Of course."

She heads into the living room, where she takes a seat on the couch and crosses one leg over the other. "Since we're heading into fall, I'd like you to find me some suede boots, brown, with no heel."

I write down her request in my notes.

"How high would you like them to go?" Given that she's older but still fashionable, I know she's not going to want them to go over her knees, but I figured I'd ask.

"Below the knee."

I nod. "That's what I thought you were going to say. Would you like me to look for a matching suede trench coat as well? I know we spoke about it this summer, wanting to add more trench coats into your wardrobe. Just unsure with the San Francisco weather if suede is the way we want to go."

She slowly nods. "Yes, look for a trench in suede. Please have it match the boots. I'm not one to spend a lot of time outside, and if I do and it rains, I'll have an umbrella."

"Great. I'll get right on that. Anything else?" I ask, looking down at my gigantic list of things I need to get done.

"I'd like some of those macarons everyone is talking about, preferably raspberry and pistachio."

"I spoke to the bakery this morning, actually, and they have set a box to the side for me to pick up. I'll have Mark deliver them." Adalade smiles, clearly pleased with my ability to anticipate her needs. It's moments like these that make me feel safe. She appreciates all that I do, which is why I know this job suits me. *I'm good at this.* My dreams to start my book truck feel less safe.

"Thank you."

I close the top of my pen and ask, "So, are we good then?"

"I believe we are," she says. "Thank you."

"Of course."

I go to stand when she says, "How are you fitting into San Francisco so far?"

She might be a demanding boss, quite needy, but she does care about me, which is probably why I don't mind running all of her errands.

"Great. Learning the lay of the land. My best friend's brother lives here, so he's been helping me. I stayed at his apartment the first few nights when my place was getting a fresh coat of paint."

"Oh." Adalade folds her hands on her lap. "Your friend's brother…" She wiggles her brows, which makes me laugh.

"It's nothing like that. He's eight years younger than me. I've known him since he was a teenager. We're friends."

"You know, my first husband was ten years younger than me. There's something to be said about the virility of a young man and their eagerness to please."

Adalade Von Herbert!

I don't think I've ever heard her talk like that before.

I don't even know how to respond, which of course makes her laugh.

"And then my second husband, well, he was six years older than me, and there's a reason why that was my shortest marriage. Wasn't quite up to the task like the previous husband. Couldn't keep up."

Well, consider me intrigued now, because never has she ever talked about her life like this.

"Wore him out on the honeymoon?" I ask.

Adalade chuckles. "Let's just say things died down after that. Thank goodness for a prenup. He was gone within months. And then there was Larry." She sighs and stares off at the fireplace. "My dearest Larry. Not the most well-endowed, but boy, did he know how to use what he had."

I can't help it; I chuckle.

She shivers and then looks up at me. "He was my friend's brother as well."

"He was?" I ask.

She slowly nods. "Twin brother. Just a year younger than me, but he rocked my world. We were friends first, and well, a relationship unfolded in front of us, and it was the best decision I ever made. Tell me, what does your friend's brother do?"

"Well, he, uh…he actually is the starting third baseman for the Bombers."

Adalade's interest piques. "The baseball team?"

"Yeah."

"Oh, that's an unexpected answer." She holds out her hand. "Please, hand me my phone. I want to get a good look at this boy."

I pick up her phone off the coffee table and hand it to her. She pulls her reading glasses from on top of her head and places them on her nose before typing on her phone. It takes her a second, but I know the moment Bennett shows up on her phone because a small gasp falls past her lips as her hand goes to her chest.

"Bower, is this him?" She turns the phone toward me, showing me a picture of Bennett, holding his bat and standing in the dugout, waiting to go out on the field. His helmet casts a shadow partially over his face while his stunning blue eyes stand out against the obscurity of his brim.

Yes, that's him.

That's my best friend's brother.

And it's hard not to notice just how attractive he is now that he's all grown up.

I've always thought he was cute, but over the last year, something has changed in him. He's grown thicker, taller somehow, and it's as if he's filled out into a man with his sharp angles, the endless beard scruff, and the way his muscles fit his body as if that's how he was meant to be this entire time. I try not to pay too much attention to it, but it's hard when he's that freaking hot.

"Uh, yeah, that's him."

"My, oh my." Adalade adjusts her glasses again. "If this was my best friend's brother, I'd be asking her when I could officially become a member of the family."

I chuckle. "It's really not like that with us."

"Which is a damn shame." She sets her phone down. "I feel like this is a big mistake on your part." Her eyes meet mine. "Do you two get along?"

"We do," I say, almost feeling dumb from her judgment. "But I'd never go there. I care about my friendship too much, and I know she wouldn't be okay with it. We…we have a really important pact that we made, and boinking her brother doesn't fall in line with that. Plus, he's just…he's Bennett. I don't see him that way."

"Well, if he's single, ask him if he's interested in a woman forty years his senior."

I laugh and pocket my list. "I'll see what I can do."

With that, I take off to the car waiting for me. The one plus about doing all these errands is that Adalade allows me to use her driver, Mark, so I don't have to worry about parking or navigating the city. If I didn't have Mark, I'm not sure I'd be as thrilled to be running errands.

"Where are we off to first?" Mark asks as he pushes off the side of the car and flips the toothpick in his mouth.

As he opens the door, I say, "Texting you details now."

"Sounds good."

He shuts the door and I pull my phone out just as a text comes in from Bennett. Speak of the devil.

I quickly copy and paste the itinerary of errands for the day and shoot them off to Mark before looking at the text from Bennett.

Bennett: Eight-year breakup? What the actual fuck?

I let out a loud laugh before texting him back.

"Everything okay?" Mark asks, looking at me through the rearview mirror.

"Everything is great."

"Then if you're ready, we can take off."

I buckle up and say, "Good to go."

As he pulls out onto the road, I text Bennett back.

Bower: Brutal, right?

Bennett: What on earth would possess an author to do such a thing?

Bower: Daring and bold, but also psychotic.

Bennett: But also, why did I like it?

Bower: SAME! Ugh, see, this is what I need in my life, someone to talk to about books. What about the sex scenes? Did you like them?

Bennett: Honestly, at first, they made me feel weird.

Bower: Tingly weird in your private parts? Yeah, that happens to me too.

Bennett: No, LOL. Although…sort of.

Bower: HAHA. Did you get hot and bothered?

Bennett: On a fucking plane with a bunch of dudes sitting around me. Nolan asked why my cheeks were red.

Bower: Why can I see that in my head so vividly? So, do you think you will read the second one?

Bennett: Already started it.

Bower: GAH! Oh my God, you're a reader and we're best friends and oh my God, we're book besties. Bennett! We need shirts and matching tote bags, and you know what? We should have a crafting night where we make bookmarks and put our faces on them. Wait, we need a name for our book club. What should it be?

Bennett: Whoa, slow down. I'm still stuck on shirts.

Bower: Catch up. We have decisions to make. First and foremost, in my most Dwight Schrute–like voice, do you want to form an alliance with me?

Bennett: *Said like Kim Halpert* Absolutely I do.

Bower: Kim Halpert?

Bennett: Fuck! I meant Jim. Goddamn phone.

Bower: We were so close to being cool and then you ruined it.

Bennett: Which means just one thing.

Bower: What's that?

Bennett: Our book club name must be the Kim Halpert Book Club.

Bower: LOL! Oh my God, yes. Can we please make shirts with Jim's face but Kim's hair?

Bennett: I wouldn't have it any other way. But to clarify, what Kim?

Bower: Kim Cattrall, what other Kim is there?

Bennett: Kim Possible.

Bower: Ooof, good point. I think we go with Kim Possible.

Bennett: Does Jim wear Kim's cargo pants and crop top?

Bower: That seems like a dumb question, Bennett. Of course he does.

Bennett: Of course, what was I thinking?

Bower: Clearly, you weren't.

Bennett: Foolish of me.

Bower: I'll forgive you because that's what book besties do. Ahh, I'm so excited. Do you think you'll read the whole series?

Bennett: If you say I should, then I will.

Bower: You know, Bennett, I think this is the start of a beautiful friendship.

Bennett: I thought we were already friends.

Bower: Just let me have my moment.

CHAPTER 9
BENNETT

"BENNETT," GRAYDON SAYS AS I'M about to exit the zoo.

"Hey, man, what's—"

He slaps a piece of paper to my chest and starts to walk away, his large, imposing body not even skipping a step. I quickly grab the paper and look down at the almost unintelligible handwriting.

Cougar Vajeen and a number.

"That's for your friend." He continues to walk away.

"Wait, are you not going to introduce me or anything?"

He spins on his heel to face me. "Is it a date for you or a date for her?"

"A date for her," I answer.

"Then good luck." With that, he keeps walking into the zoo while I'm on my way out.

I stare down at the number, the back of my neck tingling with irritation.

Before he gets too far, I call out, "Does he know?"

Shouting before he walks into a building, he says, "He's expecting her call."

And then he disappears.

He's expecting her call, words I didn't want to hear, but also words I set up myself. This is what I wanted, right? It's all part of the plan?

Then why the hell does it make me feel incredibly nauseous?

This is what Nolan suggested, though. At the time, it all made sense, and there seems to be logic behind it all…so might as well just rip off the bandage.

Not wanting to second-guess this, I pull out my phone and send Cougar's name and number to Bower before heading to my car.

There, now to finish executing the plan. All she needs to do is—*gulp*—go on a date with the douche, realize he's a douche, and then come crawling back to me and see how great a guy I am.

Seems simple enough.

Foolproof.

One of the best ideas I've ever had.

I get in my car, start it, and pull out of the parking lot, headed straight to the stadium for my game tonight. We got home yesterday, but I haven't seen Bower because we got in late and I had to report to the zoo this morning to fulfill the hours of this stupid PR bullshit, and I really didn't do much other than help prepare food for the lions. Still wondering how this is helpful for my image when there aren't even cameras following me around. It feels like court-ordered community service, not some publicity stunt that's supposed to get the fans to like the team again.

Thankfully the stadium isn't too far from the zoo. When I pull in, I nod to the security guy at the gate and then park my car next to Nolan's, who is getting out of his car at the same time.

"Fucking hell," he says in greeting once I lock up my vehicle.

He's sporting gray sweatpants, a red Pikachu shirt, and slides with socks. Large, dark sunglasses that you would only truly find on an octogenarian cover nearly half his face as he sucks on a lollipop and props his hand against my truck.

"What the hell happened to you?" I ask.

"Dude, I've seen hell and somehow resurrected myself."

"What do you mean?"

He tilts his glasses down to look at me. "Whatever you do, don't get the lamb at Quints." He presses his hand to his stomach. "Motherfucker, I might throw up again."

"Jesus," I say, taking a step away. "Can you play?"

"If Michael Jordan can play after getting food poisoning, then so can I." He grabs a hold of my arm. "But can you walk me into the stadium? My legs are a little wobbly."

He clutches on to me like I'm a life raft, and because I'm that good of a friend, I let him as we walk slowly—and I mean very slowly—into the stadium.

"When did you have Quints?"

"Last night. They were one of the only places open, and I thought, lamb kabob, why not?"

His cheeks puff out, a gurgle moving up his throat, and all I can say is fuck that, I'm not that good of a friend. I release him, taking a step back, and wince as he opens his mouth and lets out an echoing belch that vibrates my entire spine.

Jesus Christ.

"Oh fuck," he says, gripping his stomach, hunched over for a beat before he stands taller, assesses himself, and then smiles. "Shit, that… that kind of helped."

"Jesus, dude, you're disgusting."

Nolan scoffs at me. "It's a burp, nimrod. Go clutch your pearls somewhere else."

Then without my assistance, he strolls into the stadium, me walking slightly behind him.

After a few seconds of silence, I say, "So, I went through with your plan."

"What plan was that? I offer up so many successful ones, I can't keep track." He heads into the cafeteria, where he pops his sunglasses on his head and grabs a few Powerades, two for each hand.

"Oh, I don't want any."

"They're not for you," he says, walking past me again.

For someone who looked like they were about to drop to their knees and keel over, he sure seems fine now. Did he really just need to burp to solve his problems? Wouldn't put it past him. He's that kind of guy.

"You really just going to drink all of those?"

"Going to pound them."

"Don't you think that'll upset your stomach more?"

"You fail to remember I'm a different breed."

"Yeah, never fail to remember that," I say as we head into the locker room, where most of our team is chatting and getting their warm-up gear on.

Nolan heads straight for the recliners in the middle of the locker room and flops back on one, lifting the footrest at the same time. Once settled, he uncaps a Powerade and starts chugging it before flipping his sunglasses back down and then holding the bottle close to his chest, like it's a stuffed animal he can't live without.

And because I have some time to spare and apparently love the torture, I take a seat next to him.

"So, uh. . .like I said, I went through with your plan."

"Oh, right. What plan?"

"The one we talked about, where I set up Bower with someone else, so I could swoop in and look like the good guy."

"Oh, right," he says, taking another sip.

"I texted her the guy's information before I left the zoo. Graydon got it to me today."

"Who was it?" Nolan asks. "I know a few guys on the team."

"Cougar Vajeen."

Nolan straightens and flips his sunglasses up so his bloodshot eyes are boring into me. "Cougar Vajeen?"

"Uh, yeah, is that, uh. . .is that a problem?"

"Who the fuck's idea was that?"

Sweat starts to tickle the back of my neck. "Graydon. I told him I needed a douchebag, and that's who he came up with, or at least that's who his friend Hutton came up with."

"Dude, Cougar Vajeen is not the guy you want going out with the girl you have a crush on."

Panic washes over me as I ask, "Why?"

"Because, he might be a douche, but he's a charismatic one. I've seen him work his charms firsthand, to the point that with a simple wink, he's taking a girl back to his place."

"Wait, what?"

I quickly pull out my phone to…hell, I don't know, reverse my text when I see three text messages waiting for me from Bower.

Oh fuck.

Oh God.

OH FUCK!

Bower: Ahhh, you're amazing. Thank you so much.

Bower: Just looked him up, and holy shit is he hot.

Bower: Eeep! We have a date this Friday. I can't wait. Thank you!

"Noooo," I say, slouching in my seat.

"What?"

Looking Nolan in the eyes, I say, "They're going out Friday night."

"Oh…shit." He blows out a heavy breath and then leans back in his chair. He flips his sunglasses back down and uncaps another Powerade, this time handing it to me. "Drink up, dude, you're going to need the electrolytes."

"Why?" I ask.

"Because your future is filled with a lot of tears and you'll have to hydrate."

"Stop. It can't be that fucking bad." Although, my stomach is feeling like it ate some bad lamb kabobs from Quints right about now.

"You can convince yourself of that, but let me tell you, it's bad. Cougar is unmatched. He has women crawling at his feet whenever he goes out. He has his choice of anyone, and when he chooses, he goes hard. Hard with his approach and hard with his dick." Nolan lifts up, glances around, and then says, "Rumor is, he broke a woman's uterus once with his penis."

"That is not fucking true," I say, bile rising to my throat.

"Either way, the man is charming as fuck, and for someone like you, who has a massive crush on the girl he's taking out Friday, well, let's just say he's your worst nightmare, and there is nothing douchey that will deter your girl away from him. And he's only going to ruin her, because any other man won't compare. Dick is too big, man."

"You're exaggerating."

He pushes his sunglasses down his nose. "Six foot fucking seven," Nolan says. "Pecs bigger than my goddamn head. Thighs that have cracked a watermelon with one squeeze. And that dick of his? A fucking tree trunk. I've seen it firsthand. Tell me I'm lying."

"When have you seen his dick?"

"Don't ask questions." Nolan holds his hand up. "Just know your chances of being with this girl are nonexistent now. Unsure what Graydon was thinking, but welcome to the permanent friend zone, my guy."

And just like that, dread fills me along with a heavy dose of regret.

"What the fuck, man," I yell. "You were the one who told me to do this."

He presses his hand to his ear. "For fuck's sake, not so loud."

"No, you're the one who got me into this mess, now get me out of it. Tell your friend, Cougar, to cancel on her."

"No can do. He's not my friend. Also, this was not my fault."

"This one hundred percent was your fault."

"No, I told you to get someone douchey, not an Adonis with a fucking jackhammer dick. That's on you."

"You said douchey, and Graydon said he was douchey. How is this my fault?"

"It's called research," Nolan says as he takes another sip of his Powerade. "Did you even look the guy up before sending her the info?"

"No," I say, hating how hasty I was.

"That's right, because if you did look him up, you would have seen just how massive he is. And you're a big guy yourself, but to him, you're an ant. If you actually saw what he looked like, you never would have sent his phone number over."

He's right about that. If I took one goddamn second to look Cougar up, I'd have seen just how "good-looking" he is and I'd have never sent his information over to Bower. I'd have asked Graydon to try again.

But I didn't do that. No, I served Cougar up on a silver platter to Bower, practically dabbing her face with a napkin and handing her the utensils to chow down.

What a fucking moron.

"Fuck," I say, dragging my hand down my face. "What have I done?"

"Something incredibly stupid."

"Maybe...maybe they won't hit it off."

"They will." Nolan downs another Powerade. "Because I know Cougar, and there isn't one person that he doesn't hit it off with. Your only prayer now is that he won't like her. Any hope in that angle?"

I shake my head because Bower is perfect. How could he not like her? She's fun, beautiful, smart, quick on her feet, and outgoing. Nothing seems to bother her. And she's up for pretty much anything.

"She's...she's amazing."

"Says the guy with hearts in his eyes when he speaks about her."

"She is," I say, slouching more in my chair, defeat reigning over me. "They're going to hit it off, date, and he'll end up fulfilling all of her sexual fantasies, and by next year they'll be engaged and I'll be asked to give a speech at their wedding about how I set them up despite being completely and utterly infatuated with her."

Nolan pauses for a moment, staring me down through those

ridiculous sunglasses. After a few seconds, he nods. "Yup, that seems very accurate."

"I fucking hate you."

"Don't hate the plan, my man." He cracks open another bottle. "Hate the execution."

Head buried in my pillow, I take a deep breath and then sigh.

It still smells like her.

If you're thinking, *Whoa, dude, that's coming off as pathetic,* then you would be right.

It is pathetic.

And yet, here I am.

This is what I have left of her. The faint smell of her in the fabric of a pillowcase.

With one more big sniff, I get myself out of my bed and head to the bathroom, where I take care of business and brush my teeth before slipping on a pair of sweatpants that ride low on my hips from how much I've been training.

My waist has become narrower and my shoulders broader. I've seen the change slowly happen over the last two years since I've been training and eating differently. My muscles are more pronounced, my skin almost feels tighter around my bones, showing off every curve and indent. Sure, probably in the best shape of my life, but what good has that done me?

None.

Absolutely zero.

I scoop some water into my hands and spray my face and wet my hair before drying off and heading into the kitchen to make a protein drink.

Water droplets fall from my hair as I grab my milk just as there is a knock at the door.

I glance at the time and know that I didn't order anything, therefore it could only be one person.

Excitement pulses through me as I set the milk down and go to the door.

Thank God I brushed my teeth.

I open the door and standing on the other side, wearing a pair of black leggings and a white off-the-shoulder crop top, is Bower. Fuck, she's so beautiful.

"Good morning," she says with a huge smile. "I can see that you're ready for the day."

"Late night. Just got out of bed."

"Ooo, did you go out?" she asks, wiggling her brows.

"No, game went extra innings."

"Did you win?"

"No," I answer, still feeling the irritation of the loss.

"Yikes, that's not fun." She nods to my apartment. "Are you going to let me in, or are you going to make me talk to you out here?"

I push the door open and she walks under my arm, her hair brushing against my skin as she walks by, and it takes everything in me not to get hard from it.

Fuck, I'm so pathetic.

I don't see the bag she has with her until she sets it on the counter and turns toward me.

"What's that?" I ask.

"Cronuts. Want one?"

"Not really part of my diet," I say.

Her eyes scan my torso for a moment before she clears her throat and says, "I think you can spare the calories." Then she moves to my kitchen, grabs two plates, and brings them to the counter, where she dishes out two large, pink-frosted cronuts.

"Raspberry flavored," she says before lifting up and taking a seat on the counter.

Joining her, I lean my hip against the counter, pick up my cronut, and take a bite just as she does.

Her eyes widen and then they shut as she lightly moans.

Nope.

No.

Can't have her doing that.

"This is so good. It's like sex in my mouth."

"Huh?" I ask.

"Better than an orgasm."

I mean, it's good, but not that good.

"If you think this is better than an orgasm, then clearly you haven't been with the right people."

"Clearly." She takes another bite and moans.

"Can you...can you not do that?" I ask, trying to hold it together.

"Do what?"

"Moan while you eat?"

"Why? Turning you on?" she jokes.

Yeah.

I look away and she laughs, nudging me with her foot.

"Oh my God, Bennett, a food moan is turning you on."

"No, I mean...maybe, it's just...it's been a little bit since, you know, and I don't need you moaning like that. It's too sexual and you have me reading those books, and it's just—"

"They made you horny."

"Hell..." I let out a deep breath.

She laughs loudly. "Do you see why I'm the way that I am? My vibrator has had three new battery changes. I'm wearing it out."

I glance at her, not expecting her to be so candid. Then again, it's Bower. I should expect nothing less.

"Your hand must be rubbed raw." She lifts my hand to examine it. "My God, the calluses on your palms. Your poor dick. It must be like fucking a cheese grater every time you jack off." Her eyes meet mine. "Is your dick okay?"

"My dick is fine."

"Just fine?" She lifts a brow.

"Can we not talk about this?"

"Ooo, you seem to be in a mood today. Everything okay?"

No.

It's not okay.

First, you look hot as shit and you're not even wearing makeup—which of course is my favorite.

Second, you smell so fucking good that it's taking everything in me not to push you against the wall and run my tongue up your neck—or rub my pillow all over you for an extra boost in scent.

And third, you're going on a date with a guy that you're probably going to end up marrying, all because I failed to do the research before giving you his information.

"Just tired," I say.

"Well, I can leave if you want to get some more sleep."

"No," I almost say in a panic and then clear my throat. "I mean, no, it's okay. I was up anyway."

"Okay." She eyes me for a moment. "If this is about the horniness, I can possibly see if I can find someone for you."

I shake my head. "It's not. It's fine. Sorry."

"Why are you apologizing?" She nudges me with her foot. "You don't need to apologize. Honestly, I don't know what I'd do without you at this point. I'm so lucky that you live here and have been willing to help out. I thought bringing a cronut over might be nice given your sweet tooth, but I'm seeing that maybe the morning after a late night might not be the best choice."

"No, it is," I say. "Just, yeah, forget I even got weird." I look her in the eyes. "Thank you for the cronut, feel free to bring over pastries every morning if you want."

"Don't tease me. There are enough pastries in this city to try something new every day for a year. Ooo—" Her eyes widen with excitement. "We could start a food blog about pastries. Kind of like what Nolan does with his breakfast burritos."

"That would require me caring about social media, and I don't care in the slightest."

"Yeah, you don't seem like someone who would care. Maybe we can keep the reviews to ourselves. Start a notebook, rate them."

"I could get on board with that," I say and take a bite of my cronut. "What would you rate this?"

"Well, given my moaning, I would grade it pretty high. Oh, maybe we can rate it by moans? How loud and long it made me moan."

"Or we can go by stars. Stars are pretty universal." Because I don't need her moaning around me.

"Ugh, boring, but fine." She examines the cronut. "Are we talking solid one through five stars here, or can we go with decimals?"

"I think we can go with decimals."

"You're a real savior." She studies the cronut some more. "Okay, I think I'd give this a four-point-two-seven."

"A four-point-two-seven?" I ask. "How the hell did you come up with that?"

She shrugs. "Just felt right."

I shake my head because she's weird but really fucking cute.

"What about you?" she asks. "What would you give it?"

"If we're giving oddball numbers, then three-point-eight-two-three."

Her mouth falls open and she sets her cronut down. "What? Three-point-eight-two-three? Have you lost your mind? That's outrageous."

"How is that outrageous?"

"Because"—she picks up her cronut again—"this hybrid of a flaky, buttery croissant and ooey-gooey donut is easily no less than a four-point-one-seven-two-nine and you go and give it a three-point-eight-two-three?" She shakes her head. "You're no longer invited to offer ratings with that kind of tomfoolery."

"This coming from the person who uses a four-point-one- seven-two-nine as a rating."

"I'm impressed you remembered those numbers, because I couldn't have told you what it was if you asked me."

I chuckle. "My point exactly. I think decimals have to be taken out."

"Decimals are what makes the world run smoothly."

"Why are you like this?"

"Unsure." She smirks and then nudges me again. "There you are, the easygoing guy I know."

"Was here the whole time."

"No, you weren't, but nice try." She wipes her hands on a napkin.

Not wanting to harp on my weird mood, but instead, try to show her what a fun, compatible guy I can be for her, I say, "So when are you going to invite me over to your place so I can see it?"

"Ooof, that will be a little while."

My brow scrunches together. "Why?"

"Everything is still in boxes besides clothes. Haven't had much time to unpack since I've been either helping my boss, running errands, or too exhausted after the day to even think about unpacking."

"You can't live like that, Bower. You have to unpack. I can help you."

"No." She shakes her head and hops off the counter. "You've already done so much for me."

I press my hand to her hip, keeping her in place against the cabinets, her eyes shooting up to me in surprise. "I'm serious," I say, dropping my tone so it's softer. "Let me help you."

Her eyes search mine for a second before she says, "But you're… you're so busy and you've already done so much. I can't ask you to do that for me."

"You're not asking me to do anything. I'm offering."

"I know, but—"

I move in closer to her, watching her expression morph into even more surprise. "I have an afternoon game on Saturday. I can help after that. We could order pizza and tackle all the boxes. Get it done so you can retreat to a home after you get done with work."

She swallows. "You, uh, you would do that?"

"Of course I would." I release her hip. "But you're paying for the pizza."

She clears her throat on a laugh. "Okay, says the multimillionaire."

"If you want the muscles to come work for you, then you're going to have to pay up."

"And the way to the use of your muscles is through pizza?"

No, it's you.

But it doesn't seem like that's something I can ask for.

"It is. Pepperoni with mushrooms." I wink and then shove the rest of my cronut in my mouth.

CHAPTER 10
BOWER

"WHAT DO YOU THINK OF this one?" I ask Gabby, who is on FaceTime with me while I pick out an outfit to wear to my date that's happening in less than forty-five minutes. "Is it too slutty?"

"Are you wearing a bra?" she asks, moving her face closer to the phone for a better look.

"No, should I be wearing a bra?"

"I can see your nipples through that shirt from here."

I glance down at the white, gauzy material and see that she's, in fact, correct. There they are. My nipples on full display.

"Maybe it could be nice—"

"No, we're not showing nipple on your first date."

"Pretty sure you showed nipple on your first date with Ryland, and look where that got you."

"Technically, it wasn't a date at all, just a one-night stand," Gabby says just as Ryland comes on screen, grips her jaw and gives her a kiss that I can actually see melts a piece of my best friend. See, that's why I'm doing this, why I'm going on this date, because I want that.

I want a man to be so possessive that he makes me melt in front of my friend on FaceTime.

When he pulls away, he says, "It was a date."

"If that was a date, then I hope I have the same kind of date tonight, as this girl could use that kind of activity in her life."

Ryland gives Gabby one more kiss and then says, "Be responsible, Bower. Use protection."

After he takes off, I say, "Why does he treat me like one of his students?"

"Probably because you have the maturity level of one of them."

I chuckle. "You're right about that."

I move toward my closet and pull out a black top. "What about this with my black leather pants?"

"Feels very Sandy from *Grease*. Don't you have a simple dress? Maybe something with a decent neckline that doesn't make your bosom defy gravity?"

"My bosom is one of the benefits I have to offer. I should show them off."

"Not to this guy, not yet."

"What do you mean, not to this guy?" I ask, turning toward her with a red dress in one hand and a light green one in the other.

"I was looking him up, and well, he kind of seems like a player. I'm honestly surprised that Bennett suggested him, because Cougar could hurt you. Plus, with a name like Cougar, do you really think he's the type that settles down?"

"First of all, I'm not going into this date looking to get married tomorrow. I'm looking to have fun with the possibility that maybe it could lead to more. Second of all, Cougar is a hard name to pass off. I'm unsure why his parents went in that direction. Needless to say, I think he's owning it and we shouldn't prejudge him. He sounded nice in his text messages—"

"He's not picking you up at your apartment. You're meeting him at a bar."

"That's just safety. No one picks people up at their apartments or houses unless it's been at least five dates. Lots of psychos out there; can't give them clearance to an address just yet. You would know this if you didn't have a slutty one-night stand with a baseball coach."

She rolls her eyes. "It was not slutty. It was beautiful."

"He spanked you several times."

"Shhhh..." she says, looking over her shoulder. "Ryland doesn't like it when I share specifics about our love life."

"Ew, don't call it 'love life.'"

"What am I supposed to call it?"

"You can say Ryland doesn't like you to share the way you two fuck."

"Yeah, I'm not going to say that. 'Love life' is romantic."

"'Love life' made me throw up in my mouth."

"Either way, I think you need to have a plan. Is this another fling for you? Or is this a new chapter?"

I shrug. "I don't know. I guess we shall see how it pans out." Deep down, I sort of want this to be the start of something, not a random hookup, because I'm ready for that. I'm ready for something so much more, but telling Gabby that, she'll...ugh, she'll just take it too seriously and probably drive me nuts, asking me if I'm in love every two seconds, so I'm keeping those feelings close to my chest for now. I hold the dress options up and say, "Which one?"

"Light green."

"That was going to be my choice, too, but I need help zipping it. Think I can find someone on the street to help me?"

"Ask Bennett."

"Doesn't he have a game?"

"It ended really early. He should be home by now."

"Really?" I ask, surprised.

"Yeah, text him."

I pick up the phone and shoot him a quick text, asking if he's home, and when he replies almost immediately that he is, I know I've found my helper.

"He's home. Okay, well, I'll get changed and then have him help me."

"Perfect. And hey." I pause what I'm doing and look at her because she's using her serious tone.

"Yes?"

"I want you to have fun tonight, but please make smart decisions, okay? This guy…from what I've seen online, he seems like he knows how to play the game, and I don't want you to just…fall into his bed."

"Like you fell into Ryland's?" I ask with a smirk.

"Ryland was different and the circumstances were different. He wasn't a player. He was celibate and hadn't had sex for ten years—"

"That is not fucking true," Ryland says off camera, making us both laugh.

"It seems like Cougar can have a new girl every night, and I just don't want you to, you know, give away the goods so easily. If you're really looking for love, for a partner in life, then maybe just…close up shop for a bit. Make sure he's a good one before you give away the bacon."

"Are you referring to my lady parts as bacon?"

"No," she says just as Ryland says, "Yes."

She glances over her shoulder and whispers, "Stay out of this."

When she turns back toward me, I say, "I understand the point you're trying to make, and I know this might surprise you, but I made a promise with myself to not sleep with the guy for at least five dates, because if he can take me on five dates and not try to get in my pants, then he very well might be serious."

"I think that's a really good idea, actually."

"Thank you. Came up with it myself."

"Well, you're smart. I approve."

"Good, now, if you don't mind, I'm going to get dressed and then go out on my date."

"Have fun. Love you."

"Love you too."

I wave bye and then hang up. I hold the green dress up in front of me and nod.

Yup, it's going to be a good night.

Come on, Bennett, open up.

Open up.

After a few seconds of waiting, I raise my fist to knock again just as Bennett opens the door, holding his book in one hand, looking all types of disheveled as if he's been running his hand through his hair.

I love it when he's not wearing a baseball cap, because his hair is always a disaster in this cute *didn't style* way.

"Oh, hey, sorry. I didn't know it was you. Aren't you supposed to be—" His eyes scan me up and down and I watch as his Adam's apple bobs. "Whoa, Bower, you look incredible."

"Thank you. You don't think the dress is too slutty, do you?"

"Uh…no."

"Good." I turn around and lift up my hair. "Do you think you can help a girl out and zip me up? I have to grab a ride and don't want my driver thinking they're picking up a half-naked woman."

"Um, sure," he says before setting his book down on the console next to his door. He steps up behind me and grabs the small zipper, slowly pulling it up my back. "Isn't Cougar picking you up?"

"No, I didn't want him to know where I lived in case he turned out to be a psycho."

"Oh, probably smart." He finishes zipping me up and I turn to face him, straightening out my simple dress with a square neckline.

"Do I look okay?"

He takes a minute to look me over. "You look really good."

"Really?" I ask, my insecurities getting the best of me. I'm usually confident, but it's been a while since I've been on a date, and that wears on a person, so, yeah, I might be questioning myself.

"Really," he answers as he tugs on the loose strands of his hair.

"Well, that makes me feel much better, because I've been questioning every decision I've made while getting ready."

"Don't." He wets his lips. "You look incredible."

"Thank you." I let out a sigh. "Okay, I should get going. I need to call a ride and—"

"I can drop you off."

"Huh?" I ask, surprised by the gesture.

"I, uh, I was going to go grab some ice cream, so I can drop you off if you want."

"Oh, you don't have to do that."

"I don't mind," he says while slipping on a pair of slides and plucking a hat and placing it on his head. He grabs his keys, phone, and wallet and then locks up, not even giving me an option to stop him.

Well, I guess he's dropping me off.

He guides me to the elevator with his hand on my back then presses the down button.

"Uh, thank you."

"Sure," he says, as we both wait for the elevator, silence falling between us, because I was not expecting him to drive me around, and from the feel of it, he wasn't expecting to do it either.

When the elevator arrives and opens, I stop him before he can get on and say, "You really don't have to drop me off."

"And deny myself ice cream? That makes me think you don't know me at all."

"I know you, and I know you would do something just to be nice, even if it's inconvenient for you."

"It's not." He rests his hand on my waist, turns me, and we both head into the elevator, where he presses the button that leads out to the garage.

He guides me to a matte black Rivian truck, where he opens the passenger side for me, and lends me his hand to help me in. I glance at him in question, but he just smiles, as if this is all normal when it doesn't feel normal at all, but I go with it. When I'm settled in my seat, he reaches for my buckle and hands it to me.

"Safety first, Bower."

And here I thought he was going to buckle me in himself. No, that only shows up in romance novels, not real life, right?

He joins me on his side and then pulls out of his parking spot.

"Where we off to?" he asks.

"Oh, right, that might be good for you to know. We're meeting at The Powell Pub."

He glances over at me. "Really?"

"Is that bad?"

He shakes his head and presses forward. "Just...not a place I guess I'd take you on a first date—well, I mean, anyone, not just you, but I wouldn't take anyone there on a first date."

"Why not?" I ask as he makes a right onto a main road.

"It's kind of like an old boys' club, where men sip brandy and smoke cigars. Now it's a pub for all, but it still gives off those good-old-boy vibes."

"That is an interesting place to take a first date." I worry my lip, thinking about what Gabby said beforehand. "Do you know anything about Cougar?"

"Not really," he answers, his grip tightening on the steering wheel. "But Graydon thought that he might be good for you."

"Gabby was saying that he seemed like a player. Makes me a little nervous."

"Really?" he asks, stopping at a stoplight and facing me. "Want me to take you back home, or better yet, take you to get ice cream and then take you home?"

The prospect of crawling out of this dress and right back into pajamas with ice cream in hand is incredibly appealing, but if there is one thing I know, it's that I don't ever want to be the person that stands someone up. It's happened to me before and I know how bad it feels. And sure, it seems like Cougar is the type of guy who'd bounce back pretty easily, but still, I don't ever want to be that person.

"No, that's okay. I'll be fine. I'm sure it'll be a good time."

"You sure?" he asks, looking like he's willing and ready to book it the hell out of here and back to the apartment building. "Because I don't want to be the reason why you have a bad night."

"It won't be your fault if I do. It would be his. After all, he's the one who has to impress me, right?"

"Right," Bennett says, his eyes dropping to my lips for a moment before he turns back to the road. "But just in case, do you want to have a signal that you can text me in case you need me to bail you out?"

"Oh, that's a clever idea. Like if I send you an alert emoji, you know to call me and I'll pretend my aunt fell off a cliff or something."

"Jesus," he says as he makes a left-hand turn. "Maybe something a little more believable and a little less insane."

"Aunt falling off a cliff too much?"

"Just a little."

"Okay, maybe you got your head stuck in something and I have to come help you get your head out or else it's a call to the firemen."

"Why does my head need to be stuck in something? That seems idiotic."

"I wasn't talking about the head that sits on the top of your neck..."

His lips flatten, which makes me chuckle. "You're talking about my penis? What the hell would I get it stuck in?"

"I don't know. You're young. Are there any trends going around that would make you accidentally get your penis stuck?"

"No," he nearly shouts. "Jesus, Bower."

I chuckle. "Okay, so not into the penis getting stuck in something. Got it, hmm, what can you get stuck in something?"

"Nothing," he says. "Just say that I'm sick and need your help."

"Oh...that's actually, huh, that's really good. Gives me a relatable reason to leave but also makes me seem like a good person rather than someone trying to get out of a horrific date. Wonderful job, Bennett."

"Not that hard."

"What's not hard? Finding a reason why you need me? Or your penis when it gets stuck in something?"

He shakes his head as he says, "There's something seriously wrong with you."

"Are you sure you're good to go? I can still take you home."

I unbuckle my seatbelt and shake my head. "No, it's good. This is going to be fun." I look out the window toward the pub with stained-glass windows. Really wish he chose somewhere else.

"I can stick around for a second or even walk you in if you want."

I chuckle. "You're acting like a dad."

"The fuck I am," he says, utterly insulted at the suggestion. "Just looking out for you."

"Well, I'll be fine...Daddy."

One singular brow raises that makes me burst out in laughter.

"If you're calling me 'daddy,' then I can't possibly allow you to go into that bar. Off to get ice cream it is." He reaches to put the car back into drive, but I stop him with my hand to his.

"Don't even think about it," I say, then I open the door. "Thank you for bringing me here."

"Anytime," he says. "Want me to walk you in?"

I laugh. "No, I'll be fine. I promise."

"Okay, but seriously, text me anytime if you need me, even if it's three in the morning. I'm here for you."

"Thank you, Bennett." I squeeze his arm. "You're a great friend. I'd be lost without you."

His lips press together as he lightly smiles. "Anytime."

I let out a deep breath. "Okay, here goes nothing." I hop out of the car, wave to Bennett, and then head toward the front door. Large, mahogany, and heavy, it takes me a second, but I pull it open and I'm instantly hit with that day-old, musty-beer smell that seems to permeate every pub in the world.

The entire space is floor-to-ceiling wood. From the walls, to the floors, to the tables and chairs, and only the stained-glass lampshades and brass accents along the bar provide contrast.

Bennett wasn't kidding when he said it seems like a good old boys' club.

Not letting it shift my mood, I glance around the room, looking for Cougar, just as a hand is placed on my back.

Surprised, I turn around and come face to, well, chest of a man in a blue-and-white-striped shirt and navy blue capris with accompanying loafers. Slowly, I lift my eyes past a broad set of shoulders, up a thick column of a neck, to a freshly shaven jaw, slightly pointy nose, and then to a pair of dark and almost dangerous eyes.

"Bower?" he asks.

"Cougar," I say, almost feeling breathless from his sheer presence. Not sure I've ever met someone who is six seven in real life, but my God, is he tall.

"That would be me." He leans down and places a kiss on my cheek. "Great to meet you." He takes in my dress and smirks. "You look great."

"Thank you. I might have changed several times before coming tonight."

"You chose right." He holds out his arm and says, "Shall we?"

"I think we shall." I smile up at him, already mentally thanking Bennett for setting me up, because this is what I'm talking about. He seems nice, a bit of a gentleman, and he's hot.

He leads me past a few tables, and when I feel like we're going to go to the back, he makes a hard right and gestures to a stool at the bar.

Oh.

This is…this is not what I was expecting.

"Are we waiting for a table?" I ask, taking in the four empty booths in the back.

"Nah, I like sitting at the bar. Drinks come faster." He winks and takes a seat next to me.

Okay, no big deal. I like a good drink as well.

"What would you like?" he asks.

"Umm, what are you getting?"

"Blue Moon. Want one? It's the best beer, no contest."

Blue Moon? The best? Nothing against the beer company, but claiming it as the best seems odd, since you can get it pretty much anywhere. I mean, it's good, but that's a pretty big statement.

But we're going with the flow, so I say, "Then I'll take one as well."

His eyes lift in surprise. "Damn, I like you already."

If I knew agreeing to a favorite beer was the way to win a man's heart, then I wouldn't be single right now.

He flags down the bartender and puts in an order for two beers and some nachos. Then he turns toward me and says, "So, how do you know Graydon?"

"Oh, I don't know him," I say, probably confusing him. "My friend actually asked him to set me up."

"Your friend asked Graydon St. John to set you up?" His brows lift in shock. "Does he know Graydon at all? Setting people up is not his thing, not even a little. The whole reason I accepted your number was because I was curious as to who Graydon would put in the effort for." His eyes travel down my body for a moment before he says, "I can see why he'd put in the effort."

"Well, it wasn't Graydon. It was my friend, Bennett. He actually plays baseball for the Bombers."

Our beers are set in front of us and he grabs his, taking a large gulp before putting it back on the bar. "Bennett Brinkman?" he asks.

"Yes, that's him."

"He's fucking elite at baseball. Have you seen him play?"

I nod, my cheeks blushing for some reason. Maybe because I've known him for so long that when people fangirl over him, it's almost as though I feel complimented as well. That's what happens when you're super proud of someone, I guess.

"I have. He's incredibly good."

Not that I know much about baseball, but when I see him play, we're always cheering because he gets on base or makes a good play. Unsure how that compares, but from the sound of it, he seems to do much better than others.

"So good that there are already conversations about his career and where he'll end up, because San Francisco would be wasting his potential, given the cheating scandal."

"Well, he wasn't part of the cheating," I say.

"Oh, I know, but his image is almost sullied being on the team. It would be best if he was traded somewhere else."

God, the thought of him being traded actually makes my stomach churn. I haven't been in San Francisco long, but I couldn't imagine what it would be like if he was no longer here. He's...he's my friend and I rely on seeing him, even if he's in and out thanks to his job.

"He's doing PR to help the image, though."

"Yeah, same bullshit Graydon is doing." Cougar shakes his head and takes a sip of his beer. "Don't see how it's going to help. Bennett would have to come up with something really good to pull his team back to good graces, and it sucks that it's his face they're using to do so, when he wasn't the one who fucked up to begin with."

"I agree. It's not very fair."

"Although...Graydon seems to be doing a hell of a job."

"Isn't he doing something with the zookeeper?"

Cougar nods. "Yeah, a whole PR relationship."

"Oh, I thought. . .Bennett made it seem like it's a real relationship."

"Might be." Cougar shrugs. "From what it seems to me from the outside, it's a PR relationship, but Bennett probably knows him better. I don't cross paths with Graydon all too much."

"Oh, you're not friends?"

"Nah, just teammates. He's more of a recluse. The only guy he really hangs out with is Hutton. Kind of like how Asher Peppers is on the Bombers."

"Who's that?"

"The catcher. Kind of surprised Bennett didn't try to hook you up with him."

"Oh, um, that's probably because I didn't really want to date a baseball player."

"No?" He lifts a brow. "Why not?"

"Uh, not around enough," I say. "I guess with football, you don't travel as much as baseball, and well, it would be nice to have my man around."

"Your man, huh?" He slowly nods. "I like the sound of that. And you're right. The baseball travel schedule is hectic and for longer stretches. If you stick with me, babe, I could have you way more nights than any catcher ever could." He winks. "But Asher Peppers, I could see you two hitting it off."

"Trying to get rid of me already?" I ask, sipping my drink.

"Just giving you options."

"Well, then maybe you'll give me Asher's number."

He shakes his head. "No, your fine ass is staying right where it is."

"Good answer."

CHAPTER 11
BENNETT

THIS WAS THE WORST FUCKING idea I've ever had in my entire goddamn existence.

Setting Bower up with someone else, stupid idea.

Setting her up with fucking Cougar Vajeen? It's a crime.

Jail.

I should be taken to fucking jail right now.

Pacing my living room, I tug on my hair for the hundredth time as I try not to think of every minute they spend together.

Or how she's probably touching him while she laughs.

Or how he's probably checking her out...in the dress I zipped for her!

Or how...fuck, how they'll probably kiss.

He'll kiss her before I will.

Hell, I'll probably never kiss her now. I'll just always wonder what it's like to be admired by her, but never actually feel it.

Because that's my life, right? Lonely, pathetic, with no prospect of securing a date with the girl I can't stop thinking about.

That I haven't stopped thinking about for years.

"Fuck," I yell and then flop down on the couch, where my phone is.

I check the time and curse when I see that it's past ten.

Are they still out?

Did she go home with him?

Is he unzipping the dress that I zipped up for her?

Should I go down to the bar and offer to drive her home even though she's with a date?

Would that be weird?

Of course it would be weird, jackass. She's with another man.

But is he the type to drive her home?

I hope not, if he's been drinking...

Would he do that?

Fuck, I have no idea and now the questions are starting to consume me, eat away at me, and before I can stop myself, I send a text to the one person I probably shouldn't text, but I can't help myself.

Bennett: Does Cougar tend to drink and drive?

I set the phone down and rock in my seat, burying my head in my hands, agonizing over the thought of them together.

If I have learned one thing from this entire experience, it's don't take fucking Nolan's advice, because this is where it sends me, straight into a fucking agonizing torment.

My phone beeps with a response and I half wish for it to be Bower asking for a ride home or better yet, an escape from the date because it's going so badly.

But when I see it's not her, all hope is lost.

Graydon: No.

Fuck. Why did I think that he'd be the best person to help me with this? The man barely talks. Hell, if this was OC, he probably wouldn't have set her up in the first place because he'd have been able to read between the lines and come up with another idea to get Bower to like me. But if he did set her up with someone else, there's no doubt in my mind that OC would be sitting on the couch, right next to me, holding my hand and making sure that I'd be okay.

Graydon…not so much.

And yet, I can't help myself in texting him back.

Bennett: Are you sure? I dropped my friend off at a pub and just want to make sure she's safe.

Graydon: Then why aren't you texting her instead of me?

Great point.

Excellent, actually.

The man is a smart one.

Too bad for him that I'm full of desperation.

Bennett: I don't want to bother her.

Graydon: If it's about drunk driving, I'm sure she wouldn't be bothered, but grateful instead.

Another great point. He's being logical, and I'm purely emotional.

Bennett: Agreed, agreed, but I just want to feel you out and see what you thought of the situation. Does he get drunk often? And when he's drunk, is he persuasive? Does he get his date drunk as well? Does he take advantage? What are his thoughts on consent?

I press send before I can stop myself and then start pacing the living room again.

I know over the last few weeks I've gained a lot of ground with Graydon. He's come to respect me, appreciate me, maybe even consider me a friend, but I know from that text alone, he'll probably block my number.

But I had to take a chance, I had to figure it out.

After a few seconds of him not responding and me on the brink of texting him again, my phone buzzes in my hand and I see that he's calling.

Graydon.

Calling me.

I know this doesn't happen often and that he's not much of a talker, so I steady myself and try to remain calm as I answer.

"Hey, man, what's going on?"

"What's going on is that you're bothering me and I don't want you bothering me, so fucking stop it," he growls.

Yup, saw that coming.

And yet, I can't stop myself.

"Sorry about that, just concerned about my friend, you know? I have a sense of responsibility where she's concerned. I need to make sure she's safe and taken care of."

"So why did you send her on the date?"

Because I'm a moron!

"She really wants to meet new people and I trust you. I figured you would have good judgment and that you'd set her up with someone respectful. Is, uh, is Cougar respectful?" Possibly practicing the art of celibacy at the moment?

"I mean...sure," Graydon says, not sounding sure at all.

That's not reassuring.

"Sure? That, uh...that doesn't sound like you mean it, and this is my friend, Graydon. I need to make sure that you didn't do me dirty. Did you do me dirty?"

"Where the fuck is this all coming from? You asked for a number of a complete douche. I gave you a number and then I walked away. Why the fuck are you bothering me on a Friday night?"

"Well, to be fair, you're the one who called me."

"Yeah, and you're the one texting, looking for a background check on a man I barely know."

"Ah-ha!" I say with a point of my finger. "So you admit you barely know him."

"I never admitted otherwise," he counters.

True, very true…

"Listen, you're annoying the shit out of me. I want nothing to do with this. Cougar isn't dumb. He's not going to do something like drink and drive. I know he fucks a lot, but nothing makes me suspect that he does it without consent. So, if your friend ends up in his bed, that's of her own volition. Got it?"

I swallow hard, my skin prickling with nerves. "Got it."

"Good." And then he hangs up, leaving me feeling incredibly unwell.

So unwell that I walk over to the kitchen, open up the freezer door, and plop my head in it to cool my burning skin.

And as I rest there, the bag of frozen peas practically mocking me, I wonder if I should just…give up. If all of this worrying is for nothing, because let's be honest, would I ever really have a chance with Bower? Will she ever look at me the way that I look at her?

From how she called me a great friend in my truck before she went off to her date, I'm going to guess my chances are about as thin as the plastic holding this bag of peas together.

Buzz. Buzz.

A text!

I lift my head from the freezer, my excitement climbing.

It has to be her. She needs to be rescued.

And here I was, about to freeze my head into an ice cube.

Foolish behavior!

I slam the freezer door shut, grab my phone, and see that it's a text from Gretchen.

Ugh. That was fucking cruel.

Gretchen: In the neighborhood, want to talk now?

It's past ten, what the hell is she doing?
What do I care, though? That will keep me busy.

Bennett: Sure, meet you at Brewers? In five?
Gretchen: See you there.

I slip on a hat and a shirt that isn't drenched in nervous sweat and then book it down to the twenty-four-hour coffee shop that is right around the corner from me.

When I arrive, she's already sitting at a table with a cup of coffee in front of her. I offer her a nod and then fill a complimentary cup of water before sitting down across from her.

Gretchen is...tough.

She keeps us in line when it comes to this PR nightmare and doesn't let us get away with anything. We even tried to overthrow her at the beginning, tell her that we weren't into this whole zoo thing, but that did us no good. She put us in our place pretty quickly.

"So...you're unhappy."

About a lot of things, but she doesn't need to know that.

"Yeah, I just, I fail to see how working at the zoo is helping me. I know there will be video released of everything we've done, but it's quite time-consuming for me, and I don't see much return. Maybe there's something else I can participate in that would be a better fit, kind of like how Graydon is doing the social media thing with Maple."

She nods. "Yeah, I've heard from the Bombers front office that they haven't seen much pickup from what you've been doing, and I've been thinking about how I could remedy that."

"Really?" I ask, feeling hope. "Maybe you can go with someone else on the team? The whole grumpy thing seems to work, so maybe you can ask about Asher Peppers, take the Graydon route."

She shakes her head. "No, he was on the team during the scandal. We're trying to uplift a new line of faces and they're set on you. You have the most appeal to the fans right now, especially the women." She brings her drink to her mouth. "How do you feel about a PR relationship?"

"Not happening," I say, knowing for a fact that's not something I could pull off.

"Shame, oh…what about a dating show?"

"No," I deadpan.

"You don't have to actually date the person."

"No, nothing to do with my love life."

"Do you have a girlfriend?"

"No," I say wistfully as my mind goes to Bower.

"What's that?" she asks, motioning to my face.

"What's what?" I ask.

"That look. When I asked if you have a girlfriend, you said no, but there was this starry-eyed glaze in your expression."

I shake my head. "No, there wasn't."

"There most definitely was. Are you lying to me? Do you have a girlfriend? Because this is information we need to know. We have to know every aspect of your life, especially if you're romantically involved with someone because if there is a scandal or—"

"I don't have a girlfriend."

"But are you seeing someone?"

"No," I answer, which makes her study me longer than I want her to.

"You don't have a girlfriend, nor are you seeing someone, but you're practically giddy at the thought of it…"

"I'm not giddy—"

"You like someone." She points at me and then nods, agreeing with herself. "You like someone and wish they were with you, am I right? I have to be right. Am I?"

"Noooo," I drag out, not even convincing myself.

"Liar. Who is it?"

"No one."

She uncrosses her legs and leans forward on the table. "Bennett, it would benefit you tremendously if you don't piss me off. So who the hell do you like? And if you tell me no one, I will be sure to extend your PR time with the zoo into the next year."

Christ, I don't want that.

"Fine, it's my sister's best friend."

She leans back in her seat. "Interesting."

"She's currently on a date right now with Cougar Vajeen," I blurt, hating myself for it.

"Cougar Vajeen? As in the running back for the Foghorns?"

"Is there really another person with the name Cougar Vajeen?"

Her eyes narrow. "Don't get lippy with me. I'm trying to help you."

"How is drilling me about my love life helping me?"

"I'm helping your image."

"My image is fine." I slouch in my chair. "It's my personal life that's fucked up." I tug on the brim of my hat. "I was the one who set her up with Cougar."

"You set up the girl you like with Cougar Vajeen?"

"That would be correct."

"Why the hell would you do that? Do you not know his reputation?"

"I do now."

"Then why did you do it?"

"Bad advice."

"From whom?" she asks.

"Nolan Hart on my team. He said that if I wanted to win her over, I should set her up with a douchebag and then when she realizes what a douche he is, that I could swoop in and show her how great I am. So I asked Graydon to help—"

"Graydon's in on this?" Gretchen's eyes nearly pop out of their sockets, and I don't blame her; I'd think the same thing.

"He was reluctant but then asked Hutton and they got me Cougar's number, which I gave to Bower. That's her name."

She rubs her temples as if this is information that will hurt any plans she's worked on over the last few weeks.

"Who knows about this?"

"Why does it matter?"

"Because I need to know everything so I'm fully prepared. What if Cougar decides to do something stupid with this girl, then she comes to the media about how Cougar Vajeen mistreated her and then names all the people involved in setting her up with him? I need to be prepared for such an event."

"She wouldn't do that," I say. "She's a good friend."

"Good friends always turn on the famous. Textbook. So who is involved?"

"She won't turn on me," I say with conviction. That makes Gretchen pause for a moment.

"Fine, in the unlikely event that she does turn on you, who was involved in this setup?"

"Just the people I mentioned. Me, Graydon, Hutton, Nolan, and Cougar."

She types something in her phone and says, "That's way too many men to be involved in a woman's future."

"She asked to be set up," I say out of pure defense. "I want that to be clear. It was initially her idea."

"Well, that's a relief at least." She lets out a sigh and glances toward the window. "So, there's no chance you're going to be dating this girl?"

"From what I heard about Cougar Vajeen, it's probably a no," I say, my gut churning at the thought of them being together, getting married, having kids…

"But you want something to happen with her?"

"I don't see how this is relevant to the PR bullshit that I'm trying to get out of."

"It's relevant."

"How so?" I ask. "I told you I'm not doing a dating show."

"No, I wasn't thinking about that." She folds her arms, staring off in the distance, a thoughtful expression tugging on her face. "What if…" She pauses and her teeth pull on the corner of her lip. "What if we did something with you in the PR space that would possibly, I don't know… assist in your endeavors to date her?"

"I don't want to expose her to the public and use her to help the Bombers' image."

"No, that's not what I'm thinking. Graydon is already doing that with Maple. We don't want to double down on the same PR strategy."

"Okay, so then what do you mean?"

"What if we had you participate in something that she likes and that could win her over, while also uplifting the image of the team?"

"And why the hell would we do that? As if you care about my love life."

"You're right, I really don't." Her eyes scan over me. "But I care about your image because that's my job, and the way you're presenting yourself at the moment is one step up from angry troll under a bridge throwing sticks as people pass by."

"I'm not a troll."

"Your shirt is inside out."

"No, it's not," I say as I glance down at my shirt, and sure as shit it is.

"And don't tell me it's the new way of wearing it."

"Fine," I capitulate. "I might have had a bad night, but that's because it's Bower's first time going out with Cougar and I'm struggling with the thought of it, so yeah, I'm struggling—"

The door to the coffee shop opens and as if saying her name enough beckons her, Bower walks in.

"Holy shit," I whisper, wanting to duck under a table, praying to the fucking gods above that Cougar doesn't walk in behind her.

"What?" Gretchen asks, looking over to the side.

"That's her. Bower is here."

An evil smirk spreads over Gretchen's lips just before she lifts her hand and calls out, "Bower."

"What the fuck—" I start to whisper as Bower turns toward us, a crease in her brow before she recognizes me.

"Bennett." Her face lights up. "What are you doing here?"

"Uh…"

"Late-night planning session," Gretchen says with a smile and then lends out her hand. "Hi, I'm Gretchen. I'm in charge of Bennett's PR right now."

"Oh, the whole zoo thing. It's nice to meet you." She glances at me and smiles. "Well, I'll let you get back to what you're talking about. It's late and I don't want to hold you up."

"No, please join us," Gretchen says, making my cheeks burn, because what the hell is she doing? "We could use some help, actually, and since you know Bennett so well, you could be of use."

"Are you sure?" Bower looks between the two of us.

"Positive," Gretchen says.

"Okay, sure. I'm just going to grab a drink really quick."

"I can get it for you," I say, going to stand, but she places her hand on my chest and stops me.

"I got it. Thank you, though." With a wink, she heads over to the counter and my eyes trail after her, watching the way her hips sway against the fabric of her dress, how it clings to her torso and flares out at her waist.

Did he touch her?

Kiss her?

Slip his hand under the hem of her dress?

Did he tell her he'd call her later? Set up another date?

If she's alone right now, does that mean they didn't get along?

Fuck, I don't want to get my hopes up.

"If you stare at her any longer, she might disappear into thin air," Gretchen says, pulling me out of my thoughts.

I turn back toward her and whisper, "What the fuck is your plan, Gretchen?"

"Well, now that I've seen the transparent longing in your eyes, I'm going to attempt to end the agony and just tell her how you feel."

"What?" I say, my fucking balls shriveling at the suggestion. "No, you can't. Gretchen, it would...it would ruin everything. She's...she's my sister's—"

"I'm kidding, Bennett. I wouldn't do that."

My breath catches in my lungs from the panic she just put me through. "How do I know that's the truth?"

"Because it seems like the thought of her finding out about your feelings might actually give you a heart attack, and although it would tickle me to see a love connection unfold in front of my eyes, the job comes first, and giving one of my clients a heart attack doesn't necessarily scream 'good press.'"

I let out a short sigh. "Good, because she can't know."

"Ever?" Gretchen asks with a lift of her brow.

"No, not never, just...not yet. She...she still sees me as the little brother and I need to show her I'm not that man."

"Fair. So then my plan will work."

"What plan?" I ask as I hear Bower thank the barista for her drink.

"Just go with it?"

"Gretchen, I fucking swear," I say through clenched teeth just as Bower joins us, taking a seat right next to me, her shoulder brushing up against mine.

Is it dumb to think that I missed her? That all of the agonizing I've done tonight has made me feel like a lovesick puppy, looking for any kind of connection with her?

And she smells so good, just like her. I want to lean into her, run my nose along her neck, see if she smells like anyone else but her, but I refrain as she crosses one leg over the other and leans into me.

I take that opportunity to drape my arm over the back of her chair, something that Gretchen tracks with calculating eyes.

"So, why are you guys meeting so late?" Bower asks, a smirk on her lips. "Anything you're not telling me, Bennett?" She wiggles her brows and I hate that she'd ever suggest that Gretchen and I would be together.

"We're not together," I say, maybe too quickly and too high-pitched.

"That doesn't sound innocent at all." Bower laughs and then takes a sip of her drink. It smells a lot like a chai.

"We're not," Gretchen says. "Bennett is not my type."

Ouch.

Not that I really care.

But still, I'm sitting right here.

"Not your type?" Bower asks, shocked. "Is handsome not your type? Muscular? Good at baseball? Abs for days?"

"Abs?" Gretchen asks, her brow lifting. "Sounds to me like you might be the one who should date him."

Gretchen…

Bower laughs and shakes her head. "No, Bennett and I have known each other for so long, and I'm practically his grandma. He wants nothing to do with an old lady like me."

"You're not my grandma. You're eight years older. That's nothing."

"It's something, but either way, we're good friends, right, Bennett?"

So fucking painful…

"Yup, great friends."

Gretchen looks between the two of us and then folds her arms over her chest. "Friends I can work with."

"What do you mean?" I ask.

"I'm just thinking you don't want to do the zoo anymore, but we have to figure out something that will replace the zoo but still bring in good publicity. And if you two are friends and clearly have good chemistry since you're so close, it might benefit you to see you two do something together to help the Bombers."

"I don't want to drag Bower into this," I say just as Bower places her hand on my arm.

"Speak for yourself," she says. "I want to hear what Gretchen has to say. If it means you stop bitching about the zoo, then I say we hear her out."

"Bower, you're not getting caught up in—"

"Shhh," Bower says while pressing a finger to my lips. "Let the lady speak."

Gretchen chuckles, actually chuckles, can't be sure I've ever heard that sound come out of her before. "Yes, Bennett, let me speak." Knowing I won't get anywhere with these two women teaming up against me, I gesture for Gretchen to continue. "So, you two have known each other for a while now. What are some things you like?"

Bower thumbs toward me. "Obsessed with baseball. Has been ever since I met him. He's dedicated his life to the sport. I don't think there was a time where I'd visit my friend, his sister, and he wasn't doing something to better himself."

"Do you play baseball?" Gretchen asks.

"Oh no." Bower waves her hand in dismissal. "Barely understand it. I know that Bennett is good and that the fans love him. Oh, and the camera guy loves zooming in on his face when he's up to bat, because if the angle is right, you get the dark scruff of his jaw in combination with the light blue of his eyes. A dangerous blend."

"It is a dangerous blend," Gretchen says as I can feel her eyes on me. "What about you, Bower, what do you do?"

"I'm a personal assistant. My boss just moved here, actually. I was living farther up north, but she wasn't feeding her shopping addiction enough, so we moved to the city. Knowing Bennett was here, I was excited to find an available apartment in his building."

"Oh." Gretchen's brows raise. "You two are neighbors?"

"We are. I bring him sweets in the morning when he's barely made it out of bed. He loves sweets, especially pastries. He didn't get to have them growing up, so I'm filling him up now."

"Why couldn't you have pastries?" Gretchen asks.

"Couldn't afford them," I say, not wanting to go too much into detail about it.

"Maybe you can do something with sweets," Bower says.

"Perhaps." Gretchen gives it some thought. "What else do you two do together?"

"Other than hang out?" Bower shrugs and then her eyes widen. "Oh, wait, we read together."

"You read together?" Gretchen looks to me for confirmation.

"Not like...read together, but we read separate books and talk about them."

"We have a book club between the two of us, and get this, he reads romance."

"Really?" Gretchen sits taller.

"Yup, our book club is called the Kim Halpert Book Club, long story, but he's reading a baseball series right now and he cried while reading it."

"No, I didn't," I say.

"Wait, you didn't?"

"No, you might have been thinking about yourself."

"Huh, maybe. Either way"—Bower turns back toward Gretchen—"the books make him incredibly horny."

"Bower," I say as Gretchen laughs some more.

"This is the kind of thing I was looking for."

"A horny Bennett?" Bower asks. "I don't think he gets out much, so he's got to be revved up and ready to blow...if you know what I mean."

"Oh, I know exactly what you mean." Gretchen winks.

"Hey, can we not talk about my...desires?"

"Desires." Bower snorts and covers her nose. "Why did you choose that word?"

I pull on the brim of my hat and mutter, "No fucking clue."

Should have left the minute Bower showed up.

Gretchen starts typing away on her phone and says, "This is really, really good stuff and something we can use."

"We're not telling the public that I'm horny," I say.

Gretchen winces. "Gross, Bennett. Of course we wouldn't. People don't need to know about your lack of sex life."

"Extremely blue balls," Bower says, a smirk on her face.

"Extremely is a bit...extreme," I say. "Also, can we stop talking about my balls?"

"I'd prefer if we did," Gretchen says as she finishes typing on her phone and then looks up at the both of us. "This is what we're going to do. Bennett's going to form a book club, we will create social media accounts for it, and you will start recommending two books a month to read and then discuss them with Bower on video."

"She doesn't need to be—"

"Oh my God, I'd love that," Bower says, gripping my arm. "I've always wanted to start a book club. I thought it would be great to go with my book truck idea that will never happen, but at least I can cling to a book club."

Book truck idea? What's that?

"Perfect. It's settled." Gretchen starts to gather her things. "Come up with a name that I can approve, and the Kim Halpert Book Club is not it. I'd like to see this up and running in a few weeks. Once I see you have committed to this idea, Bennett, then I can reduce your time at the zoo. And when the time is right, I'll involve Graydon and OC in the book club to spread the impact. This will be great to capture the female audience, especially since you're such a heartthrob already."

"Ooo, is he?" Bower asks, looking far too excited about it. "I bet you're an inspiration for sports romance authors."

"Most likely," Gretchen says, looking between the two of us.

"Any chance we can secure some sort of shirtless campaign for him? He has amazing abs. Go ahead, Bennett, show her your abs."

"I'm not showing her my abs."

"Go ahead. Don't be shy." She turns to Gretchen. "They're great. A set you can lose a finger in, the divots are so deep. Go on, Bennett, flash her."

"I'm not flashing her," I say, clamping down on my shirt. "We're not doing a shirtless campaign."

"Actually, a shirtless campaign is not a bad idea. Let me talk to some magazines and see what we can do."

Bower claps. "They won't regret it. Oh!" She holds up a finger. "Have we considered a dating show?"

"Oh my God." I groan and then lift out of my chair, pulling Bower with me. "We're leaving."

I tug her toward the door, Gretchen chuckling as Bower calls out, "Consider the dating show. Women will be pleading at his feet to ease the blue balls."

Jesus.

Christ.

CHAPTER 12
BOWER

I THREAD MY ARM THROUGH Bennett's as together we walk along the streets of San Francisco toward our apartment building.

"A book club. That's so much fun. We have to be thoughtful about what books we pick and should probably focus on sports romance since that ties in well with what you do. Maybe we can pick the books you've already read so there isn't pressure to have to finish the books you choose that month and you can be ahead of the game."

"Yeah, probably," he says, seeming distant. It gives me pause.

"Is everything okay?"

"How was the date?"

"Oh. Um, it was fine." I shrug, thinking about Cougar and how it was just…eh. There wasn't much we could talk about or much we had in common.

"Just fine?" he asks as I feel his eyes on me.

I cling tightly onto his arm as I say, "Yeah, just fine. We didn't have a lot in common, but we did talk a lot about football, and I don't really know sports, so that was kind of weird."

"Sorry. I should have set you up with someone you have more in common with."

"It's fine. We're going to go out again."

He pauses and turns to me. "You are?"

"Yeah."

"Why?" His brows pinch together.

"Why not? We're not committed to each other, just having some fun."

"But if you have nothing in common, why still see him?"

"Because I think we're just at the tip of the iceberg. I could sense that he was guarded and maybe I was a little guarded myself. He already texted asking if I could go out next week, so we're looking to see where that takes us, but he was open about seeing other people, and I'm chill with that."

"Wait." Bennett shakes his head. "I thought you were looking for a relationship, not a fling."

"I am," I say. "But sometimes relationships start off as just getting to know each other. Listen, who am I to stop him from seeing other people? I have no hold on him."

"Does that mean you're going to see other people?"

"Perhaps." I shrug. "I mean, I can't put all my eggs in one basket, right? Just trying to be breezy about all of this. I think once I start putting pressure on myself, that's when nothing happens. So just letting the universe take hold of my love life, you know?"

He guides us toward the apartment again. "I guess so."

Noticing how firm his jaw is and the stiffness in his body, I ask, "Are you okay? You seem tense. Is this about the book club thing? I don't have to do it—"

"I want you to do it," he says quickly. "With me. I want it to be something we do together."

"Really?" I ask, excited that he said that, because I felt like I was clinging to something that maybe I wasn't necessarily invited to, but more so invited myself.

"I'm not doing it alone, and I feel like you bring the best out of me, which will help."

I pause our walk again and turn toward him. "That's a really nice thing to say, Bennett."

"It's true," he says, his eyes meeting mine.

For some odd reason, my cheeks blush from the compliment. "Well, thank you. That's really sweet."

He smirks and then pulls me into a hug, which I graciously take. His arms wrap around me like a protective shield as I place my cheek against his chest and just sigh into his hold. He's so much bigger than me that it truly feels like a hug from Bennett garners me all the protection that I need.

When I pull away a few inches, I look up at him and he smiles down at me. "Thank you."

"For what?"

"For being there for me. You've always checked in on me throughout the years and now that I've moved here, you're watching over me even though you don't have to. I appreciate you, Bennett."

He softly smiles. "I appreciate you, too, Bower."

I return his smile and then pull away, looping my arm through his again.

As we walk toward our apartment building, he says, "There is something I want to ask you about."

"Oh? Is it did I kiss Cougar?"

"No."

I glance up at him. "Because I didn't. I want to take things really slow with him because he seems like a bit of a player, at least from what Gabby informed me, and I don't want to be that girl. If he's interested, then he's interested and we will be slow about it."

He lets out a deep breath and nods. "Yeah, that sounds like a really clever idea. Smart, actually. I'd take it as slow as you can with him."

I chuckle. "The way you say that almost seems like you don't want me to be intimate with him at all."

"Just trying to protect you," he says as we reach our apartment building and the doorman opens the door for us.

"I appreciate it, but that clearly wasn't what you were going to ask me."

He pushes the button for the elevator and it opens right away. I press the button for his level and his level only, figuring there is more for us to talk about, and he doesn't seem to mind.

"No, that wasn't what I was going to ask you."

"Okay, so what is it?"

He tugs on the back of his neck and says, "Well, you mentioned something that one night that you slept in my bed about wanting to do things you can't do. I can't really remember the specifics, and then today, with Gretchen, you said something about a book truck but it never happening."

"Oh." I nod and look away, feeling slightly embarrassed that I got so excited I let that slip.

"Yeah, 'oh.' What were you talking about?"

The doors part when we reach his floor and I follow him to his apartment, where he lets us both in and I head for his couch.

He follows right behind, sitting next to me.

I scooch in close and face him while he turns slightly on the couch to look at me. "So...what were you talking about?"

"You're going to think it's stupid."

He slips a finger under my chin and says, "I'd never think anything you dream or wish about is stupid, unless it's becoming one of Cougar's groupies."

I chuckle. "You're the one who set me up with him."

"Yeah, and I might be regretting that now."

"Oh?" I snuggle into the side of his couch, feeling so much comfort in his place. I haven't made my apartment feel like home just yet. It's just a place to sleep, not a place to live. "Why are you regretting setting me up?"

"You could do better."

"Is that so? With whom?"

He shakes his head. "Stop changing the subject. Tell me what you were talking about."

Sighing, I say, "It's just something I've been thinking about for a while.

Gabby knows all about it and has encouraged me to do it and to move to Almond Bay to see through my plans."

Bennett rolls his eyes. "Of course she told you to do it in Almond Bay. But how come you told her and not me?"

I shrug. "I don't know. Sometimes I feel like I bother you. You're so busy and everything, and even right now, you should probably be going to bed, but here I am, inviting myself into your apartment—"

"I brought you in here, and I'm never too busy for you, Bower."

I smile softly and press my hand to his. "You're such a good friend, Bennett."

His lips slightly purse before he says, "So what is this idea?"

"Since books have taken over my life, I thought it would be fun to own my own little book truck where I can show up to different places and people can buy books from my truck, like a mini storefront that travels to different trade shows and has a social media following."

"Like a food truck, but for books."

"Yes, exactly," I say. "And it would just be romance books, and I could sell all the bookish things as well and have an online storefront too. I don't know, just seems like fun and I've saved up quite a lot working with Adalade. She pays me well and pays for a lot of my expenses. So I've stashed away money and, well...I don't know...that's the dream."

"So why don't you do it?"

"It's not that easy. It will take a lot of work, and who knows if that's something San Francisco wants, you know? I don't want to put in all this time and fail."

"Who's to say you'll fail?"

"There is a high likelihood that it would fail. Twenty percent of all small businesses fail after the first year."

"Yeah, but that's also an eighty percent success rate. Why aren't you paying attention to that number?"

"Because my dad was part of the twenty percent," I say softly. "I saw what he went through, all the time and energy he put into his idea, only for it to crumble at his fingertips. He had to work his ass off just to support his family." I shake my head. "It's terrifying. I don't want to follow in his footsteps."

"Just because your dad failed doesn't mean you will. You can't let his past dictate your future."

I nod as I feel a bout of emotion hit me, so I turn away from him, avoiding those understanding and sincere eyes of his so I can calm my racing emotions.

"Hey, did I say something wrong?" He tugs on my hand, entwining our fingers.

"No," I say as my eyes well up with tears and I beg myself to keep it together. "It's just… I remember those days." A tear drips down my cheek and I quickly wipe it away as I feel him move in even closer to me. "I remember the arguments between my parents, the yelling and uncertainty. They were stressed from my father's failure. There wasn't much joy, and well, I don't want that for me."

"There's a difference, though, Bower." He turns my head so I have to look at him. "You don't have a family—you don't have dependents relying on you—so if it's something that doesn't work out, it's not going to have the same impact that it had with your family, right?"

I nod, because he's right about that.

"And also, you don't have to quit your job while you figure this out. You can still work for Adalade, start putting everything together, and on the weekends, you can work on your book stuff. That way you have the safety net in case something doesn't work out." He cups my cheek and speaks with such sincerity. "But I believe in you, I believe you can make this great, and we can use the book club as a platform to help raise awareness of your book truck."

"Oh, I wouldn't ask you to do that."

"You're not asking. I'm offering."

I shake my head. "You've already helped me out with so much."

"Because I want to," he says, his hand still cupping my cheek. "I want you to succeed. I want to see you happy. I want you to accomplish your dreams. You were there for me and Gabby for so many years. You helped us, even if it was as simple as letting Gabby bring home soup from the restaurant. You were there for us. Let me be there for you."

My lips lightly tilt up into a smile. "I guess that's what friends do, right?"

He slowly nods, his Adam's apple bobbing as he swallows. "Yup, that's what friends do."

I move in close and wrap my arms around him, pulling him into a hug. "Thank you, Bennett."

His hands fall to my back as he holds me tight. "Anything for you, Bower. Anything."

I pull away. "I'll give it some thought. Not making any promises, but you drive a hard bargain."

"I only have one requirement."

"What's that?" I ask.

"That you stay here in San Francisco. Can't have you moving out to Almond Bay if you start a book truck."

I chuckle and stand. "You might have to go into a bidding war with your sister."

He stands as well and turns his hat backward, looking so incredibly adorable. "My money is on me." He winks and then takes my hand, leading me to his front door. *How did he know I needed to talk about this tonight?*

The night with Cougar was okay, but I didn't get the sense that he truly wanted my opinion on anything. The conversation was light. And that doesn't surprise me. But with Bennett? He wants to know what I'm actually feeling. He's so invested in what I'm invested in. *Despite growing up without parents.* Gabby's love held this man together. I must acknowledge that with her someday.

If I'm honest, I don't want to leave. I want to stay.

I want to ask if I can spend another night in his bed, where comfort seems to consume me.

But that would be weird, right?

He has a life, and it doesn't revolve around me.

"What's going on in your head?" he asks.

"Huh?"

"I can see it in your expression. You're thinking about something."

"Oh, nothing you need to worry about."

"It's cute that you think you can get away with that answer."

I take a step toward his door. "Seriously, don't worry about it."

He snags my hand and twirls me back toward him. "I'm worried about it, so tell me."

Why is he like this? So kind, caring, thoughtful.

Maybe because his sister is, but where did they get such personality traits? They grew up in a horrid foster care system. They fought and clawed their way to get out of it and then supported themselves while achieving their goals together. You would think they would be jaded assholes and against the world, but they're not. They care about others, especially me. It can be overwhelming to know you have such positivity cheering you on.

"It's nothing important. I just haven't set up my apartment yet and I was thinking about how comfortable your place is and how I don't want to leave—"

"Then don't," he says, almost looking hopeful.

"Bennett, you have a life that's outside of me and you have to get to bed. You have games almost every freaking day and the last thing you need is your sister's friend crashing at your apartment."

"Why don't you let me tell you what I want and you stop telling me what I need?"

Oh…

That...that catches me off guard, because Bennett doesn't usually use that tone of voice with me, nor does he say harsh things like that.

And yet...why did I like it?

"You're right. I'm sorry," I say. "What do you want?"

"I want you to feel comfortable, and if that means staying here tonight, then you're staying here."

I tug on the corner of my lip, hating that I'm putting him in this situation.

"It's fine. My apartment is just full of boxes is all. Seriously, don't worry about it."

I head toward his door again and to my surprise, he follows right behind me.

"What are you doing?" I ask, looking over my shoulder.

"Wait right here," he says and then disappears down the hall of his apartment. Within seconds, he's back and he's holding his cell phone charger and a toothbrush.

"What are you doing?" I ask.

"Going to your apartment for the night. Let's go. I have to get to bed, and the longer you take, the longer you're making me stay awake."

"Bennett, be serious."

He grips my chin, forcing me to look him in the eyes. "I'm dead fucking serious, let's go."

Umm...

Okay.

The thrill that just shot between my legs is criminal, because this is Bennett, for crying out loud, but the way he just said that, the look in his eyes, the control and strength he's exuding? It's...oh God, it's making my heart race.

Jesus, maybe I should have spent the night with Cougar, as it seems like my body might have needed it.

I swallow and nod, not wanting to make him madder, and I head out of his apartment, him following me after he locks up. We take the elevator up one floor and he trails behind me when we reach my apartment. I unlock it and then turn toward him.

"It's just boxes and stuff, so don't judge me."

He nods toward the door. "Let me in."

Right.

Bennett has morphed into an alpha male for the night, so I open the door and he pushes it wider as I turn on the hallway light and notice all the outfit changes I made, scattered all over the living room.

Shit, I forgot about that.

"Uh, don't mind the clothes." I start gathering them. "Just had a hard time picking out an outfit." I glance over my shoulder, where he's taking in the apartment. It's smaller than his, but it has plenty of light during the day and a white kitchen, which I love. And it's just the right size for what I need. "It's, uh, it's smaller than yours, and it doesn't help that I haven't unpacked or really settled anything in its rightful place." I stare at my couch that's in the middle of the living room, the TV that's still in its box. God, he must think I'm a freak. "Just been really busy is all."

He moves deeper into the living room, to the mantel of the fireplace, where a single picture frame decorates the top. It's a picture of him, Gabby, and me at a fair in Almond Bay. I'm in the middle, clutching both of them.

He picks it up and examines the picture.

"That goes with me everywhere," I say. "One of my favorite pictures. It reminds me of the small family I've put together that's outside of my own."

He glances up at me. "It's the only family I have."

And that makes my heart ache. "If you want, you can have it."

He shakes his head. "Nah, you keep it. It will remind you of me when I'm gone."

I chuckle. "As if I could forget about you. You text me all the time."

"Eh, you text me."

I smile and push at his shoulder playfully. "No, you text me."

"Fifty-fifty."

"It's so not fifty-fifty, but whatever."

Happy that the mood is a touch lighter, I show him my bedroom that is currently a mattress with bedding.

"Where's your bed?"

"It was broken in the move, so I have to get a new one. Haven't done that yet." I sigh. "I do so much for Adalade during the day that the last thing I want to do when I get home is situate myself, you know?"

"I get that." He looks around some more. "But you can't live like this."

"I know. I'll work on it."

"I can help."

"Bennett." I tip my head to the side. "No, you have done enough. You shouldn't even be here right now, but I'm being a baby."

"Benefits me." He moves into the bathroom, where he plucks my toothpaste from the corner of my counter.

"How does this benefit you?" I ask.

Smirking, he says, "When I go out of town, I won't feel guilty asking you to do shit for me."

"At this point, I'm going to be in your debt for at least a decade."

"Just the way I like it." He winks and then turns back to the mirror, where he brushes his teeth.

With that, I go to my closet, where my clothes are strewn all over, and I grab a pair of pajama shorts and an oversized T-shirt before heading back into the bathroom, where Bennett is finishing up.

"Um, can you help me with my dress?" I turn my back toward him and feel his body move closer to mine, the heat of it overwhelming as his hand falls to my hip.

Chills break out over my skin as he slowly raises his other hand to the zipper of my dress.

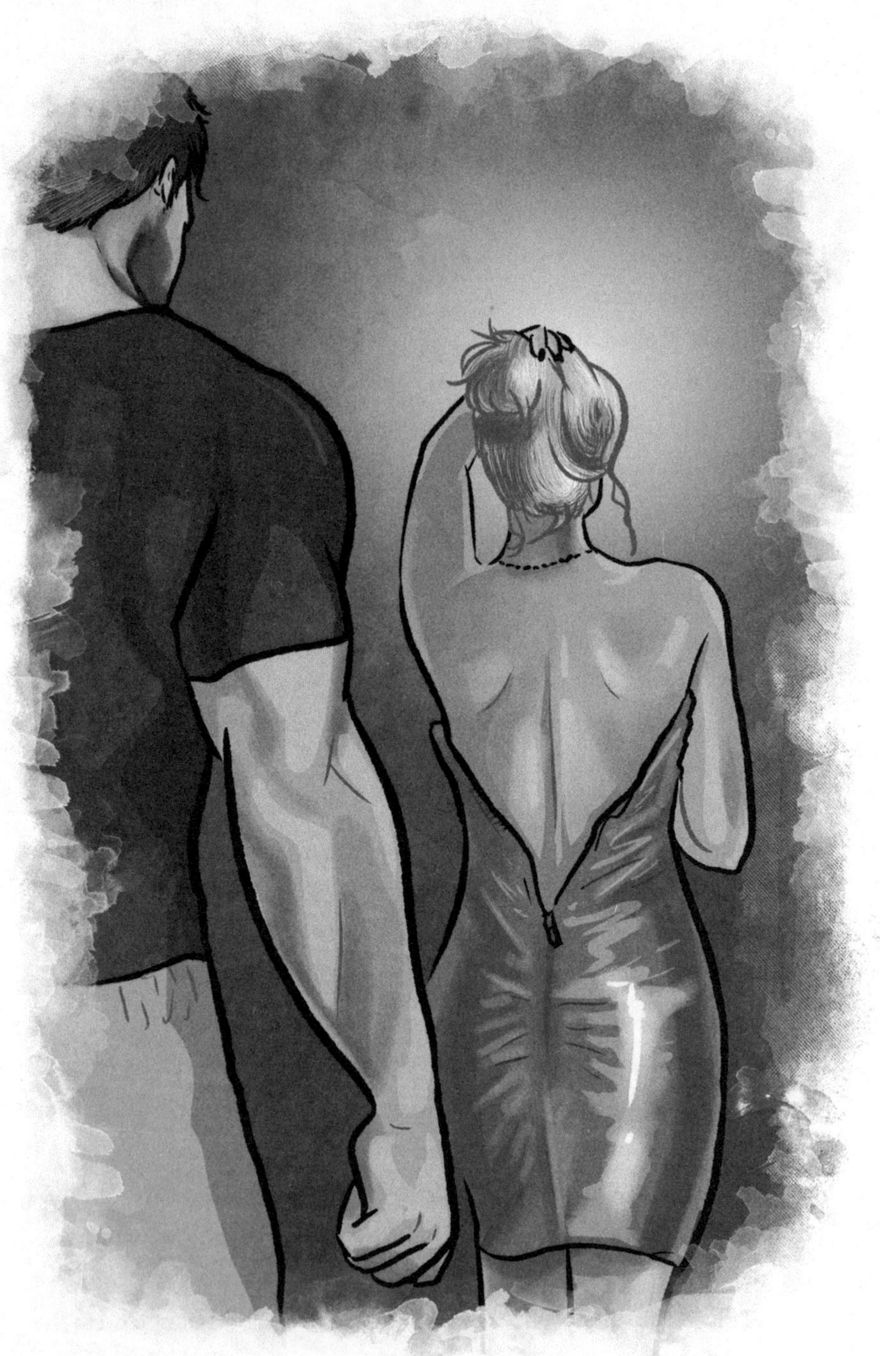

What the hell is going on with me?

"Sure," he says softly and then slowly...and I mean, slowly, tugs down the zipper of my dress, one tine at a time, before it's all the way undone, my dress barely hanging on as I turn back around to face him, his eyes lasering in on me, the light blue almost looking dark.

"Um...thank you," I say, my voice going dry for some reason.

"Anytime," he says and then moves past me and heads toward my mattress on the floor.

I quickly shut the bathroom door and set my clothes down, taking a deep breath.

What the hell was that?

He unzipped my dress and my body is acting like he just licked every inch of my skin.

I take a few more deep breaths, steadying myself before I get ready for bed, taking care of my makeup and making sure to spend some extra time scrubbing my face and applying my lotion so I can gather myself.

Once I'm ready, I turn off the light and head into the bedroom, where Bennett has lost his shirt. I spot it folded neatly next to the mattress... along with his sweatpants.

Oh God, why does that make things...different?

I don't know. It just does. Then again, he probably doesn't want to sleep in bulky sweatpants. I don't blame him.

"Figured this is the side that was open, given your things were on the other."

"Yup, you guessed correctly," I say as I feel my nerves humming, which is so weird, because this kind of stuff has never bothered me before. I'm usually unfazed about everything, and yet, Bennett in my bed, in nothing but his underwear, has my mind whirling and my body buzzing.

Which needs to stop.

This is not a big deal.

This is just two friends seeking comfort. Or perhaps one friend seeking comfort from another friend.

Either way, get your life together, Bower.

I move to my side of the bed, slip under the covers—with help from Bennett, of course, because that's the kind of guy he is—and then I turn off the light and face him.

"My bed isn't as comfortable as yours."

"Well, you could have stayed at my place, but you forced me to follow you."

"I didn't force you."

He scoffs. "As if I was going to let you be alone after that look you had in your eyes. Nah, not what I do."

"Because you're a good guy. Your sister would be proud, although not sure how she'd feel about this."

"I think she'd be grateful that I was taking care of you."

"Yeah, but I don't think she'd like that you're taking care of me in your boxers."

"Boxer briefs."

I roll my eyes. "As if it matters."

"It does. Boxer briefs are far more attractive than boxers. Boxers are… clunky. There is one guy on my team who wears them and every time I see him in them, I wonder if he's okay."

"Really? Who?"

He shakes his head. "Can't tell you. That's locker room confidentiality."

"Oh, sure, so if I asked you who has the biggest penis on the team, you wouldn't say that either."

"That I can answer, because it's me."

I laugh…louder than what I think he was expecting, because in the moonlight, I can see the irritation in his brow.

"That's what any guy would say."

"Yeah, but I'm not just any guy, and I'm telling the truth."

"Have you measured your penis next to others?"

"We have to," he answers. "At the beginning of the season, we all line up naked and we measure dick size. It determines the batting order."

I pause for a moment because I know nothing about baseball, absolutely nothing, but that doesn't seem like it would be real.

"You're lying."

"How can you be sure?"

"I know," I say, turning away from him and grabbing my phone. I shoot a text to Gabby.

Bower: For baseball, do all the guys measure the size of their dicks at the beginning of the season to determine the batting order?

"Texted your sister."

He smirks. "I look forward to her answer."

"As do I," I say just as my phone buzzes.

Gabby: Where on earth did you hear that from? Your romance books? No, Bower, that's not what they do. Dick size has nothing to do with earning your position in the lineup. Are you losing it?

I gasp as I turn the phone toward Bennett, who starts laughing.

I push at his chest. "Great, my friend thinks I'm losing it."

"She thinks you're losing it every day."

He takes my phone from me, leans over, his bare chest pressing against me as he plugs my phone back in, and then lies back down, still facing me.

"You can't say things like that, because if I don't fact-check, then I could say some pretty dumb shit on the streets, and is that what you want?"

"I think no matter what, if you're uncertain about something, you should fact-check it."

"Excuse me for believing the baseball player."

He chuckles. "Not a smart move."

"Clearly," I huff as his hand falls to my hip, catching me off guard. He pulls me in closer to him and then to my utter freaking surprise, he leans forward and presses a kiss to my forehead.

"Night, Bower."

My...my breath catches in my lungs from the feel of his lips on my skin, from the warmth of his body so close, wrapping me up into what feels like a comforting blanket that I never want to leave.

Clearing my throat, I say, "Good night, Bennett."

Then he closes his eyes, but keeps his hand on my hip, holding me close enough that if I wanted to, I could lean forward and press my head to his chest, but not too close that he's forcing me to be with him.

A comfortable distance that has my mind screaming with questions.

Questions I don't think I should be answering.

CHAPTER 13
BENNETT

OC: What are your thoughts on vibrators? As a man, would you use one?

Graydon: Why is this something you're texting us?

OC: Because we're in a sacred group together, the Gladdy Daddies if you don't recall, which means it's a safe place and we can talk to each other about these types of things.

Bennett: I'm all for them.

OC: See? A confident man, talking about things that he's not ashamed to talk about.

Graydon: I'm not ashamed to talk about them. I just don't want to talk about them with you.

OC: Why not?

Bennett: Maybe because—and I mean this in the nicest way possible—you tend to make a big deal about things, and if Graydon were to say he likes playing with a vibrator on himself, you would probably wave a flag around with the news printed all across it.

OC: DOES HE LIKE TO USE A VIBRATOR ON HIMSELF?!? Did he tell you that? I will fucking flip my shit if he told you that.

Graydon: I did. Bennett and I have a separate thread that doesn't include you and we discuss use of vibrators without you.

OC: I am dead inside.

I LAUGH TO MYSELF AS I slip my socks on, getting ready for the game tonight.

Bennett: He's kidding, we don't. We just talk about sexual positions.

OC: I'm not kidding, I will not be able to handle the demise of the Gladdy Daddies. It *will* be the death of me.

Graydon: Then get your shit together and stop asking us about things I don't want to talk to you about.

OC: To be fair, I wasn't aware vibrators were off-limits with you. I did hear you have sex six times the other night when I stayed the night at your place.

Graydon: And didn't I say to never fucking talk about it?

Bennett: He did.

OC: Sorry that I was impressed. Six times…I think I've gone five. That's a lie, it was four. Fine! It was three, but I could have gone four. She was just raw.

Graydon: For the love of fucking God.

Bennett: Dude, the raw comment…not necessary.

OC: You're right, that was on me. I retract the raw comment.

Graydon: You can't retract. It's already out there.

Bennett: We already saw it.

OC: Then I'll be sure to never say it again. Please don't punish me. You're all I have.

Bennett: Shouldn't your season be starting soon? You need more friends.

Graydon: I second that.

OC: Fucking rude, my guys. We have bonded over so much. The zoo, the use of vibrators, Maple and Graydon's love affair that I had a hand in making happen, and you can deny that shit as much as you want to, but it's true. And Bennett's sister's friend…

Bennett: You've done nothing for that.

Graydon: Because you haven't told us anything.

OC: Graydon, I'm clutching my pearls, as that sounds like interest to me.

Bennett: Nothing is going on. So drop it.

I set my phone to the side and lean back in my chair just as Nolan walks up, holding a burger in one hand and a Coke in the other.

"Peanut butter burger with pickles. Dude, it's blasphemy that this is so good." He holds it out to me. "Want a bite?"

"I'm good." I study the meal. "Are you going to be okay to play? That's pretty heavy, dude."

"I once had a twelve-ounce steak, fries, and a giant slice of chocolate cake before a game. I hit two doubles and made a diving play. Nothing is going to stop this brick house," he says as he takes a seat next to me and kicks his feet up on the locker. "How's life, my man? You never told me how the date went for your girl."

"She's not my girl."

"Not yet."

Yeah...not yet.

"So, how did it go?"

I shrug. "They have nothing in common, but they're going to casually see each other while seeing other people."

"That's fucking great," Nolan says.

"How is that great?"

"Simple—she can still see him, find out how much of a douche he is, while you swoop in and continue to charm her. She's going to be in your arms in no time."

I mean, she was sort of in my arms the other night when I stayed at her place. I pushed my limits and placed my hand on her hip, hoping that I wasn't going too fucking far, but she didn't seem to mind. I probably wouldn't have been able to stop myself either way.

"Don't know about that. She still sees me as a friend."

"Then text her a dick pic," Nolan says, mouth half-full of burger.

"Have you lost your fucking mind? You should never send an unsolicited dick pic to anyone, let alone to your sister's best friend."

"Pretend like it was an accident and that you meant to send it to someone else."

"Get the fuck out of here." I push at his chair, rolling him away from me.

"Ask anyone. It's a great idea." Just then, Asher Peppers walks by in nothing but his baseball pants and socks. "Right, Peppers? Dick pics are where it's at."

Asher pauses for a moment and turns on Nolan. The cold, blank stare that he gives everyone, the one that is absolutely terrifying, nearly slices Nolan in half. "Don't fucking talk to me."

Then he storms off to the corner, where he secludes himself.

Nolan twirls toward me and mouths *Yikes* before taking another bite of his burger.

At least we can agree on that.

My phone buzzes next to me and I almost don't look at it because I don't want to deal with the Gladdy Daddies right now, but I see that it's Gabby, so I pick it up.

Of course she's calling.

"Hey, Gabby," I say as I lean back in my chair.

"Hey, how's it going? How is Seattle?"

"Good," I answer. "Nothing special."

"Says the guy who hit a home run yesterday."

"Just another day at the office."

She chuckles. "I'm not sure if you'll ever boast about yourself."

"No need when you do it enough for me."

"True. Anyway, I know you have to get ready. I was just calling because I was hoping we could visit you when you get back. Ryland wants to take me on a little getaway and thought that a few nights in San Francisco might do the trick since my brother and best friend are there."

"I'd love that," I say, excited to see my sister and her husband. "Is Mac going to come too?"

"No, she's staying with her aunt and uncle. Ryland wants an adult getaway."

"Enough said…please, enough said."

She laughs. "We're going to be staying at Hayes's apartment because he's nice like that, but I'd love to get together and maybe come see a game or two."

"I'll get you tickets."

"Get three. We won't have many nights there, and I want to spend as much time as I can with Bower as well, so I'm going to drag her to a game."

And just like that, butterflies erupt in my stomach, like they always do when I know Bower's coming to a game.

"Sure. Just send me the dates."

"Of course. Ahhh, I'm so excited. I miss you."

"Miss you too, sis."

"Okay, I'll let you go. Good luck tonight. I'll be watching."

"Like you always do."

"Love you."

"Love you too," I say and then hang up the phone.

"Ooooo," Nolan coos. "Who do you love?"

"My sister, you fuck," I say, throwing a roll of athletic tape at him and making him laugh.

"Is she single?"

"You know she's married, and even if she was single, you would be the last fucking person I'd even consider letting her date."

He grips his heart. "That hurts, man. That really hurts."

Bower: Are you still awake?

Bennett: Just got back to my hotel. What's up? Everything okay?

Bower: Yeah, everything's fine. I've been attempting to unpack ever since your sister told me she was coming to visit.

Bennett: I told you I'd help you. I couldn't the other night like we planned because of a last-minute team meeting, but I said I would make it up to you.

Bower: And I told you I didn't need the help.

Bennett: I'll be back tomorrow after the afternoon game. I can help tomorrow night.

Bower: It's fine. I've got it. I was texting you because I was wondering if you have any tools.

Bennett: What do you need tools for?

Bower: Hanging things and maybe building a side table.

Annoyed, I exit the text thread and call her.

It takes her two rings before she answers. "Bennett, I will not take a lecture from you about tools. You either have them or you don't."

"Bower, I will not take a lecture from you about not needing help. If you're building things, at least let me help with that."

"I don't need some big, strong man to help me. I can do this on my own."

"You think I'm strong?" I smirk as I lie down on my hotel bed.

"Oh my God, can you hear my eyes rolling? Of course you're strong. I'd be lying if I said otherwise."

"You would be. Glad you can admit it."

"Seriously, Bennett, can I use your tools? I have a date tomorrow morning and want to make sure I hang something before that."

My brow furrows.

A date?

In the morning?

With whom?

"You have a date?" I ask.

"Yeah, with Cougar. We decided to do a breakfast thing. It was my suggestion. I thought if I took him out of his playboy atmosphere, he might be more down-to-earth and willing to open up."

Don't like the fucking sound of that.

"But either way, can I borrow your tools?"

"You can borrow them with my supervision, tomorrow, after my game."

"Bennett," she groans.

"Don't you have other things you can do?"

"Yes, but I don't want to do those things."

I chuckle. "Too bad. You're doing them. When I get back tomorrow, I'll build and hang your other items, okay?"

"Fine, but only because I'm tired and don't want to fight anymore."

"Would you call this fighting? Or me trying to be a good guy and you not letting me?"

"Oh, Bennett, there's something you need to learn about women. We are *always* right."

"Yeah, Gabby taught me that a while ago."

"Best you remember it."

Chuckling, I ask, "How was the rest of your day?"

"Oh, you know, fine, until this guy called me instead of texting me back. You know I don't like to talk on the phone if I don't have to, but you and your sister seem to forget that."

"I like hearing your voice," I say before I can stop myself, causing there to be a blip of silence between us.

Fuck.

Why did I say that?

I was just so comfortable, so relaxed, that I forgot—

"Ugh, fine, it's nice to hear your voice as well. I think I've become accustomed to it."

In the words of OC, my dick just got hard.

A huge smile stretches from ear to ear as her words are burned into my brain.

It's nice to hear your voice as well.

Unsure of the meaning behind all that, but I'm going to take it as a solid win.

"Not a bad thing to become accustomed to."

"I guess not."

"Other than the annoying guy with the nice voice calling you, what was the rest of your day like?"

"Busy with errands, of course. Oh, and Gretchen emailed me all the NDA things and paperwork."

"Did she?"

"Yeah, the basic stuff that you have to sign when working with a celebrity. I sent it to Adalade's lawyer, who's looking it over for me, just to make sure I'm not signing my life away to be in a book club with you. By the way, did she send you the possible names for the book club that she came up with?"

"No. What are they?"

"Oh my God, Bennett, they're terrible."

"Tell me," I say as I put the phone on speaker and start getting ready for bed.

"Well, the most obvious is Baseball and Books."

"Oh fuck, she did not suggest that."

Bower laughs and it's the most beautiful fucking sound ever. "She did. It was on the top of her list."

"That's embarrassing for her."

"That's what I thought." I can practically envision her curling up on her couch in those pajama shorts and oversized shirts she likes to wear, talking to me. Makes my fucking heart all warm and tingly just thinking about it.

"What were the other ones?"

"Bombers Book Club, which is just as lame. And then there was Bennett's Book Club, which...boo."

"Yeah, not great."

"And the best is when she put all three together and suggested Bombers Bennett's Book Club. Or, if you will, Triple B Book Club."

"Oh, for fuck's sake."

She laughs some more as I start to brush my teeth. "Yeah, it's so bad. I told her I'd think on it and talk to you. And I'm telling you right now, I will not be a part of a book club with that name. I'm just daring enough to go against Satan herself and call it the Kim Halpert Book Club before Triple B."

"Is that what we're calling Gretchen? Satan?"

"Ehh, might be a little harsh, but if she keeps it up with those horrible names, I might call her that out of spite."

I chuckle and then spit the toothpaste out of my mouth. "I dare you to call her that to her face."

"Just so she can scratch my eyes out of their sockets? No, thank you."

"Probably a smart move. Either way, do you have any ideas for the name?"

"I've been brewing some things up, but I'm not ready to present yet. In the meantime, are you still reading your assigned books?"

"I am."

"Did you get to the scene where they're on the kitchen floor and she sticks the vibrator up his ass?"

"I did," I say, my cheeks flushing.

"Thoughts?"

"You want the truth?"

"Always."

Smiling, I lean against the bathroom counter and say, "It made me hard as fuck."

I wait for her reaction, because I know it's daring, but I think these are the moves I need to make with her. Get her thinking about me in a different way.

"Oh my God," she whispers. "Why did my nipples just go hard?"

I let out a wallop of a laugh as I make my way back to the bed and strip out of my clothes, even my underwear. I stretch out along the mattress and place one hand behind my head as I continue to talk to her.

"You trying to tell me something?" I flirt.

"I think my body is trying to tell you something." She laughs, but it almost sounds like a scared laugh.

"Good to know." Not wanting to go much further with her, because I think I got what I wanted with that comment, I say, "Okay, I'm headed to bed."

"Right, me too, now that you won't let me use your tools."

"Tomorrow, you and me. It's a date, okay?"

I hear the smallest intake of breath as she says, "Okay."

"Night, Bower. Sweet dreams."

"Umm…night, Bennett."

I hang up, set my phone down, and then grip my goddamn cock. Because if there is one thing I know for sure, hearing that little gasp at the end of that phone call, it made me hard as stone.

CHAPTER 14
BOWER

THIS WAS A TERRIBLE IDEA.

A morning date?

There is nothing pleasant about this.

Because he has to be at the stadium at seven this morning, we're meeting at a smoothie bar close by at five thirty.

Five thirty!

No one looks cute at five thirty, me included.

I dragged my half-dead carcass out of bed at four forty-five, blasted my face with cold water, praying my eye bags away, and then threw on some tinted moisturizer and a touch of blush, and then apologized to my eyes as I coated them in mascara.

The hair, well, it's currently propped up on the top of my head in a mess, secured by a clip.

And the outfit, it's the best he'll get from me. Leggings, an oversized off-the-shoulder sweater, and—as the British would say—a smart pair of trainers.

No idea why I'm channeling the British at the moment other than the fact that I'm delirious and want my pillow.

My Uber drops me off at the smoothie bar, and I stumble out of the car with a thanks and right myself on the sidewalk. From the window, I can see Cougar sitting at a bar-height table with two smoothies. He asked for my order ahead of time, which I thought was considerate.

Adjusting my top to show off a little more shoulder, I head into the smoothie bar and right to him. He's on his phone, but when he looks up and spots me, he lifts off his chair and comes up to me, placing a kiss on my cheek in greeting.

"I'm surprised you're here," he says.

I try to hide my exhaustion and slap on a smile instead. "Did you think I was going to stand you up?"

"Not many women would meet at five thirty in the morning for a date."

"Well"—I take a seat—"I'm not like many women."

"I see that." He smirks and hands me my smoothie. "Berry blast with whey protein."

"Thank you." I take a sip and let the cold of the smoothie attempt to wake me up. Should have ordered the coffee one. What was I thinking?

Clearly I wasn't thinking at all.

"So, what have you been up to since I last saw you?" he asks.

I swallow some more smoothie and say, "Putting together my apartment."

"Did you just move?"

"I did. From up north, actually. I've been here for over two weeks now and I haven't really set up my apartment. My boss keeps me really busy, and by the time I get home, I just want to relax."

He nods. "Understandable."

"But my friend is visiting me and her brother, and well, I can't have her coming to see me living in an apartment full of boxes. She'd be very disappointed."

"Do you need help?" he asks, shocking the hell out of me, because last time I was out with Cougar, I'd have bet my entire paycheck that Cougar is not a guy who lends a hand. Which in the grand scheme of things, with that knowledge, why would I go out with him again? The answer is...no idea.

But he's already surprised me. Maybe he really needed to be pulled from the bar atmosphere. Perhaps, he's more human in the morning and not so…playboy-ish.

"I'm good. Bennett's going to help me tonight with some things."

"Who's Bennett?" he asks.

"From the Bombers. You know, the guy who gave me your number."

"Oh, right." He chuckles and sips his smoothie. "It's early, brain isn't fully working. That's cool that he can help."

"Yeah, he lives on the floor below me, so it's easy for him."

"Nice." He glances in the other direction. "How close are you guys?"

"What do you mean?"

He shrugs. "Just seeing what kind of competition I'm up against."

"Oh." I laugh. "He's just a friend. Also, shouldn't I be the one asking you about competition?"

He twirls his smoothie cup on the table. "Yeah, let's not go there."

"That's what I thought."

He smirks at me. "But to be honest, I haven't been out with anyone since our date."

I press my hand to my chest. "Consider me flattered, but feel free to explore. I don't want to tie you down."

"You don't?" He raises a brow.

"I'm still getting to know you." I smile. "I need to see if you're worth tying down."

"Oh yeah?" That seems to bring a joyful challenge to his eyes. "Tell me, how can I prove that I'm worth it?"

"Not agreeing to a five thirty in the morning date is the first thing you can do."

"Hey, this was your idea. I told you it would be early."

"I didn't think this early." I lean forward on the table and whisper, "I almost fell asleep in the Uber on the way over here."

He chuckles. "What time do you usually wake up?"

"Not this early. I have to be at my boss's house around eight, which means I'm usually up by seven."

"Not bad."

"Yeah, so four forty-five is criminal."

"Consider me honored that you were able to make it, then."

I take a sip of my smoothie. "You know, you're more down-to-earth this morning."

"It's because I haven't fully woken up yet."

"Oh, is that how it works? Once you fully wake up, your inner douche comes out?"

Both his brows raise. "You think I'm a douche?"

Taking my chances, I say, "Our first date you bragged about your football stats, and for a girl who could not care less about sports, it came off as extremely douchey."

"Women fawn at those stats."

"And what was the first thing you learned this morning? I'm not like other women."

"I guess you're not," he says with a smirk.

"This is stunning," Adalade says as she marvels at a burgundy cashmere sweater I found that I knew she'd love. "The color is so rich."

"I thought it would look perfect on you with a pair of brown boots and your brown silk skirt."

"Yes, oh, beautiful. I love it."

"I'm glad," I say as I take a seat on the couch next to her, pleased with the shopping I did for her today. "So then I just have to take the tweed jacket back?"

"Let me think on it for the night and I'll let you know."

"Great." I glance at my phone, noticing the time and a text from

Bennett saying that he's done with his game and should be heading home soon. "Your dinner is on its way—steak salad with pickled onions."

"Thank you, dear."

"And if that's all, I'll pack these clothes back up and then head out."

"Yes, that should be all."

"I'll just put them back in their bags and take care of them in the morning while you decide on that jacket, if that's okay with you?"

"Yes, please just put the bags in the entryway closet."

"Of course," I answer as I start packing things up.

"While you do that, I was hoping to talk with you."

"Oh?" I ask as I gently fold the cashmere sweater and put it back in the tissue paper the store wrapped it in.

"Yes, I've been invited to a dinner, a quaint one, no more than twenty people, and I was hoping that I could bring you along."

"Sure, what day?"

"It's Thursday night, but I have an ulterior motive for going."

"You know I love the drama."

She chuckles. "There is going to be a man there, his name is Draco Humphrey, and I was hoping to catch his eye."

I pause and look up at Adalade, who is blushing. "Excuse me?"

She dismissively waves her hand at me. "Oh please, do not make a big deal of this."

"Adalade, I thought you never wanted another man in your life ever again."

"That was until I found out Draco would be at this dinner."

"And how do we know Draco?"

"I went to high school with him. He took me to a dance once, but his family ended up relocating and I never saw him again. My dear friend Gert said that he moved to San Francisco and that she invited him to the dinner party."

"So, do you want me to go to talk you up?"

"Yes." She nods. "But I don't want it to be obvious, so I asked Gert if you could come and bring a date."

"A date? Why would I need a date? I could just go as your assistant."

Adalade shakes her head. "No, that would look pretentious, and Draco, well, he's quite down-to-earth."

With a name like Draco, I'd think he's running a Fortune 500 company in a high-rise, but okay.

"So bringing your assistant wouldn't be down-to-earth?"

"No, it would seem desperate, and I'm a lady if anything."

"You are," I say. "Okay, so you want me to bring a date so it looks like I'm part of the dinner party and not an assistant following you around, trying to talk you up."

"Exactly."

I nod. "I see what you're trying to do. I think I could maybe ask Cougar."

"Who is Cougar?"

I finish packing up the last piece of clothing and say, "This guy I've been sort of seeing. We've only had two dates, one of them being this morning."

"A morning date?"

I roll my eyes. "Please, don't get me started. It was my idea and it was terrible because I had to meet him at five thirty to make it work. Bad choices all around. Either way, he might be available."

"What does a guy with the name Cougar do?"

"He actually plays for the San Francisco Foghorns."

Adalade straightens up. "My dear, do you only know professional athletes?"

"Does seem that way, doesn't it? Bennett actually set me up with him."

"And how do we feel about Cougar?"

I shrug. "I think he has good moments."

"'Good moments'? That doesn't seem too convincing."

"We're still trying to get to know each other. We were both so tired this morning that I don't know if I was able to get a good assessment of him. Then again, I thought he was more normal this morning than he was the other night. So, we will see."

"Do you think he'd be embarrassing at the dinner? Because that is not something I can afford."

I shake my head. "No. If anything, he might be able to help out because he's a professional football player and that's intriguing."

"That is true. Well, if you think he'll do, then I say we go for it."

"Great. I'll get the details from you tomorrow and start working on preparations. I'm assuming you're going to want to find something nice to wear?"

"I think that cashmere sweater might be exactly what I need."

Proud, I say, "Good, I'm glad." I grab the bags and offer her a smile. "See you in the morning."

"Yes, see you in the morning, dear."

"Why do I smell tacos?" I say as I enter my apartment.

"Because I got some for us," Bennett says, popping out of the kitchen and looking so freaking cute in a pair of joggers, a plain black shirt, and a backward hat.

We exchanged keys to each other's apartments, which has been incredibly useful, especially when he's out of town.

I might have snuck into his place once and spent the night because I love his bed so much, but shhh, let's not tell him that.

Not that he'd mind.

I fear if I did tell him, he'd just give me his bed.

I walk up to him and wrap my arms around him, giving him a big hug. "Thank you, I'm starving."

His hands slowly slide down my back as I start to pull away, but not fully as I look up into his eyes. The scruff on his face is thicker than normal and his eyes look tired, like he hasn't slept really well.

"Are you okay?" I ask.

"Great," he says, his thumb rubbing over my back.

"You look tired."

"Can't hear that enough," he says with a laugh.

"Sorry, didn't mean it like that. Just want to make sure you're good."

He nods. "Yeah, should be an early night for me so I can catch up on some sleep. Which, speaking of sleep." He takes my hand in his and pulls me toward my bedroom, where he opens the door and reveals a brand-new midcentury modern bed.

"Oh my God, Bennett, what did you do?"

"Do you like it?"

"Of course I like it," I say, moving in closer and running my hand over the white oak that matches the two nightstands on either side perfectly. "This is gorgeous. Why did you do this?"

"Because you needed a bed and I know you would have been embarrassed if Gabby saw your place without one."

"Bennett, this is . . . this is really sweet." I close the distance between us and cup his face before lifting on my toes to place a soft kiss on his cheek. "Thank you so much."

He clears his throat. "Of course."

"Have you tested it out?"

"No, didn't want to get my scent all over your bedding."

"I wouldn't mind." I wink. "I like your scent." Then I throw myself onto the bed and mold right into the blankets and mattress. "Oh my God, Bennett."

He tugs on the back of his neck as he says, "Can you refrain from saying, 'Oh my God, Bennett,' while lying in your bed?"

I laugh. "Don't be a prude." Then I tap the bed next to me, welcoming him in.

He joins me, moving in close so our shoulders are touching.

"Isn't it amazing?"

"It is." His fingers brush up against mine. "Almost feels exactly like mine."

"It does." And then I pause for a moment. "Wait…" I turn toward him and prop my head up on my hand as I stare down at him. "Bennett…"

"What?" He can't hide his smile.

"Did you give me your bed?"

"No."

"Bennett…"

He laughs. "I like you, Bower, but I don't like you that much. I might have purchased some things to resemble my bed, though, because after I slept here the other night, it was no match to what I have going on in my apartment."

"I know this, but you didn't have to purchase things for me."

He shrugs as if it's not a big deal. "If I can't spend money on the people I like, then what the hell am I going to spend money on?"

"I'll pay you back."

"The hell you will. This is a housewarming present, and if you pay me back, I'll be thoroughly insulted."

Ugh, stubborn man.

"Fine, then at least let me pay you back for the tacos."

He rolls his eyes. "Sure, Bower, you can pay me back for the tacos."

"Ha, I knew I'd crack you."

Chuckling, he gets out of bed and then tugs me along with him. "Speaking of tacos, they're getting cold. Come on."

His fingers tangle with mine as he tugs me toward the kitchen and I allow it, because…I'm hungry.

He brings me to the counter and then to my surprise, lifts me up and places me on the cold quartz.

"I have a table, you know."

"Yeah, that's full of boxes. This is easier." He hands me a to-go box and then picks one up himself, flipping open the lid to reveal five shredded-beef tacos.

"Oh my God, it smells amazing." I flip open my lid as well and my mouth starts to water. I take in the three tacos he got me and silently laugh, because he knows I wouldn't have consumed five, like him. "Where are these from?"

"One of my favorite places, about a mile away. The dipping sauce is fucking phenomenal."

"Is that what this is?" I ask, pointing to a container that's next to my tacos.

"Yup. It's messy, so be warned." I watch him dip his taco in the sauce and then take a huge bite, nearly devouring half of it.

Jesus.

After he chews, he says, "I also got some pastries for dessert."

That makes me laugh, because I wouldn't expect anything less from him.

"Surprised you didn't start off with dessert."

"We have to earn it by putting this apartment together." He glances around. "Which, by the way, what did you do while I was gone?"

I scoff. "Uh, I did a lot."

"Uh-huh, and what exactly did you do?"

"I organized my clothes, which was a big job, and I put away kitchen stuff."

He nods. "Okay, that's progress."

"See? I did things."

"Well, we can finish everything else tonight."

"I just need some help hanging some things. Don't worry about the boxes. I can handle that."

"Why don't you let me decide what we do and what we don't do?"

"When did you become the boss?"

"When you decided to ask me for help."

He winks and it's so…not adorable, not cute…Good God, is it…is it hot?

When he smirks I feel my stomach erupt in butterflies.

Yup.

Yup, it's hot.

CHAPTER 15
BENNETT

BOWER WIPES HER FACE AND sets her to-go box down. "That was so good." She presses her hand to her stomach. "I'm going to need their information so I can get that every night."

"If you get it every night, you better get some for me as well," I say as I lean my hip against the counter, facing her.

"You're not home all the time."

"Stick it in my fridge."

"Ooo, I like when you talk dirty to me."

"Excuse me?"

She laughs. "Didn't you think that sounded dirty?"

"Gabby's right. You read too much."

"Never," she says, chin lifted high. "By the way, what are your thoughts on Boobs and Balls Book Club as a name?"

My expression falls flat. "Are you serious with that?"

"Depends if you like it or not."

"No."

"Then not serious." Her smile stretches across her face, and it takes everything in me not to sigh at the sight of it.

Fuck, she's so beautiful it actually hurts.

"I think we need to keep thinking. By the way, how was the date this morning?"

Please don't say he kissed you.

Please say it was awful and that you never want to see him ever again and that you actually have been harboring feelings for me this entire time.

Does that sound pathetic? Probably, but I don't care.

"Note to self: Never have a morning date ever again. I met him at five thirty."

"Oh fuck, why?"

"Because he had to be to the stadium by seven. We had some smoothies and talked." She shrugs. "He wasn't spouting off his stats, trying to impress me this time, which made him seem more normal. Actually joked around a bit."

My hand clenches at my side from the thought of him making her laugh. "Think you'll see him again?"

"Yeah, probably. I was actually going to ask him to go with me to a dinner my boss asked me to go to."

My jaw tenses as a full-blown stream of anger pumps through my veins.

"What kind of dinner?" I ask in a controlled voice despite the war going on in my body.

"Adalade's trying to impress some guy she knows from high school. When she told me, I was so caught off guard because she swore she'd be single forever, but then all of a sudden Draco is back in town and she's singing a new tune."

"Draco?"

"Yeah, that's his name. Either way, she wants to impress him at this dinner party and asked if I'd go to help her look good. She wants me to take a date so it doesn't look like she brought her assistant to talk her up."

"Makes sense." I swallow the lump in my throat. "So you're going to take Cougar?"

Can't stand the thought of her going to an intimate dinner with him, where I'm sure he'll have his hands all over her, probably whispering in her ear, making a goddamn move every chance he gets.

Fuck, makes me want to lose my goddamn mind.

"I think so, unless you want to go." She laughs it off as if it's a joke, but I don't find anything funny about it.

"When is it?" I ask.

"Bennett, I'm only kidding. I know you have baseball."

"When is it?" I ask again, not fucking around. Hell, I'll pretend to be sick if I need to.

"Thursday, but—"

"I'll be there."

For once in my life, the baseball gods have aligned, because I have an off night on Thursday and no travel, which is rare. So I'll be damned if she takes anyone but me.

"But don't you have baseball?"

"Off night," I say.

"Oh, well, you don't want to spend your off night with me."

My brow furrows together. "I have spent almost all my off time with you."

"I mean at some stuffy dinner party."

"You will be there, right?"

"Of course," she answers, looking confused.

"If you're there, then I know I'll have fun."

Her head tilts to the side. "That's very flattering. Are you trying to flirt with me?"

Panic erupts in my chest because *oh fuck, oh fuck…*

But then she laughs. "Just kidding, you would never flirt with an old bag of bones like me."

Little does she fucking know.

"And I don't like to ask you for one more thing, but honestly, it might be best that you go with me because I still don't know Cougar that well and what if he says something out of line and ruins Adalade's chances of impressing Draco?"

"Wouldn't want that."

"Think you can be on your best behavior?"

"Depends, what do you need from me?"

She crosses her legs on her counter and says, "Well, someone by my side that acts like a date. There might have to be some touching. Are you okay with touching?"

Fucking yes.

I shrug. "That's fine. You touch me all the time and I somehow manage."

She scoffs. "You say that as if it's torture."

"I wouldn't say torture, but pretty damn close to it."

"You're going to have to suffer a night of it, so get ready."

Trust me, I am. Already thinking about all of the goddamn touching.

"And then just be a good conversationalist, which I know you are. I can send you a write-up about Adalade so you know more about her and can help talk up how great she is, especially about her charities."

"What kind of charities does she work with?"

Bower softly smiles. "Foster care kids."

"Really?" I ask, feeling my throat grow thick.

"Yes. She's on the board for a few. I can let you know which ones."

"Please do, as we might support the same charities."

"That would actually be pretty amazing."

"Was she in foster care?"

Bower slowly nods and then gets off the counter. "She was, but it was different back then for her. She doesn't talk about it much, but I just know she wants to help reshape the system she grew up in and that's what she focuses on."

"That's awesome." I smooth my hand over my jaw. If there's one thing I've been intentional about, it's using my income to support those with less. I don't advertise who I support, as that would just be a dick move—*insincere*—and seem as though I'm only giving for the kudos.

Gabby and I grew up with nothing, and if I can help others not experience such destitution, I will. I wonder if Adalade knows of other places I could support that would help more. "I'd like to get to know her better, too, if that's all right with you. I'm always looking for people to partner with."

"Of course, I'm sure she'd love that. Hey, have you ever told Gretchen about the work you do for foster kids and their families?"

I shake my head. "No, that's not something I want her using to get in the good graces of fans. That's personal."

"I get that. You're right. Sorry I suggested it."

"Don't apologize."

She smiles softly. "So, do you think we should hang some things?"

"Yes, because I want dessert, but we're not allowed to have any until we've done some damage."

She clasps her hands together and says, "Then let's get to work."

"Graydon, if you could put your hand on OC, that would be great."

"I'm good." Graydon stuffs his hands in his pockets, clearly not into this whole publicity shoot for the zoo. I think it's the third one we've done, and I can't imagine why we have to keep doing it. Maybe because Graydon wouldn't know a smile if it saved his fucking life.

"Graydon, just touch him so we can get this over with," I say, my back starting to cramp up from twisting in a weird way as I sit on this godforsaken golf cart.

"Listen to the young one," OC says and then whispers, "Touch me."

"Making it worse," I say.

"Get the fuck away from my face," Graydon says as the photographer lowers the camera.

"Gentlemen, please."

"Switch it up. I'm not touching him."

The photographer presses her fingers into her forehead as Gretchen walks up, clearly not happy with any of us.

Then again, none of us came here in a good mood.

Graydon is in a bad mood because something happened with Maple, quite sure they broke up.

OC is still suffering from—in his words—a major heartbreak. The girl that he likes and planned on getting back together with is now engaged. Mind you, she lives in Vancouver and he lives here. Sure, it sucks, but dude, move the fuck on.

And I'm pissed because Cougar invited Bower out to another early morning date and she accepted. Gabby and Ryland arrive today and I was excited to see them, but this puts a damper on things, because three dates? Three fucking dates?

What does that mean?

Does she actually like him?

Every time I ask, she doesn't really seem that excited about the prospect of dating him, and yet, she's waking up at four forty-five to go on a date with him.

That has to mean something.

"You three are blowing this photo shoot," Gretchen says, looking none too pleased.

"Why are we even doing this? We've done two already," Graydon asks, ever the grump.

"Because we're constantly adding images to the zoo socials and creating content around these photo shoots, hence why we did individual shots before this. Are you really that immature that you can't suck it up for a few minutes and take a picture?"

"The fucking golf cart is too small for all of us," Graydon says, gesturing to the cart. He's right, it's like clowns piling out of a clown car.

"It's pretty tight," I add, keeping my tone even. "Cramping up my back."

"Yeah, same," OC says, raising his hand.

Gretchen sighs and then says, "Fine, head back to the greenroom and we'll figure something out."

"I have to leave in about thirty minutes," I say.

"Which means when we have a new setup ready to go, you three will be cooperative." She shoos us with her hand. "Now go get some sugar in you so we can finish this up and I can go home and take a bath."

"Are you going to use bath salts?" OC asks.

"Get out of here," she nearly shouts, causing us all to move toward the room that's set up as a greenroom. It's normally used for events, but the photo shoot has taken over.

Graydon slumps in a chair while I grab a pack of fruit snacks and OC snags a donut.

"Want anything?" I ask Graydon.

He just shakes his head and crosses his arms over his chest. OC takes a seat next to him, apparently testing his life span, and I sit across from them.

I check my phone for texts, but when I come up short, nothing from Bower, I grumble under my breath.

"So I know why Graydon is grumpy and I know why I'm contemplating my life choices, but what's up with you?" OC asks.

"Nothing," I say, staring off into the distance.

"Yeah, not buying it. Does it have to do with the sister's best friend? What's her name again?"

"Bower," Graydon says, surprising us both. I might have mentioned her name a few times, but I didn't think he'd remember.

"Right, Bennett and Bower," OC says. "Does it have to do with her?"

I stay silent because I don't think I'm ready for this, for them to be involved.

But after a few seconds, OC gasps. "It does. It has to do with her. What happened?"

"Nothing," I say. "Absolutely nothing."

"Oh no." OC winces. "Did you make a move and she rejected you?"

"No."

"Wait." Graydon scratches his cheek. "Bower is the sister's best friend? Then why was Cougar talking about her yesterday?"

"Cougar Vajeen?" OC asks, sitting on the edge of his seat now. "Is it the same Bower?"

I sigh heavily and say, "Yeah, same Bower."

"Wait, you had me set Cougar up with the girl you like?"

"What the hell?" OC asks, outraged. "You had Graydon set someone up for you and you didn't involve me? What the actual fuck? You know I like that kind of shit."

"Yeah, too much, and I thought you'd be annoying about it, hence why I just asked Graydon."

"But why would you have me set her up with someone else?" Graydon asks.

"Because I got some bad advice."

"You sought advice outside the Gladdy Daddies?" OC asks. "From whom? Also, serves you right. You know you only get the best advice from us. Now look at you, sending the girl you like out on a date with one of the most notorious players in the Bay Area. Pretty fucking dumb if you ask me."

"I don't tend to agree with him, but yeah, that's dumb," Graydon says.

"I know," I growl. "I don't need the reminder."

"Who gave you the advice?" OC adamantly asks.

"Nolan."

"Nolan Hart?" OC asks, jaw slightly parted. "The guy who walks around in crop tops, chewing wads of gum, and giving everyone who walks by him a finger gun?"

"Do you know him?"

"No, but my algorithm sure does and is always showing me videos of him."

"You know, it's catered to keep showing you what you watch the most. Very telling, man," I say.

"I watch because I want to see if I could pull off the crop top."

"Absolutely not." Graydon shakes his head.

"No chance in hell, man."

"I have abs." He lifts up his shirt, showing us his stomach. "I could put on a good show."

"It's not about abs. It's about aura, and you're not a crop-top-aura kind of guy."

"Facts," Graydon says.

"Well, fuck both of you, but we're getting off track. I want to get back to why we're setting Bower up with Cougar Vajeen."

I scrub my face with my hands. "Because I can't tell her how I feel because she still sees me as the kid she first met, so Nolan said I should set her up with someone not good enough for her and then I can swoop in like a hero and show her how perfect I am for her."

"Huh..." OC thinks about it for a moment. "Actually, not a bad plan."

"The only problem is he set her up with Cougar, who is known to charm," Graydon says.

"You're the one who told me he'd be perfect," I practically shout.

"Because you didn't give me all the details. You said douchebag, and he's the epitome of that. If I'd have known your entire plan, I'd have probably chosen someone like...Kent Ronald."

"Ohhhhh, Kent Ronald would have been a great choice," OC says.

My anger gets the best of me and I say, "Why the fuck is this happening? She had her third date today. Third. What does that even mean? Every time I ask her how her date went, she just says okay and that they don't have that much in common, but she keeps going out with him."

"Maybe it isn't really a date," OC says. "If you know what I mean."

"I will fucking murder you," I say through clenched teeth.

"Whoa, whoa, whoa, that's a bit harsh. I'm just saying out loud what this big guy is thinking."

"Is that what you're thinking?" I ask Graydon.

"It would track with him."

"Oh my fucking God," I say, popping out of my seat only to start pacing in front of them. "Are they having sex? Do you think they're having sex? She said she was taking it slow. I don't even think they've kissed, but do you think they're doing it?"

OC winces and looks over at Graydon, who presses his lips together.

"Fucking fuck!" I yell before I feel everything around me collapse.

I'm such a goddamn moron.

CHAPTER 16
BOWER

"DON'T EVER LEAVE ME EVER again. You live here now," I say to Gabby as I loop my arm through hers and hold on to her tightly while we make our way through the Bombers concourse.

Ryland's behind us, carrying our food and drinks, because he insisted, not because we forced him, although I do enjoy him being a pack mule so I can gush with my best friend.

"You're the one that left me," Gabby says.

I shake my head. "No, you got married and traded me in for a more muscular, grumpy version."

"I love him, but he never could replace you."

"Keep saying that to me. I need the reassurance."

She chuckles and then leads us down the stairs to our seats. Bennett must have pulled some strings, or he straight-up paid for it, but he got us great seats, ten rows back from the first base on-deck circle. Ryland and Gabby were, of course, frothing at the tickets, while I just admired their appreciation for good seats.

After we've sat down, we fit our drinks into the cupholders. I grab my hot dog and hand my phone to Gabby. "Can you take a picture of me with my hot dog?"

"Sure." She chuckles. "Do you want the field in it, or just you and your hot dog?"

"With the field." I roll my eyes. "I want to do a front and a back picture to send to Bennett so he can see the shirt I got to wear."

While I was out making the rounds for Adalade today, I had Mark drop me off at a sporting goods store, where I bought a shirt with Brinkman and his number, twenty-two, on the back. It's a bit tight, because it's a kid's size, but it was either that or a size way too big for me.

"You're going to send it to Bennett?" Gabby questions.

"Uh, yeah, so he can see that his neighbor supports him."

I hold up the hot dog and she snaps a picture before I turn around, my hair to one side, and she takes another picture.

When I grab my phone from her, I motion for her and Ryland to get together. They're both in their Bombers gear, twinning and looking so adorable.

"Smile." I take the picture and then open up my text thread with Bennett. I include all the pics and tell him we plan on being the loudest.

Once I'm good with that, I put my phone to the side and take a huge bite of my hot dog, staring out at the well-manicured field.

"Wow, that grass is so—" I pause when I turn and see Gabby and Ryland both staring at me. "What?" I wipe at my mouth. "Do I have ketchup on my face?"

"What's going on?" Gabby asks.

"What do you mean?"

"You just sent Bennett a picture of you."

"Uh, yeah, because I'm wearing this shirt and I'm at his game."

"That's...very girlfriend-like of you," Ryland says, picking up his beer and sipping from it.

I scoff, because he has completely lost his mind.

"Girlfriend of me?" I ask. "Uh, no, it's not. First, I'm seeing someone sort of—kind of—second, I'm just being a friend, and there's nothing girlfriend about me and Bennett."

"Are you sure?" Gabby asks. "Because that would be...well, it wouldn't be right."

"Of course it wouldn't be right. He's eight years younger than me, your brother, and not my type." Ehh, maybe a little my type. The dark hair, light blue eyes, and thick scruff... God, so hot...

I mean, not him, just that aesthetic of a man.

Bennett is... Sure, he's attractive and the muscles don't hurt, but like I said, not my type.

Did you believe that? Because I didn't.

"Well, all of that," Gabby says. "And the fact that you've been in his life for so long helping me take care of him. You made me that promise one night when we were working at the Olive Garden, and I wasn't sure I was going to make ends meet."

As if I could forget the promise. I remember that night. I found her sobbing in the back of the stockroom and when I asked her what was going on, she was at her wit's end, unable to make rent and didn't know what to do because her sketchy boyfriend at the time took money from her.

"I promised that no matter what, I'd take care of Bennett."

"And when his apartment was broken into and...and they robbed him blind, that was...my lowest moment, Bower. But you promised you would help take care of it, and you did. You helped with filing the police report, even though it was months later. That's the friend I need. I don't...I don't need a friend trying to hook up with my brother. I need you by my side, like you always have been."

"And I am," I say. "Nothing has changed. It's you and me."

"I know, I just...I don't know, for a second, I freaked out. I'm sorry." She shakes her head. "God, what a weird way to start a visit." She laughs nervously.

I take her hand in mine. "You're good. Bennett and I have been spending a lot of time together because he's the only person I know here, but there's no need to worry. We're just friends and we'll keep it that way." I smirk. "I'd like to set him up with someone, just like he set me up, but I don't know anyone."

"Maybe we can make him a dating profile," Gabby says with excitement.

"Oh my gosh, I love—"

"Nope," Ryland says, draping his arm behind Gabby. "Not going to let that happen. Let the boy figure out his own love life. He probably hasn't put effort into dating because he's coming toward the end of his season. He's focused, and he's gained so much popularity that it will be harder for him."

"Hmm, I didn't think about that." I bite my hot dog.

"Yeah, me either."

"Good thing you have me," Ryland says, looking completely in his element.

"Maybe the guy you're seeing knows of someone. Maybe he has a sister," Gabby suggests.

"I can ask." I think about it. "Ehh, maybe I'll wait. I'm still getting to know the guy."

"Didn't you have another date?"

"We've had three," I say, as if that's an impressive thing, but it's really not, because two of the dates I've only been half-awake.

And the only reason I went on the second morning date was because Cougar said he liked it so much he wanted to do it again. Being the sucker that I am, I caved and said I couldn't wait.

"Three, that's so great. Have you guys kissed yet?" Gabby fully turns toward me now, blocking out Ryland, but he doesn't seem to care as he continues to watch the grounds crew prep the field. And this is why I didn't tell her I was looking for something more serious, because...the questions.

"No," I say. "Haven't really had that feeling, you know?"

"Really?" Gabby asks, her confusion actually kind of comical. "That's very unlike you, looking for a feeling."

"A feeling of attraction," I clarify, not wanting her to get too excited again. "I think I might be broken."

"No, not broken."

I slowly nod and dab my napkin at my mouth. "Yup, broken, because I haven't thought about him naked once, and you know how much I like to think about dicks."

"Jesus," Ryland mutters off to the side.

"I like to think about them penetrating me and tickling me and rubbing all over my face."

"Can you not?" Ryland asks, leaning forward. "There are people around us."

"And they're paying attention to the game, not to us," Gabby says and then turns back toward me. "So you haven't been thinking about his penis in your mouth?"

"For the love of God," Ryland grumbles.

"No," I say, panic hitting my voice. I haven't been able to say this to Bennett, because that would be weird, and I haven't had a chance to catch Gabby up, and there is no way in hell I'd say this to Adalade, so I'm finally getting it all off my chest. "I have not had any visions of his penis near me and it's…it's disturbing."

"This conversation is disturbing," Ryland says.

"Shhh…" Gabby shushes him with a finger. "Watch your sports."

"This is your sports too."

"Yes, but my favorite player is still in the locker room, so I can focus on my friend right now." Turning back toward me…again, she says, "It does seem like you might be broken. Maybe it's all the romance you've been reading. It's desensitized you."

I shake my head. "If anything, it's made me hornier. I just don't know if I'm into this guy."

"Which is odd, because he's hot, tall, muscular—"

"Sitting right here, babe."

Gabby turns to Ryland and kisses him on the lips, like full-on open-mouthed kiss that makes him clear his throat when she pulls away. "And I love you so much."

Happy with that, he goes back to drinking his beer but keeps his arm draped over her chair, never letting her forget who she belongs to.

And that, right there, is what I want.

I want that all-consuming love where there's a healthy possessiveness between two people, where you stake a claim, letting everyone else know that the person you're with is off-limits.

I want to feel the passion they feel, I want to be able to freely kiss, with open-mouth kisses and tongue and get lost in the moment in public without any repercussions.

I want to feel loved.

Held.

Cherished.

And when I'm with Cougar, I'm just not there. Yet.

"Maybe he's not the guy for you," Gabby says.

I shrug. "I don't know. I'm going to go out with him again, as he texted asking when I'm free."

"Really?"

I nod. "Yeah, he started chatting during our last date and maybe he sees me differently, like...I don't know, like I'm not like the other women he's dated who probably go out with him for one thing."

"The sex."

My lips thin. "You don't have to put 'the' in front of sex."

"Feels more official that way."

"Yeah, perhaps. Either way, yes, maybe he's used to women like that and I'm just not her, so he finds me fascinating."

"Probably. And that's something to hold on to. It's nice to be fascinating."

"Yeah, I guess so." I sigh and look out toward the field. "Just wish being fascinating came with dick tickles."

"Don't call it that," Ryland says.

"Sir." I lean forward, looking him dead in the eyes. "May I remind you, once again, this conversation does not involve you. So keep that trap shut or I'm going to swap seats with your girl and you'll then have the utter joy of cradling me for the next three hours."

He turns away and goes back to observing the field.

"That's what I thought." I sigh and say, "Now, where was I?"

"Dick tickles," Gabby says.

"Right." The crowd cheers as the Bombers take the field to do some warm-ups, my eyes finding Bennett immediately as he jogs out to the outfield grass, where he tosses the ball with Nolan Hart. I can tell it's Nolan from his tattoos.

A group of women huddled against the netting catcall out to them, waving signs and making complete asses of themselves. If I know anything about Bennett, it's that he won't pay attention to such blatant behavior.

He's sophisticated.

He's—

"He looks so much bigger," Gabby says. "Every time I see him, I swear he's packed on another ten pounds of muscle."

I can vouch for the muscles, as I've seen him with his shirt off. He has a lot of them.

But this is the first time I'm noticing that he has quite the ass. Very round. Has it always been that round? Has he always had an ass? Maybe it's his tight pants that are accentuating said feature. Or the way his broad shoulders tug on his shirt, forcing the fabric to narrow down around his waist.

Oh, you know what, it's probably the belt. Unsure if I've ever seen him in a belt. Well, that's not true. I've been to games before and he's worn a belt, but maybe I'm used to him in street clothes, because he's not walking around the apartment in his baseball uniform. That would be quite comical if he did.

Either way, he probably did gain ten pounds of muscle, but it's ten pounds of ass muscle, because that junk in the trunk was not there before.

"Seems regular to me," I say, just to make sure she didn't somehow read my thoughts about his ass. Not that I'm attracted to his ass. I just noticed it, but given Gabby's reaction earlier, I don't want her to know that I noticed his ass.

So…there you have it.

Although…it is a nice ass.

But that's all I'll say about it.

"You know, baseball can be quite thrilling," I say as I sail some popcorn straight from a plastic helmet directly into my mouth.

The score is tied. I think it's ending soon, something about last inning, perhaps. And there's a runner on second with one out.

"Shhh…" Gabby says, sitting on the edge of her seat. "Bennett's getting on deck."

I look straight ahead and watch Bennett step outside of the dugout, slipping his helmet on simultaneously with one hand, his forearm flexing as he does so. He rests his bat against his leg as he adjusts his batting gloves, tightening them around his wrists before picking his bat back up and strengthening his grip around it.

My eyes travel the length of his back, how his shoulder blades pull at the fabric and once again…his butt on full display.

I really think it's the belt.

Has to be.

Going to make a note to ask him where to get such a belt, because I wouldn't mind a little pop of the booty like that.

The batter swings, hitting the ball straight into the ground, which I think baseball fanatics refer to as…wait for it…a grounder. The guy in the middle, I want to say shortstop, grabs the ball, scares the base runner back to second with what I can only imagine would be a growl, and then throws the batter out at first, yeeting the ball with all his might.

Quite an impressive display of athleticism.

Unfortunately, it didn't assist in us winning.

Now, according to the giant screen right in front of me, there seem to be two outs. That guy still on second who might have pissed himself, can't be sure, and our boy is up.

Some lucky motherfucker with a mic announces Bennett's name, his number—which is twenty-two because that's the day he and Gabby left foster care—and his walk-up song plays.

It's some techno beat drop that gets the stadium going every single time and they accompany the drop with a light display, which of course gets my nipples hard.

I glance to my left, where Gabby and Ryland are both on the edge of their seats, holding hands, looking so adorably nervous.

So I cup my hands around my mouth and shout, "Come on, Bennett! Make Mommy proud!"

Smirking, I see both Ryland and Gabby turn their heads toward me, causing me to laugh.

"Mommy?" Gabby asks.

"Just trying to lighten the mood. Did it not work?"

She chuckles and shakes her head, turning back toward the game.

With one foot in the square thing that all players must stand in when attempting to whack the ball, Bennett stares at his bat held in front of him like a sword, ready to slay the mighty beast.

My guess is he's whispering sweet nothings to a piece of wood, convincing it that now is the time to make a significant impact.

Some drunk guy to the right of me shouts that Bennett sucks.

BOMBERS
BOMBERS

A lady down in front pumps her fists in the air like she's at the club.

And a vendor—who I like to consider a good friend of my wallet—shouts about peanuts.

The dramatics.

Finally, after mentally making love to his bat, Bennett steps into the square of truth—truth because we shall see if making love to wood pays off—and he gets into position to slay.

I'll be honest, despite not being overly involved in the sport, I do enjoy the tension of it all.

Will he or won't he?

Will he be a hero?

Or will he be like the guy before him, getting thrown out by a yeeting clown in the middle of the field?

Only time will tell.

The pitcher fingers the ball, lifts his leg like he's blowing a fart, and then sails the ball toward Bennett at such an enormous speed that I'm unsure how anyone can track such a thing.

The man dressed in armor, let's call him the king of the court—others might refer to him as an official of some sort—sticks his hand out to the side, showing off his finger guns.

Ah-ha, I know what that means.

It was a strike.

"That's not good," I say.

"It's fine," Gabby says. "He likes to take the first pitch most of the time unless it's a fastball, but that was a curve and he's not going to waste a swing on a curveball if he wasn't clocked in on it. It was a good take."

No idea what she just said, but I clap anyway and shout, "Great take, great take." I point toward the field, talking to the people around me. "He meant to do that."

They all look at me as if I've lost my mind.

And perhaps I have.

I am slightly intoxicated.

I have had far too much cotton candy—two bags, yikes.

And I think the popcorn is sitting awkwardly in my system.

Not to mention I feel restless. I've been sitting in this seat for so long that—

The crack of the bat pulls me out of my thoughts as the crowd erupts.

What happened?

Where did it go?

Everyone stands, so I do the same, no problem in being a follower at this moment.

And then, before I can even make sense of what's going on, Ryland and Gabby are screaming, jumping up and down, and…ew…making out.

What the fuck is wrong with them?

I look out toward the field, where I see Bennett casually trotting around the bases while his teammates are billowing out of the dugout, bouncing up and down and throwing…is that gum? I hope they pick that up, because what a waste.

"He did it," Gabby screams, excusing herself from Ryland's mouth for a second.

"Did he win the game?" I ask.

"He hit a home run! Yes, he won the game. That's why it was so smart that he let that first ball go. He knows he can't do much with a curveball unless he needs to, so he zeroed in on that fastball and took it yard."

Took it yard, what a weird term.

Either way… Yay, Bennett!

You, your bubbly ass, and your lover—his bat—did it.

Now, let's go to the bar!

CHAPTER 17
BENNETT

Bower: We're in the back. Be prepared: Your sister is drunk and very handsy. She's been shoving her tongue down Ryland's throat every chance she gets. I might throw up.

CHUCKLING AS I RIDE DOWN the streets of San Francisco in a professional car service, because I knew we would be hanging out after the game and I wanted some drinks, I stare down at the picture that Bower sent me before the game.

The picture of her wearing my number on her back.

It made my gut clench, because fuck, it looks so good on her. Too damn good. And all it did was remind me that I want her, don't have her, but if I did have her, that is what my life could be like.

Bower in the stands, cheering me on, wearing my number…eating a hot dog.

It made me long for something I so desperately want, something I'm hopefully working toward, despite fucking Cougar being in the way.

The entire game, anytime I thought about her being there, watching me, my mind kept going toward what I talked about with the guys. Does she like him? Have they kissed? Are they getting serious?

All things I don't know.

BRINK
22

All things that fuel the rage that lives deep inside me.

But maybe I could get some info from Gabby, because there is no doubt that they've talked about it. I just need to unearth the truth.

The car pulls up to the side of the street, in front of the bar that Gabby and Ryland chose. I tug on the brim of my hat, attempting to hide my face. It's dumb, because I'm easily recognizable in a hat, and then I thank the driver before getting out.

I keep my head down as I enter the bar and then walk all the way to the back, where a rope closes off the rest of the place to the public.

The security guy protecting the area gives me one look and nods before saying, "Great game."

"Thanks, man." I pat him on the shoulder as he lets me in. I finally look up and the first person I see is Bower. She's sitting up on her knees, in the booth, holding up a shot and looking me dead in the eyes.

Her Bombers shirt clings to her, highlighting her breasts while showing off about two inches of her stomach. Her hair is wild, curled and falling over her shoulders. The lights bounce off her glossy lips, making them look irresistible, and the expression of utter happiness when she spots me creates a sense of *mine* in my head.

"Bennett!" she shouts, keying Gabby and Ryland into my arrival.

Gabby flies out of her seat, completely drunk, and wraps her arms around me, giving me a huge hug.

"My baby brother, the game winner." She sloppily kisses my cheek and then grips my shoulders as she pulls away. "You're amazing."

"And you're drunk." I laugh.

She pats my chest. "I am, but you're catching up. We have drinks ready for you."

She tugs me toward the booth and Ryland, also looking lit, pulls me into a hug and pats me rather aggressively on the back. Whispering in my ear, he says, "I love your sister so much."

Chuckling, I reply, "Good thing since you married her."

"Very good thing." Then he lets go. "Good game." He then grabs Gabby and pulls her into the booth and starts kissing her, which she obliges, tongues and everything.

Jesus.

I glance at Bower and she mouths *Told you so*.

I walk up to her and to my pleasure, she gives me a hug as well. My hand briefly skims her bare skin before she pulls away and winks at me. "Hell of a game, laying off that curveball only to take the fastball yard for a walk-off game-winning home run."

I raise one brow. "Did my sister tell you to say that?"

"I memorized what she's been repeating in between making out with Ryland. Did I do a decent job?"

"Very good," I say.

She smirks and with a flirtatious wink, she says, "It was a really good game."

"Did I impress you?"

"Tremendously." Then she tugs on my hand and has me sit right next to her. Ryland and Gabby are still going at it, so Bower turns toward me, holds up a shot glass to me and says, "Bottoms up."

"What is it?"

"Does it matter?"

"I guess not."

And with that, I tip the liquid back and swallow.

"Never have I ever…uh…licked ice cream off a person's body," Gabby says with a giggle and then turns to Ryland, who rolls his eyes and takes a sip of his beer.

Oh, for fuck's sake.

"Ryland Rowley, that wicked tongue of yours strikes again," Bower says. "So far we've learned that you have licked Gabby—"

"Don't need the recap," I say, holding up my hand. "For the love of God, no recap."

Bower bumps her shoulder with mine, her hair brushing up against me, the sweet scent of her shampoo so goddamn intoxicating. It smells sweet like coconut with some sort of rich musk, fuck if I know, but I'm going to tell you right now, if I ever see a coconut in person, I'll probably get hard.

"Okay, your turn," Gabby says, pointing to me as she waves back and forth.

Finally. I swear she and Bower have been going back and forth for the last ten minutes, not letting me or Ryland say anything, not that Ryland would, he's just over there, feeling up my sister every chance he gets. It's weird, not just because that's my sister, but because he's my former coach as well.

"My turn?" I ask, trying to play it off as if I haven't been waiting for this goddamn moment once I figured out what I wanted to ask. "Uhh…never have I ever…kissed someone on the lips in the last three weeks."

Gabby and Ryland both groan while Gabby says, "You did that on purpose to make us drink."

Yup, that's exactly why I did that.

Please note the sarcasm.

As they both drink, my heart beats wildly in my chest as I turn to Bower, waiting for her to take a sip.

But when she remains still, joy erupts through me because that means she hasn't kissed Cougar.

"You're not drinking?" she asks me.

"Nope," I say. "Haven't had the time. What about you?"

She shakes her head. "Sad day for me, no kisses."

"And no dick tickles." Gabby laughs.

"Dick tickles?" I ask.

"She's right. No penis has been inside of me for a while. More sad news, I know."

Clearing my throat, I say, "Not even with Cougar?"

"Dry as a bone," Gabby announces. "But she's going to try to make it work with him, right? Because there's potential."

And then Gabby just fucking pisses all over my joy.

"Are you?" I ask.

Bower shrugs. "You went through all that trouble to set things up for me, might as well give him another try. We might be getting to a place where things move along."

Not what I wanted to hear.

"'Might' being a strong word," Gabby says as Ryland kisses her neck. Jesus, slow down, dude. "She said when she's near him, she feels nothing, as if she's broken inside."

"Okay, okay," Bower says, waving her hand at Gabby. "We don't need to talk about my lack of sex life or the fact that my ability to be aroused has fallen off the face of the earth. Back to the questions." She turns to me and says, "Never have I ever come in my pants."

I roll my eyes and take a sip of my drink as Gabby says, "Ewwwwww."

"Oh please," I shoot back. "As if you've never."

"I haven't." Gabby tilts her chin high in indignation.

"Bullshit," Ryland says. "All those times I fingered—"

"For the love of God, we're done," I say, ending this godforsaken game. I down the rest of my drink and then let out a deep breath. "I have to get to bed or else I'm not going to be able to play tomorrow."

"Why, will you be in trouble?" Bower cutely asks.

I shake my head. "No, just can't function when I'm extremely hungover."

"This coming from the guy who doesn't have an ounce of a hangover the next day," Bower says.

"That's what being twenty-four will do to you," Ryland says and finishes his beer as well. "We need to go anyway." He wraps his arm around Gabby and whispers something into her ear that makes her giggle.

Fucking gross.

I pull my phone out and order up the car. I turn to Bower and ask, "Want to catch a ride with me?"

"Obviously."

"Good, he's right around the corner." I stand and then help Bower out before giving Gabby and Ryland a hug goodbye. They need some time alone.

Because the bar is so crowded, I take Bower's hand and weave her through hordes of people, not stopping when I'm noticed, but keep moving forward until we're outside and my driver pulls around just at the right time. I open the door for her, let her in, and then follow in behind.

"That was very quick," she says, surprised.

"He was waiting for me."

"How nice." She yawns and leans her head against my shoulder. "I'm exhausted."

"Same." I put my arm around her and she snuggles into my chest, and that's where she remains until we reach our apartment building.

For a moment, I think I'm going to have to carry her up, but she stirs awake and takes my hand as I walk her into the building and to the elevator.

"Can I just come to your place?" she asks on another yawn.

"Sure," I say, welcoming the idea.

"Thank you."

When the elevator doors part, I help her to my apartment, where she heads straight to my bathroom.

"Let me grab you a shirt. I, uh, I grabbed a few things the other day for you in case you ever decided to stay the night. There's face wash and a toothbrush and anything else you might need in there. Drawer on the right is yours."

"I adore you," she says right before she shuts the bathroom door.

Excited but also exhausted, I grab a Bombers shirt she can borrow and then quickly change out of my clothes, leaving me in just my boxer briefs. I plug my phone in and then once she opens the door, the bathroom smelling like fresh toothpaste, I hand her my shirt.

"Thank you," she says as she goes into my room and starts to undress.

Jesus.

I quickly shut the door to the bathroom, because I might be infatuated with her, but I'm not about to take a peek when I'm not offered a show.

So I get ready for bed while she gets changed. I take a few extra minutes just to calm myself before I exit the bathroom, where I find her already in bed, curled up.

That's what I want.

Right there.

Her, in my bed, no one else's. Just the sight of her under my blankets, sleeping on my pillow, gives me fucking hope.

Turning off the lights, I slip under the covers as well and turn toward her, only for her to turn her back toward me and then push up against my chest.

Does she want me to snuggle?

What would she do if I put my arm around her? Would she care?

Would she even notice in her state?

I bite down on the corner of my mouth, contemplating until she answers the question for me. She reaches for my arm and places it around her waist, pulling herself in even closer.

And then in the sweetest, softest voice, she says, "Night, Bennett."

Fuck, this is amazing.

Pressing my face into her hair, I say, "Night, Bower."

"Death," Bower says as she appears in the living room, her hair sticking up in all directions, a wince across her expression, and a light smear of mascara under each eye.

I chuckle as I lean against the counter of my kitchen in a pair of sweatpants, sipping my coffee.

"What can I get you?"

She plops down on the couch and says, "A shovel for my grave."

"Don't have a shovel, but I have some greasy hash browns warming in the oven and some strong coffee."

"I'll have to settle." She drapes her arm over her eyes and groans. "Why are you not even affected a little? You drank more than I did."

"Technically, you were drinking during the game too." I prepare a platter of hash browns and some coffee for her and bring it over.

"Which I realize now was a bad mistake."

I sit down next to her and hand her the mug of coffee, and when she doesn't take it, I jokingly ask, "Do you need me to feed it to you?"

"Through an IV, thanks."

I laugh and she takes the mug, her head resting against the couch. "God, why do I do this to myself?"

"Because my sister was letting loose for the first time in probably a year and you were joining in."

"That's very true." She lolls her head to the side and looks at me. "Ryland was a horndog last night."

"Don't remind me. Fucking keep it in your pants, dude."

"I found it endearing."

"Endearing? I saw far too much of my sister's tongue last night."

She chuckles and takes a sip of her coffee. "I don't know. It's nice to see her so in love. I only wish I had something like that. Made me kind of jealous, you know?"

"You want that?" I ask, interested to know what her dreams are when it comes to a relationship.

"I do. I want someone to want me that much, someone who finds it nearly impossible to keep their hands off me. Someone who worships me."

Turn your head, babe. I'm right here.

"Are you not finding that with Cougar?"

I kind of already know the answer to this, but I want to double down on it since my emotions got the best of me yesterday.

"I don't know." She sighs. "I mean, I can see potential there, but it's moving at a snail's pace, which is great, because maybe that's what I need, to spend time developing a friendship before jumping in right away."

"I get that," I say, not overjoyed by her answer.

"What about you?" She slightly turns toward me and I reach for the plate of hash browns, offering her one. As she grabs one, she says, "Last night you said you hadn't kissed someone in three weeks. Do you really go that long without…you know, doing anything?"

"I mean, there's always self-pleasure."

She smirks. "Yes, well, we all seem to be taking part in that, but you know what I mean. You're Bennett Brinkman, and you just won the Bombers game last night. There has to be a bunch of women waiting to grab your attention. Are you just not interested?"

"Not really interested in the women who throw themselves at me."

Clearly, I only like the ones that are putting me firmly in the friend zone.

She leans her head to the side, studying me for a moment. "Are you still hung up on that crush you had?"

Ha, if she only knew.

"I mean…yeah."

"It's been so long. Why haven't you moved on?"

I wet my lips, wishing I could tell her the reason, wishing I could look her in the eyes and tell her that it's her, but the timing isn't right. I don't think I've done enough to get her to break, or to accept my feelings without being scared.

I need a little bit more time.

"Why haven't I moved on?" I ask, giving it some thought. "Why would I let go of someone who means so much to me? There might still be a chance for me to figure things out with her."

"There is?" she asks, looking far too excited for me. "Then why don't you just go for it?"

"It's complicated, but maybe…maybe soon I can."

"Well, I will need all the details when it does happen." She takes a bite of her hash brown and moans. "Oh, this is perfect. How did you know I'd need this?"

"Because I know you pretty well at this point, Bower."

"You do." She flashes me a smile. "By the way, you never responded. Did you like my shirt last night?"

I pick up a hash brown as well and take a bite. "I did," I answer. "Do you think it would fit me?"

She scoffs. "Maybe one pec, which by the way, when did you get an ass?"

"What?" I laugh, nearly choking on my hash brown, because I never thought I'd hear her ask that.

"I was watching you yesterday and all of a sudden my eyes were fixated on your rear end and how pronounced it was. I don't ever remember you having an ass like that. Was it the belt you were wearing?"

"Uh…no."

"Oh my God." She covers her mouth with her coffee mug. "Do you stuff down there?"

"For fuck's sake, Bower."

She chuckles and then groans when she realizes it's too much for her head.

"I've been doing a lot of squats and lunges, building up my legs, which in return, builds the muscles in my glutes."

"Well, send me your routine, because a girl would like a rounded rear like that."

"Uh…thank you."

She smirks and then clinks her mug with mine. "You're welcome."

CHAPTER 18
BOWER

Bower: Are you sure you still want to go to the party tonight?

Bennett: Yes.

Bower: Because you can back out if you want.

Bennett: I said I'd go.

Bower: Okay, well, it's on a rooftop and it's businesswear, so suit coat and button-up. Do you have that?

Bennett: Did you really ask that question?

Bower: Right, dumb question. Okay, I'll be at your place around six. That work?

Bennett: See you then.

I SET MY PHONE DOWN and scan the notes I took while Adalade dictated about everything she'll need for a gala she's attending in a few days. I glance down at my bags, counting them and checking off my list, the hostess gift being the most important errand I ran today.

I had to pick up some sort of silver platter that I was told would be perfect. Looks like a useless piece of serveware, but what do I know?

I said bye to Gabby yesterday. She was suffering just as much as me after our night of drinking, but she also had a huge smile on her face and I knew exactly why. Of course, that made me jealous all over again.

Either way, it was good to see her and Ryland and remind myself that I'm looking for something like they have.

This is why I'm attempting another date with Cougar.

I check my phone for the time, just as my phone buzzes with another text from Bennett.

My stomach flips for a moment as his name reminds me of how we cuddled the other night.

Sure, I was drunk.

Sure, I probably should have gone to my apartment.

But there was so much comfort in having him there, and well, we're friends. Friends cuddle, right?

Close friends, at least, and that's what we are. We're very close.

Bennett: Did you see Gretchen's email?

Bower: No, am I going to be upset?

I'm about to go check, but he calls instead. Damn Brinkmans always call.

"What did I tell you about calling?" I answer playfully.

"And what did I say about hearing your voice?"

"When you put it like that...what's up?"

"She named the book club and started social media for us, as well as posted a graphic."

I startle to attention. "Wait, seriously? What's the name? Is it lame? Is it Kim Halpert's Book Club?"

"It's Books with Bombers," he says flatly.

"Ugh, I hate that. That makes it seem like it's your whole team. Is it your whole team?"

"As far as I know, it's just me."

"Why would she do that?"

"According to the email, we were taking too long on a name and she took matters into her own hands. She also announced what book we're reading."

"She did not!" I gasp. "How dare she. This was our thing, not hers. What book did she pick?"

"The baseball romance I already read."

I bring my hand to my chest. "Well, thank God for that. Still, I think I might type her back and scold her for such brazen behavior."

"Good luck. She's fucking brutal, so I don't think she will give a damn."

"Yeah, and I don't think I have it in me to actually scold."

He chuckles, the sound so deep and rumbly. "All bark, no bite?"

"Precisely," I answer just as Cougar walks into the restaurant wearing his workout gear and a backward hat. Although, his hat makes him look like he has a bit of a pickle head. He can't rock it like Bennett.

"Hey, sweetheart," he says as he leans in and presses a kiss to my cheek.

"Sweetheart?" Bennett asks. "Who is that?"

"Oh, meeting Cougar for a quick lunch."

"You are?"

"Yup, so I should go. I'll check the email and we can discuss later."

"Okay, yeah."

"Bye, Benny Boo Boo," I coo into the phone as he says bye. I hang up and set my phone down, bringing my attention to Cougar, who has commandeered the chair across from me, slouching his large body and manspreading for the entire restaurant. "You're two minutes late."

He smirks. "Couldn't find parking. Were you pining to see me?"

Actually…no.

But then again, we're trying here, so I say, "Of course."

His smile lights up his face just as the waitress takes our order, something Cougar already prepared for when he knew we were coming here.

When she takes off, Cougar studies me for a moment before he says, "Think you'll come to a game this season?"

That feels like it came out of nowhere.

"Do you want me to come to a game?" I ask.

"Of course, I'd want my girl there."

"Your girl?" I ask with a raise of my brow. "How many girls are you calling your girl?"

He looks to the side. "Honestly?"

"Yeah, honestly."

"Only you," he answers, and for some reason, I don't believe him.

"How could you say that? We've only been on a few dates. We're not committed to each other. You're seeing other people, so how can I be your girl?" I say it in a teasing way, but I actually mean it, because he can't assume that when there hasn't been one part of our relationship where we've committed to each other.

"But you're not like the other girls I see," he says.

"I know! You already told me that. But how do you mean?"

"You're grounded," he says, his expression turning serious. "You don't play into my bullshit and haven't attempted to take my pants off."

I chuckle. "Imagine the gasps we'd hear if I did try to take your pants off right here in the restaurant. There would be pearl-clutching all over the place."

"Yeah." He picks up his fork and starts flipping it through his fingers. "You're girlfriend material, Bower."

And the way he says that, with the tilt of his head and the sincerity in his voice, it should get me excited. It should tell me that I'm headed in the direction I want to go, where Gabby and Ryland are, but...I just...I'm not convinced.

"I think that's the first time someone has called me that," I say.

"Maybe you've been going out with the wrong people."

Seems like I might still be making poor choices, but then again, I'm not being fair. He has good qualities. Our last date, we made progress. I felt like I got to know him a little better. I just feel like...like there's something holding me back and I can't quite pinpoint what that is.

Clearing my throat, I say, "Uh, your first game is Sunday?"

He nods. "I can get you tickets if you want."

"Yeah, I think I'm visiting a friend," I lie, because the thought of going to a game to cheer on a guy I barely know, it just doesn't sit well. It's not like going to Bennett's game. The other night was so much fun. And not just because I was with Gabby and Ryland, but I actually liked watching him play. I liked cheering him on.

I can't imagine doing that with Cougar.

"You think?" he asks, his brows shooting up.

"I mean, I'm waiting to hear back from her, but it's pretty set in stone."

"Ah." He nods as the waitress drops off waters for us. "Is that real, or are you avoiding me?"

"Would you be offended if I was avoiding you?"

"Maybe a little," he says, but he tacks on a smile.

"Then no, I'm not avoiding you."

He chuckles. "How come I don't believe that?"

"Trust issues?" I playfully ask before taking a sip of my drink.

"Funny." He nods at me. "What do I have to do to get you to a game?"

"Why do you want me at a game so bad?" I ask, wondering why this is important to him.

"So I can show off to you." *Ah, there it is. It's not about me. It's all about him.*

"I'm unimpressed by sports."

Although, I was pretty impressed by Bennett's home run. That was incredible. The ball seemed like it sailed forever.

"Really? Not even a little bit in awe over what I can do with a football?"

I shrug. "Not to sound like a dick, but not really. I'd be more impressed to see what you do with the popularity you've gained through playing your sport. What are you doing to give back?"

He slowly nods but doesn't say anything.

"Sooo...are you going to answer the question?"

"What question?"

"What are you doing to give back?"

"Oh." He scrubs his hand over the side of his cheek. "I do sick kid hospital visits."

Sick kid hospital visits. Wow, what a way to put it.

"Do you have any charities you help? Anything that speaks to you? For instance, Bennett works with a lot of foster care charities."

"He does? You don't ever hear about it. There are clips of me talking to kids in hospital beds."

I try not to flare my nostrils, because that's a dense comment. Kids in hospital beds? Those kids are ill and going through such a tough time. For him to just throw it out like that is insensitive.

"You don't have to record yourself doing good to prove that you're a good person. You know it in your heart that you're doing the right thing and helping, and that's what should matter."

"I can see that."

"So then, if you were to put your name behind a charity, what would it be?"

His lips purse as he thinks about it. "What would yours be? Help me out."

Seeing that he's actually genuine about it, I say, "Well, I really have started to love to read, so maybe I'd focus on that, bringing the love of reading to kids, helping out those who don't have access to books or might not know how to read."

He slowly nods. "That's actually a pretty cool idea."

I smile softly from the compliment. I mean, he has his moments where I can see a glimmer of hope for there to be something between us, and maybe that's why I keep holding on.

"So, what would you do?"

"I like animals." He shrugs. "Maybe something with them."

"There you go." I gesture toward him. "Maybe you should have been the one doing the zoo stuff and not Graydon."

He chuckles. "You are so right about that. Maybe I can trade positions."

"Would you?" I ask, curious.

"I would, but I don't see him giving up time with the flamingo girl. Plus, it would be cool to have my own thing."

"Are you really thinking about it?" I ask.

"Yeah, I probably should." He shifts in his seat. "My mom would have liked me to do something like that."

"Would have?" I ask. "Sorry if this is insensitive, but has she passed?"

"Yeah, a few years ago. Suffered from a blood clot bursting in her cranium. We tried to save her, but it was too late."

"Cougar." I reach across the table. "I'm so sorry."

"Thanks, but she was big into animals. It's where I got my love for them, and well, she'd probably like to see me doing something in that realm."

"I think that would be so beautiful."

"She really liked the Sheldrick Wildlife Trust."

"What's that?" I love seeing this different side of him, where he's clearly lowering his walls, talking about his mom and animals. It's endearing, human…real.

"An orphaned elephant and wildlife rehabilitation center in East Africa. I should reach out to them, see if they need anything."

"Now that would be a great way to spend your off time."

"Well, besides with you." He winks.

With a flicker of amusement, I say, "Yes, besides with me."

I check the mirror one more time, tamping down some wild hairs that seem to want to frizz out on the crown of my head, and then adjust my top.

I chose to wear a pair of wide-leg black trousers and a black backless long-sleeved top that shows off maybe an inch of my stomach. If my pants were high-rise, I wouldn't be showing any skin but my back, but this is fine. It's chic.

I paired the outfit with some three-inch leopard-print heels and a black clutch. My hair is curled in waves and pinned down tightly, framing my face, but then loose in the back. Pleased, I head to Bennett's apartment, not bothering with the elevator, but taking the stairs instead.

After my date, I updated Gabby about how it all went and how there was maybe a slight hint of interest on my end when I learned that he was, in fact, not all douchebag.

But the smallest of hints.

Of course Gabby took that as we're getting married and gushed for a solid ten minutes while I curled my hair.

Married, no.

But another date? Possibly.

Attending one of his games? Not yet.

When I reach Bennett's apartment, I knock on his door. Technically, I could walk in, because I have a key, but what if he's naked or not ready? I don't want to be that person.

After a few seconds, he opens the door and a wave of his breathtaking cologne hits me. It's woody, spicy, and sensuous. *Good God, the man smells divine.* My eyes then focus on the stylish, incredibly handsome man in front of me.

Dressed in a black suit with a black button-up and black shoes, he looks all sorts of mysterious with his thick scruff caressing his jaw, but he still has his youthful innocence with his icy-blue eyes. And when his eyes hungrily take in every inch of my outfit, my stomach churns with anticipation.

I haven't felt this kind of anticipation in an extraordinarily long time.

And I shouldn't be feeling that about my best friend's brother.

"Hey, you," he says, stepping up and pulling me into a hug.

I melt into his chest, my arms clinging on to him as I take a deep breath and soak in his scent, not to mention that he seems a little possessive of me, and I kind of love it. It might sound crazy, but I'm so glad he's going with me, instead of Cougar, because at least I can be more myself tonight while I attempt to help my boss.

"You smell good," I say as his hand lands on my bare back, his fingers flexing into my skin.

"I was about to say the same thing about you," he says as his thumb rubs along my spine, sending a straight shot of lust between my legs.

Oh my God, is that all it takes? A thumb rub?

Get it together, Bower.

"You also look fucking gorgeous." He pulls away to look me in the eyes. "Then again, you always do." He winks and then turns away, where he grabs his phone off a side table, leaving me in a state of…uh, what did he just say?

No, don't look too much into it.

He's a nice guy and that's what nice guys do. They say nice things.

Right?

And friends do the same thing. They say nice things.

"Ready?" he asks, and then threads our fingers together, locking up his apartment.

"Uh, yeah," I answer, caught off guard for more reasons than one.

He holds my hand the entire way down to the lobby, acting as if this is an actual date. I did tell him there would be touching. Perhaps he's practicing. "I got us a car service again, just in case there are drinks there."

"Smart," I say as he brings me out onto the street, where a black SUV waits for us.

The driver opens the door and I get in first, Bennett following behind. Once we're settled, he turns toward me. "How was your day?"

"Um, it was good," I answer as his eyes are intent on me.

"Just good?"

I shrug. "Nothing exciting happened."

"Didn't you have a date?"

"Oh, right. Yeah, that was nice. Cougar opened up and seemed more human today."

"Nothing like date number four to realize the guy you're seeing is human."

I chuckle. "Never said I was good at this dating stuff."

"You probably are with the right man," he counters.

And for some reason, that hits home, because I think he might be right about that.

"What about you? How was your day off?"

"Wasn't a true day off. I still worked out and took some batting practice."

My expression flattens. "Bennett, that's not a day off at all."

"Can't really take many days off in baseball; have to keep up reps."

"Really? I know nothing about baseball."

"You can come with me one day, if you want? To take some batting practice, maybe show you some mechanics."

For some reason, that actually excites me.

"Tell me when, I'm there."

"Yeah?" His expression softens. "I'll send you some days. You can even come before a game, in the morning."

"Will you give me a tour of the stadium?"

"Do you want one?"

"I do," I say, excited at the prospect.

"Then it's a date."

It's a date…

Why does that give me so much joy and not an ounce of trepidation? With Cougar, I was coming up with any sort of lie to not go to his game, but Bennett…he's different.

Maybe because it's Bennett, and if I can trust any man, it would be him. There's no pressure when I'm with him. Familiarity, perhaps? Or maybe because he's not just trying to score or impress me. He's not saying all the words to get me into his bed. *And then leave.* He's just…Bennett. We have history, a solid friendship. Trust.

Yeah, that's it. Isn't that what every woman wants in a friend?

CHAPTER 19
BENNETT

THE MOMENT I HEARD SHE was on a date with Cougar, my entire day was flipped upside down. I honestly had no intention of going to the stadium because our manager does ask us to take rest days, but I had to blow off some steam.

I was irritated.

Frustrated.

And fucking annoyed.

Because I couldn't believe she was on another date with him, let alone him calling her fucking sweetheart.

Sweetheart.

What the actual fuck?

That word, hearing it directed from another man to my girl, lit something inside of me.

I was ignited and ready to fucking blow.

I refuse to let her grow attached to someone else right in front of my fucking eyes. Not happening, which means I'm not holding back anymore.

And it starts tonight.

"This is incredible," Bower says as we make our way out to the private rooftop where the dinner is being held.

Brick walls line the perimeter mixed with potted plants and string lights. There's a long dinner table in the middle, decked out with candles, moss centerpieces that run the length of the table, and earth-toned dishware. The wooden chairs that line the table are all eclectic in their own way, while olive-green velvet table linens soften the setting.

It's the perfect atmosphere for me to make my move.

Not to mention we're supposed to act like a couple, so I'm going to take advantage—as much as she will allow.

"Bower," an older woman in a silk skirt and sweater says, walking up to us. Her skin appears soft, but with laugh lines in the corner of her eyes and mouth. Her hair is solid white and tied back into a low bun, while her lips are dusted in a rosy pink. She gives off elegance but with a hint of kindness in her eyes. "Thank you for coming."

"Of course." Bower, in her mouthwatering shirt, turns toward me and says, "Bennett, this is my boss, Adalade. Adalade, this is Bennett."

Adalade slowly looks me over, a smile pulling on her lips. "Bennett, it's so nice to meet you. Bower has said such wonderful things about you."

"I can definitely say the same," I say, taking Adalade's hand and giving it a gentle shake. "Thank you for moving to San Francisco. You really did me a solid by bringing Bower closer to me."

Adalade chuckles, her hand to her chest. "My, what a charmer."

"Only speaking the truth," I say as I wrap my arm around Bower.

"Well, then maybe Bower needs to consider that you could be more than friends."

Now that's what I'm fucking talking about.

"Oh stop it," Bower says, her cheeks actually red. "We're here to play matchmaker, not the other way around. So tell us where Draco is."

Adalade sighs. "Sadly, he had to cancel."

"Oh." Bower looks up at me, as if questioning why we're here. "I'm sorry to hear that. Do you want us to go?"

Adalade shakes her head. "Absolutely not. You both dressed up. You look stunning, and I want you to have a good night."

"But are you going to be okay?"

"Of course. It's a beautiful night and I'm surrounded by people fascinated to hear my story. It's a dream. But you must know, I told our host, Anita, that you two are a couple." She winks. "Don't let me down."

"We won't," I say and then take Bower by the hand and lead her over to the quaint bar by a large lounge.

"I'm sorry," she whispers after I order two glasses of wine for us.

"Sorry for what?" I turn toward her, my breath catching in my chest from just how goddamn perfect she is.

Makeup, no makeup. Sweatpants or dress. She's stunning at every angle. And tonight, under the string lights, she's just so perfect.

"For making you come tonight when the guy didn't even show up."

"You act as if this is a hardship for me."

"It's your night off. I'm sure the last thing you want to be doing is wearing a suit and standing on a roof with a bunch of people you don't know."

"The way I see it is I get to hang out with you, drink some fancy-as-shit wine, and eat probably one of the best meals we're ever going to have. Also, I probably would have been hanging out with you anyway, so we're just in a different setting."

She glances back at the dressed-up table. "It does look like it's going to be a fancy dinner." Then she looks at the bar. "And the wine does seem fancy." And then her eyes set on mine. "And I could have seen us reading together tonight."

"Exactly, which means...you shouldn't be apologizing." The bartender sets down two glasses of wine and I give him a twenty before handing Bower a glass. I clink mine with hers. "To an evening full of the unknown."

She smirks. "To the unknown."

"Thank you so much."

"Of course," I say, with a smile.

"Sorry to bother." The woman, who came over looking for a picture, walks right up to Adalade and gushes.

"I think that's about everyone." Bower glances around the rooftop, taking in the small crowd. "I don't think one person missed out on taking a picture with you."

"Once one person figured it out, they all fell in line after that."

"I would have thought people who hang out with Adalade wouldn't have wanted a picture with you. No offense, but they just don't seem like the sporty type."

"It's not my baseball talent that brought them in."

"Oh yeah?" she scoffs. "What is it, then?"

"My stunningly good looks."

Bower rolls her eyes. "Full of yourself much?"

"I thought you liked hanging around douchebags," I counter, surprising her.

"Oh, you're going there, huh?"

I finish off my wine just as a waiter brings us both our fourth glass of the night. We went through our second when a man named Ira was telling us all about investing in bonds. And our third was consumed while speaking with a woman about her late husband, Ronald, who she's grateful died before her, because now she gets to live her life, attending rooftop dinner parties.

Got to love a bitter widow.

"Just unsure what you see in him."

"You set me up with him."

"Mistakes were made. I can admit it."

She smiles over the rim of her wineglass. "Big of you." She shifts a little closer, close enough that I can rest my hand on her hip, and I do just that as I stare down at her. "And if you think I can do better, what does that entail?"

"First of all, not a guy named Cougar. His name alone doesn't pass the orgasm test."

Her mouth falls open before saying, "Oh my God, I forgot I told you about the orgasm test."

I slowly nod. "Yeah, you did. And there's no way you can moan his name and it will sound appealing. Cougar is not the kind of name that rolls off the tongue in a sexy way."

"Not so much. Okay, what else?"

Taking the bait, I say, "You need someone who can take care of you, not because you need it, but because you deserve it." Her expression softens. "You need someone who's infatuated and not asking you out to morning dates because that's what's easiest for them. You need someone who'll put in the effort, like the things you like, and be there for you when you need it the most and the least."

"To name a few things." She shakes her head. "Men like that don't exist." I'm about to tell her the fuck they don't when her eyes snap to mine and she says, "What about you? What's on your list of the perfect match for you?"

"Why would I tell you that?"

"Uh, so I could help you find someone."

"I don't need help. I already know what I want."

She rolls her eyes. "Are you talking about your crush? Because it's never going to happen unless you make a move."

"Well aware."

"So, are you going to make a move?"

"I am." I nod, causing her eyes to widen in surprise.

"Oh my God, really? When? Who is she? Can I be there when you do it?"

"Bower, Bennett, dinner is about to be served," Adalade says with a knowing smile, the kind of smile she only shares with me.

Bower turns to me and says, "This isn't over."

I finish off my wine, and she does the same before I take her hand and lead her to the table. We're sitting on the end, so I pull out her chair for her and help her down before taking the seat right next to her. I then capitalize on the moment and drape my arm over her chair, tugging her in closer.

Our host, Anita, introduces the chef she hired for the night, and he spouts off the theme of the dinner, his inspiration for each platter, and where he found the ingredients so they're as fresh as they can be.

Once he's done, our glasses are refilled and I'm feeling buzzed as I lean into Bower and whisper, "Never had steak tartare. Have you?"

"I don't even know what that is."

I chuckle. "Looks like we're about to find out."

Waiters place a petite-sized plate in front of us with what looks like one bite of red meat and a quail's egg over easy resting on top.

"That is the smallest piece of meat I've ever seen," Bower whispers, making my chest rumble with laughter.

"Thank fuck you're saying that about the food on your plate and not the dick in my pants."

Her eyes widen even more before she snorts, covering her nose and attempting not to draw attention to us as the rest of the dinner party all engage in mature conversation. Something about an art gallery they went to.

"Grateful I didn't take a bite when you said that, or else tartare would have flown out of my nostrils."

"Shame, would have loved to see that." I stab the meat with my fork and wolf it down in one bite.

The texture is off for me, but the flavors are decent. When I swallow, I press my lips to her ear and say, "That was fucking slimy."

"If you don't like slimy things, how are you going to impress your crush?" she asks, tucking into the tartare herself.

I've turned toward her, completely blocking off the rest of the group, which doesn't seem to bother anyone as we separate from the pack and form our own dinner party of two.

"What the hell does that mean?"

"It means..."—she sips her wine and then wiggles her brows—"going down..."

"Why the hell would you call that slimy?"

"Well, if the juices are really flowing, it could be a mess."

"The best kind of mess," I say. "And the juices would be flowing, so much that she's practically fucking my face as I go down."

I watch her carefully. There's a small hitch in her chest, a pause in her breathing before she takes another sip of her wine.

"That's, uh, that's great for her, then. We appreciate a king who will go down. Do you, uh, do you do that often?"

"When I'm with a girl, yes."

"Good for you." She gulps some more wine. "Really, really great. Pleasuring your partner is the way to go. Some might say the best way to go; others might say the only way to go—"

"You're rambling," I say as I let my finger twist a piece of her hair.

"Because I wasn't expecting you to...to, I don't know, say you like eating women out."

"Favorite dessert." I glance around the rooftop. "Think they're serving up pussy tonight?"

"Bennett," she shout whispers, her face turning bright red. "Oh my God."

I chuckle and lean back in my chair, completely pleased with myself.

"The tartare was eh-eh," Bower says. "And the deconstructed Caesar was like sucking on a fish, but this pasta, fucking hell, I might propose."

"Too late, I already did and it accepted. Save the date for November eighteenth. It's going to be the wedding of the century." I finish my last bite and hold back my moan, because damn, that was good.

The chef made it in front of us, wheeling out a giant block of cheese and dropping the spaghetti in the center, swirling it around, and then serving it on a plate for each of us.

"Think the chef will let me tongue the cheese wheel?" Bower asks.

"Ask. If he says yes, I get first dibs."

"You don't get first dibs. It was my idea."

"Yeah, but that's my goddamn wife, and I'll be damned if she's tongued by anyone else."

Bower lets out a wallop of a laugh, drawing the attention of everyone at the table.

"Bower," Adalade says with amusement. "Please, tell us what has you laughing so hard?"

Yeah, Bower, go ahead and tell her…

Bower dabs her napkin at her lips.

Pauses.

Glances at me with a devilish smirk and then says, "Bennett was just telling me how much he wants to tongue the cheese wheel."

Oh.

My.

Fucking.

God.

I didn't think she was going to tell the truth.

The table goes silent and I know we're both drunk at this point, but for fuck's sake, have some goddamn decorum.

I stiffly turn toward the table, ready to apologize for how crass that was, until Adalade holds up her wine and says, "Get in line, buster, the tonguing will be done by me first."

Bower clamps her hand over her mouth as the entire table erupts in laughter.

"If anyone is tonguing the cheese," Anita says, "it would be me. I paid for it, therefore I am the rightful owner."

"Some might consider that prostitution, Anita," an older gentleman says.

"Fine by me." Anita tips her wineglass back, taking down the rest of her drink. When she's done, she waves her finger around the table. "Another round for the group."

"How long have you two been together?" Anita asks, motioning to me and Bower.

Dessert has been served—no, it wasn't pussy, but rather a raspberry sorbet that melted on my tongue—and now we're all drinking our lives away, enjoying the evening under the stars.

Honestly, I didn't know what to expect when it came to dining with a bunch of people I didn't know, but I don't think I've had this much fun in a while.

The group is witty, not at all prudish as I'd expect, and all out for a good time.

"Only a few months," I say as I tug Bower out of her chair and directly into my lap. She comes willingly and loops her arm around my neck, so I wrap my arm around her waist.

"Only a few months?" Anita runs her tongue over her teeth. "Seems like years to me."

"We've known each other for several years," I say. "And then one day, she gave me a chance after I've been pining for her for so long."

"Isn't that the sweetest?" Anita brings her attention to Bower as she says, "Why did it take you so long to give in to this man?"

"Didn't want to get in the way of his dreams," Bower says, as if it's the truth, not some fabricated lie to placate the group sitting around a dinner table with us.

"So darling." Anita pats her chest. "And look at you two now, happily in love."

"Yup," I say, looking Bower in the eyes. "Happily in love."

She smiles, her cheeks going pink as she clears her throat.

"I remember Bower telling me all about Bennett," Adalade says, swirling her wine in her glass. "It almost seemed like he enamored her. Then, how could you not be? The man is the whole package. Sweet, interested, infatuated, handsome…"

"Can I get that in writing so when she gets mad at me, I can remind her why she's with me?"

Adalade chuckles. "Want me to write you a letter of recommendation?"

"That would be greatly appreciated. I can't have this woman running away from me."

"Oh she'd never," Anita says. "I can see the way she looks at you, and that means wedding bells should be coming soon, right?"

"Oh, I don't know about that—" Bower starts to say, but I butt in.

"If I knew she'd say yes, I would have proposed already."

Her head snaps to mine and all I do is smile up at her fucking gorgeous face, because facts.

I would.

I'd propose so fucking hard.

Because if I know anything, it's that I want to spend every spare waking hour I have with her. I've thought this for so long, but now that she lives close and that I've been able to spend even more time with her, the addiction I have for her has grown to where I crave her before bed, when I wake up, before games. I want to text her when I'm gone, call her before I go to sleep, and FaceTime her when I wake up so I can see how rumpled and warm she looks in her bed.

I want to spoil her, be the one who makes her throw her head back and laugh.

Fuck, I want to be the one that calls her pet names, not some jackass who has no right being near her.

"Oooo, looks like there needs to be a discussion had between you two," Anita says.

"Yes," Kent clucks, his body swaying back and forth from the port he's been consuming all night. "They need to discuss the love affair he's having with the cheese." He hiccups. "Because he was eye-fucking that wheel."

I snort, along with Bower, while the rest of the table joins in the laughter.

Because Kent is so not the man you would expect to say the words *eye-fucking*. He has a toupee, for fuck's sake!

And I know because he told me.

When the laughter dies down, Bower holds up her hand and says, "You know what? I'll be the bigger person and step aside. Who am I to be the one who gets in between a man and his need to tongue his cheese?"

"And that's why he's in love," Anita points out as I look up at Bower. "Because she's willing to step aside so he can truly be happy."

If only she knew what would truly make me happy...

"You, my dear, truly dazzled," Adalade says while holding Bower's hands. "I know there was no purpose in you being here, since Draco did not show up, but I know for certain I'm the belle of the ball because you were my guest."

"Thank you," Bower answers with drunken sincerity. "It was such a fun night."

She shivers, so I take my jacket off and drape it over her bare back. She glances up at me with a look of gratefulness.

"Yes, thank you for tonight," I add. "I had such a good time."

"I'm glad you could spend your night off with us." Adalade pats my cheek. "You're a good one, Bennett. I just hope you find that girl you're looking for, because you truly are a catch." Then she smiles wickedly. "If I was fifteen years younger, you very well might be going home with me."

I chuckle and say, "And I'd take you up on the opportunity."

"Hey," Bower says, her face cutely scrunched up.

"What's your deal?" I ask with mirth. "You're the one always saying we're the best of friends. A guy needs to strike when he's admired."

"He's very right about that," Adalade says while I feel Bower study me, but I don't give her any indication of nerves.

Even though I feel like fucking melting right here, right now, because it was a bold statement, a statement that if she takes it to heart, she will see that I have been waiting for my moment with her.

"Anyway, thank you for coming. Feel free to take the day off tomorrow, Bower. You've done a lot for me today." With that, Adalade places a kiss on both of our cheeks and then takes off.

So I wrap my hand around Bower's, my coat still draped over her shoulders, and I lead her to the elevator that takes us to the lobby.

I texted my driver that we'd be leaving, so when we reach the front of the building, he's waiting with the door open.

I help Bower into the car and then follow in behind her.

Once we're buckled, I say, "I liked Adalade. Think she was serious about dating me?" I wiggle my eyebrows and Bower's lips turn flat.

"She is far too old for you."

"I don't know. I think we could make it work. She seems pretty interested."

"Not happening." She shakes her head and crosses her arms.

"You seem pretty adamant about that." I poke her side, causing her to laugh.

"The last thing I need is for my boss to date you. You're so clingy and needy that Adalade will have me running all around San Francisco to purchase items for you."

"I'd make sure of it."

Her eyes widen with mirth as her mouth curves up. "You wouldn't."

"Oh, I would. I'd be persistent." I press my hand to my chest. "Oh, my dearest Adalade, Daddy needs those special pastries from an hour away. Please send your minion to go get them."

"Ew, do not call yourself Daddy."

I let out a boisterous laugh.

"And there is no way I'd go get them."

"Then enjoy your unemployment, because I'd demand it," I tease.

"Fine." She lifts her chin in indignation. "Then I'll move to Almond Bay and be with your sister, win her over, and make sure she never speaks to you again."

"You wouldn't."

"Oh...I would."

"Wow." I shake my head. "Didn't think you would stoop that low."

"Says the guy threatening to date my sixty-six-year-old boss."

"Age is just a number."

And I fucking mean that.

"Well, it's not happening. Keep your willy and your cheese-loving tongue to yourself. My boss is off-limits."

CHAPTER 20
BOWER

BENNETT AND ADALADE…IMAGINE.

No, I couldn't.

But just the thought of it, it…triggered something inside me that I didn't like. Dare I say…jealousy?

I know, I know.

I'm losing my mind. She could be my grandma, and he's, well, he's a friend and maybe, maybe the jealousy is because in this scenario, they find love and I don't, despite trying so hard.

Is that it?

God, I hope so.

Because any other form of jealousy is just not acceptable.

The elevator door dings and Bennett walks me up to my apartment door. When I reach it, I turn toward him, his jacket still draped over my shoulders. "I have cupcakes."

His eyes light up.

"Really?"

"Yes. Red velvet with cream cheese frosting because I knew you were doing me a favor and I wanted to thank you for it."

"You chose correctly," he says with a smirk.

So I unlock my door and we both enter my apartment.

"Am I going to ever get my jacket back, or are you going to keep it?" he asks while I move into the kitchen and grab the cupcakes from the fridge.

"I believe it's mine now."

With the cupcakes and napkins in hand, I head toward the couch, where he follows me. I take a seat on one side and he sits directly in the middle right next to me, comfortably, without even thinking about it. He's been that close all evening, close enough that I could smell his cologne, I could feel his heat, and study every angle of his face.

He takes a cupcake from my hand and peels the wrapper off before taking a huge bite.

"Whoa, that's quite the bite."

"You shaming me?" he says around his mouthful.

"No, just surprised is all." I take a bite of mine but not as large as him.

"You know how I am with sweets." One more bite and it's almost gone.

"Well, don't expect to come over here looking for more because you just devoured—" He shoves the rest of the cupcake in his mouth and then smiles at me. "Oh my God, why are you a child? You're going to choke."

"No, I'm not," he says, cupcake falling out of his mouth and making me laugh.

"You are, and I doubt I'll be able to save you because you're so much bigger than me."

He chews, swallows, and then says, "Which means stealing your cupcake will be very easy for me."

"Don't you dare." I shift away from him, only for his eyes to light up with laughter. "Bennett…"

He lunges at me and I quickly fall off the couch, on my ass, his jacket falling off me as he trains his eyes on me, ready to pounce. I attempt to get off the ground, but he's on me faster than I can even consider my next move. He grabs one of my legs and drags me right toward him, shocking me with his strength.

I playfully yell, attempting to palm his face as I hold my cupcake as far away from him as possible.

"Don't you dare."

"Your cupcake is mine."

"Never!" I yell, shifting underneath him and scooting farther away, only for him to climb on top of me, straddle me, and hold me in place. "No, this is my cupcake. Mine."

He grabs the arm holding the cupcake and brings it up to his mouth.

"Bennett, don't you dare."

He opens his mouth wide, and out of pure defense, I shift under him and with my other arm, push at his chest, forcing him to his back as I reverse our position, so now I'm on top and he's on the bottom.

"Ha-ha!" I say in triumph and then take a bite of my cupcake. "Nice try. Not as strong as you thought you were."

"I guess not," he says, not looking too upset about me taking him over. "I am upset that you won't share your cupcake."

"Don't eat yours so fast and I won't—"

He snatches the cupcake out of my hand, making me screech. "Hey, give that back." I shift on top of his lap, reaching for the cupcake that he's holding above his head.

"It's mine now."

"No way." I lean forward, my chest pressing against his face as I reach for the cupcake.

"Hell, if this is what you plan on offering, then you can have your cupcake back," he mutters under me.

I snatch the cupcake and shove the rest in my mouth before he can try to steal it again.

"I'm not even mad about it," he says as his hands land on my hips, holding me in place, right on top of his lap.

I chew, chew…chew, and once I swallow, I say, "I think you motorboated me."

"You were the one who shoved your tits in my face."

"I wasn't shoving them in your face. I was reaching for my cupcake."

"Mm-hmm," he says as his thumbs dig into my hips, something that makes my entire core throb.

Jesus, what is wrong with me?

I should probably get off him.

Send him on his way.

Thank him for a lovely night and offer him sweet dreams.

And yet, I don't move.

I stay put, straddling him in just the right way...

"I just like how you happened to pin me down despite me being much bigger than you," he playfully says.

"It's not my fault you folded like a feather," I counter, shifting on top of him.

"Maybe I wanted to be folded by you."

"Oh? For what reason?"

"So you could straddle me like this," he answers, his eyes never moving from mine.

My hands fall to his chest. "And why would you want that?"

"You tell me," he says, shifting my hips so they smooth over his bulge.

His exceptionally large bulge.

My eyes widen as I feel him rub right between my legs and it's...oh fuck, it's such a good feeling.

Holy shit...so good that I allow him to move my hips again, rubbing the length of him between my thighs.

My skin breaks out into a sweat as that telltale feeling of being instantly turned on pulses through my veins and sends my mind into a frenzy of needing more.

So much more.

And when I grind on top of him for the third time, the juncture between my thighs prickles in excitement and I can feel myself grow wet, as I take it upon myself to move my hips, slowly, torturously, but just enough for my body to feel all of him.

All.

Of.

Him.

God, I know I should stop, that I shouldn't even be straddling him, but maybe it's the wine, or the fact that I'm so freaking horny, or that this feels so damn good that I might lose my mind. Either way, I can't stop myself, but truth be told, he's not stopping me either.

He's not telling me to get off him.

He's not lecturing me about whether or not we should be in this sort of position.

No, when I look him in the eyes, it almost seems like he wants this just as much as I do.

"What's happening?" I ask as I grind down on him, his teeth pulling on the corner of his lip. So freaking sexy.

"It seems like you're trying to get yourself off," he answers, his cock so fucking big.

"I shouldn't." I squeeze my eyes shut for a moment as my stomach clenches, needing more.

"But you are."

I nod, dipping my head forward.

Stop, Bower.

Stop what you're doing and remove yourself.

But...God, I don't want to.

I want this.

I need this.

I need to get off.

So I use his chest to support me while my hips move faster, his length driving along my clit, creating such delicious friction.

"Fuck, I need to stop."

"Then stop," he says, his hands finding my hips again, but instead of stopping me like I thought he would, he encourages me to move faster, to grind down harder on him, to use him the way that I want to.

"I...fuck," I whisper as what feels like every cell in my body starts to tingle.

No, I should stop.

I shouldn't be riding him.

I shouldn't be using him.

I shouldn't be...

"Oh God," I moan as his hips thrust up against me.

Fuck, yes. I can't stop. It's too fucking good.

My fingers curl around the fabric of his shirt, bunching it in the middle of his chest, tugging on the buttons until one of them pops open. A small gasp pops out of me as I stare down at his small patch of exposed skin.

Tan, strong...

And then to my horror, I undo the rest of the buttons, ripping his shirt open until his bare chest is visible and fully on display.

He does nothing about it, other than encouraging me with his hands and smirking up at me.

So, being completely out of my mind, I let my hands run up his exposed chest, feeling every contour and divot, the thickness of his pecs and the stiffness of his abs.

"Fuck, your body is incredible," I say absentmindedly as I lift off his lap for a second and then lower back down, letting his hard length spark a fire that I need to chase.

His hands slide up to my waist, where his fingers glide against my exposed skin, the heat of his touch adding to the inferno building inside of me.

"God, I...I should stop. Tell me to stop, Bennett."

"No fucking way," he says as he thrusts up at me, pulling a moan past my lips.

"Fuck, I shouldn't... Oh God." I squeeze my eyes shut and dig my fingers into his skin as I rotate against him with force, his hard, thick cock hitting me in just the right spot as I ride out the feeling, the friction billowing between my legs until I'm panting and every last piece of me feels like it's pulling into my center.

"Goddamn it," I whisper as my body tenses.

"Fuck," he whispers, his hips moving with mine, the quiet sound of his pleasure sending a wave of chills over me, and it's so simple, so small, but it's what I need. It turns me on more than anything else and I grind down on him a few more times before I'm losing myself in the feel of my orgasm tipping me over the edge and sweeping me up into a blissful state of mind where there's nothing but me and Bennett and the way he's making me feel in this moment.

"God, Bennett," I moan just as he stills beneath me and groans, the sexiest sound I think I've ever heard as he comes as well, leaving us both in a state of shock.

His hips lower from where they were tipped up into me and I loosen my grip on his chest, taking in the red marks I left on his skin.

And then, as if we both know it at the same time, our eyes connect and I can see the desire in his.

And yet, I feel the confusion in mine.

I wet my lips, catching my breath as fear starts to ratchet up my spine, because this…this shouldn't have happened. I don't know what I was thinking. I don't know—

"Don't," he says, breaking my thoughts.

"Don't what?" I ask, worry tugging at my heart.

"Don't overthink it," is all he says as he sits up and then helps me off him gently. As he stands, he takes my hand with him and pulls me to my feet. Then he brings me into a hug, where he kisses the top of my head. My mind's racing, my feelings are pulsing, my regret so heavy, but my need to do it again even heavier.

When he pulls away, he smirks at me and says, "Catch you later, Bower."

Catch you later?

Wait…

That's it?

He doesn't want to talk about it?

He doesn't want to deconstruct it at all?

Possibly make a pact to never do it again or never to speak of it to Gabby?

No, instead, he heads toward my door, leaving me perplexed and satisfied at the same time. When I glance down at the ground, I see his discarded jacket, so I call out to him, "Bennett, wait."

He looks over his shoulder. "Yeah?"

"Your jacket."

He smiles, his handsome face nearly splitting me in half as he says, "It's yours now, beautiful."

Then he takes off, the door to my apartment shutting behind him.

I plop down on my couch and push my hands through my hair. "What the hell did I just do?"

"What on earth are you doing here?" Adalade asks as she comes into her kitchen, where I'm making a batch of her favorite blueberry crumble muffins.

"Just working," I say, mixing the batter by hand, feeling insane while I do it because I'm attempting to mix away the fear building inside of me.

Because I did something bad last night.

Very bad.

So bad that I don't think it's forgivable.

"I told you to take the day off."

I shake my head. "Didn't want it. Thought it would be better to come in and work, because work is what makes this country function, right?

We need everyone to work and when everyone works then we have a stable economy and a stable economy means good things and good things means—"

"What happened?" Adalade says, pressing her hand to my arm, stopping me from overmixing the batter.

"What do you mean? Nothing happened." I try to smile, but it feels more like my teeth are trying to pop past my mouth with a massive underbite.

"Sweetie." She gently takes the bowl from me and sets it down on the counter. "Something happened, because I can see the panic in your eyes."

"You can?" I ask, scared now that I won't be able to mask this feeling if Gabby calls, and I can only miss a few of her calls before she starts to worry.

"Yes, I can, so tell me what happened."

"Nothing…nothing happened." I shrug, the truth eating away at me.

"Now, Bower, I've known you for a long enough time to know when you're lying, and I'd appreciate it, as your boss, if you wouldn't lie to me. You don't want to form distrust between us, do you?"

"No," I say, guilt consuming me.

"Then I'm only going to ask one more time. What happened?"

I let out a large sigh and then word vomit all over her, because she asked for it, and she's right, I can't lie. "Oh my God, Adalade, I'm so fucked, like majorly fucked, and I don't know what I'm going to do about it because I could lose my friendship and I don't want to lose my friendship, but oh my God, I can't stop thinking about it, about him and the way it felt and I want more, but I know I shouldn't have more, and I just think it's because I'm horny, not because I like him or anything like that. At least I don't think I like him, even though he's sweet and kind, and handsome and has the best fucking body I've ever seen, but I don't *like* him, but I lost control last night and oh my God, I dry-humped him." I nod. "Yes, you heard that right, I dry-humped him, on the floor of my apartment, just humping my life away, clothes and all, no shame. Nope, there I was, on top of him, grinding against his dick, tearing his shirt open—" My hands go to my mouth. "Oh my God, that's right, I tore his shirt open, like he was the main event of a *Magic Mike* show. Oh my God, what is wrong with me? Maybe the romance novels are getting to my brain and I thought it was appropriate to just dry-hump a man on the floor of my apartment without any thought or care. And I haven't heard from him, even though he texted this morning, so I guess I did hear from him, but I didn't read it, okay, I did, he said good morning, but I didn't respond, okay, I might have. I sent a heart emoji because I didn't know what else to say, but he didn't respond to that and now I'm here and I don't know what to do."

I take that moment to slide down the face of the cabinet until my butt hits the floor.

"Well." Adalade clears her throat. "That was a lot to take in."

"You shouldn't have asked."

"No, no. I'm glad I did." She motions for me to stand. "Come sit down, as I'm not about to have this chat on the floor."

I follow her over to the kitchen table and we both take a seat, me slouching, her poised like the posh socialite she is.

"Now, when you say 'he' and 'him,' are you speaking of Bennett or someone else?"

"Bennett," I groan, hating that I even have to say that out loud.

"I see, and remind me why this is a problem? Because everyone loved you two together last night. We thought you were so adorable."

"It's a problem because he's my best friend's little brother, eight years *little*, Adalade, and I promised her that I'd always protect him, and dry-humping him on my living room floor is not protecting him. That's taking advantage." My hand goes to my forehead. "Oh my God, I took advantage of someone younger than me. I should be put in jail."

"My goodness, Bower, get a hold of yourself. If he's eight years younger, that makes him twenty-four, a very acceptable age to be dry-humping."

"Do you know what's not acceptable? Dry-humping your best friend's brother. That is not acceptable in any way."

"I don't see an issue with it."

"Adalade," I groan. "It's so bad. Like...really, really bad. She will lose her mind if she finds out."

"Are you going to tell her?"

"What?" I feel my eyes pop out of their sockets, practically winking right against Adalade's semi-wrinkly skin. "Have you lost your mind? Of course I'm not going to tell her. That would be the worst idea ever."

"Then what are you worried for? Do you think Bennett will tell her?"

I grip Adalade's arm in a panic. "Oh shit, I don't know. Do you think he'd tell her? He tells her almost everything. What if...oh my God, what if he already told her? What if she's on her way to San Francisco right now to punch me square in the nose? I know I seem tough, but I can tell you right now I will not take well to a punch to the nose. I bleed easily."

"Where on earth is this coming from? Honestly, dear, this is very unbecoming."

"I'm sorry, I'm just...I'm losing it. I know I am. I'm freaking out." I lean in closer and whisper, "And do you know what the worst part is? I really liked it. Like...liked it so much that I haven't stopped thinking about it." And in even more of a whisper, I add, "And he was huge. I felt just how big."

Adalade cracks a smile. "I wouldn't expect anything less from him."

I prop my elbows up on the table and bury my head in my hands. "Adalade, what the hell am I going to do?"

"Great question, I'm glad you asked. First, you're going to relax, because the sister won't find out."

I pop my head up. "Wait, but what if he told her?" I spot my phone on the counter and quickly grab it. There's a text from Bennett.

"Oh my God, he texted me."

Calmly, Adalade says, "And what did he say?"

I open it up and read it out loud. I'm going to be at the zoo today and then I head straight to the stadium. Late game tonight. Didn't want you to think I was avoiding you. Can we meet up tomorrow, maybe read some books together for the book club?

"That sounds very sweet."

"Is it? I can't tell. Is he playing games?"

"What on earth? No. That was very straightforward."

"Do you think he told his sister? You know what? I'm just going to ask him."

"I don't think that's a good idea. You don't want to get the sister involved."

I look Adalade in the eyes, hoping I don't get fired after all is said and done, because this is extremely unprofessional of me. "She's already involved because she's the sister and the best friend. There is no scenario where she's not involved."

"She might know the both of you, but that doesn't mean she needs to know the both of you together."

I shake my head. "We're not together. We just had a drunk night. Too much wine. A cupcake got in the way and then his hard dick just...ugh, never mind. I can't talk about it or my mouth will start watering again." I look right at Adalade and add, "But I want to say this, and it's probably what's freaking me out the most: I went on several dates with Cougar and there wasn't even a glimmer of a spark, but one dry-hump session on the floor with Bennett and it was like fireworks shooting off in my stomach. Which is bad. I can't be having fireworks where he's concerned. Maybe I need to dry-hump Cougar."

"Do you think that will help?"

"No," I groan as I send a text to Bennett.

Bower: Did you tell your sister about last night?

Adalade leans over and reads my text. "Bower," she reprimands. "You didn't even answer his question. Don't you think that's a little rude?"

"Uh, don't you think it's rude that he didn't acknowledge what happened?"

"He's probably being a gentleman and knows you're freaking out and is attempting to calm you in a way that feels natural."

"It didn't work."

My phone buzzes so I quickly open up the response, letting Adalade read it as well.

Bennett: Why the hell would I tell her about that?

"See," Adalade says. "You have nothing to worry about."

I stare down at his text, my mind racing with even more fear and uncertainty now because…

"Do you think there's a tone in his text?"

"What?" Adalade asks.

"Look, he said, 'Why the hell would I tell her about that'—it almost seems like he's insulted I'd bring it up, or even mention it, like…like it was a mistake to him or something."

"Oh boy." Adalade sighs. "You know, dating was so much easier back in the day. Now you have too many factors that could ruin it."

"We're not dating," I say just as my phone buzzes again.

Bennett: You never answered me. Are we on for tomorrow?

I bite my bottom lip, staring down at the message.

"You know, for a guy who seems quite adamant about seeing you, I wouldn't think what he thought you guys did was a mistake. It seems like he wants to make the most of the opportunity, or if anything, just bring things back to normal."

Maybe she's right, maybe he does want to bring things back to normal. That would be very Bennett of him.

"We do like to read together," I capitulate.

"See." Adalade gestures. "He's probably thinking that you guys had a little fun, but it doesn't change anything, that you're still friends and that's how you'll remain."

I perk up a little bit. "You think so?"

"Absolutely. The dry-hump was just a blip, and you two will still remain friends."

"Yeah...friends."

CHAPTER 21
BENNETT

"OH MY FUCKING GOD, SHE dry-humped my dick last night," I say as I sit down next to Graydon and OC.

OC is midsip of some water when he tears the bottle away and does a spit take, spraying Graydon in the arm.

"What the actual fuck," Graydon says, his eyes burning with flames.

OC is wiping the water off his chin, completely unaware of his impending death as he says, "Who did? Bower? The sister's friend? Please, for the love of fuck, let it be Bower."

I nod. "It was Bower."

Graydon grabs OC by the collar and brings his face almost nose to nose with his. "Get me a towel, now."

"But—"

"Now," he growls.

"Right." He shakes off Graydon and holds up his finger. "One second. Don't start without me. I want to hear everything."

OC takes off toward the bathroom while Graydon turns to me. "Tell me everything while he's gone."

"Brutal," I say on a laugh.

"The fuck sprayed me with water. He deserves to miss out."

Graydon is on a whole other level of grumpy today.

Today we're signing our pictures we took at the zoo for an off-site fundraiser. Everyone who comes gets a picture, but we're waiting on

Gretchen to bring them and she forgot Sharpies as well, so we have a little bit of time in between, something apparently Graydon is not pleased about.

"I got the towels," OC yells as he runs toward us, holding them in the air before he plops down in his seat and starts dabbing at Graydon.

Graydon rips the towels from OC's hand and says, "Don't fucking touch me."

"Jesus fuck," OC says, backing his chair away. "It was just water."

"That was in your goddamn mouth."

"For less than a second. Talk about sensitive." OC thumbs toward Graydon and rolls his eyes.

"I'd be careful, dude," I say to OC as Graydon keeps his eyes on OC the entire time.

OC glances toward Graydon and I see the bob in his throat before he brings his attention back to me. Funny thing is I've seen OC play hockey, I've watched clips, and he's a goddamn beast on the ice—brutal, actually—a goddamn menace, but for some reason Graydon has a hold on him.

"Hurry up and tell us what happened before Gretchen gets back. You know she won't let us fucking talk about it. She's all business."

Not able to contain myself, I say, "We went to a dinner party last night where we had to pretend we were a couple. I got to touch her, and she sat on my lap. Fuck, it was amazing. Of course we drank a lot and when we got back to the apartment building, I walked her to her apartment."

"To dry-hump?" OC asks.

"No. She bought cupcakes as a thank-you for helping her out."

"Were there actual cupcakes or was it *her* cupcake she was offering up?"

"Clearly it was actual cupcakes, you nitwit," Graydon says.

"You don't know that. She could have easily—"

"It was actual cupcakes," I say.

"Huh, imagine that," OC says contemplatively.

"Anyway, we were sort of playfully wrestling over the last bite of hers and we wound up on the floor, her on top of me, and fuck, the minute I felt her ass on my lap, I got hard."

"Ahhh, to get hard. What's that like?" OC asks wistfully as he stares up at the ceiling.

"What the fuck is wrong with you?" Graydon asks.

"Grace broke my dick, that's what's wrong with me. But this isn't about me." OC signals me to continue.

"Anyway, she started moving over my lap. I guided her with my hands and then she started going faster and faster until...well, you know."

"You came in your pants," OC finishes.

"Christ." Graydon rolls his eyes and leans back in his chair.

"Yes, to state the obvious."

"Please tell me she came as well," OC says in a panic.

"Yeah, solid question," Graydon surprisingly offers.

"Thanks, my man." OC offers a fist bump, but Graydon just pushes his hand down.

"Of course she came. She was the one who got off first."

"Hot." OC nods. "Also, dry-humping, ridiculously hot. Do you and Maple do that?" he asks Graydon.

"Ask about my girlfriend's sex life one more time, see where it gets you."

OC winces and then turns back to me. "So what does this mean? Are you two an item now? Have all your fantasies come true? Do you think you're going to propose soon?"

"Jesus," Graydon mutters as I shake my head.

"That's the thing, after it happened, I just got up and left."

OC's mouth falls open and I can see from the disagreement in Graydon's expression that he doesn't necessarily condone that decision.

"Why the fuck would you leave?" OC asks. "Dude, that was your in. After you dry-hump, you're supposed to take your clothes off and then do the real thing, not fucking leave."

"I was giving her space," I say, even though I know it probably wasn't the right decision in normal circumstances, but things with Bower are not normal. There is nothing normal about it, hence why I've taken my time.

"Space to go spend time with Gator?"

"Who the hell is Gator?" I ask.

"Fuck, what's his name?"

"Cougar," Graydon helps.

"Right." OC pats Graydon's shoulder. "I knew his name was some sort of animal. Anyway, are you going to push her toward Cougar?"

"No, why the hell would I do that?"

"I don't know. Why the hell would you get her off and then just leave? You seem to be making stupid decisions."

"He's right on that," Graydon says, shifting in his seat.

"Wow, you actually agreed with me."

"Make a big deal about it and I won't do it again," Graydon says, holding his annoyance at bay, at least for now.

"I'm taking this slow and being deliberate about how I handle this. I know she's freaking out right now and I'm trying to keep her calm. I think pushing her any further than what we did last night wouldn't have been good. I already saw the panic in her eyes after all was said and done. So I'm taking this one step at a time. I texted her this morning and asked her to hang out with me tomorrow."

"What did she say?" OC asks.

"She said yes."

"Well, then...that's fucking great, right?"

"I think so. Like I said, I have to take this step by step. Keep letting her know that I'm interested, and then when the time is right, strike."

"Seems like a good plan," Graydon says.

"Really?" I ask. His approval means something, because he doesn't fuck around like OC.

"Yeah." He rubs the side of his jaw. "I could see this working out for you."

"And when it does"—OC swirls his finger in the middle of us—"the Gladdy Daddies will be groomsmen."

"I seriously hate you," Graydon says on a groan, just as Gretchen walks in with Sharpies.

"No, you don't. You love me."

"He doesn't," Gretchen says, placing markers in front of all of us. "It's hard to find someone who actually likes you."

"Jesus Christ, woman," OC says, absolutely offended. "You weren't part of the conversation."

"Don't need to be a part of it to know the facts." She plops a stack of pictures in front of each of us. "Now get signing."

Bennett: Think you can record a video with me tomorrow for Gretchen?

Bower: Yeah, I can.

Bennett: Are you okay with being in it?

Bower: Does Gretchen want me in it?

Bennett: I think so. I can ask.

Bower: I doubt she wants me in it. But either way, I can help.

Bennett: What if I want you in it?

Bower: Sometimes we don't always get what we want, Bennett.

Bennett: I don't know. Seems like I'm getting the things I want lately.

Bower: Did you send me cupcakes?

Bennett: I did. Felt bad that I wrestled for yours.

Bower: There is half a dozen here.

Bennett: Yeah, heard there's a cupcake thief in the building. Wanted to make sure you had enough in case they strike.

Bower: LOL. I'll be sure to safeguard them.

Bennett: Probably best.

Bower: Aren't you about to play a game?

Bennett: Yes, but you texted.

Bower: That's flattering.

Bennett: It's the truth.

Bennett: Please tell me you ate at least three cupcakes tonight.

Bower: If I said four, would you judge me?

Bennett: No, I'd be impressed.

Bower: Good. I was eating my feelings.

Bennett: Everything okay?

Bower: Everything is fine. Great game, by the way.

Bennett: Don't skip over the eating-the-feelings part. Do you want me to come to your apartment?

Bower: No. I'm good. Don't worry about me.

Bennett: Bower, seriously.

Bower: Seriously, Bennett. Don't come over here, okay?

Bennett: I don't like that.

Bower: I know, but sometimes you have to deal with things you don't like.

Bennett: Would you tell me if I could help?

Bower: I would.

Bennett: Then I guess I have to live with that. Are we still on for tomorrow?

Bower: We are.

Bennett: Okay, I'll come to you. Have a good night, Bower.

Bower: You too.

Bennett: Sweet dreams.

CHAPTER 22
BOWER

OKAY, I CAN DO THIS. It's just Bennett. I've known him for a long time, a very long time. I shouldn't be nervous or—

Knock. Knock.

Oh God, that's him. I'm going to puke.

No, keep it together.

Oh fuck…oh fuck…what do I say to him?

Stop it. He's your friend. Nothing has changed.

But we humped!

Deep breaths, you're fine.

Like I said, you can do this.

Should I be concerned that I'm having a full-on mental breakdown conversation with myself?

Honestly, not enough time to even go there.

On a deep breath and shaky legs, I open the door to my apartment, Bennett's addicting scent assaulting my senses right before he steps in, closing the space between us and pulling me into a hug.

And that's all it takes for everything to feel normal.

I wrap my arms around him, press my cheek to his chest, and let him just hold me like he's done so many times in the past.

The unknown of what today would bring made me feel nutty inside, like I was losing my mind, but right now, in his arms, it all feels normal. Like nothing happened at all and it's just two friends hanging out together.

When he pulls away, he smirks down at me, his handsome face shadowed under the brim of his hat. "Where are the cupcakes?"

I gasp and push away. "Nowhere."

"Liar." The glint in his eyes is so playful that once again, he eases the tension that I was creating.

He goes into my kitchen, finding the box on the counter. He flips open the lid, only to gasp when he sees nothing is in there.

"What the hell? Why would you keep the box if the cupcakes are gone?"

"I don't know, to be mean?" I say on a wince.

"That was fucking mean." He sets his backpack on the counter—which is new for him—and pulls out his phone. He starts typing away and I lean over his shoulder to see what he's doing, but he blocks me out.

"What are you doing? Calling the police to arrest me?"

"If anyone is going to put you in handcuffs, it's me," he says, shocking me just as he looks up and winks, and then goes back to typing on his phone.

I swallow the lump of desire forming in my throat from the very idea of being handcuffed by him.

"There," he says, putting his phone in his pocket.

"Did you order more cupcakes?"

"I did. And if you're a good girl, I'll share." The way he said "good girl" an octave lower, I swear I felt a chill race up my spine. He hops up on my counter and grips the edge, flexing his triceps, as well as the strength in his thick forearms.

Jesus, Bower, stop checking him out.

What is wrong with you?

"So." He twists his hat around, facing it backward so I can see his beautiful eyes better, a brilliant shade of blue that's so striking, you can get lost in them in seconds. You're never ready for it, but when you do get lost, it's temptation right in front of you.

But when you're ready for the intensity of the color, it's hard not to get lost in it, to want to explore the depths of it and make a road map to his very soul…

"Are you okay?" he asks, snapping me out of it.

"Huh, what? Yeah. Are you okay?"

He chuckles, the sound so freaking sexy that it actually makes my knees want to wobble, a—dare I say it—swoon, ready to sweep me right off my feet.

"I'm good. You just were staring there for a second."

"Oh, uh, I was thinking."

"Thinking about what?"

"Cockroaches," I say, the first thing coming to mind.

His nose scrunches up. "Why were you thinking about cockroaches?"

"Why not?"

"Because they're gross."

"You know, cockroaches are always so hated on. It's rude if you think about it. Why can't they have a normal life like the rest of us?"

"Because they're gross."

"Ugh." I roll my eyes and lean against the counter. "Cockroach hater."

"Yeah, not sure you would find many cockroach lovers."

"Oh yeah? I bet you're wrong. There are many cockroach lovers out there in the world. Clubs actually devoted to the love of those brown insects and given your disgusting display of prejudice, I might just take you to one."

"Yeah, you do that, Bower. Take me to a cockroach club, where they probably let cockroaches squirm all over your body."

I full-on shiver, causing him to laugh.

"That's what I thought." He hops off the counter and takes my hand. "Come on, let's get this video over and done with."

"Gretchen approves," Bennett says as he rests on my couch.

"Thank goodness for that, as we wouldn't want to disappoint

Gretchen." I bring over two glasses of chocolate milk and set them on the coffee table, where the cupcakes are waiting for us. "Now listen," I say, holding up my finger. "I think we need to have some ground rules before we consume."

"Yeah?" he asks, draping his arm over the back of the couch, his shirt stretching out over his broad chest. "What kind of ground rules?"

"First of all, this cupcake is mine, and this one is yours." I point to each cupcake. "And it is your responsibility to remember that. Second, there will be no stealing of the cupcakes. Once you consume your cupcake, that's it, you're done. Understood?"

"Afraid I'll snatch yours?"

"Yes, and even though I had six cupcakes in the last twenty-four hours, I refuse to let you take this away from me."

He cutely chuckles. "Got it."

"Oh, and there will be no…shenanigans."

He lifts up his cupcake and pulls off the wrapper. "Please define 'shenanigans.'"

I eye him. "You know what I'm talking about."

"Ehh, not really. There could be a bunch of things you're referring to—"

"The dry-humping, Bennett. There will be no dry-humping."

He chuckles. "Ahh, that. Yeah, I wasn't going to go there again."

His comment should make me happy.

It should actually make me feel elated, but in fact, it's quite the opposite.

My first instinct is to ask why the hell not?

My second instinct is to dry-hump his stupid face, just to show him what he's missing out on.

But thankfully, I strapped on my brain today and I'm thinking quite clearly, because I nicely smile and say, "Great. Glad we cleared that up."

"Same." He takes a bite of his cupcake and smiles at me while he chews.

My lips are pursed, not entirely happy with his easygoing attitude. Then again, I'm just going to go with it, because it would be ludicrous to fight with him about his nonchalance with the dry-humping.

Maybe it didn't mean as much to him as it meant to me?

Wait, did it mean something to me?

I don't think so, I mean...it was the first time I've gotten off in a long time that didn't require help from my hand.

And sure, it was erotic in a taboo kind of way. Dry-humping my best friend's brother has a bit of a naughty allure to it, as if I was fulfilling some sort of fantasy I didn't know I had.

But that's it. Therefore, I should be perfectly fine with the way he's acting.

"Should we read now?" he asks, breaking up my thoughts.

"Sure," I say, shoving the rest of my cupcake in my mouth and reaching to the coffee table to grab our books.

Bennett is still working on the baseball series I told him to read. He's on book five, my favorite because there's a scene in there that lives rent free in my head, one that we already talked about and that he already read, the kitchen scene with the vibrator. Chef's kiss.

As for me, I'm starting a new hockey book.

I hand him his book and he gets comfortable while I move to the other side of the couch.

"What are you doing?" he asks.

"Uh, I'm about to read, just like you."

"No." He shakes his head. "What are you doing all the way over there?"

"Trying to get comfortable. Do you want me to read next to you, shoulder to shoulder?"

He plops a pillow on his lap and says, "No, come lie down."

I glance at the pillow and then back at him. "On your lap?"

"Yeah."

"Is this your way of getting me to motorboat your crotch?"

"What?" He lets out a boisterous laugh. "No, I just thought it would be nice for you to stretch out your legs."

That actually would be kind of nice.

Not thinking much of it, I move back to his side, turn on the couch so my head is resting over the pillow on his lap, and then get comfortable.

"You good?" he asks, once I part open my book.

"I am, and you?"

"Perfect," he says as he holds his book with one hand and then rests his other hand on my stomach.

His palm spans from my waistband to the underside of my breasts, almost short-circuiting my brain from his warm touch. And here I thought the dry-humping filled a hole inside of me. Nope, he just busted it wide open, as I can feel my skin twitch with excitement.

It's just a hand, Bower. A hand on your stomach. Get a grip.

Taking a deep breath, I focus my attention on the words in front of me, and start reading, allowing myself to get lost in the story.

My mind gets so lost in the story that I forget about everything around me.

The cupcakes.

The dry-humping.

The man whose fingers are slowly sliding across my waistband…

My eyes pause on a sentence, my breath hitching into my chest as his fingers slide across a small patch of exposed skin. Why the hell does that feel so damn good?

I glance up at him, as much as my eyes will allow, only to find that he's not paying any attention to me but is enamored in his book. As if the slide of his fingers is just an absentminded gesture rather than one with purpose.

Therefore, I shouldn't think much of it.

Right?

With that settled, I go back to my book, to a scene where the hero and heroine are in a sauna together. They're fake dating and he's ten years older than her. He's trying to keep his hands off her, but she's making that exceedingly difficult when she starts stripping in the sauna.

His eyes are focused on her tits.

His mouth's watering from the thought of sucking on them.

His cock's hardening as she approaches, closer and closer and…

Bennett's finger glides just under the waistband of my shorts, making me still, my pulse skyrocketing from a comfortable rhythm to an all-out erratic throb.

The swipe…minuscule. The impact…enormous.

Others might not have even noticed, but not me. It was as if he burned me with one gentle stroke.

I can still feel it, the tip of his finger has found itself past the waistband of my loose shorts. Static, resting, but it's there. I'm not dreaming this, I'm not—

Swipe.

Oh.

My.

Fucking.

God.

My clit immediately starts throbbing, my nipples harden, and suddenly I'm sweating everywhere. This should not be happening. I should stop him. I should flee and move to the other side of the couch. I should put an end to this madness, and yet, I wait on bated breath for the next swipe, the next… something, anything, but as the seconds tick by and he does absolutely nothing, I resign myself to the fact that maybe it was just a spasm of his finger, or perhaps that's just as far as he'd go, which is probably for the best.

Wait, I know it's for the best.

I turn back to my book and reread what I've already read because I need to get back into the scene.

She's naked.

Her tits.

He wants them.

Right, okay, she moves closer to him, her hands falling to his thighs as she spreads his legs open, making room for her body. She wets her lips, her eyes on his straining cock, stretching up toward her, waiting for her mouth—

Swipe.

A gasp almost falls past my lips, but I hold it back as his hand moves an inch farther, now a few centimeters above my pubic bone, just close enough to make me fucking mad with need. Because now all my brain can think about is that he's almost there.

So close.

With a thrust of my hips, he might actually caress me.

My eyes squeeze shut as I contemplate what to do, my clit still throbbing, my mind playing games as I feel like he's moving again...is he?

His finger twitches again. This time it feels closer, so much closer.

No, I'm thinking things.

He wouldn't go there, would he?

Maybe he's technically already there.

Either way, I need to just—

His hand lowers, now right above my slit, his finger toying with me there, brushing up against it, but never truly grazing, turning me on to the point of no return. I can feel how wet I'm getting, how much I want this, need this.

I want him to pleasure me, his fingers to glide along my slick, wet...

His fingers press a millimeter farther, right at the edge.

And uncontrolled by me, my legs fall open, giving him access if he wants to go any farther.

Which I wait for.

And wait.

And wait, until I find that he's not going to do anything. He brushes his fingers over my pussy, but never *in*. He grazes and teases and edges, but when it comes to actual pleasure, he won't make that move.

Maybe that's something I'm just going to have to live with.

Maybe that's all this is, him trying to see how far he can push me.

How far he can torture me.

Swipe.

My lips press together, my heart racing now, just as his finger slowly—and I mean *slowly*—slides along my slit, all the way down, and then all the way back up.

Motherfucker.

It's all just surface level, but it's enough to make me forget all reasoning as my legs fall even wider apart, giving him all the access he needs as my breathing hitches.

And then he does it again, slides his finger along my slit, barely grazing my clit before he pauses, and then to my surprise, presses his whole palm against my pussy.

I can't breathe.

I absolutely can't fucking breathe as he holds still, doesn't move, just cups me, to the point that I swear if he paid attention, he could feel me throbbing against him.

Can he feel how wet I am?

Can he see how hard my nipples are?

Does he see the pleasure and pain he's giving me all at the same time?

I can't even look up to see if he's noticing what he's doing to me. If he sees the war raging inside of me, even though it's a pretty heavy one-sided war right now, the bad choices taking the win at the moment.

His finger slides along my slit again, but this time, he presses down, the pad of his pointer finger lightly dancing over my clit before he repeats the move, up and down, up and down.

"Fuck," I groan, unable to hold back as his featherlike touches start to make me mad with desire.

So mad that I drop my book and slide my hand down his forearm, to the top of his hand that's touching me. With my finger on top of his, I push him farther, sliding him all the way down, and all the way back up.

"Yes," I whisper as I release and he repeats the technique, not just focusing on one spot of pleasure, but giving me full range, all the way to the back and to the front. Inside and out.

Gliding, sliding, thumping, his technique is unlike anything I've felt before and it's probably why it's making it feel like he's pulling every last ounce of control from me, like he's gathering every nerve, muscle, and bone and twisting it in the best way possible, to the greatest feeling that makes everything feel numb even though the pleasure is so intense.

"Fuck…yes," I say as my hips thrust up into his hand. "Make me come."

I can't even think about the fact that I just said that to Bennett.

Not even a little.

Because my mind is racing, racing for pleasure. Racing for a man I shouldn't be with.

Racing with the idea that this is what it's supposed to feel like.

Attraction.

Temptation.

Desire.

It's supposed to make you lose your mind, to forget all outside perspective and just feel.

And that's exactly what he's doing.

"Fuck…Bennett," I say as he dips his fingers inside of me, two of them, grazing my inner walls before he pulls out, tapping along my clit with short precise strokes. My gasp is caught on my lips as he slips two fingers inside me again and curls up, only to pull out and vibrate his fingers against my clit.

It pulls at me.

Tugs.

Wars against my ability to hold strong.

But I can't. It's twisting and pulling, and fuck...I'm going to come.

My brain starts to muddle into darkness. My focus is right between my legs as he builds me up and up and up until...

"Fuck!" I yell as I crest, my orgasm yanking me from reality and right into a space where only white-hot pleasure exists.

And I ride it.

I ride that feeling, humping his hand over and over again until there's nothing left to give.

"Oh...my...God," I whisper as my legs clamp around his hand for a moment, my body trying to calm down from the shock.

After what feels like minutes of me throbbing against his palm, Bennett slowly removes his hand, and as I glance up toward him, looking for any sort of answer, he brings his fingers up to his mouth, staring down at me as he sucks them, lapping up every last drop of arousal.

And it's the hottest thing I think I've ever seen.

"Fucking perfect," is all he says as he snaps his book shut and then gently lifts me up before he stands from the couch.

He's leaving again?

He must see the confusion in my eyes, because he smirks down at me, and then once again brings his fingers to his mouth, where he sucks them for a second longer before he says, "Tastes like fucking joy."

Then with a wink, he heads toward the door and I don't know what possesses me, but I hop off the couch and head toward him, blurting out, "You're just going to leave?"

"Have to get to the stadium but going to need to take care of some business beforehand." He glances down at his lap, where his cock is pressing so incredibly hard against his jeans that my mouth waters. "Catch you later, beautiful."

And then with that, he's gone.

CHAPTER 23
BENNETT

"WHY THE SMILE?" NOLAN ASKS as he sits next to me while Asher warms up in the cages. I'm next, so I put my batting gloves on and get ready.

"Am I smiling?"

"Big time," Nolan says as he pulls a toothpick from his pocket and places it in his mouth.

"Didn't think I was," I say as I feel my cheeks stretch, a smile most definitely on my face.

"You're still doing it. You're smiling."

"Can't I smile while watching Asher hit?"

Asher doesn't even glance at me when he says, "No," in his gruff, take-no-prisoners voice.

"See, you're making the scary man uncomfortable." Nolan gestures to him. "So either cut the smile or tell me why the hell you look like a goddamn clown."

Keeping my voice down, I say, "Things might have gone a little further with Bower."

He slaps his hand to my chest and shouts, "Shut the fuck up. Did you bang her?"

"Dude."

"Can you two fucking leave?" Asher asks, looking like he's ready to shove his bat up our asses.

"Sorry," I say and then get up and head to the hallway, Nolan remaining where he is and crossing one leg over the other, playing with the toothpick in his mouth.

"What the fuck, man?" I ask, hands spread.

"Do you want me to come with you?"

"Why else do you think I got up?"

"I don't know." He shrugs. "Bathroom?"

"Get the fuck out of here," Asher shouts, gripping his bat intentionally, like he's going to snap it in half over Nolan's head.

"Jesus," Nolan says, getting up. "Get laid, man."

Then he joins me in the hallway and leans against the wall. "He's such a dick. You shouldn't let him push you around like that."

"I'm giving him space."

"He doesn't need space; the dude needs friends." Whispering, Nolan says, "Can't trust guys with no friends, like what the fuck does he do with his spare time? Work out? Have you seen his forearms? They're like fucking bazookas."

"He has friends, doesn't he?"

Nolan shakes his head. "Nah, he's always been a loner. He just needs some fucking love on his dick. He never goes out after games, he never—"

"Maybe he has a girl at home that no one knows about. Also, why do we care?"

"You're the one who asked."

"I didn't ask anything."

"Whatever, dude, I'm getting bored. Why are we out here?"

"Jesus," I mutter. He's almost as bad as OC. "You were asking why I was smiling."

"Right." He takes the toothpick out of his mouth and flicks it into a trash can before pulling a green Lifesaver from his pocket. Does he just collect free items from the hostess stand when leaving restaurants? Is an Andes mint next? "So, did you bang her?" He props one foot up against the wall behind him and crosses his arms.

"No. But I did do something else."

"And that is..." He motions with his hand for me to continue.

"I don't feel comfortable talking about it. I don't want to invade her privacy like that."

"For fuck's sake, I'm your therapist; you can tell me."

"You're not my therapist."

"Your sex therapist."

"Also no."

"Fine, I'm the asshole who helped you get to where you are now, and if you don't fucking tell me, I'm going to find a way to get her number and text her myself."

Even though I know he wouldn't do that, I know that he could, so I quietly lean in and say, "We were reading books and I fingered her."

Nolan slowly nods. "Nice."

Uh, was kind of expecting a grander reaction than that.

"That's all you have to say? 'Nice'?"

"I'm not about to be some giddy asshole. Good job fingering her, man. Maybe next time you can use your dick."

"Are you serious right now? You've been a part of this fucking pursuit from the beginning."

"Was I, though? Didn't you start liking her at sixteen?"

I drag my hand over my face. "Never mind. Jesus, way to ruin a good thing."

I start to walk away, but he grabs my shoulder. "What's next?"

"Huh?"

"With her." He rolls his eyes dramatically. "What's next with her?"

"I don't know."

"You have to have a plan. You can't just wing this."

"I have so far and it seems to be paying off."

He shakes his head. "You lucked out, man. She dry-humped you and that was pure fucking luck and wine and you know it. You took your chances and fingered her—can't stand the term by the way—and that seemed to pan out. The next move is the most important move."

I hate to admit it, but he might be right. I was able to pass off the dry-humping and get her into a position where I could make the next move, but that was a big one, a big one that she allowed. But my next move is the most important.

"So, what is it going to be?" He nudges me. "You dry-humped her, you fingered her, now you can go all the way and shove your dick in her, or you can take the half step before that."

"What's the half step?" I ask.

He rolls his eyes as if I'm a fucking moron. "Eat her out, man."

He pats my chest and then pushes off the wall.

Just as Asher exits the cages, Nolan calls out, "I've got next."

Eat her out?

Would she even allow that?

Fuck, I want to, desperately. But that's a huge step. Wouldn't kissing her be easier than that?

I chase after Nolan, who is loosening up his back in the cages.

"What about a kiss?" I ask through the net. "Wouldn't that be better?"

He shakes his head and gets in his stance just as a ball is thrown to him and he grounds out. He swears under his breath and loosens his arms for a second.

"No, my man. A kiss is intimate. That's easily last. Use your lips…on her lips."

He swings and cracks the ball up the middle.

"It's the only way. Trust me on this."

"I trusted you on Cougar," I counter.

"Yeah, and look at where that got your fingers. Right in her pussy. You're welcome."

"Look at this," Gretchen says as she plops a manila folder in front of me.

I'm exhausted from the game last night. It went extra innings and we wound up losing. It was a tough loss because we're on the edge of making the playoffs, and right now, every game matters. Every fucking game.

I stare down at the folder and say, "It's a manila folder."

"Don't be a smart-ass. Flip it open."

Groaning because I'm not in the mood for Gretchen's theatrics, I flip open the folder only to find a write-up of Books with Bombers.

Social media handles.

Pictures.

Followers...

"What the hell?" I say, zeroing in on the number. "Is that really ten thousand followers on Instagram?"

"It is," she says. "And about ninety-eight percent of them are women."

"Probably because I'm reading romance."

"That and because you're nice to look at."

I scoff at her. "Give them more credit than that."

"True. Apparently the first book you recommended is a well-known start of a series. Many comments from readers looking for a space to talk about it. Which is why I need to set up a date with you that would work to have a book club night. We're also coming up with merch that we can ship out to the first one hundred members who join your Patreon."

"Don't people have to pay for that? I don't want to make money off anyone."

"Technically no, but we're going to have a pay tier."

"What? No." I shake my head. "I'm not taking money from people."

"Calm down." She plops in the seat in front of me. "All proceeds will be donated to one of the foster care charities you work with. I just need you to pick which one, or you can divvy up the money to all three. Up to you."

"Oh." I lean my forearms on the table in front of me. "Will they be told that's where the money will be going?"

She nods. "Yes. If you would like to add a backstory, you can. Up to you. I know you like to keep that side of your life private, although I think it would be helpful to bring awareness, but again, that's totally up to you."

See, just when I start to think that Gretchen is the bad guy, she really isn't. She wasn't the bad guy when it came to Maple and Graydon, and she's not the bad guy here. Under all those black pantsuits and slicked-down hair, she really does have a heart.

"Let me think on it."

"Fair enough." She clears her throat. "Now, I plan on partnering up with a local bookstore, preferably indie, so we can also support small business. I'm still looking around, trying to see which one would be the best fit but—"

"I have one."

"Really?" she asks, crossing one leg over the other. "Which one?"

"Uh, well, it's still kind of in the works, but I know it'll be amazing."

"What do you mean…in the works?"

"Don't worry about it." I stand from the table and rap my knuckles on the surface. "Good talk, though. Have to get ready for the game."

"When will you tell me the store? I have to keep this going. We have traction, Bennett."

"I know. Just…let me feel it out first. I can chat next week."

And then without another word, I take off and pull my phone from my pocket as I head toward the locker room. I didn't think this thing was going to blow up, but now that it has "legs," I think we need to run with it, and I have the perfect way to do that.

I shoot off a text, my smile growing wider as I think about how great this could be.

Bennett: I need to talk to you tonight. Coming to your apartment after the game. Super important.

CHAPTER 24
BOWER

"IT'S IMPORTANT?" I SAY, PACING Adalade's living room. "What does he mean by 'important'?" I pause and turn to her, tears filling my eyes. "He told his sister. I know he did. And now he's letting me down gently, telling me that she never wants to see me ever again."

"Why is that where your first thought goes?" Adalade says as she folds one of the cashmere sweaters I found for her today.

"Because that would be the only important thing he could talk to me about. He said it was urgent, which means...oh God, she's coming here to punch me in the face."

"Dear God in heaven, girl." Adalade practically snorts in exhaustion. "If you weren't so damn good at your job, I'd have fired you over this nonsense. You're a smart woman; start acting like one."

"I am. That's why I've thought this through. This is the only conclusion I could come up with."

"Really? Out of all the things he has to talk to you about, maybe he enjoyed your special book reading time so much, and he wants another crack at it."

Yeah, I told Adalade what happened, because she's the only one I can talk to at this point and she's invested. It was awkward at first, but then she told me a story about how she used to dabble in a good diddle—her words—back in the day, and well, that made it awkward. My story was nothing in comparison to hers.

"I don't think he'd text about that. We barely spoke about the dry-humping. I doubt he'd talk about the…the…"

"The diddle."

"Sure," I capitulate. "The diddle. I mean, we haven't talked about it since it happened…or talked much at all, to be honest. Ugh, that's a lie. We chatted this morning, but it was just him. Wait, that's a lie too. I told him about the donut I ate, he got mad at me for not sharing, and then said I owe him one, and instead of giving him one like an adult, I left one at his doorstep, bolted, and texted him while I was on my way here."

Adalade picks up her iced tea. "You're exhausting."

"I know. I hate myself for it." I take a seat on the couch with her and lean my head against the back. "Why did I dry-hump him? None of this would have ever happened if I had just gotten off him the minute I had my cupcake, but noooooo, I had to let my horny flag fly and grind down on his penis like it was my own fuck pillow."

"Just be happy it was his lap and not his face. I heard that's a new trend—humping faces."

"Where the hell did you hear that?"

"Oh, I don't know. I think Mark was telling me about it, a whole sit-on-my-face moment."

"Mark your driver?" I ask, horrified. "He should not be talking to you about that kind of stuff."

"I'll have you know, just like yourself, I've given Mark quite a bit of advice, which has scored him a girlfriend. He actually tested the sit-on-my-face trend with her and it was well-received but quite a commitment, and since you're not in the business of committing to a handsome professional baseball player with a knee-melting smile, it's best it was his lap."

"I…I don't even know what to do with that."

"Well, then, if we're done here, I think I'll have some chicken salad for lunch and then you can be on your way."

Sighing, I stand but then turn toward her. "What do you really think it was?"

"I don't know, but given the upward trend of your interactions, I'd guess that he might want to ask you to sit on his face. I'd be open to it."

"Adalade." I let out a deep breath. "With all due respect, you have not been helpful."

She chuckles and examines her nails. "Just wait. I bet I'm right."

"There is no way you're going to be right about that."

I'll be honest, the one thing I hate about his schedule is that he gets back home so late after his games. There are times when he doesn't, because thank God, we're on the West Coast and games start earlier than, let's say, the East Coast, but still, the process for him leaving the stadium after all is said and done could be shortened.

I glance at my clock again. My nerves are fried at this point because I've been through every scenario in my head and know for a fact what Adalade said is not true.

Which means one thing—this has to be about Gabby.

Knock. Knock.

Once again, I'm going to throw up.

Whatever you do, Bower, do not fall for any funny business. He's your friend's brother, he's your friend's brother, he's your—

I open the door and…

Fuck, why is he so hot?

"Hey, you," he says with a nod before stepping into my apartment.

He must have gone home and changed, because he's in a pair of gray joggers, a black T-shirt, no hat, but his hair is still wet from his shower and twisted and styled every which way, while he smells like fresh soap, an intoxicating aroma that has my nipples pebbling to attention.

"Why does it look like you've seen a ghost?"

"What?" I ask. "Me?" I nervously laugh, as if I'm attempting to hide a murder and the murder weapon is in my pocket. "There's, uh, there's no ghost here."

"Bower?"

"Huh?" I ask, attempting to smile.

"Why are you being weird?"

"Wow." I cross my arms over my chest. "Care to tell me why you've decided to be so rude?"

"What?" His brow creases.

Yeah, what?

I wave my hand dismissively at him. "That's neither here nor there. What's important is that it doesn't happen again."

"What doesn't happen again? Sorry, not following."

"You know, the thing."

"What thing?"

I circle my hand around, as if that's giving him the answer. "The…thing."

"Bower." He cutely scratches the top of his head. "What are you referring to?"

He's going to make me say it, isn't he? Of course he is. He's an immature little punk, that's what he is.

"You know…the diddling."

"The diddling?"

It takes him a moment, but then a wicked smile passes his lips.

"Beautiful, I wasn't even talking about that. But if you want to, I'd be more than happy to oblige."

"No, no." I wave my hand through the air. "Not necessary to talk about it, honestly. I haven't thought about it at all."

"Yeah, I can tell." His smile grows wider.

"It really is just one of those things that happened, and then poof, oops, out of the memory, not logged away or anything. Just poof and it's gone."

"Because of how bad it was or how insignificant it was to you?"

"What? No, that was phenomen-uh, wait, umm...yeahhh," I drag out. "Actually, it was pretty insignificant, so if you could not tell your sister, that would be great."

He purses his lips for a second before he closes the distance between us, pinning me against the wall.

And the devil be damned, my body heats up within seconds.

Freaking seconds.

My hands turn clammy.

The back of my neck warms.

My mouth goes dry.

And as he lowers his head, closer and closer, my entire insides start to thrum with want.

With need.

With so much yearning that I should not take from this man, but so much that I want to.

"Insignificant," he whispers as his lips caress my ear. "My fingers were fucking drenched, Bower. That doesn't seem insignificant to me."

I can feel my stomach quiver, the spot between my legs throb, my skin prickle.

"Um, yeah...I don't know what to say to that."

And I don't, because his proximity is frying my brain.

All rational thoughts have completely gone out the window as I attempt not to throw myself at him.

"Tell me you were lying. That it was significant."

"No," I say as his hand finds my hip, and my body begs for his hand to slip down my pants again.

"Why not?" His lips caress my ear, sending body chills down my arms and legs.

"Because if I do"—I take a deep breath—"I fear it will happen again, and it can't happen again."

"Mm," he rumbles in my ear. "And why is that again?"

"You know why," I say as my hand presses against his chest, attempting to push him away. Instead, my fingers glide over his muscular chest.

"Can't recall, actually," he says.

"Bennett?" My palm glides over his pec.

"Yeah, beautiful?" he says, the nickname he's used four times now, filtering right past the cobwebs and dreariness of my sex life and straight to my freaking soul.

"We shouldn't—" His lips barely pass over my cheek, not kissing, just a whisper of their presence. "Fuck, we...can't..."

I'm throbbing.

So fucking bad.

My legs want to spread, my heart is nearly beating out of my chest, and I'm buzzing to strip down to nothing and just rub my body all over him.

Every last inch.

"But you want to?"

"Doesn't matter what I want."

"Sure as fuck does to me," he whispers, his lips pressing against my lobe before he pulls away so I'm forced to look him in his beautiful blue eyes. His hand lifts and he pinches my chin with his forefinger and thumb. "But that's not why I came here."

My breath feels short, but the brief distance allows my brain to function again. "Oh, not to, uh, not to chat about that? Because your text made it seem like that's what you wanted to chat about, like you told your sister or—"

"Let's get one thing fucking straight." His anger rolls in, surprising me. "Whatever the hell goes on between you and me doesn't apply to my sister. She's not a part of this. She doesn't make decisions for either of us. And if I want to read a book and then fuck you with my fingers, then that's what I'm going to fucking do, and she's not going to hear a word about it. Understood?"

Oh my God, I think I might have just orgasmed.

The power.

The strength in his words.

The conviction.

The protection.

God, why does he have to be so hot, so attractive, so everything I think my body and my mind want? And why is he off-limits? Although, is he really? I haven't told him to stop. I haven't truly ended anything that he's started, but rather, I've indulged.

"I said, understood?" he repeats, pulling my attention back to the present.

"Umm, ye-yes," I stutter.

"Good." He then puts a few inches between us and takes my hand in his, the anger vanishing as he says, "I spoke with Gretchen."

Clearing my throat, I nod, feeling fuzzy and like I just had whiplash. "Okay."

"And the book club is taking off and she wants to sign on with a local bookstore that can help distribute the books."

"That sounds—"

"And I want it to be you."

My brow creases. "But I don't have a bookstore."

"Your book truck," he says, looking like I'm the confused one here.

"Bennett, that's just a dream. It's not actually real."

"But you can make it real. This is the chance, the opportunity you need to push you in that direction."

I shake my head. "I don't know about that. I'm not ready. There's so much that goes into it and—" His fingers silence my lips.

"There's always going to be reasons not to try, Bower, but you can't let those cloud your vision. You know what you want, you've done the research, and you can make this happen. I know you can."

"I don't know. It all seems too quick and I'm not sure I really want to do this—"

"That's a fucking lie and you know it. You've dreamed of this book truck for a while. You have the money for it, the capability, and the plans. You just need to take the leap and execute. Trust me." He looks me dead in the eyes. "I wouldn't push you to do it if I didn't think you could."

I bite down on my bottom lip and look away.

Could I?

Could I actually put this together?

I have the logo designed, the name, the truck even. I just have to make the leap.

"I can see you thinking about it," he says, moving in close again. "Bower, I know you can do this. I fucking know you can. Gretchen wants it done in a week, but I know that's too soon. I'm going to hold her off, because I want your grand opening to coincide with the book club."

"That's a lot of pressure, Bennett."

"The kind of pressure that's worth it," he says as his thumbs slip under my shirt, causing my head to fall back to the wall. "This is what you've wanted for so long, so don't be scared now that there's an opportunity." He swipes his thumbs across my hips. "And I'll be here to help you."

"You're going on a long away trip tomorrow." Just the thought of him being gone for ten days actually makes me feel sick. And that's what should scare me the most, because have I really grown so attached to him that I can't fathom him being gone for ten days?

This is bad, so freaking bad, and yet, as his hands play with me and he moves in closer, I don't stop him. I let it happen, because I know, deep down inside, even though I know my friend would not approve, I want him.

I squeeze my eyes shut from that realization.

I want Bennett.

I want his hands on me.

His mouth.

His tongue.

I want to feel him, every hard, muscular inch.

I want to feel him near me, on me…in me.

I want to know what it's like to be worshipped by him and not just in small pieces. I want all of him. I want to be controlled and possessed.

And the craving for it has grown each and every day, as well as the fear.

"Just because I won't physically be here doesn't mean that I still won't be able to help."

"Help in what capacity?"

"Any capacity you want," he says, his thumbs hooking on the waistband of my shorts and tugging them an inch lower.

I suck in a sharp breath, my mind starting to go fuzzy again. Seems to happen whenever he gets this close. "I don't know, Bennett."

"What don't you know?"

"I don't know anything at this point," I say, my hand on his chest. "And when you're this close, it's hard to think. It's hard to even compute what you're saying."

"Do you want me to back away?"

Yes.

No.

But also yes.

But fuck…ugh, no.

"I'm taking your silence as an answer," he says, tugging my shorts down another inch so that they're barely covering my front now.

My mouth waters at the thought of what he can do, the ache inside of me growing so intensely that my legs feel wobbly and my core twitches, waiting for his touch.

"I'm so confused," I say, finally finding my voice.

"Confused about me?"

I shake my head but then nod it. "I shouldn't want this, want you. I know I shouldn't. And yet…"

He wets his lips, his eyes going feral as he says, "But you do."

Maintaining eye contact, I do the one thing I probably shouldn't. I nod.

The smallest of smirks peeks past his lips before he whispers, "Good."

And then he goes down to his knees and pulls my shorts with him, as well as my underwear, exposing me right in front of his face. He helps me out of my clothes, deposits them to the side, and then lifts my leg over his shoulder.

He looks up at me for a moment, hunger in his pupils, and he pauses, waits for me to tell him no, but for the life of me, I can't.

I know I should, but I can't.

I'm so desperate for him to make me feel alive again that I don't say one fucking word.

And he runs with it.

He brings his mouth right up against my pussy, and he kisses me gently. Immediately, I grow wet, my arousal spiking with just one simple kiss. His hand smooths over the back of my thigh and up to my ass, where he grips it tightly, right before he parts me and his tongue slowly drags over my clit.

"Fuck," I whisper as my hand falls to the top of his head.

He must enjoy the encouragement, because he pushes my leg open more, the one on his shoulder, and he moves his tongue in even deeper, applying more pressure and hitting me in just the right spot for the sweetest torture ever.

It's heaven, feeling him between my legs, the scruff of his jaw over my sensitive skin, mixed with the warmth of his mouth and the soft, yet firm press of his tongue. It's a dream, something that hasn't been done to me in so long that I actually want to cry because I miss this.

I miss having a man lap at me, like I'm his favorite dessert.

I miss being desired like this, like he can't get enough.

And I miss the feel of being taken, in the middle of the day, without a thought or a care of the time, what's happening around us, and who could possibly disturb us.

This is hot.

Raw.

Sexy.

And I don't think I'll ever be able to stop him, because I don't want to.

"Yes," I moan, my body shaking from holding myself up with one leg.

His hand continues to squeeze my ass as his other hand travels up my thigh, just below his tongue, and then slowly he inserts what feels like two fingers inside of me, curving them up toward my G-spot.

"Fuck," I squeak as my body convulses from the feel of his fingertips playing with a spot that has never been touched before. "Oh fuck, Bennett."

My pussy clenches as he laps at my clit, over and over, his pace picking up as he swipes his fingers, creating a maddening feel of euphoria to build and build and build in the pit of my stomach.

Consuming and billowing and developing into something bigger than I ever expected. A feeling so overwhelming that my body grows wet with need. Sweat dots my upper lip, and my pussy starts to clench around his fingers, my orgasm imminent.

"Oh God, oh fuck," I moan, my fingers digging into his hair.

His tongue grows stiff, now focusing on my clit, flicking over and over again, heightening my arousal until every muscle in my body turns to mush and the only feeling that exists is pooling between my legs at a rapid rate, stealing my breath.

My thoughts.

"Right there, Bennett," I moan. "Please don't stop. Fuck, don't stop."

He increases the intensity, faster, harder, matching each stroke of his tongue with his fingers until a shot of light bursts behind my eyelids and I tip over the edge, my orgasm ripping through me and tearing me into what feels like a million pieces.

"Oh my God!" I yell as my body convulses and I ride out my orgasm on his tongue, taking every last ripple of pleasure until there is nothing left inside of me.

After a few seconds of catching my breath, Bennett stands and then gently places a kiss on my forehead.

"Think about the book truck," he says, bringing this full circle as I still try to figure out what he just did to me, how he just rocked my world within minutes.

And then he takes off, leaving me shortless and satisfied in my apartment.

I lower to the ground and press my hands to my face.

Bennett Brinkman just tongue-fucked me. I just came over his stunning face. How did that happen? And why the hell was it SO good? I've been with a few men. I love sex. *But that?* He hasn't even kissed me, and yet, three times his only focus has been on giving me pleasure.

He knew what he was doing, all right. And good God, I so want that again.

God, I'm so fucked.

Because all I can think about is how desperately I want to return the favor.

CHAPTER 25
BENNETT

"GOOD GAME," I SAY TO Asher, who is passing me, fresh from the shower, looking like he wants to wring everyone's neck that talks to him, despite being the guy who hit the game-winning single.

He grumbles something under his breath, but I can't quite make out what it is and don't even bother trying.

We leave tomorrow first thing in the morning and have a game tomorrow night. We don't typically leave the morning of a game, but the team voted on it since the next city is only an hour-and-a-half flight and families wanted to spend more time with each other. Given that we're coming up on playoffs and our tanks are pretty much drained right now, management will do just about anything to keep us happy.

But the rule is we're not to go out, and if there is any talk of going out, you will have to deal with management in the morning.

"Fuck," Nolan says, dropping down next to me in nothing but a thong. He's been on a hot streak lately, and he swears it's because he's been wearing a thong for the past ten days. Whatever makes him fucking happy, I guess. "I really wanted to go out tonight." He leans in and whispers, "Want to chance our luck?"

"Absolutely not," I say, thinking about how if I had it my way, I'd be going back to Bower's apartment and cuddling into her. But one small step at a time, which I think has been working, by the way, because fuck, I can still taste her on my tongue and she tastes fucking incredible. So damn good that I can feel an addiction take root and I'm looking for my next hit.

"I knew you were going to say that. You're too fucking pure."

"Also, going out would let the team down, and is that the kind of guy you want to be, Nolan?"

He glances down at his barely covered dick and says, "None of this is the guy I want to be, but here I am." He gestures toward his crotch, and I shy away from looking because one accidental spotting of him in that thing is enough.

"Are you going to go take a shower?" I ask, because fuck, I don't want to see it anymore.

"Is that what you want?"

"I just want you away from me, showered, and tucked into your bed so you can wake up at a decent hour and make the plane for our game tomorrow."

"Seems like a lot of work. Want to do it for me?"

"I'm good." As I'm freshly showered, I slip my shirt over my head, so ready to get back to my place.

"Are you off to go see her?" Nolan asks, picking up a bat from my locker and resting it right on his dick as he pretends to stroke it.

I snatch the bat from him. "Don't fucking do that with my shit." I set it down and then add, "And no. Getting some sleep and letting the heart grow fonder with my absence."

"Really? Hell, if I were you, I'd try to at least get a handy before I went off for ten days."

"Yeah, well, you have no respect for yourself."

He laughs. "Dude, it has nothing to do with respect and everything to do with getting off with some hot chick. If you're going to respect anything, respect the dick. When was the last time you actually came all over your goddamn stomach that didn't include your hand and some lotion?"

Well, if he takes out that scenario…

"That's what I thought. A long-ass time, right? If I were you, I'd march my ass right to her apartment and look for some assistance in the matter."

"It's not like that," I say. "This is about her and winning her over. I'll get my dick rubbed off at some point, but not now. I'm too fucking close and I don't want to scare her away."

"Are you sure? What happened that makes you think you're close?"

"Nothing you need to know about," I say.

"Holy fuck." He stands and presses his hand to my chest. "You ate her out, didn't you?"

"Leave me alone."

"You fucking did." A huge smile crosses his face. "You fucking ate her out and you liked it and she liked it. Didn't she?"

"We're done."

I pocket my phone and my wallet and turn to head out of the locker room when Nolan squats into sumo position, just his thong-covered ass out, and starts twerking while bouncing forward and singsonging, "He fucking ate her out. He fucking ate her out."

"Jesus Christ," I mumble before moving away from him and his celebration that some of the other guys take part in. If there is one thing I know for sure, it's that Nolan Hart is easily the life of the party.

And that I fucking ate her out!

My driver drove me today because I was packed and ready to board the plane after the game, only to find out that we weren't leaving until the morning, which means, my driver is driving me home now.

I kind of fucking like it, though. Not having to mess around with traffic after a game. I can just decompress in the back while he deals with weaving in and out.

Also, it gives me a chance to catch the "daddies" up.

Bennett: Things have progressed with Bower. Book club is taking flight, not as popular as your social media launch, Graydon, but we'll get there. Gretchen is getting Bower involved in the book club and I might have fucking eaten her out.

I lean my head back, just as there is a text, buzzing my phone in my hand.

OC: Who did you eat out? Gretchen? Did she taste like burned popcorn? Because that's the feeling I get from her.

Graydon: Why the fuck would he eat Gretchen out? Clearly he's talking about Bower.

OC: From his sentence structure, one could assume the subject (Gretchen) is the one who he's performing the tongue action on, the eating out.

Graydon: But the last proper noun in the sentence is Bower.

OC: She's the secondary, Gretchen is the subject, therefore making the reader lean into thinking she's the one Bennett stuck his tongue in.

Graydon: You've lost it.

OC: You need to get educated.

Bennett: For fuck's sake, who cares! I ate Bower out. That's what should matter right now.

OC: It would if you structured your sentence properly. I know text messaging allows for a lack of punctuation, but don't *assume* I know what you're talking about, because you will just make an ass out of you and me.

Graydon: Want to move to a separate chat without him in it?

Bennett: Yes.

OC: Wait, please no, don't leave me! I'm sorry. I'm lonely and depressed and you both have lives and I have nothing, absolutely nothing, which makes me so pathetic and lonely, and the only thing keeping me going are the typing challenges I've been doing online, perfecting my words per minute to sixty-five. Shooting for sixty-nine, if you get my drift.

Graydon: I don't know what to say to that.

Bennett: Sixty-five, respectable.

OC: Thank you. It's all about relaxing in the wrist.

Graydon: And we're leaving.

Pumping with adrenaline from the win earlier today, and my game win, I enter my apartment and kick off my shoes, dropping my bag off at the front door because I know that I'll just pick it up in the morning.

I brushed my teeth at the stadium, so I pull my shirt over my head and walk into the bedroom just as I come to a complete stop, my life nearly leaving my lungs when I see a lump in my bed.

"Jesus," I say when I notice that it's Bower.

She lifts up, looking so adorable in one my shirts and her hair tied up on the top of her head.

"I should have texted you. I'm sorry."

"Don't apologize," I say, the shock of finding her slowly dissipating as excitement takes its place. "Everything okay?"

She nods and looks away, almost as if she's embarrassed.

"Doesn't seem like it."

"I shouldn't be here," she whispers and then glances over her shoulder at me. "But I couldn't stop myself from coming over." She swallows. "You're leaving for ten days and I just thought, well, that maybe we could cuddle before you leave, nothing else."

"As if you have to ask," I say, wanting to pin her to my bed and thank her for coming here tonight. I wasn't going to push my luck, but thank God she didn't mind.

I get rid of my socks and pants and then I slip under the covers with her, lying on my back and reaching my arm out for her. She curls right into my side and rests her head on the crook of my shoulder and places her hand on my chest.

"Thank you," she says on a sigh, as if she's the most content she's ever been.

"Anytime you want this, you tell me," I say, kissing the top of her head.

"Don't say that. I'd be here every night."

"You say that as if it's a bad thing."

"You know it is," she says, uncertainty in her voice. "You know damn well I shouldn't be here, Bennett."

"I don't, actually, because last time I checked, you're a grown woman who can make her own decisions."

"If she finds out, she won't speak to me again."

"That's not going to happen. She loves you."

"She trusts me and she shouldn't," she says as her hand slides down my chest and straight to my stomach as her finger swirls around my individual abs, causing my stomach to concave from her touch.

"Why?" I ask as she swirls the tip of her finger one by one farther south as she goes until she reaches my waistband, and that's when I go from semi-hard to fully erect.

"Because, she has no idea how much I want you and how much I'm willing to cross the line."

And then her hand slips past the waistband of my boxer briefs and the palm of her hand flattens over my length.

Mother of fucking God.

The amount of times I've dreamed of this, thought of her touching me, wanting to be with me, fucking maddening. And now that it's finally happening, it's hard to contain the euphoria flowing through me.

"God, you're huge," she says as she presses a kiss to my chest and lightly caresses my erection that's growing harder and harder by the second. "And I know I shouldn't be doing this, but I can't stop." Her mouth moves down my pec as her body slides along my side until her lips are caressing my abs.

"Fuck," I whisper, her mouth so goddamn close.

Her tongue peeks out, swiping along each divot, swirling and kissing, driving me fucking nuts as her fingertips lightly graze my cock, up and down…up and down…up and…

"Jesus," I groan as her hand connects with my balls. I spread my legs, giving her room, and she climbs between them, positioning herself right below me.

She cups me and then rubs her thumb along my seam, slowly spreading and playing with my balls in a way that I've never fucking felt before. She's gentle but also knows what the fuck she's doing, because she has my dick twitching against my stomach and my stomach hollowing with need.

Her fingers move toward the back of my balls and right to the spot behind them where her thumb applies pressure, swirling over and over again, creating a whirl of need inside of me that has me begging for her mouth as pre-cum pebbles at the tip of my dick.

"Bower," I breathe out, my hands clutching the sheet beneath me. "Please."

I glance down to catch a smirk pass her lips before she lowers her mouth to my length, peeks her tongue out, and runs it along my shaft, all the way up to the tip, where she lightly flicks the underside while still playing with my balls, creating a soft friction that will easily be the death of me.

The teasing.

Taunting.

Playing.

I'd half expected her to just deep throat me and get me off in seconds, but Jesus, this...this is fucking phenomenal.

She has me panting and she's barely touching me.

She has me begging and she hasn't even sucked me in.

She has me wanting to bury myself so far deep in her throat that I fear what will happen if she actually takes me in her mouth.

Her tongue moves back down my length, to the base, and then slides over my balls, along the seam, creating a feral feeling deep within me that escapes through a long, guttural groan. I drape my arm over my eyes, the feeling almost unbearable as pleasure continues to shoot up my spine with every slide of her tongue or thumb over my balls.

And she doesn't stop. It's constant.

Building and building, to the point that my balls tighten and I can feel my body preparing to come.

"Beautiful," I say, breathless, air barely getting into my lungs. "Please... fuck, I need your mouth."

She pauses her strokes and then takes a long, languid lick along my balls, up my shaft, and then she opens her mouth and takes me all the way to the back of her throat until I hear her gag.

"Motherfucker," I croak as I lift up on my elbows to watch her take me in again, her head bobbing, up and down, her tongue running along my cock, her teeth barely grazing. "So fucking good, beautiful. Take me... take me deep."

She pulls up, licks the tip, swirls her tongue around, and then buries her mouth over my cock again and then swallows when I'm balls deep, and that's all it takes. My body grows stiff and my orgasm teeters, ready to fall over.

"Bower, babe, I'm about to come."

She pulls up, licks the tip again, and starts pumping me hard at the base, squeezing and tugging me so rapidly that I know it's any goddamn second, and then she captures the head with her mouth and sucks.

She sucks so hard that I black out, my breath escaping my lungs just as my body stills and the pressure builds up in my cock right before I nut all over her tongue.

"Fuck...me," I groan while she licks me clean. All of my dreams have come true as she pulls away and sits up on her knees to stare down at me. With the back of her hand, she wipes her mouth and then smiles.

I knew if I ever had the chance of being with Bower, I knew it would be fucking good, but this, this was incredible.

She starts to move, but I sit up and grab her hand.

"Don't go," I say. "Just give me a second."

I lift off the bed, grab a fresh pair of boxer briefs from the dresser and go to the bathroom, where I clean up quickly and take a few seconds to catch my breath.

Okay, this is not what I was expecting when I came home. Hell, I wasn't even expecting to see her tonight, so I need to tread carefully. I don't know what my next move should be, and I wish I had my phone with me so I could text the Gladdy Daddies or even Nolan, but I'm shit out of luck, so looks like I have to handle this on my own.

On a deep breath, I exit the bathroom to find Bower sitting in the same position on my bed. I go to her just as she lifts up and says she needs to go to the bathroom.

So I sit on the edge, pleading with the universe to keep this going, because not only is she the fucking woman of my dreams, everything I could ever want, but she just rocked my world to the point of no return.

When she exits the bathroom, she leans against the doorframe in nothing but one of my T-shirts that falls down to her knees.

Hoping for the best outcome, I say, "Will you stay?"

"I shouldn't," she says.

"But will you?"

She looks away, indecision written all over her expression. Her teeth pull on the corner of her lip as she says, "Just to snuggle. I can't...I can't have you do anything other than that."

"If all you're offering tonight is for you to sleep in my arms, then consider me fucking lucky," I say.

Her arms unlock from where they're poised at her chest and she walks up to me, offering me her hand, so I take it and help her onto the bed and under the covers. I lie flat on my back and she curls up to my side, resting her head in the crook of my shoulder like she did when I first got here.

I wrap my arm around her and hold her tight, not wanting to ever let go now that I've had her, tasted her, been with her.

"I don't know what's happening to me," she softly says, her hand gently on my chest. "I shouldn't have these feelings, but I can't stop myself. Something changed, Bennett, and I'm so conflicted, confused, and the one person I'd talk to about this, I can't talk to about it at all. And the second person I'd talk to is you and I can't—"

"You can," I say, feeling guilty that I put her in the position. She's been so resistant, so scared, and I kept pushing her, but only because I felt there was something there, something between us.

"No, I can't talk to you about it."

"Why not?"

"Because it's about you."

"So, it's open communication. That's how it should be between us, open. No secrets, no boundaries, nothing held back."

"I don't know what that's like," she says softly.

"Would you be willing to try with me?"

"I shouldn't be trying anything with you." She shifts her head, growing even closer.

"And yet, you are, aren't you?"

"I don't know," she says. "I'm so confused, Bennett. Torn. And I should leave right now. I should go, but I don't want to. I want to stay here, with you and just...just forget about everything else."

"Then let's forget. Let's forget together." I rub her back, wanting to soothe this nagging ache she's living with, that I've brought on her.

She wraps her arm around me and plasters her body against mine, and that's how we spend the night.

Together.

Forgetting the rest of the world.

CHAPTER 26
BOWER

BENNETT'S ALARM SOUNDS OFF, STARTLING me awake from where I'm comfortably sleeping on his chest.

"Shit," he grumbles as he picks up his phone and turns off the alarm. "Fuck, I'm sorry. Early plane this morning."

"It's fine," I mumble into his chest as his hand rubs up and down my side. "I get it." I slowly lift, the ache of staying in the same position all night hitting me in the back.

"You can stay," he says, tugging on my hand.

"No, I should get back to my place, take a shower, and get started with my day."

"Bower, it's five thirty."

"It's fine." I slide out of bed and look around the bedroom, unsure what I'm trying to find. I didn't bring anything here with me besides my phone and keys, so I pick them up from the nightstand and turn to leave just as Bennett comes right up to me.

"Bower, please don't pull away."

I look up at him, into those sultry eyes, and feel the pull toward him that I've felt the last few weeks. The one that I was attempting to mask as friendship but have realized is not friendship at all.

It's lust.

Yearning.

The need for so much more from him.

Wetting my lips, I say, "Even if I tried, I know I couldn't pull away. I'm drawn to you."

A sense of relief seems to wash through him as he tugs me into a hug and kisses the top of my head.

"We'll work through this," he says. "Promise, okay? Just trust me."

I nod, even though I feel so unsure.

He takes my hand in his and guides me toward the front door. "Want me to walk you to your apartment?"

I shake my head. "No, you have to get ready. I'm good."

"Are you sure?"

"Positive." I squeeze his hand and move away from him, offering him a smile. "Safe travels, Bennett."

"Thanks," he says as he releases my hand, looking pained that he had to do so.

And with one last tight smile, I head back home, taking the stairs so I don't have to wait for the elevator. When I get to my apartment, I head straight for my bed, place my phone on the nightstand, and bury my head in my pillow, where I let all my emotions go.

I allow myself to feel, to sob, to cry until I don't have any tears left. *Because how can something that feels so, so right also feel so incredibly wrong?*

I stare at my computer in front of me, at one of the book trucks I've been thinking about purchasing. I haven't taken the leap yet because I can't seem to put together a solid thought.

Everything feels muddled.

Out of place.

Not right.

I'm itching on the inside but burning on the outside.

I'm disappointed in myself but thrilled at the same time.

I'm concerned for my friendship but also dying to talk to my friend.

To sum it up, I'm not doing well.

And the pressure of it all keeps building up to the point that I crash out and cry.

I've done it three times already, twice in Adalade's house and I've been able to hide it, but the third one, well, it happened right here in this coffee house.

At least Adalade didn't have to see it, because the last thing I want to do is explain to her what's going on, especially after the last few conversations we've had.

So, here I am, sitting alone, attempting to follow through on a promise I made to myself but can't possibly figure it out—

"What are the chances of running into you here?" a familiar voice says.

I glance up to see Cougar, standing in front of me with a to-go iced latte and a smile on his face.

"Cougar," I say, surprised. "What are you doing here?"

"Grabbing some caffeine in between practice and film review." He nods at the seat in front of him and I gesture for him to take a seat. "What about you?"

"Attempting to get some work done."

"Attempting, huh?" He slouches in his chair like he always does. "Why does that sound like you're not getting anything done?"

"Because you would be right about that. I've gotten nothing done."

"That seems like shit." He nods toward my computer. "What are you doing? Maybe I can help."

I chuckle, the sound feeling foreign because I couldn't imagine chuckling with my state of mind, but who says that? Who says they can help with someone's work?

Cougar, that's who.

I turn my computer toward him and say, "Attempting to pick out a truck."

He sits up and leans forward, taking the computer from me, and says,

"Would you look at this shit?" His eyes zero in on the screen. "What the fuck are these things?"

"They're called mini trucks, and their beds are converted to have shelves in the back."

He scrolls through the page, passionately interested, which makes me smile. "How the fuck do I get one?"

"Cougar." I chuckle. "You're too big to drive one of those. You would never fit in one."

"The hell I wouldn't. I could get one of these and hand out signed jerseys from the back. It could be the merch mobile." His eyes light up. "The Cougar mobile. Fuck, sweetheart, this has to happen. I can get it wrapped to look like a cougar as well." He clicks on something and turns it toward me. "This one, right here. Perfect. Give me ten of them."

"Oh my God, you're so ridiculous," I say, shaking my head.

"Ridiculous or genius?" he asks.

"Ridiculous."

He shakes his head and then sips his drink. "You're hating because you're jealous."

"I'm telling the truth because there is no way you would be able to drive that thing, let alone give away merch. You would be mauled by fans."

"I see no problem with that. Got to love all the love."

"Okay, fine, get one. Let's see you go through with this idea."

His lips purse to the side and then he says, "Damn, you know I'm all talk."

I laugh because he truly is just…to say it nicely, an idiot.

There's nothing complicated about him.

He's unapologetically him.

And there might not be much substance to him, but sometimes easy is best.

"What do you need this truck for?"

"You're going to make fun of me."

His eyes pop open as he points to his chest. “Me? Make fun of you? Come on, I have better people to spend that kind of energy on. So tell me, what it’s for?”

I take my computer back and say, “Promise you won’t make fun of me?”

“Promise.”

“Fine.” I shut my computer and fold my hands on top of it. “It’s supposed to be a book truck.”

His brow furrows together. “What do you mean by ‘book truck’?”

“I’d sell books from it. Kind of like a food truck, but instead of food, it would be books.”

“Is that a thing?” he asks. “Like...people read?”

Oh, Cougar.

“Yes, they read.” I chuckle. “It’s actually quite popular.”

“Really?” he asks, absolutely stunned as if this is new information to him.

“Yes. Very popular.”

“Huh.” He scratches his cheek. “Do you read?”

“I do.” I nod, finding so much humor in this interaction. “Do you not read?”

“Sweetheart, I can’t tell you the last time I even picked up a book that was not a playbook. Not even sure I can read at this point.”

“You can read.”

He shakes his head. “Doubtful. I don’t think I have the attention span to be able to complete a book.”

“It does require attention to be able to finish one.”

“The only reason I haven’t drifted off during this conversation is because, well, for one, you taught me about mini trucks, and two, you’re hot to look at.”

I smirk. “Well, I’m flattered that my hotness can keep your attention.”

He tips his drink toward me and says, “You’re welcome.”

Unbeknownst to me, this is kind of what I needed. A mindless conversation with a guy who just might have more interest in what he looks like in the mirror than the words on pages in a book.

And I'm grateful for this little encounter. I needed to smile.

I now understand why there haven't been chills or goose bumps whenever I've been around Cougar, though. Is he still hot as hell? Yes. But do I want more substance in a man that Cougar just doesn't have? Also yes. I've made a friend, and I'm okay with that.

He takes a look at his phone and mutters, "Shit. I have to go. Same time, same place tomorrow?" He stands. "Maybe I can help you pick out the colors for your mini truck while I convince you to come to one of my games."

"You can try to convince all you want, not saying it's going to happen."

"Can I at least convince you to go with the Foghorn colors? That would be a sharp fucking truck."

"I was thinking more on the pink side."

"Should I convince the Foghorns to change their colors then to match your truck?"

"I'd love to see you try."

He winks. "If anyone can do it, it's me. See you tomorrow, sweetheart."

Then he takes off and for a moment, I can't help but wonder, did I just agree to another date with Cougar?

Bennett: How was your day?

I stare down at his text for the fifth time, knowing I need to answer. I promised him I wouldn't shy away, push away, flat-out disappear, but God, wouldn't that be easy?

It would be painful, quite sure my body would hate me, but the mind and heart would appreciate such a move.

Then again, I can't be that person.

Gabby would hate me even more if I didn't treat her brother with all the respect he deserves.

So I take a seat on my couch and let out a deep breath as I text him back.

Bower: Pretty decent, how about yours?

Sure, it's a lie, but telling him that I cried three times because I'm so confused by my thoughts and feelings doesn't really seem like a great opening line.

Instead of texting back, though, he calls.

Of course he would. He always does.

Just keep an even voice and everything should be fine. Slapping on a smile, even though he can't see me, I say, "Hello?"

"Hey, Bower," he answers, his voice deep, as if he's talking to me shirtless and in bed.

"Umm...hi," I say awkwardly because, well, I nearly sucked the man's dick off last night and just from the sound of his voice, I want to do it again.

And again.

And fuck...again.

"Oh no, you're not going to make this awkward, are you?" he teases. That lightens my mood only slightly.

"You're the one who called when we were texting. If anyone made it awkward, it was you."

"Sorry that I'd prefer to hear your voice."

"Apology accepted."

He chuckles and I can practically feel the rumble of his chest from here. It takes everything in me to keep my legs closed.

"There she is. See, it doesn't need to be awkward between us."

"Bennett, I sucked you so hard I made you squeal. It will always be awkward."

His laugh is a belly laugh now, which makes me smile. "I did not fucking squeal, despite wanting to badly."

Feeling slightly more comfortable, I cross my legs and place a throw pillow on my lap, getting more comfortable.

"I could sense the squeal when I started playing with your balls."

"That's what happens when a man has never been touched there before."

I gasp. "Seriously?"

"Seriously. You were my first."

"I oddly take pride in that. I can't believe no one has ever played with your balls before. God, it's one of my favorite things to do. I love edging."

"I could tell." He clears his throat, making me laugh. "Fucking made me black out, beautiful."

"Yeah, well, just repaying the favor," I say, feeling shy, wondering why our conversation went in this direction. Maybe it's for the best, because what we've been doing has been very unspoken, and now, well, getting it out in the open only makes it feel slightly better.

"Why didn't you let me repay the favor last night?" he asks.

"Afraid I'd want more."

"What the fuck is wrong with that?"

I press my lips together and lean my head on the back of the couch. "I think more would lead to kissing and we haven't kissed yet because, well...that seems intimate, like crossing the line. Which seems ridiculous in the grand scheme of things. I mean your dick was in my throat last night, but, kissing, that's...that's growing a relationship."

"And that scares you?"

"It does."

"And you were afraid if I returned the favor, that's where it would have led?"

"I know it would have, especially since my control around you is wafer thin."

"Maybe that would be a good reason to let loose and kiss me."

I shake my head even though he can't see me. "No, I can't."

"Not yet?" he asks.

"I don't know. I can't think about it. I'm taking this one day at a time."

God, today, it felt like one minute at a time.

"That's fair," he says. "Were you nervous that we would have gone all the way?"

"Yes," I answer. "I've thought about it all day and I'm just not…I don't think—"

"You don't need to explain," he says. "Seriously, Bower. I get it. And I don't want you feeling like I'm pressuring you."

"I don't feel that at all. Not even a little."

"Good, tell me if you ever do."

"I will." I let out a deep sigh. "God, I don't want to talk about this. I've thought about it all day and I'm just fried at this point. Can you…can you tell me something stupid?"

"Something stupid?" he asks, and I can hear in his voice he's really thinking it over. "Let me think…Oh, you know how you asked me if I could set you up with Nolan when you first came out here?"

"Yes," I say.

"Well, good thing I didn't because he has been wearing a thong every day during his hitting streak, and my guess is, if you two were dating, he'd be dipping into your drawers."

I let out a laugh, the weight on my chest slightly lifting, just what I need. "He would have gotten his hand slapped. No one touches my underwear but me."

"Yeah? What about me?"

I smile to myself. "Only when you're pulling it off."

"There's my girl," he says with all the joy in his voice.

I jot down the make and model of the two trucks I like in my notebook along with the dimensions. Okay, I've been able to narrow it down to two, which is impressive given how many options there were, but I like this, I think.

I stare at the options, overthinking maybe a little. Either one would do the job. Both have complimentary reviews; now I just have to pick one and be done with it.

"Interesting. I didn't think you'd show up." I lift my gaze to find Cougar standing in front of me with his coffee and what looks to be a tub of protein powder. He clenches it and says, "The store next door was having a mega sale. I might make millions, but I like saving a buck." He plops down in the chair across from me and sets his garbage can–sized protein on the table.

"Why didn't you think I was going to show up? You were the one who interrupted me yesterday. This is my spot. You're just taking over."

He leans back in his chair, studying me while sipping his coffee. "You're quite sassy, you know that? Any other woman would be fawning over me right now."

"And what did I say from day one, Cougar? I'm not like every other woman."

"You're right about that." He nods toward my notebook. "So what do you have going on in there?"

"Picked out two book trucks to choose from."

His eyes light up. "Really? Which ones?"

Once again, I turn my screen toward him and say, "I'm either going with the 210 Express or the 1180 Deluxe."

"Oooo, solid choices, solid choices." He clicks away on my computer, taking time to examine them. "You know, I can't see where you could go wrong with either of them. Although, the deluxe has those old-timey wheels with the white interiors. That's sick. But they might cost more to replace."

"You think so?" I ask.

"Oh, for sure. Any sort of specialty tire will cost you more. Which means, your deciding factor is going to be if you want the fancy, expensive tires for the look, or if you want to go with the express and save money on tires in the long run."

"Huh, I never looked at it that way."

"And that's why I'm here," he says with a very cocky but cute attitude.

"I do like the whole aesthetic of the fancy tires. I think it could bring a vintage retro vibe that I'm going for, but then again, could I still achieve the same vibe if I went with the regular tires?"

"Depends on what the rest of the setup is going to be. What's the look you're going for?"

"Well, I was thinking about getting the truck wrapped in a vintage teal, even though I thought it would be pink. I think the teal would be more eye-catching with the rest of the look. And then I would have touches of mustard yellow and pink."

"Nice. I like that. What's it going to be called?"

"Umm, I was sort of thinking about calling it The Whimsy Wagon."

"The Whimsy Wagon," he says, testing it out. "Shit, sweetheart, that's cute."

"You think so?"

"Hell yeah."

"I have a logo. Do you want to see it?"

"You do?" His eyes light up. "Fuck yeah, let's see it." I grab my computer and pull up the logo I had made a couple of months ago. It's the first time I'm showing anyone, and frankly, I couldn't care less if Cougar likes it, because I like it.

I turn the computer toward him and watch his smile grow as he reads the tagline out loud. "Whimsy, spice, naughty, and nice." He nods. "That's solid."

"You like it?"

"Yeah, that shit is good."

Would prefer for him not to call it shit, but I get it.

"Thank you."

"And sure, the retro tires would look good with the logo, but you can get away without that shit. Maybe add something to the logo so it's not just words."

"I thought about that, but I couldn't come up with a good mascot, if you will."

"Sweetheart, it's right under your nose."

"What? A book?"

He shakes his head. "The wagon. Once you pick out the one you want, use The Whimsy Wagon as the mascot. That shit will sell."

Dear God in heaven, he's right.

Something I'd never expect to say about Cougar.

But there he is, a marketing genius.

"And the merch could be so cute."

"The cutest." He winks and then sips his coffee.

Huh, he has been surprisingly helpful.

Bower: Did you really send me cupcakes?

Bennett: Yeah, I don't want you forgetting about me.

Bower: You really think that's going to happen? You're on my mind all the time.

Bennett: Good or bad?

Bower: Maybe a little bit of both.

Bennett: I guess I'll take it. You're on my mind all the time too.

Bower: Good or bad?

Bennett: Always good.

Bower: I guess that makes me a bad person, huh?

Bennett: No, I know what I've wanted for a very long fucking time, and you're still trying to figure it out.

Bower: What do you mean a very long fucking time?

I stare down at the text, my heart racing as I try to decipher what he's saying when, of course, my phone rings.

"Is this how it's always going to be?" I answer. "You're going to call instead of text?"

"When I'm desperate to hear your voice, yeah, and that's pretty much all the time."

"Good to know." I head to my bedroom after locking up for the night and flop back on my bed that Bennett bought for me. "So, what do you mean a long fucking time?"

"Remember when I told you that I had a crush?"

"Yeah, the main reason why you haven't had a girlfriend all these years."

"Exactly. That crush, Bower, that was you."

What?

No, that can't be right.

"Bennett, seriously—"

"I'm being dead serious, Bower. Ever since I met you, I felt… attached, and I know that might freak you out, but I'm willing to risk it at this point to show you how fucking serious I am. This isn't some conquer-my-sister's-best-friend moment. No, this has been an ongoing crush that has only grown stronger and stronger over the years, especially as we started to get closer. And then when you moved here, well, I've just felt itchy and anxious but so fucking excited because I've been able to steal little moments with you. Little moments that have turned into big moments. The kind of moments I never thought would happen."

"Bennett," I say, feeling completely speechless and slightly bamboozled. *I'm his long-term crush?* Can that truly be possible? So all this time he's been…what, waiting for me? Am I really the reason he hasn't dated?

And if I'm that important to him, why Cougar? *This is crazy.* "I…umm, I don't know what to say."

"You don't need to say anything. I just want you to know where I'm at, in case that changes any of the bad things you're thinking about."

Maybe…just a little. Because there was the fear about this just being some sort of fling for him and then what do I do if I grow attached and then he ditches me for some younger model? What would I say to Gabby?

"I guess it's, umm, it's nice to know where you stand."

"Ask me anytime. My position isn't going to change."

I really don't know what to say to that because it's all so overwhelming. Everything with him is overwhelming, but sometimes in a good way and sometimes in a scary way.

"Maybe…maybe it's good that you're on a long road trip," I say and I can practically hear his disagreement through the silence. "Just so we can give each other a second, you know?"

"Do you need a second?" he asks, trepidation in his voice.

"Honestly, Bennett, I don't know what I need, and I hate that, because I'm the first person to chastise a heroine in a book for not knowing what they want when the hero is so incredible, but now that I'm in this situation, I have so much internal conflict, and I'm just trying to figure it all out."

"I get that." He clears his throat. "Maybe this will help."

Then he hangs up on me.

Wait, seriously?

Did he really just—

My phone buzzes not with a phone call, but with FaceTime.

Oh…

I sit up in my bed and answer the call, his handsome face coming into view, as well as his bare, bulky chest. My mind immediately falls to the feel of him, the comfort he provides, the way I can snuggle into him and feel completely protected from the world.

I let out a dumb sigh and say, "I miss you."

And that stuns me, because it's the first thing that came to mind.

Not the worries.

Not the insecurities.

But rather *him*, just him and what he represents in my life at the moment. Comfort, joy. . . relief.

He smiles softly. "Miss you too, beautiful."

And that nickname. I've never been a big nickname person, but with him, it's different. It feels different, like that word has been held for him by the universe, and the only time it sounds right is when he says it to me.

"Why are you so hot?"

He chuckles, his smile making me yearn that much more.

"You think I'm hot, huh?"

"Are you really going to fish for compliments?"

"When you're unsure and thinking things through, absolutely. I have to give myself some solace from the thought of coming back and you not wanting to see me."

"That would never happen."

"You sure about that?" he asks, placing his hand behind his head, showing off the boulder in his bicep.

Ugh, yum.

"Positive," I say, my eyes roaming on the bits and pieces of skin he's showing off. What I wouldn't give for him to get completely naked and just walk around for me, or better yet, make himself get hard while I watched—

"What the hell are you thinking about?"

"Huh?" I ask, snapping my attention back to him.

"You're licking your lips and staring."

"Am I?"

"You are. I feel like a piece of meat in front of a starving lion."

"Well, you show up shirtless to a FaceTime and that's how you're going to be treated, like a piece of meat. I'm sure it would be the same if the situation was reversed."

"Bower, if you showed up to a FaceTime shirtless, there is no way we'd be jabbering away. No, I'd have you playing with yourself in no time."

I press my hand to my chest. "Phone sex? Honestly, Bennett. Where are your manners?"

"Manners don't exist when the girl you're talking to looks like you."

My cheeks flame from the compliment. "Well, that was very… flattering."

"Wasn't looking to flatter you, was looking to tell the truth."

"I see." I glance away, his honesty so refreshing from anyone else I've ever dated—eh, are we dating? I don't think so, we're just…seeing what happens, right?

"Why the frown?" he asks, not letting me get away with anything. *Quit being so observant, you punk.*

"Nothing," I answer.

"Do you really think the 'nothing' answer is going to work on me? You should know me better than that."

He's right. He'd never let me get away with that.

"Ugh, you're right. So annoying." I wet my lips and then say, "This thing between us, is it dating?"

"I'd prefer for it to be, but I don't want to freak you out because we haven't really established any ground rules. But if I had it my way, yes, we would be dating. And I'd take you out to dinner, worship you, and fucking kiss you whenever I want." He drags his hand down his face. "It's fucking killing me that I haven't kissed you yet."

"You've kissed me in other places."

"Don't fucking remind me. I swear to you there are times when I feel like I can still taste you and I wind up going hard because of it. Fuck, Bower, I was hard at BP this morning."

"What's BP? Is that a social engagement or something?"

He chuckles. "Batting practice, babe. You know, if you're going to consider dating me, you should really get to know some baseball terms."

"I know enough," I say. "I know that you play third and that you hit the ball hard and far, and that the thing on your hand is a baseball glove."

"Wow, who says you need an education in the sport? You could be teaching the course."

I huff on my nails and then buff them off on my shirt. "You don't need to tell me twice. Sign me up. I'll get all the lemons ready to go for the season, which… Is the season almost over?"

"Yeah, heading into the playoffs in a week and a half."

"Oh wow, is your team in it?"

"So far, yup."

"Really? Well, that's exciting. And you're going to play third in those games?"

He chuckles. "Yeah, beautiful, I'll play third."

"Aww, look at you go. Playing third in the playoffs. You are quite the accomplished man."

"Yeah, if only I could get my sister's best friend to fall for me, then I'd truly be accomplished."

CHAPTER 27
BENNETT

"CHORIZO HAS TO BE THE most underrated meat," Nolan says. His mouth is full of breakfast burrito. "No one gives it enough credit."

"That's not true," I say as I suck down a protein drink. "Almost every breakfast burrito has chorizo in it. It's not underrated at all, rather it's used very—"

"Okay, dweeb, enough with the stats," he says before taking another large bite and moaning while exaggerating an eye roll of pleasure.

Why do I hang out with him? It's a solid question that I'm uncertain I could answer.

He dabs at his face with a napkin and then says, "Got one of the worst blow jobs of my life last night." He swallows his food and continues. "It was like she was trying to play my dick like a trombone, which I was into at first, the stroking and sucking at the same time, can't complain, right? But then she started humming."

"Humming can be nice," I say, engaging for God knows what reason.

"Yeah, that's what I fucking thought until I figured out what song she was humming."

"What was it?" I ask.

He places his forearm on the table, glances around the cafeteria, and then leans in closer. "'Seventy-Six Trombones' from *The Music Man*." I'm about to tell him I don't know what song he's talking about, but then he starts humming it for me, the melody familiar in my head.

"Wait, I know that song."

"Everyone fucking knows it. It's catchy as shit. But do you know what is not catchy? Humming it on someone's fucking rock-hard cock. Do you know how difficult it was to maintain an erection while she's down there, turning my dick into an instrument from *The Music Man*?"

I snort, because that shit is pretty funny.

"Difficult," he answers.

"Did you maintain?"

"Of course." He scoffs. "If anything, I'm a goddamn professional and refuse to let a good boner go to waste. So I went with it, and as she was blowing me, I closed my eyes, pictured a band formation, and started marching along. My fear now, though, is that whenever I see a marching band, specifically a trombone, I'm going to get hard."

"But I thought you said it was the worst blow job of your life. Wouldn't a trombone scare you away, rather than turn you on?"

"You would think." He pats me on the shoulder. "But my mind works in crazy ways."

"Don't I fucking know it."

"What about you? Get any good head last night?"

"Dude, you know I'm going after Bower."

"Yeah, but that doesn't mean you have to be celibate."

"No, it doesn't, but I also have no interest in fucking anyone else."

"Does she know that?"

"Yeah, she does."

"And she feels the same way?" he asks. "Because I saw some pictures of her in a coffee house with Cougar, them laughing, looking all cozy."

I scoff. "That shit is old."

He shakes his head. "From two days ago, man."

"What? No, you read it wrong."

"I fucking didn't. I take my celebrity gossip seriously and the girl that

I follow, that is 99.9 percent accurate on almost everything, had pictures of them looking all giddy at a coffee house."

A hint of panic surges through me as I say, "Show me."

"Can't take my word for it, fine." He sets his burrito down, wipes his hand on a napkin, and then types away on his phone until he finds what he's looking for. He turns the phone toward me and I take it from him, zeroing in on the screen and the pictures taken of Cougar and Bower at a coffee house, laughing and looking at her computer together. I glance down at the date and see that it was two days ago, the same day I FaceTimed her.

I shake my head, confused. "This can't be right. She didn't tell me anything about seeing Cougar."

"Do you think she'd say that? Especially when you come off as desperate and needy as you do?"

"Fuck off," I say as I zoom in on the pictures. Shit, they do look happy, like they're having a fun time, and of course, that makes me physically ill. Is she really seeing him and possibly thinking about seeing me at the same time?

Are they actually dating?

Or just talking like me and Bower?

Oh fuck…has he…has he kissed her yet? If the answer is yes, it very well might downright destroy me.

"From the green—ill—look in your expression, I'm guessing this is not what you were expecting."

"Not even fucking a little." I take a screenshot of the pictures and then text them to my phone. Then I toss his phone back to him and bury my hands in my hair. "Fuck, do you think they're dating?"

"I don't know. What has their relationship been like?" he asks. "From what you told me, it was casual, right?"

"Yeah, casual." I think about it for a second, trying to recount what she's told me about them, but I can't fucking remember a goddamn thing.

"At least I thought it was casual. Hell, they were going out on morning dates, like five-thirty kind of shit."

"What the fuck is that?" Nolan shakes his head. "Nah, that's not serious. That's tagging her along."

"Really?" I ask, with a bout of hope I shouldn't cling to, but it's all I have at this moment.

"Yeah, no one serious about dating someone is going to only do morning dates. That's like the courteous date time. Hell, five thirty is not even courteous, that's the pity date. The date you go on, hoping they don't show up."

"I think it's because it's the only time he had available."

"Nah, he could make it work and he's choosing not to. Now, the question is...where is her head at? Also, you might want confirmation where his head is at, because those pictures don't seem like an early morning date. More like lunchtime."

"How can you even tell? They're in a coffee house," I say.

Nolan rolls his eyes as if I'm the biggest fucking idiot he's ever met. He pulls his phone out again and goes to the pictures. "See this guy at the table next to them? Classic ham-and-cheese sandwich with soup. No one is eating that at five thirty in the morning. Easily an afternoon date, and if he's moving her up to the afternoon, then that means she's moving up on his list of interest. When these pictures are taken at night, that's when you need to start shitting yourself."

Yeah, already fucking there.

"How do I get confirmation?"

"Ask Graydon to ask him."

I sarcastically laugh, because imagine. "You really think Graydon St. John is going to ask Cougar about his love life?"

"If the price is right, he might." Nolan takes a bite of his burrito and moans again. "Seriously, I'm going to start campaigning for chorizo."

"It doesn't need a campaign," I nearly yell, frustration taking over. "It's a wildly popular breakfast meat."

Nolan has the burrito halfway to his mouth as he stares at me from my outburst. He slowly lowers it to his napkin on the table and says, "Hey, motherfucker, don't take your frustration out on me. Be grateful I'm here to support you in your time of need." He clears his throat and offers me a bite of his burrito. "To calm your nerves."

Lips pursed, I get up and slam my chair into the table before taking off toward the locker room, my mind whirling with possibilities and my stomach queasy with the idea that she might still be interested in Cougar.

And where is his head at? How convincing is he? Would he be able to win her over, despite the history we have together?

Fuck, why don't I know anything about him?

No, the better question is: Why did I follow Nolan's stupid advice and set them up to begin with?

I pull my phone from my pocket and stare down at the screen, a picture of me and Bower as my wallpaper igniting the simmering rage deep inside me.

Fuck, I have to find out.

No, I need to find out.

And it seems like there's only one way to do so…

CHAPTER 28
GRAYDON
(YES, GRAYDON, JUST GO WITH IT.)

"ONE OF YOUR GLADDY DADDIES texted you," Maple says as she takes a seat on my lap and curls into me as she hands me my phone.

I set my phone down, not giving one shit that they're texting me, because I have my girl in my lap, in my house, sitting on my couch, which means everything is right in the world.

"Are you not going to answer it?"

"Why would I?" I ask, running my hand up and down her back.

"Because it had the word 'help' in capitals."

"It's probably just OC being dramatic about something stupid. Not in the mood."

"I think it was Bennett."

Well, that is different. Still, not in the mood, though.

"I'm sure he's fine." I move my mouth to her neck, kissing her while my hand glides up the back of her shirt.

"Graydon," she says, pulling away to look me in the eyes. "Weren't they the ones that helped you when we were going through a rough patch?"

"No." I bring my mouth back down to her neck or at least attempt to as she pulls away once more.

Goddamn it.

"Graydon, seriously, you should see what he wants."

I love this woman, so fucking much. She's my everything, and one of the reasons I fell in love with her is because of her kind and caring nature. It's sexy as hell, but right now, that attribute is acting as a giant cock block, and I know she won't let this go. That's the kind of person she is, so I grumble and pick up my phone.

Satisfied with my choice, she curls back into me as we read the text together.

Bennett: HELP! Nolan showed me these pictures of Bower with Cougar. They were taken two days ago. I FaceTimed with her that night and it was great. Now I'm worried that she's still seeing him. And I very well might have a heart attack. What do you think is happening in the pictures?

I click on the pictures just as OC texts back. Maple and I examine the pictures together.

"It seems like nothing," I say. "Why is he worried?"

"I don't know," Maple says. "They're leaning in toward each other and she's smiling rather brightly. And..." She zooms in. "Is he staring at her breasts?"

I look a little closer, amazed that she could notice that.

"Only a girl would fucking point something out like that," I say as I open the text thread to read OC's text.

OC: He's fucking staring at her tits! That's what's happening in these pictures.

"Jesus...Christ," I say as Maple laughs.

"What does that say about OC? Perhaps more observant than you."

"Yeah, that's it," I answer sarcastically as my phone buzzes.

Bennett: Fuck, I didn't even notice that. That means he's interested, right?

OC: You're a man, you tell me.

Bennett: Shit. Fuck! What am I going to do? Before I left for my trip, we, uh...we did some things and we've been talking every day. I just assumed that when I got back, we would pick up where we left off, but this, this has thrown a wrench into my plans. Graydon, man, I need your help on this.

"Aww, he sounds so panicky. Answer him."

Grumbling again, because this is not how I wanted to spend my evening, I text him back so I can get this over and done with and get back to my girl.

Graydon: What do you want?

"Graydon, that wasn't nice. He's clearly panicking."

"What?" I shrug. "I asked him what he wants."

"I know, but you could have been nicer about it."

"Maple, that's how I respond. If I sugarcoated it, he'd know it wasn't me."

My phone buzzes again.

OC: He's clearly in pain. He needs your strong chest to cry on. Want to meet up at Graydon's house and talk this through? I can bring muffins.

"Oh, that would be fun," Maple says.

"No." I shake my head. "Not fucking happening. And the fuck if OC is bringing muffins."

I go to type back just as Bennett responds.

Bennett: I'm out of town, you fuck, remember?

Relief washes through me.

OC: Shit, really? Well, uh…Graydon, I'm here.

"What?" I ask, just as the doorbell rings. "Mother…fucker," I growl.

Maple places her hand on my chest and says, "Stay calm."

"Do not let him in, Maple. I'm not fucking kidding. I don't want him in here."

"We can't be rude, Graydon." She starts to get off my lap as the doorbell rings again. I grip her hip, keeping her in place.

"He doesn't know we're home. He could go away."

"I can see your car in the garage," OC yells through the door. "Let me in."

"I'm going to fucking kill him."

"Graydon, please," Maple says, hand on my chest, straddling me now. "We won't keep him long. I'll tell him I have to get to bed early, and as a reward, I'll let you do anything you want to me tonight."

"I was going to do that anyway," I say, smoothing my hands over her perfect ass.

"Yes, but I'll wear whatever you want, maybe even strip for you."

Hell…

She smiles and presses a quick kiss to my lips. "I'll consider the blank stare on your face as a deal."

Then she gets up and goes to the door, where she lets in OC.

"For a second there, I didn't think you guys were going to let me in." OC laughs as he comes into the living room with a pink box. "Brought muffins, big guy." I try to convey through my eyes that one wrong move will find him face first in my goddamn carpet. He slowly nods. "Got it, not happy that I'm here, but might be good for Bennett, because he seems to be struggling."

He takes a seat across from me and flips open the box of muffins before taking one, and I stare him down as he takes a bite like a normal goddamn human—unlike the last time I watched him eat a muffin, which…not going there. I don't want to be reminded.

"Anyway, shall we, uh…text him?"

"Don't mind the growls," Maple says, sitting back down on my lap and placing a soft, promising kiss on my lips that soothes me. "You know how he can get."

"I do," OC answers, eyeing me still.

I go back to the text thread and read Bennett's reply.

Bennett: I know you're going to fucking hate this, Graydon, and you might block me after the ask, but I'm desperate and you should know I'd never ask you to do this unless I was desperate.

"Oh shit, what is he going to ask?" OC asks, before taking another bite of his muffin and crossing one leg over the other, acting as if he's watching a soap opera play out on his phone. "The anticipation is killing me."

Our phones buzz.

Bennett: Could you ask Cougar where he thinks his relationship with Bower is? And ask if he's kissed her? Or fucked her? Or touched her? Or fucking anything? I need to know what's going on.

"Absolutely not." I shake my head and set my phone down.

"Graydon," Maple says with disappointment.

"Really, man. You can practically hear the squeak of desperation in his voice from that one text. It probably took a lot out of him to make that ask. If he asked me, I'd do it."

"Because you're a gossiping ninny with nothing better to do than insert yourself into your acquaintances' lives."

OC's face falls flat. "Acquaintance? Really? That hurts." He leans forward and adds, "Also, 'ninny' is a great word, not even offended. Delighted, actually."

"Jesus Christ. Maple, make this end."

She rubs my chest and softly says, "I think you should do it."

My eyes zero in on hers as I try to convey to her that's *not* happening, but of course, she doesn't take shit from me, and she leans in close to my ear and says, "You know that thing you've been wanting to do with me? If you do this for Bennett, the answer is yes." And then she bites down on my earlobe, making me go fucking hard right in front of the muffin-tonguing nimrod.

I shift, letting her feel just how much that excites me, which of course makes her chuckle into my ear.

"Are you two saying dirty things to each other?" OC asks, watching us with one brow raised and a whole lot of interest on his face.

Maple pulls away and says, "Just making promises if he's a good boy."

"I like the sound of that. What kind of promises? Maybe I can have some input."

"Eat shit and rot," I snap at him, causing him to lean back.

"Jesus. The anger issues are unbecoming," OC says and then holds the pastry box to Maple. "Muffin?"

"I'd love one." She smiles and takes one, unwrapping it while wetting her lips.

Fuck…

Am I really that much of a sucker for her that I'll do anything to make her happy? To make me happy?

She lifts a piece of the muffin to my lips and gently inserts it into my mouth, leaving her fingers for me to suck on for a moment before she drags them away from my lips.

Yup.

I'd do just about anything.

Fuck.

"Fine," I grumble. "I'll do it."

"I knew you had a heart in there," Maple whispers before picking up my phone and texting Bennett back.

Graydon: It's Maple. Graydon would be more than happy to chat with Cougar tomorrow. I'll make sure he reports back with the correct information. As for Bower, if you want, I can introduce myself and kind of feel her out as well, that way you have information from both sides.

"How the hell are you going to do that?" Graydon asks.

"Shhh," she says, pushing more muffin into my mouth. "Let me handle this. I know what I'm doing. You just need to worry about talking to Cougar."

"And how the hell do I talk to him?"

"I'll send you questions. It will be easy."

"I mean...how can you go wrong when you have prepared questions?" OC asks. "Seems like we're all going to win after this."

Maple: Approach him calmly. Ask him how his day is going, how he sees the season faring, and then casually ask about the date you set him up on. Stay light and breezy, and you can't mess this up.

OC: Agreed. Light and breezy, Graydon. Light and breezy.

Graydon: Why the fuck were you included on this text thread?

Maple: I thought it might be helpful.

OC: Yeah, because she sees my value, something you tend to look past every chance you get.

Graydon: I hope you gag today.

I stuff my phone in my pocket, hating every goddamn second of this, and begrudgingly walk over to Cougar, who's currently doing bench presses in the weight room.

"Need a spot?" I ask.

"Sure," he answers. "Thanks."

Not something I'd normally do, but I keep thinking about the promises Maple made me. *That* has propelled me to step out of my comfort zone.

He pumps out four more reps and then I help him set the bar on the rack before he sits up and turns toward me. "Thanks."

"Yeah, sure," I say, awkwardly standing there, unsure how to make the transition from not ever communicating with this guy to his love life.

"You okay?" he asks, eyeing me skeptically.

"Yeah."

"You sure? Because it sort of seems like you're just standing there, like you're either constipated or you want to ask me something."

This is exactly why I didn't want to do this. I didn't want stupid questions. I didn't want to have any sort of interaction, and lastly, I'm not fucking good at this shit. It doesn't come natural to me.

"Are you constipated? Because I have some prunes in my locker. I tend to eat them when I get to the stadium to keep things loose before the game, get all the weight out, if you know what I mean."

Jesus Christ.

"Not constipated," I answer. Just extremely uncomfortable.

"Okay," he drags out. "So then is there something I can help you with? Because you're acting weird."

"No, I'm not."

"You are. You haven't moved. Quite sure you haven't blinked."

I've fucking blinked.

At least I think I have.

Fuck, now I'm super aware of my blinking. Am I doing it too much?

"Uh, are you winking at me?"

"What? No."

"It feels like you are."

This isn't going well. Just ask him and get it over with and get the hell out of here.

"That girl you're seeing, are you fucking her?" I ask rather abruptly.

"Whoa, okay, that came out of nowhere."

"Uh, a requirement from Coach," I say, not really sure what I'm saying because I don't like our coach, nor would our coach ever ask about our sex lives, but here we are. I blame Maple. She did not prepare me enough.

"What is a requirement?"

"Wants to know who is fucking. So, are you?"

His brow furrows, looking so fucking confused. Don't blame him; I'm just as confused. "Why the hell would that matter?" he asks.

"Curfew," I say, just pulling shit out of my ass. "He's, uh, considering it."

"The fuck he is." Cougar stands, anger flashing through him. "Who else knows about this? Because we can cause a scene in his office."

"No one," I say quickly, a hint of nervous sweat beading on my upper lip. Fuck, this isn't going as planned. The last thing I need is Cougar spreading a lie about our coach that started with me. "He asked me to keep it quiet, but because you won't answer the question, I had to tell you."

"Oh." He glances around the weight room. "Well, thanks for keeping me informed. Are you taking care of it?"

"Sure," I say, wanting to add a heavy eye roll, but hold back. "Just answer the fucking question so I can move on."

"Right, uh, am I fucking the girl you set me up with? No. But I have been meeting up with her at lunch."

"Have you kissed?"

"Huh? What does that have to do with anything?"

Great question.

Let me just call up Bennett and fucking ask him.

I grip the back of my neck, frustration pricking at my skin. "Kissing leads to fucking."

"Oh, right. Uh, no, we haven't kissed. It's platonic right now, but I think I want to move it forward. I really like her, and I think she really likes me too. So I guess kissing soon and then fucking."

"Great." Then without a second word, I take off, because I got what Bennett wanted, no need to dive deeper.

"Is that it? What about curfew?" Cougar asks as I walk away.

I spin on my heel and point at him. "Keep your fucking mouth shut about that or I'll make sure it happens."

"Hey." He holds up his hands. "You're the one that told me about it."

"And I'm the one who's telling you to shut the fuck up about it. Now add tens to that weight and get benching. You bounce off defenders like a goddamn lightweight. Put more fucking muscle on."

"Fuck you," he says as I exit, thinking about how much Bennett owes me for that.

And how quickly I'm going to cash in with my girl the minute I see her.

CHAPTER 29
BENNETT

Graydon: They're not fucking. They haven't kissed. He has seen her for some lunch dates. Plans on fucking her.

I READ OVER GRAYDON'S TEXT five fucking times, each time making me more and more ill. I'm also full of rage.

OC: When does he plan on fucking her? Is he going to seduce her first with a kiss and then undress her? Will the fucking happen at her place or his? And did he say no kissing at all, or has there been light nibbling?

Maple: I think no kissing means no kissing at all, but can you clarify, Graydon?

Graydon: How did you get involved in this text thread?

OC: We needed our Gladdy Mommy. She's handling the vagina side of this.

Graydon: Don't fucking call her a Gladdy Mommy or refer to her vagina in any way, you fucking pervert.

OC: Whoa, slow down, big guy.

Maple: Graydon, he wasn't talking about my vagina, and I kind of like Gladdy Mommy, as it makes me feel like I'm part of the gang.

Bennett: Yeah, he was talking about the vagina I want. Don't fucking do that or you'll find my fingers through your eye sockets.

OC: The violence in this group is getting out of hand. I'll have you know, Graydon, I gagged on my fucking toothbrush the other day and I blame you.

Graydon: Good, I hope it happens again.

Maple: Graydon, you're being rude.

Bennett: Can we please get back to what we're supposed to be talking about, for the love of fuck!

Maple: He's right, you two are taking away from the information.

OC: Yeah, Graydon, stop taking away from the information.

Graydon: I swear to fucking Christ…

Maple: Okay, settle down, both of you. From what Graydon told us, we know that they have not been intimate in any capacity just yet, but he wants to move forward. Now what we need to figure out is if she wants to move forward on her end.

OC: Exactly, Mommy.

Graydon: DO NOT FUCKING CALL HER THAT!

For the love of God. I hate them, all of them.

Maple: You said she's going to be at the coffee house on 4th Street, right? I can stop by tomorrow with those cookies and make a special delivery from you like we talked about. Then I'll probe for some information.

Bennett: Thank you, Maple.

OC: Uh, I think you should thank Graydon as well.

Graydon: Not that I want to agree with him, but yeah, where the fuck is my thank you?

Maple: You'll get it tonight. Don't worry. You did good, Graydon.

OC: **Whispers** I think it's sex.

Bennett: Everyone knows it's sex. God, you're so fucking irritating sometimes.

Graydon: Glad you can finally see that. Thought I was the only one.

Maple: He can be quite annoying.

OC: Maple!

Maple: Sorry, OC, it's true. But back to Bennett. I'll get the information you need tomorrow. As for now, go about as if everything is normal.

Bennett: So, should I call her tonight?

Maple: Absolutely. Don't even think about him. Focus on wooing her instead.

OC: Woo the fuck out of her!

OC: Graydon…

Graydon: Jesus. Woo her.

"Hello," Bower says as she answers my FaceTime call. I didn't even bother with texting tonight because I wanted to see her face. Hell, I wanted her to see my face.

I set the phone on the counter, propped up against the bathroom mirror, leaning forward so she can see my face, as well as my chest, flexed abs, and the V in my hips from my low-slung towel.

"Hey, beautiful," I say as I grab some lotion.

"Umm…what, uh, what do you have going on there?" she asks, looking so fucking cute with her hair in a clip and her face freshly washed.

"Applying some lotion. Needed a second shower tonight, as I felt like I didn't get all the dirt off me."

"Mm, well, I don't mind a second shower."

I raise a brow as I rub lotion on my arms. "You getting a free show?"

"Yeah, don't mind if I do."

I'm so fucking confused. This is what it's been like since I've been gone. There's been flirting, some serious conversations that have led me to believe that she'd give this a try, so the whole Cougar thing is throwing me off. I know she spoke to him about dating other people, but that's not going to work for me.

I want her for me, and for me alone.

"I think you missed a spot on your nipple. Might want to rub that again."

I pause, which makes her laugh.

"Go ahead." She bites the tip of her finger. "Rub your nipple for me."

"Bower."

"Huh?"

"I'm not about to rub my nipple for you."

"What if I asked you to rub your dick instead?" she asks.

I'm applying lotion to my stomach when I stop. "Are you serious?"

"I mean, I was joking, but the serious look on your face makes me believe you'd do it."

"I'd do pretty much anything you want," I say, feeling my dick starting to grow hard from the thought of it.

"Besides lotion your nipple, I guess."

"Because how is that sexy to you?"

"Is it sexy to you?" she counters.

I think about it, because if she was standing in front of me, topless, lotioning her nipple, I'd probably have the hardest fucking time keeping my hand off my dick.

"Uh...yeah," I answer, my mouth growing dry the more I think about it.

She chuckles. "That's what I thought. You're too easy, Bennett. Then again, so am I. And I'm so horny. I've been reading this book, and I swear, it's one chapter of plot and one chapter of sex, flip-flopping consistently. I used my vibrator this morning just to ease some of my tension."

My dick grows even harder.

"Why didn't you call me; let me watch?"

"Guess I didn't think about it." She smirks. "Would you have watched?"

"Are you kidding me with that question?" I ask as I pick up the phone and head to the bed, where I whip my towel off and climb under the sheets.

"Perhaps." She smirks and then sets her phone down so I'm staring up at the ceiling.

"Uh, not the view I was looking for."

"I know. Give me a second." I hear her rustle around and then after a few seconds, the phone moves again and seems to be propped up against the lamp on her nightstand, but she's still not in view.

"What are you doing?" I ask just as I hear the sound of a vibrator turn on. "Bower," I groan. "Are you fucking kidding me right now?"

"Do you have a problem with this?"

"Uh, fuck no," I say as I whip off the blankets.

"Then let me see you."

"Uh, you're the one not showing yourself."

"For good reason."

"And what's that reason, because my tongue has been all over your pussy."

"Just...because."

"Valid argument." But because I don't want to ruin this moment and what she's giving me, I decide to give her the full show. I set the phone up on the nightstand and prop it against the lamp as well, then I stand in front of the camera, showing off my entire naked body, erection and all.

"My God, Bennett, you're so freaking hot." She lets out a moan along with a sigh. "Are you going to stroke yourself?"

"Do you want me to?" I ask.

"I do."

"Good, because I'm hard as fucking stone." I start to stroke myself, already turned on to the point that I'm able to use some pre-cum to help my hand glide.

"You have a huge dick, Bennett. I love it."

"Well, you taste like fucking heaven, and I wish you were here right now, because I'd be doing all the work with my tongue, not that vibrator."

"I'd use the vibrator on you," she says, still not showing her face. It's driving me nuts, because I just have to go by the buzzing sound and her breathless tone.

"Where?" I ask, squeezing my dick a little harder.

"I'd love to try it anywhere you'd let me. Would you, Bennett?" She practically moans my name. Fuck, I want to hear it again, just like that, full of desire and need.

"I would, anywhere you fucking liked."

"Mmmm, I love that. I love that you would let me play with you."

"All fucking day, babe," I grunt. "Torture me, edge me, make me beg—whatever you want."

"Would you return the favor?"

"You wouldn't be able to leave until I did."

She moans some more. Her breathing's become erratic, which spurs me on, my legs starting to grow numb.

"Come…forward," she says. "I want…oh fuck, Bennett, I want to see your hand move…" She pauses. "Oh God, I'm going to come. Show me your cock, up close. I want to watch."

I step forward, bringing my cock and hand right into frame, and I start pumping myself, harder, faster. So much that I bend over and place my hand on the nightstand, my abs flexing as my cock strains for release.

"Shit, Bennett, oh God, yes. You're so big. So hot. Fuck!" she screams and then a moan falls past her lips, her orgasm sending her.

"Yes, baby, that's it. Come for me."

"Fuck," she breathes, her vibrator still going, giving me an image of her riding her hips against the device, taking every last ounce of pleasure while her moans continue to fall past her perfect lips.

And it sends me over the edge, my cum shooting all over my hand and down my length while I continue to pump, the image of her face in my head the entire time until I'm completely sated.

That's when she picks up the phone and smiles at me.

I let out a heavy breath and say, "There you fucking are."

She smirks. "I like the thought of you coming, using only the image you can conjure up in your head of me."

"Trust me, been doing it for a while. Nothing new here."

Her cheeks redden as she pushes a stray piece of hair behind her ear. "Well, it was new for me."

"And would you do it again?"

"I think I would." She smiles at me, making me fucking melt. "I'll let you go clean up and get to bed. Have a good night, Bennett."

"Would be better if you were here with me."

"Looks like you'll just have to warm your bed by yourself." She winks and then blows a kiss. "Night."

"Good night, Bower."

I hang up and groan as I go to the bathroom to clean up. That was… unexpected. Amazing. Fucking insane, but was that just because she was horny or because she wanted me?

She didn't show herself. Was that because she was remaining guarded?

I know she hasn't done that with Cougar, but fuck, I feel like she's giving me little inches, but not the whole thing, and it's making me feel nuts. I want all of her, and I'm not sure what it's going to take to earn that.

I know she's had relationships before and I haven't, but is this how it normally is? When Gabby and Ryland committed to each other, they were all in. Am I wrong to expect Bower to be the same? She's said she can't stay away from me, but will that just be physically? Is that all I mean to her?

CHAPTER 30
BOWER

I CAN'T BELIEVE I ORDERED the truck.

I actually put money down and I'm supposed to pick it up in a week. Then I take it to the body shop and get it wrapped. This is all so... intimidating.

And I'm attempting not to feel like a failure, but it feels almost impossible to war with all the emotions.

Either way, I put the money down, I applied for an LLC, and I bought the domain name for The Whimsy Wagon.

I also told Gretchen I was going to need some time to get things set up, but that maybe by next month, I could be the featured bookstore. She seemed okay with that, at least that's what it seemed like after rereading her incredibly curt email of "Sure."

Bennett gets back from his road trip in three days, and part of me is nervous to see him, because I'm unsure what I'll do. I know I shouldn't do anything, maybe offer him a high five and "nice to see you," but I think we all know at this point that is not going to happen, which makes it all so much worse.

I haven't really spoken to Gabby in a week, well, ever since I showed up in Bennett's bed, the night before he left, because I don't know what to say to her. I'm bursting at the seams here with no one to talk to. And I don't want to keep talking to my boss about it, because I'm quite sure she's getting tired of my dramatics. Don't blame her, though. I'm tired of them too.

"Um, excuse me," a woman with blond hair says as she stands in front of me with a box of cookies from one of my favorite bakeries. She looks vaguely familiar, but I don't think I've met her before. "Are you Bower?"

"I am," I say, confused as to how this woman knows me while I sit here in the middle of the coffee shop.

The woman smiles and sets down the cookies. "These are from Bennett. He asked me to bring them to you." She leans forward and holds out her hand. "Hi, I'm Maple. I'm actually Graydon's girlfriend."

"Graydon from the Foghorns?"

She nods. "That very one."

"Wait, you're Flock and Tackle. That's right. That's why you look so familiar. My God, when you two launched your social media together, I was all over that shit. My little romantic heart was going crazy. Ugh, you and Graydon are so cute together."

"Thank you," she says sweetly. "I like to think we're cute together too."

"You got the whole grumpy-sunshine vibe going. Really cute."

"Yeah, he's pretty grumpy. I genuinely believe he only smiles for me at this point."

"But how cute is that? You're the only one who brings him joy. Makes you special."

"That it does. Although, you're pretty special if you have a guy calling in favors to send his girl cookies."

I take a look at the box, my mouth watering from already knowing what's inside. "He had you get these and deliver them? That's a pretty bold ask."

"May I have a seat?"

"Oh, of course, please."

She takes a seat and then says, "It was a bold ask, but I felt like I owed him. He helped out a lot when Graydon and I were going through a dark time. And he said he just wanted to make you feel special, which I thought was cute."

"Well, he did. Do you actually mind taking a picture of me with the cookies and I'll send it to him?"

"Of course," she says as I hand her my phone.

She snaps a picture and I send it over to Bennett with some kiss emoji and a thank-you. When I'm done, I flip open the box, revealing my favorite Twix-flavored cookies. The shortbread base with the caramel and chocolate, ugh, divine.

"Here, have one. They're so good."

"Oh, I don't want to take one of your cookies."

"Do you have the time?" I ask. She nods, so I hold out the box to her. "Then you can have a cookie."

She smiles and then takes one, pulling a napkin from the napkin holder and then setting her cookie down.

"Thank you."

"Have to spread the love. Also, I can't eat all of these by myself. The man keeps feeding me pastries, and I fear it might start showing."

She chuckles. "I doubt it." She takes a bite and her eyes light up. "Oh my God, this is so good."

"You're welcome for your new addiction."

She examines the cookie. "Seriously." Once she swallows, she says, "Honestly, I was surprised Bennett asked me to help him out."

"Oh, why? Are you two not that close?"

"I mean, I wouldn't say best friends, but it's not that. I just thought you were seeing Cougar is all."

"Yeah, I mean, sort of but not really. It's kind of weird."

"I like weird, explain."

Honestly, given all the emotions I've been through, it might help to just get it all out there to someone who doesn't quite know the situation.

"Do you mind if I drama dump on you?"

"Do I mind? Absolutely not. I spend my days with flamingos and then a grump at night. I'd love a little human interaction that involved actually talking."

"Well then, hold on, because I might just word vomit on you," I say as I cross one leg over the other. "Long story short, Bennett is the brother of my best friend. He's eight years younger and I've known him ever since he was sixteen."

"He's twenty-five now? Right?"

"No, twenty-four. But close. He seems so much older, but yeah, there's a significant age gap here."

"But you're friends?"

"Yeah. We used to text a lot because he'd tell me what was going on with Gabby, his sister, and if she needed any help that she wasn't willing to ask for since it was just the two of them. No parents. Anyway, as time went on, we grew closer and closer, and when I moved here, it just felt natural to meet up with him, because we're friends and he's the only one I know in San Francisco."

"Makes sense."

"Well, the first time I saw him, it was like...I was trying to get to know him all over again. And not in the emotional or mental sense, but...physically. He had changed so much that it truly threw me off. I found myself touching him more, holding his hand, hell...sharing a bed because I found comfort in him. Anyway, I really wanted to start dating someone because I thought all these feelings I was developing were because I haven't dated anyone in a while, so I asked him if he could set me up with someone."

"Which is why he went to Graydon and Graydon set you up with Cougar."

I nod. "Yup. And sure, Cougar is hot—he's tall and muscular, but he's kind of...boring. Like it almost feels like there's not much going on up there."

"I haven't actually met him, but Graydon has mentioned something along the same lines." Glad I'm not the only one who noticed.

"We went on a few dates that seemed to be okay. There were good moments and moments that really did nothing for me. But then he ran into me, here, at the coffee house and well, he surprised me."

"In what way?" Maple asks.

"He was thoughtful and endearing, and he cared about what I was doing. He actually helped me out a bit and I realized that maybe I judged him or didn't give him a chance to be himself."

"Ah, I see, so you like him then."

"Well, I don't know. I like him in the sense that he's a nice guy, I think." I ponder that for a second, because what is really wearing me down are the feelings I have for Bennett. I look Maple in the eyes and say, "Can I be completely transparent with you even though I just met you?"

"Please, I can tell you need to talk this through."

"I do and I really don't have anyone to talk to because the two people I'd talk to about this are the two people I can't."

"That's so hard. I'm sorry."

"No need to be sorry. I put myself in this situation." I take a bite of my cookie and sigh as I stare out the window for a moment. "I like him," I say finally. "More than I probably should, and it's eating away at me. I don't know what to do about it."

"Who? Cougar?" Maple asks.

I shake my head. "No, Bennett. I think Cougar is a failed attempt on my part to convince myself that there are other options out there."

"A failed attempt? So are you not going to go out with him anymore?"

"I don't know," I say, so conflicted. "There are things about him that I know I like, and the more I get to know him, the more I see him differently and not as the boring asshole I initially went out with. And he also keeps showing me a different side of him. Makes me think he puts up this front so he doesn't get hurt, you know?"

"Yeah, I get that. When I first met Graydon, I couldn't see past his grumpiness and negativity. But once I got to know his story, once I saw beyond the facade, I couldn't stay away."

"Makes sense."

But I know I don't feel I want to keep delving into Cougar's psyche to see if I'm genuinely missing something I shouldn't miss. Is that the key to this issue? Or do I ignore that?

"But with Bennett, there's no trying. We get on so well. I don't have to peel back the layers. What you see is what you get." I trusted him at Adalade's function. No question. "It's just me and him, and it feels easy and flawless and like it's where I'm supposed to be."

"So then why are you keeping Cougar around?" she asks with curiosity. *Because what if there is no one else out there who would deal with my crazy?*

And that thought just annoys me. I do not *need* a boyfriend to make me feel complete. I know this. I respect women who choose to be single rather than compromise when they don't find someone they desperately love. But I would *love* to find love. Being the person who loves unconditionally is something I crave. I want to build a life with someone and be their person. *I want to feel treasured.*

Maybe, quite possibly, Cougar is not that man for me, but what if we just need more time for things to truly click? He might get into reading eventually. He might become less self-absorbed. What would it harm to spend more time "trying"? He believes I'm girlfriend material, and I feel that's quite transformative thinking.

"Because I know that out of the two of them, he's the one I should be with. Bennett is technically off-limits. And I know that if I were to fully go all in on Bennett, that I'm risking so much—a friendship that means the most to me—and then what if things don't work out? What if I hurt him? That's two people I lose, two people I need in my life." Cougar is the safe option. "Cougar has grown on me. He's the one I know my brain is telling me to go with for now."

"But your heart is telling you otherwise," she says gently. And that does me in. Tears spring to my eyes.

"Fuck, I'm sorry." I grab a napkin and dab at my eyes. "You just met me and here I am, spilling my woes and crying in front of you. Not the kind of delivery you were expecting, huh?"

"I'm actually glad Bennett asked me to deliver the cookies, because I'm always looking for new friends. I moved here recently as well, so it's great to meet new people."

"You did?" I ask, still dabbing at my eyes.

"Yeah, I was living in Peru for a while, researching the flamingos, but the grant ran out, and well, I had to come back. I got a job at the San Francisco Zoo, and that's where I met Graydon. It all worked out and I wouldn't trade it for anything, but I know what it means to have people to talk to when you're going through something."

"Thank you. That means a lot."

"How about this? We exchange phone numbers and maybe we can meet up for coffee or something." She gestures to all my paperwork on the table. "It seems like you're doing a lot and you might need a friend to be there for you."

"I do." I nod, more tears springing to my eyes.

She smiles and then gets out of her chair and comes over to me, offering me a hug. "It will work out. I'm sure you'll figure out a way to make the most of your feelings and what you're going through."

"Thank you," I say just as she releases me. "If you were me, what would you do?"

"That's a tough question, because I don't know the extent of your relationship with your friend. Do you really think she'd be mad at you, or do you think that's something you've developed in your mind? And I don't want that to sound offensive. I just know how I can get sometimes."

"No, I know what you mean. And it's not something I've developed in my head. She outright told me he was off-limits."

"Oh, I see." Maple glances to the side. "That is quite a situation, and I can understand why Cougar seems like the simple option."

"It's the option where people get hurt the least."

"Besides Bennett," Maple points out and it feels like a gut punch, because she's right. He's the one who would get hurt in the scenario where I stop involving myself with him. But maybe...maybe he'd thank me in the long run.

"I think he'd recover," I say, not really believing the words that are coming out of my mouth. "He's young. He has plenty of options. I might be the one he wants now, but I might not be the one that turns out to be his forever, and that's okay."

That sentence, it feels bitter on my tongue, like it doesn't belong there, like I'm allergic to such a thought.

"Well, either way, if you need someone to talk to about it all or just to hang out, or if you ever want to feed the flamingos, I'm your girl."

"Thank you, Maple. I'm so glad Bennett asked you to deliver cookies to me."

She smiles softly. "Me too."

"Surprise!"

I nearly fall down the stairs of my apartment building when I see Gabby waiting outside.

"Oh my God, Gabby, what...what are you doing here?"

"Ryland's sisters had to come here for a meeting about expanding their store into a possible little pop-up that involved meeting with Hattie's best friend's husband, and well, you get it, they had to come here and I begged to catch a ride. I'm here for a few hours. Want to grab lunch?"

"Uh, yeah," I say, still shocked as she screeches and comes up to me, pulling me into a hug. Fear washes through me, because the last time I saw her, I hadn't touched her brother the way I have now and I feel like she can see it all over my face.

When she pulls away, she asks, "Where do you want to go? We can either find a place or we can eat in and just hang out at your apartment."

Fuck, is there anything in my apartment that would make her think I went down on her brother and sucked him until he came in my mouth?

I can't remember, therefore, I don't want to risk it.

"There's actually a great sandwich shop around the corner that I'd love to take you to."

"Sounds perfect." She loops her arm through mine and says, "Lead the way."

Trying to calm myself and remain as cool as possible, I make our way down the street and to the right while she clings on to me.

I should feel excited, thrilled that my best friend is here, but instead, it's like a giant elephant is crushing my chest, making it nearly impossible to breathe, because I broke her trust. I'm deceiving her and that...that fucking hurts. And seeing her in person, it just brings the truth of it all to the forefront.

No more hiding.

Now I just have to lie to her face.

"So what's been going on?" she asks. "Anything fun and exciting happening? I feel like we haven't chatted in forever."

"Yeah, been quite busy," I say, swallowing the lump that's in my throat.

Do not fucking cry, Bower. Get through this lunch, cry after, but do not break down in front of her.

"Adalade putting you to work?"

"Yeah, and I've been working on that book truck thing."

Gabby perks up. "Really? Oh my God, tell me more."

"So he helped you find a truck?" Gabby asks as she dips her spoon into her squash soup. We both went for the squash soup and grilled cheese, something I knew she'd like. And then we opted for water.

I've kept the conversation pretty neutral, focusing on anything and everything but Bennett, so that's why we're talking about Cougar now.

"I mean, I narrowed it down to two and then he pointed out the difference between the tires. It was helpful, and he offered up the idea of the truck being the mascot in the logo. Just supportive all around."

"Sounds like a bunch of green flags to me." She wiggles her brows.

If only she knew.

Cougar is a combination of green, beige, and red. Red flags as in warnings to me that I don't believe there is much chemistry there, but then again, it feels like all my chemistry is pent up and just explodes whenever I'm around Bennett.

"When are you two going out again?"

"Um, I think tomorrow night," I say. "He asked me out."

"Ooo, that's exciting. And you said you two haven't kissed or anything, right?"

"Yeah, we've been taking it slow, but it's been nice, because I've been able to get to know him, and that feels important."

"Very important. I got to know Ryland while his dick was in me, but it seemed to work out." She winks, causing me to laugh. "Oh look, you do know how to laugh."

"What do you mean by that?" I ask.

"I don't know. You just seem off."

Because I think I like your brother and I don't know how to handle that.

I'm trying to push him away, but I don't want to.

"Bennett feels off too."

My skin crawls to attention as the back of my neck heats up. "Really?" I ask, the lump in my throat growing, my emotions starting to tug on my resilience. "What, uh, what makes you think that?"

"Just hasn't been as talkative. I called him the other night after his game and he was really rushed with me. Seemed like he had somewhere else to be." She gasps and then says, "Oh God, do you think I called him while he had a girl in his hotel room?"

And just like that, I feel like I'm going to throw up.

The thought of Bennett with someone else actually causes me physical pain. His lips on someone else, his hands...his cock.

Him panting, sweating, writhing with another woman, I can't...God, I can't even think about it.

"That would make him get off the phone quickly. Don't blame him, though, talking to his sister would probably dampen the mood. But I'm glad he's getting out there. I mean, I'd prefer him not randomly sleeping with women, because I don't want him getting caught up in something he can't handle, but I do think he needs to let loose."

"Yeah, that, uh, that's probably good for him."

"How is he doing?" she asks, laying her arm on the table and leaning slightly more forward. "I worry about him a lot. I know he's doing well with baseball, but sometimes I wonder if he's having a real life outside of baseball. He's been grinding for so long. I want him to let loose."

"I get that. He, uh, he seems like he's doing fine," I answer, keeping my mouth shut about the dinner I took him to, the dry-humping, the fingering, him going down on me only for me to reverse it and go down on him. Not to mention the phone sex.

Fuck, I'm the worst friend in the world. She'd hate me if she knew.

"I'm just glad you're here to watch over him and make sure he's okay. Being so far away, I worry, you know? I don't know what I'd do without you."

"Yup." I wet my lips and stare down at my soup.

"Hey." She touches my arm. "Everything okay?"

Don't cry.

Don't fucking cry.

Instead, I plaster on a smile and look up at her. "Everything is great. Sorry, my mind is just getting lost in thoughts."

"In Cougar thoughts." She chuckles and then winks before taking a sip of her drink.

Yup…in Cougar thoughts.

Be casual, but get in and get out. Don't say anything you'll regret. Gabby is counting on you.

Bower: Thank you for the cookies. I'm trying to control myself. I've only had one and I put the others in the freezer.

Bennett: You're welcome. Maybe when I get back, we can defrost two and have them together.

Bower: Maybe.

Bennett: Why doesn't that sound very promising?

Bower: Nothing we need to talk about now. I actually have a lot to do. Just wanted to shoot you a quick text to say thank you. Good luck tonight.

Bennett: Wait, Bower, is everything okay?

Bower: Yeah, it's fine.

Bennett: Why doesn't it sound fine? Can I call you?

Bower: No, I really have things to do. I'll talk to you later.

Bennett: Bower, wait, talk to me. What's going on? Was it the cookies?

Bennett: Bower, please pick up your phone.

Bennett: Please.

Bennett…I can't. Your sister is counting on me. I just…I can't.

CHAPTER 31
BENNETT

I FLEE FROM THE LOCKER room, needing some space from everybody, and I walk down the hall of the home team's stadium and find a quiet spot where I lean against the wall and then sink down to the floor.

What the hell happened from last night to just now?

The only person that would be able to tell me other than Bower is Maple, because she was the one who saw her today.

So I send a text to the group thread.

Bennett: OC, I'm going to have to ask you to please not be dramatic right now. I can't fucking take it, please. Maple, I need to know what happened when you delivered the cookies, because Bower is pretty much detaching from me right now.

I wait for a few seconds and OC is the first to respond, of course.

OC: What do you mean?

Bennett: She thanked me for the cookies and then she just blew me off. Didn't want to talk, said we could talk later. I don't understand.

OC: Fuck, that's not how we wanted things to go.

Graydon: Hold on, Maple is finishing up some supplements for the flamingos and then will respond. But she did say she learned some things that could be helpful...possibly hurtful.

"Fuck," I say, dragging my hand over my face. Why did we have to have a ten-day away trip now? Why? Right when I was making fucking progress with her. I know this is the second-to-last game tonight, and then we have an afternoon game that will get us home earlier tomorrow, but fuck, it feels like a goddamn eternity.

My phone buzzes again and Maple is the one who texts. Thank fuck.

Maple: First of all, she's so sweet and kind. We exchanged information so we can meet up once in a while, as we both thought we needed to make more friends. I want to be honest about that, because moving forward, if she's trusting me as a friend, I don't want to give away her secrets.

OC: An honest woman.

Yeah, but not fucking ideal for me.

Maple: I will say this. She's really torn. She really likes you, Bennett, more than she said she should, but your sister is getting in the way of those feelings. And Cougar, well, she has grown to know him better throughout the weeks that they've hung out and she said recently he's been really helpful and she's seen a different side of him.

Graydon: Their relationship is platonic.

Maple: Which means she's getting to know him on a different level and vice versa. She finds him funny at times, and he's starting to let his guard down and show his true self, which is what she likes. But when she's with you, it's different. There's comfort there, like that's where she belongs. She's very conflicted.

I tug on my hair, my mind fucking going crazy as my body itches with annoyance. What would have happened if I never actually set her up with Cougar? Did I really fuck this up for myself? Am I the fucking reason why I'll never truly have a shot with her?

OC: But did it seem like there was a chance for Bennett?

Maple: It did, but I could see her pulling away. I could see her sparing him from the disruption everything would cause. I don't know how helpful this is, Bennett, but I know there are feelings there for you. It just depends on if she will allow herself to feel them or not.

OC: How do we get her to feel them?

Graydon: I think he pushes for it. I don't think he lets up, because when I was pushing Maple away, that's what she did. She hung on, knowing there was a future there. Bennett, you need to do the same.

Maple: I agree. I think you fight. If you really like her, and I know she likes you, then you need to make her understand that you both can work through her fears.

OC: Agreed. I don't think this is over. I think this is just the beginning and how you handle this moving forward will set the tone for your relationship. Fight, man. Fucking fight.

I let out a deep breath and rest my head against the wall, letting their words sink in and calm my raging nerves. They're right, if I want this, then I need to fight. I need to show her that I'm the one. And the minute I get back from this away trip, that's exactly what I plan on doing.

The phone rings and rings and rings.

"Hey, you've reached Bower. Sorry I missed your call, but feel free to leave a message and I'll get back to you as soon as I can. Thanks."

I clear my throat as the phone beeps, telling me to leave my message. "Hey, Bower, it's me. Wanted to give you a call after my game, see how you were. Our texts earlier left me worried, so I'm just checking in. Give me a call when you can. See you soon."

I jump off the treadmill after warming up my legs, needing to get nervous energy out this morning, and I grab my phone and head toward the locker room. Last night we lost. I played like shit, and we're so close to making the playoffs. We're in a tie right now for the wild card seed, barely hanging on by a thread. It would be incredible if we made it, given everything the team has been through, but then again, we're still a little disconnected and we make a shit ton of mistakes we shouldn't.

Staring down at my phone, I check to see if there are any messages from Bower, and when I see nothing, I know that she's avoiding me, because she'd have at least texted me by now. I try not to let it bother me, but instead, keep pushing forward like Graydon said.

So I call her.

It rings and rings and rings and just when I think it's going to voice mail, she answers.

"Hello?"

"Hey, Bower," I say, feeling awkward all of a sudden, like I'm back in high school trying to talk to a girl.

"Hey, uh...how are you?"

"Doing better now. Just wanted to call and see how you're doing."

"Fine," she says, sounding weird. Not her normal, bubbly self.

"You don't sound fine."

There's silence for a moment, and then I hear a sniffle, and my heart nearly rips out of my chest as I pause in the hallway.

"Bower," I say, panic in my voice. "What's going on?"

"It's nothing, I'm sorry, I'm just…fuck, I need to go."

"No, don't fucking hang up, Bower. I'm not kidding. Tell me what's going on."

"Bennett, I can't…I can't do this and I'm sorry. I know…I know you have feelings for me, but it's just so complicated and I don't want you to get hurt—"

"Then what the hell are you doing? You're seriously going to tell me this over the phone?"

"Because you come home tonight and I don't…I don't want you to…to…"

"To what?"

"To think that, that there's something between us."

"But there is and you'd be lying to my fucking face if you told me otherwise."

"I know, but I think we just need to have some…some distance, okay? That's why I answered the phone, to tell you that we shouldn't, umm…we shouldn't—"

"Say it to me without crying, Bower. Tell me to leave you alone without crying."

She sniffs, takes a second, and then I hear her crying again.

"You can't. You can't fucking say it, because you don't want to say it."

"Bennett, please."

"It's not over, Bower. I don't know what has happened in the last twenty-four hours, but I'm not going to let you just push me away when I know you don't want to."

"Please don't make this harder. I just…I just need space. Okay?"

"No."

"Bennett..." She starts crying again, and the sound rips me in half. I don't want to upset her, but I'll be damned if she's going to choose this future for us.

"It's not over, Bower. Not even close. And I will not allow you to push me away without looking me in the eyes and doing it. You owe me more than that."

"I...I can't do this." And then she hangs up. Disappointment rushes through me.

I stare down at my phone, at the picture of me and her that I have on my wallpaper, my grip tightening.

This is not fucking over.

Over my dead body will I allow her to end us, especially without a solid explanation.

I head back to the locker room just as my phone buzzes in my hand. My heart leaps in my chest, hope spiraling through me that it's Bower calling back, but instead, it's Gabby.

I sigh and lean against the wall as I answer the phone. "Hey, Gabs."

"Oh my goodness, as he lives and breathes. I didn't think you still talked to your big sister anymore."

"Sorry, things have been crazy." I push my hand through my hair, my mind still racing over Bower.

"I know. Playoff run is hard. But you're almost there."

"Yeah, pretty close. We have to win this afternoon," I say on automatic.

"You will. Although, what happened last night? Not to make you feel bad or anything, but yikes, brother."

"Not my best showing. Put in some extra work this morning, though, warmed up my legs and about to hit the cages to focus on some extension in my swing."

"Smart. You always put in the work. It will pay off. Ryland also said you're slicing a little, pulling your shoulder out before you should. Keep it tight."

"Tell him thank you. I'll work on that in the cages."

"I know you will. By the way, I was in San Francisco yesterday. It's a shame you're on a long away trip. I could have stolen you away for a second."

"Wait, you were?" I ask. "Did you see Bower?"

"I did," she says. "We had lunch at a sandwich shop around the corner from your apartment building. The soup was so freaking good, and Bower caught me up on everything she's doing. Her book truck and how she put in an order for it, and the name, ugh, so cute. Oh, and she showed me the logo that Cougar helped her with." A spike of anger shoots up my spine from the mention of his name. Hell, from the mention of the book truck and how she's done so much, apparently, and not said a goddamn word to me.

"Cougar helped her?" I ask, trying not to say it with a clenched jaw.

"Yeah, he helped her pick out the truck and offered suggestions for the logo. Seems like they're getting along nicely. It's good to see her find someone. I know she's been looking to be in a relationship for a bit, and Cougar, he's a good one. It's so sweet that you set her up."

My tongue glides over my teeth as I try not to break a fucking blood vessel. "Yeah, didn't, uh, didn't know things were getting serious for her."

"Well, from what she told me, they're taking it slow, but I think that's how the best relationships form—well, besides me and Ryland, but we are the exception. Anyway, I asked her if she was going to bring the book truck out to Almond Bay and she said she was considering it. She might move. Isn't that amazing?"

Consider me fucking blindsided, because what the actual hell is happening?

I leave for ten days and feel like my entire life just exploded in front of my face.

"Bennett?"

"Yeah, sorry, uh, one of the guys was asking me something. That's, uh, that's great. Hey, I hate to cut this short, but I think it's my turn in the cages."

"Yeah, of course. Just glad to hear your voice. Maybe next time I'll catch you in San Francisco."

"Totally. Love you, Gabby."

"Love you too. Kill it today."

"I will."

Then we hang up and for the second time in ten minutes, I lean against the wall of the tunnel and slide down to the ground. My world's crumbling around me, and I have no idea how to fucking stop it.

I just need to get home.

I need to get home and see her and fix all of this.

CHAPTER 32
BENNETT

I DON'T THINK I'VE EVER raced off a plane the way I did once we landed after our game.

We won, but I didn't give a fuck. I was rushing all my teammates in the locker room after, getting them on the plane, saying people wanted to get home to their families and the short hour-and-a-half flight felt like fucking five. Once we landed, I bolted and told Nolan to grab my shit for me, and thankfully he agreed to it. *And without the expected theatrics.*

It's now eight at night, I'm flying through my neighborhood and booking it up to my parking spot, where I throw my car into park and then get out, locking it as I hustle over to the elevator, with one thing on my goddamn mind: Bower.

I just have to talk to her.

Once I talk to her, then everything will be okay.

I fucking know it.

I get in the elevator, punch the number of her floor, and then rapidly press the close door button on the elevator that I swear doesn't work.

As I ascend the building, I think about what I'm going to say to her, how I'm going to approach her, possibly even beg if I need to. I'm not opposed to it.

The elevator doors part and I make my way around the corner to her apartment, where I step up to the door, take a deep breath, and raise my hand, about to knock—just as it opens, surprising me.

"Oh, Bennett," Bower says, shocked and looking fucking gorgeous in a red dress that forms to her stunning frame. Her hair's curled in droopy waves and red lipstick paints her lips, making them look irresistible.

"Bennett, my man," a guy says, stepping in behind her. *Fuck.* "Dude, I'm so glad I'm seeing you in person." Cougar comes up to me and pulls me into a hug. "Thanks for hooking me up with your friend. Seriously, you did me a real solid."

When he releases me, I feel like he's taken every ounce of breath straight from my lungs.

"Bennett, you're back," Bower says, seeming uncomfortable.

"I am," I say, looking between the two of them, clearly on their way out to a date. "Uh, Bower, can I talk to you for a second?"

"We're actually on our way out," Bower says.

"It's okay, sweetheart," Cougar says. "I'll pull the car around." Then to my fucking horror, he leans in and presses a kiss to her cheek before patting me on the back. "Meet you downstairs."

Then he takes off, leaving me in the hallway with Bower, looking so damn fine, but not for me. For another man. The thought of that breaks me inside.

"I don't want to keep him waiting," Bower says, shifting on her feet, unable to look me in the eyes.

I don't know how to handle this. I wasn't expecting to find her going on a date with another man. Out of all the scenarios I ran through in my head on the plane ride back home, they never involved this, so I've lost all ability to speak. I'm so fucking caught off guard.

I want to tell her that I'm the man for her.

That she needs to give me a chance, to show her that we can make this work.

That there is no one on this fucking planet who is going to treat her the way I will.

That we're meant to be together, and the sooner she realizes that, the better.

But every time I try to form a sentence, the pain of seeing her with another man, calling her sweetheart, kissing her...an aching pain I've never felt before ricochets around my ribs, nearly bringing me to my knees.

"Bennett, I really need to get going." She looks me in the eyes, and when I don't say anything, she starts to walk past me, but I stop her, my hand to her stomach, pulling a small gasp from her lips.

"Don't," I say, my voice raspy, full of emotion. "Don't go."

"I have to."

"No," I say. "You don't have to go, Bower. You can stay here, with me, we can figure this out."

"Bennett, you know—"

"I like you," I say, turning toward her now and gently moving her up against the wall, cradling her beautiful face in my hands. "I like you so fucking much, Bower. You've always been the girl I've wanted, but I've been waiting for my turn to make a move. To show you that I deserve you, and I know I've taken so long, but I wanted...I wanted to make sure you'd give me a chance." Nerves bloom in me as I find my words and throw my heart out on the goddamn table. "I want you, no one else. It's always been you, and I'm begging you to just give me that chance, to show you I'm the man you need."

Her lip wobbles as she tries to look away, but I don't let her. I keep her eyes on me.

"Please, beautiful. Stay with me. I know you. I know there's still so much more for me to get to know, but I want to be the one who champions you. I want to support all your dreams and walk beside you. I want to enjoy reading books with you, pleasuring you when you need it. Let me be the one to spoil you, to worship you. Let me be the one that gets to sleep next to you and wake up next to you in the morning. You're it for me,

Bower. No one will ever own my heart like you do." I press my forehead against hers, our noses almost touching. "Don't go out with him. Be with me, Bower. With me."

She tugs on the corner of her lip, her indecision written all over her face.

"Please," I whisper, one hand on her cheek, the other on her hip.

"Bennett...I...I can't," she says, breaking the contact between us and moving to the side.

"Bower, you can't leave. You don't like him. I know you don't."

She walks backward, swiping at her eye, where a tear almost crests over. "It doesn't matter, because you and me, it can't happen. I need to move on."

"But I know you don't want to or else you wouldn't be this upset. Please, Bower."

She pauses, her eyes watering as she takes a step forward, hesitant, so I help her to close the distance as well.

"Bennett...I..."

"Just give me a chance, please, baby."

Her hand falls to my chest, her eyes searching mine, so much indecision heavy in them.

"I want you, all of you, no one else," I say as her hand crawls up to my neck. "I promise I'll take care of you, be the man you deserve."

Her watering eyes search mine as she cups my cheek.

She wets her lips.

"Please," I whisper, feeling defeated in the worst way possible.

And then, she leans in and presses the softest fucking kiss to my lips, so soft that I barely feel it, making it seem like I'm living in some sort of fever dream before she pulls away.

"Please just let me be," she says before releasing me and stepping back. "Let me go, Bennett."

And then she's gone.

Leaving me completely heartbroken.

I got so close…and she just took it all away.

"Thanks," I say to OC, who hands me a beer and then takes a seat next to me on the couch.

After Bower left and I gave her a solid ten minutes, sitting outside her door, to change her mind, which she never did, I texted OC and asked him to meet me at Maritime, because if I am going to be in anyone's company, it's going to be with the guy who is also nursing a broken fucking heart.

"What happened?" he asks, leaning back on the couch with me as we stare out at the crowd.

"She's out with Cougar, after I begged her not to go. After I basically tore my heart out of my chest, handed it to her, only for her to push it away and leave. But not without dusting a feather of a kiss across my lips."

"Oh fuck," he says, sipping his beer. "Dude, that's…that's brutal."

"Yeah, I know." I take a large gulp of beer, not interested in getting drunk tonight, but also not fighting the idea either.

"What did you say to her when you were begging?"

"I told her all the things I've been dying to say to her but have never said out of fear that it would scare her away, and well, it did exactly that."

"I don't think it scared her away," he says. "She wouldn't have kissed you if it did."

"True."

"Why do you think she kissed you?"

"Because she likes me," I say, knowing deep in my soul that it's the truth. "There's no doubt where her feelings are. She wouldn't have been so emotional if she didn't like me. She's just not going to take the leap and risk it to be with me, and I think that's what fucking hurts the most. Because I'd take the leap. I'd do just about anything to be with her."

"That's because you're in love. Did you tell her that? Did you tell her you love her?"

I shake my head. "Nope. Thought that would be a surefire way to get her to run as fucking fast as she could away from me. At least when I told her I liked her, she just walked."

"Shit, dude. That's brutal. I'd like to say that the pain slowly eases, but I'm still living in it. At least Bower just went out on a date. My girl is getting fucking married to someone else."

"With my luck, Cougar is proposing tonight." I drag my hand over my face. "Fuck. I feel sick." I set my beer down and rest my forearms on my thighs. "As much as I'm grateful you're here, I think I want to be alone."

"I get it," he says.

"Sorry for dragging you out here."

"Don't apologize. I'll grab a car with you."

"Sure."

Together, we head out of the bar as he types away on his phone before handing it over so I can enter in my address. As we wait outside, I stick my hands in my pockets and look around.

"Where the fuck do you think he took her? Do you think she's snuggling into him, whispering into his ear?" I clench my hands in my pockets, wanting to punch my hand through the fucking brick wall behind me.

"Thinking about them together is not going to do you any good. Been there, done that."

"He doesn't even fucking deserve her," I say, my anger getting the best of me. "He doesn't know her like I do. He doesn't understand what she likes and doesn't like, but then he's able to fucking help her with her book truck idea. Fuck!" I yell as I tug on the brim of my hat, starting to lose it as the pain and the unknown collide together, creating a war within me.

"Car service is here," OC says as he nods toward a black Suburban.

We both get in the car, but I sit in the far back, away from the driver as OC joins me.

"Can you turn up the music up front, man?" OC asks the driver.

"Sure thing," he says, moving the music to the front so we can talk softly and he can't hear us.

"I'm not in a good headspace, man," I say, my leg bouncing, my energy dark, pushing me to make a mistake, to do something I shouldn't.

"That's why you need to get home and just fucking chill. Take a shower and then start at it with a clear head tomorrow."

I grind my teeth together. "I don't think I'll get any goddamn sleep tonight. I'm buzzed, ready to wear through a goddamn wall, do damage. I want to do damage. I want to feel pain other than the pain that's tearing at my heart right now."

"I get that, more than anything. But it's not going to help, and the last thing you need right now is bad press. Gretchen would lose her shit."

"Fuck Gretchen."

"Yes, I agree. Fuck Gretchen, but Graydon would say the same thing. You need to handle this internally. Texting me was smart. In the morning, you can text Graydon and get his advice as well, but taking this out in public, making a scene, not fucking smart, man. That's how professional careers plummet, and what's going to hurt more than not having the girl is not having the girl and losing all the hard work you put into getting to where you are."

I know he's right. If I did something stupid, like lose my shit in public, it could have severe consequences and ruin the years of sacrifices and hard work that becoming a professional baseball player required, as well as all the sacrifices Gabby made for me. And I couldn't do that to her.

So even though I'm itching to just take someone out for no other reason than expelling energy, I know I need to go back to my place, sit on my goddamn hands, and just stare at a wall until I'm calm.

Not wanting to talk, I spend the rest of the car ride staring out the window, trying not to let my mind race to that red dress she was wearing, or how that red lipstick would transfer over to Cougar when she kisses him, or how she might get out of that dress later.

Instead, I attempt to practice steady breathing while OC reads me an article about Maple and Graydon and their social media presence, something I couldn't give two shits about at the moment.

When we pull up to my apartment building, I offer OC a nod with a curt thanks and then get out of the Suburban before heading up the steps to my building.

What if the date was shit and she's home already?

What if I run into them in the hallway?

What if they came back early and she invited him to her apartment and they're there right now, fucking making out on the goddamn bed I got her?

I punch the elevator button to go up and immediately get in, pressing the button to my floor. Someone asks me to hold the elevator, but I pretend I don't hear them as I click on the button to shut the doors sooner. Thankfully it works this time.

As I ride up the elevator, I'm tempted to call Gabby, to grill her on what else Bower told her about her life and to ask what the hell Gabby said that would make Bower have this complete one-eighty. She was sucking my dick off before I left, and now she's on a date with another man.

How the fuck does that work?

When I reach my floor, I unlock my door, and I don't bother turning the lights on as I toss my keys and wallet on the table next to the door, lock up, and then head straight to my bedroom, where I flip the light on, only to find Bower curled up on the bed, wearing a pair of shorts and a T-shirt.

Holy fuck, she's...she's here.

In my bed.

Not with him.

Chills spread across my limbs from the mere sight of her, that's until

I notice her tear-stained cheeks and bloodshot eyes highlighted by the lamp on the nightstand.

Did he do this to her? I'm going to fucking kill him.

I rush over to her and sit on the bed, placing my hand on her hip as I say, "What did he do to you?"

She shakes her head, more tears streaming down her face as she says, "Nothing, he did nothing."

"Then why are you crying?"

Realization doesn't quite hit me that she's here, in my apartment, out of that dress, no makeup on her face, and looking like she's been crying for an hour, but she is.

She's fucking here.

What does that mean?

Whatever it is, I can't get my goddamn hopes up, because I don't think my heart can take getting dragged twice, well...three times in one day.

"Bennett." She sniffs and wipes at her eyes. "I...I think I'm falling for you." My breath escapes my lungs from those six words.

I think I'm falling for you.

Fuck, how I bled to hear those words from her, for so damn long, and now that she's said them, it doesn't feel real.

"And I can't stop that feeling, no matter how hard I try or what I tell myself."

My heart hammers in my chest, joy ready to burst out of me, but I hold back, because she's crying about it, which means she could say the words but still take them away from me. Like she did only a few hours ago. *"It doesn't matter, because you and me, it can't happen. I need to move on."*

She shakes her head, tears spilling down her cheeks. "I can't like you, Bennett. I fucking can't, but every time I breathe, I swear I can smell your cologne. Every time I eat something, I swear I can taste you on my tongue. And every time I close my eyes, you're there, in my dreams, waiting to hold me, love on me. You're everywhere, no matter how much I try to avoid it and it's...it's plaguing me. Eating me alive, making it so I can't even function without thinking about your smile or the way you touch me. Just make it stop. Please...please make it stop." She starts sobbing and then pulls her knees to her chest and buries her head in her hands. "I want it to stop."

Fuck.

That kills me.

I can't take seeing her like this, in so much pain. As much pain as I was in, this is worse. This makes me ache in a way I've never felt before, like someone is slowly, torturously ripping out my heart one second at a time, tugging and pulling so slowly that I feel every last ounce of agony.

I need it to stop. I can't see her like this, feeling like this, so I do the one thing I know to do. I kick off my shoes and socks and then slip under the covers and pull her onto my lap, where she curls into my chest and fists the collar of my shirt as she continues to sob.

I rub my hand soothingly up and down her back, kissing the top of her head, and trying to take that pain away from her any way that I know how.

I try to ease her agonizing.

I try to make it fucking better even though I don't know how.

She likes me but doesn't want to. That's a hard reality to face, because I want nothing more than to take her and make her mine. But she wants me to give her up, and I just don't know if I can do that. She lives and breathes under my skin, always. I'll never be able to shake her.

"I don't want to like you, Bennett."

"I know," I say calmly.

"I don't want to think about you."

"I know," I repeat, her words like a knife slashing over my chest.

"I don't want to have this burning ache inside of me every fucking time I see you." She lifts up, her eyes glossy with tears, her lips trembling. "But I do. I need you. These last ten days were torture. I thought about you all the time and wanted you here, with me, right here, in your bed."

"I wanted that too, baby," I say softly, my hand slipping under her shirt to rub her bare back. "I was agonizing over not seeing you every day."

Her lip trembles some more as tears spill down her cheeks. "I can't have you. I can't...have any part of you. Not these strong, comforting arms. This handsome, sincere face. These soft, addicting lips..." Her fingers brush over my face, her breath catching as she stares at my mouth. "I can't have any of it, but I want it. I want you, all of you. I want to be able to stop pretending like I don't feel anything, because I do. I feel so much for you, Bennett."

"Then allow yourself to feel—"

She shakes her head. "I'll lose Gabby. I can't lose her. And I promised her I'd take care of you, watch over you. I promised, Bennett. From when I first met her, I told her I'd be by her side, helping her with you."

My brow furrows. "I don't need to be taken care of. I'm a grown-ass man who can make my own choices, and it's about time she realizes that and you realize that because I choose you, Bower."

She continues to shake her head. "Don't...please, don't say that. Please."

I can see her will slipping, her wall cracking, and maybe this is not the right thing to do, given her moral dilemma, but to hell with it if I'm going to let a promise she made to my sister dictate what happens between us.

I slip my finger under her chin and force her to look me in the eyes. On a deep breath, I say, "You're it for me. Where I'm concerned, I'm done searching. I've found who I want, and I won't let some idle promise stop me from taking what I want. I'm not going anywhere, Bower, and I'm not going to stop." And then, I take a risk and bring my mouth to hers, a centimeter apart, waiting for her to say no, to stop me, but when she doesn't say anything, I press my lips to hers and feel her melt into me the moment our mouths connect.

She moans softly, the sound so sweet, so fucking sexy while she shifts on my lap, straddling me. Her hands fall to my face, where her thumbs

slide off my cheeks and her mouth opens while kissing me, intensifying our connection.

Fuck, she tastes amazing.

Feels amazing.

And as she continues to kiss me, dragging her tongue across mine, light bursts behind my eyelids, like fireworks setting off all throughout my body, igniting something deep inside me that feels like I've been repressing for so long.

My hands fall to the hem of her shirt and slide underneath the fabric, where my palms grip her sides and my thumbs land just below her breasts.

Euphoria takes hold of me as our tongues tangle, my mind realizing that this is what I've been dreaming about for so long, and it's so much better than I ever could have imagined. She's so good at kissing. She's soft but demanding with her tongue. She takes her time but then rushes quickly when she wants more. She's relaxed but then tenses when her hips shift over my growing erection.

My hands slide higher up her shirt, connecting with the underside of her bare breast, pulling a moan from her as she lifts away for a moment, our eyes connecting. And then to my surprise, she lifts her arms over her head and I take that as a sign to take her shirt off. So I grab the hem and slowly pull it over her head until her torso is completely bare to me.

My eyes fall to her chest, to her perfectly round, full tits.

Fuck.

Me.

"Jesus Christ, you're so hot." I cup her breasts, letting my thumbs trail over her hardening nipples. Her head falls back as she moans and her hips shift over my hardened cock, rocking ever so slightly, making me break out in a sweat, because I need this. I need her. To be inside of her. Claim her, let her know she's mine and no one else's.

So I tip her to her back and hover over her as I yank my shirt over my head and deposit it to the side. Her eyes fall to my torso as her hands trail to my jeans. She pauses before she undoes them and then with her feet, pushes them down my legs. I finish taking them off only to go back to her, where she pushes down my boxer briefs as well, freeing my cock.

Once those are off, I lean down and press kisses all along her neck, her chest, and then take her right breast into my mouth, sucking on her nipple gently while I roll the other between my fingers.

"Fuck," she whispers, her back arching. "Yes, Bennett."

I lap at her nipple and then give the other the same attention, tugging lightly with my teeth before I suck it into my mouth. I get lost in the feel of her, in the way she molds into my touch and forms with my body.

I get lost in the way her hand grips my cock between us and plays with the head, her thumb swiping over the tip a few times.

I get lost in her moans, in the sweet sounds she makes when I lightly nibble on her delicate skin.

And when I trail my mouth between her breasts, down her stomach to her shorts, I get lost in taking them off, spreading her legs, and then burying my face in her pussy, where I lap at her with long, flat strokes, enjoying every fucking second of being the man who gets to do this.

"Bennett, fuck...right there. Oh God, right there." Her hand falls to my hair as she tugs on it and then pushes my head down, keeping me in place while her legs tremble against my ears. I glide my palm up her body to her breasts, where I play with them, taking one of her nipples between my forefinger and thumb and rolling it ever so slightly to hear her hiss with pleasure.

"Yes," she says, her hips rotating now against my tongue. "Don't stop, Bennett. Please...ahhh, right there. Faster."

Wanting to follow her every direction, I still my tongue for a second and then make short, tight flicks over her clit, applying pressure at the same time, which pulls a long moan from her as she lifts up on her elbows.

I pull away for a moment and say, "Grab your knees and spread, baby."

She takes her knees in her hands, spreads her legs and then I go back to her clit, lapping at her, tasting her arousal with every stroke. It's intoxicating, making me feel so fucking dizzy with desire that I start to lose my mind with need.

"Fuck, yes, yes, Bennett. Oh God, I'm going to come, oh fuck…oh God! Yes! Yes! Fuck!" she yells as her body starts to convulse and she's coming on my tongue, her arousal drenching my fucking face and I love it.

I lap up every part of her until her thighs are squeezing my head and she can't take the pleasure any longer.

"Fuck," she whispers, her breath ragged as she starts to fall back down from her high. "Oh my God." Her head lolls to the side as her eyes open and she finds me, fucking satisfied that I could do that to her.

She pauses for a moment, catching her breath, and then she lifts up and pushes me down on the bed, her mouth finding my neck, my chest, down to my abs, past my belly, and then that sinful mouth of hers collapses over my cock, taking me deep in one fucking dip of her mouth.

"Motherfucker," I groan, my arm draping over my eyes. "Fuck, baby, you're so good."

She bobs up and down over my cock, bringing me to the back of her throat and then releasing, repeating the process over and over again. She builds me up, bringing my orgasm to the forefront of my brain, but never actually tipping me over, rather edging me as she pulls all the way off my cock, swirls her tongue around the head, and then takes me all the way to the back of her throat again.

My goddamn toes curl as she drags her teeth along my length, pulling off and then dipping back down. She's relentless, building my orgasm up and up until I can feel the need to fucking burst, and that's when I stop her.

"Bower, stop, babe, please…stop." She pauses, her eyes full of concern, as I lift up and cup her cheek. "I'm so fucking close, but I want to come inside of you."

Her eyes search mine for a second before she wraps her hand around the back of my neck and kisses me. She kisses me with such force that I fall back on the bed and then roll on top of her. I spread her legs apart and as her tongue molds with mine, I line up the tip of my cock at her entrance.

I pull up for one second as I say, "I'm clean, babe. I want to feel all of you. Are you on birth control?" She nods.

And I take that as the go-ahead.

"Eyes on me," I command as I start to enter her.

Her breath catches, her mouth falling open as she gasps from my entrance.

"Relax, Bower. Let me in, beautiful."

She takes a few deep breaths and with every exhale, I slide in farther until I'm halfway there. She's so fucking tight that it's making me sweat.

Wanting to help her relax even more, I kiss her. I kiss her deep and long and swipe at her mouth with my tongue until I feel her finally relax, allowing me in. I let our tongues tangle, our breaths mingle until she's completely sated and I can bottom out.

"Oh my...God," she says, her breaths short and labored. "Fuck, you're huge." Her teeth pull over her bottom lip for a moment before a smile breaks across her lips. "Jesus, you feel so good." She shifts her hips and moans. "Oh my God, yes, fuck, you're so big, so fucking big." She moves her pelvis and her smile grows even more, as if she's realizing my cock is the best thing that's ever happened to her. "Fuck me, Bennett. Fuck me hard."

Christ, she doesn't have to say that twice.

I lean back, take her hips in my hands, and I steady her right before I start moving in and out, angling my hips down and rubbing her in just the right spot.

"Fuck, yes. Oh my God, this is amazing."

She's so tight, so warm, squeezing me with every thrust that I have no control, it's like an addiction every time I push into her, this overwhelming sensation of needing to repeat that feeling of her gripping on to me, fucking me with her squeeze.

"Fuck," I yell as I start moving her body on my cock, lifting her up and down, up and down, her pussy crashing all around me, her tits bouncing with my thrusts, her head thrashing to the side, her smile so goddamn beautiful that my orgasm starts to build at the base of my spine.

So, I grab her legs and spread them as wide as she will allow and then get up on my knees and start pounding into her, our bodies slapping together, our moans mixing. It's so fucking erotic. There's no control and we're both chasing the same thing, the pleasure that's about to implode on us and fucking change us forever.

"Yes, Bennett. Fuck me. Fuck me hard, yes, right there. Oh my God, oh my God, fuck…you're so good. You're…so…good."

She starts to tighten around me.

"You there, baby?"

"Yes," she cries out. "Fuck, I'm going to come. Harder, Bennett. Fuck me harder!"

I pound into her relentlessly, sweat forming on my brow as I try to hold back my orgasm, but the feeling is too fucking good. Her pussy is so goddamn soft, so tight, that my balls squeeze, my cock swells, and just as I shoot into her, her pussy clamps around my cock and she screams out my name. "Bennett! Fuck, I'm coming."

Her pussy contracts around my cock and with one final thrust, I spill into her with such force that everything around me turns to black.

"Mother. Fucker," I cry out, my body shaking with hers as we both ride out our orgasms, every last fucking drop until we're both exhausted and I collapse on top of her.

Her hand slowly glides over my back as I regain consciousness, my fucking head dazed and dizzy from the most incredible orgasm of my goddamn life.

"Jesus," I whisper as I lift up to look her in the eyes, hoping and praying I don't see regret. When our eyes connect, all I can see is satisfaction. So I lean down and gently kiss her lips.

And she kisses me back.

I linger there for a few seconds before I gently pull out of her.

Whispering, I say, "Wait right here." I place a kiss on her forehead and then take off to the bathroom, where I clean up quickly and then bring her a washcloth.

Once she's cleaned up, I help her out of the bed so she can go to the bathroom as well.

While she's taking care of things, I lie back on the bed, my hands digging into my hair, as I try to come down off this high. But it feels impossible, because I've wanted this for so long that part of me is wondering if I actually am dreaming or if this is real.

When the door opens to the bathroom and my eyes fall to Bower, naked and so fucking beautiful, walking toward me, I know this isn't a dream. This is real.

I hold out my hand and she takes it, sliding over me and into my side, where she curls up against me. I wrap my arm around her, and she settles against my chest as I pull the blankets up and over us.

I kiss the top of her head and ask, "Do you feel okay? Can I get you anything?"

"No. Just stay here, with me."

"Okay," I whisper as I kiss her head again.

I love you, Bower. So fucking much.

I want to tell her.

Fucking badly.

I want her to know how strongly I feel about her, how much I've been wanting this, how I'm so grateful she gave me a chance, but I don't want to scare her away. I have her now, in this moment, and I don't want to do anything to disturb it, so instead of cutting my heart open and bleeding all over her, I hold my tongue and drift off to sleep, my girl in my arms, and peace finally pushing through me.

CHAPTER 33
BOWER

WHY AM I STILL SO horny?

Bennett just made me come so hard that I could feel every organ in my body shake and yet, as I lie here next to him, my body is tingling and I want more.

I've never felt this way before with someone.

And that's why it scares me, why I know I need to stop, but I can't. There is this magnetic force pulling me closer and closer to him with every breath I take.

When he came to my apartment as I was leaving with Cougar, it was like he stole my heart in that moment, ripped it right from my chest and coveted it, marked it as his. The pleading in his eyes for me to stay with him, it gutted me. But I knew it was wrong, I knew I couldn't accept what he was offering, but then at the last minute, when I was walking away, something inside me told me to not let go without a taste, just one taste.

Because maybe it was all in my head, this desire I was building up, maybe I just had to redirect it to Cougar, but I needed to know, so I leaned into him and dusted my lips over his, a kiss so light that anyone else would have felt nothing, but in that millisecond of my life, I felt everything.

I felt my body take flight, my heart pitter-patter harder than ever before, and my soul screaming at me that he's the one. *He's the one you've been searching for, waiting for.* But fate is so cruel, because there are consequences in being with him, consequences that marched my feet away from him and toward Cougar.

But the moment I got in Cougar's car and he started to drive away, I knew it was wrong. So when we arrived at the restaurant, I turned toward him and couldn't hold back the words from coming out of my mouth.

"I can't do this. I like someone else, and I'd be leading you on if I went on this date."

The words just flowed, as if I had zero control over them. And I felt guilty, for many reasons. Guilty for leading Cougar on. Guilty for canceling our date. Guilty for crossing the boundaries I set with Bennett, but as I went back to my apartment to change and take my makeup off, I didn't want to get into my bed, I wanted his.

So on a shaky breath, I went to his apartment, looking to sob into his arms, but he wasn't there.

Which, of course, led to fear.

Fear that he was out with someone else after I turned him down.

Fear that he wouldn't be coming back that night.

And that fear gripped me to the point of making it hard to breathe, so I sought comfort. I climbed into his bed, only for him to return and find me.

From there, everything felt so muddled until the moment he entered me. That was when everything changed. All the worry, the anxiety, the fear, it was washed away and I felt pure joy.

I felt like I was coming home.

Like I found the missing piece in my life I've been searching for.

Now, cuddled into him, his breath evening out, his heart pounding against my ear, I know there is no avoiding this. I can't keep trying to push him away, because my soul is going to keep bringing me back to him. So instead of trying to ignore this magnetic pull I have toward him, I'm going to embrace it while trying to figure out how to make this work.

Because I have to. I know I can't keep up the charade I've been living.

The last ten days felt like torture not having him around. Then seeing him in the hallway, begging for me to stay with him, I felt like I was denying my lungs air.

Every man up until him has been mundane and hasn't fulfilled my desires. . .until Bennett came back into my life. I should have known that first day, when I moved to San Francisco, that buzzing feeling I felt inside wasn't the thrill of a new chapter. It was the thrill of being close to my person.

I drag my hand down his stomach, over his delicious abs and right to his cock that is already growing hard again.

God, there's something to be said about being with a younger guy.

"Fuck, baby," he says as my fingers dance over his length before I grip him and start pumping. "Goddamn it." He shifts and then melts into the mattress as I lift and stare down at him.

He's so fucking hot.

From his angular jaw to the scruff that I can still feel rubbing between my thighs, to his stunning eyes, so sensual when they look at me when he's deep inside of me—he's intoxicating.

I straddle his legs, still pumping his length.

Cockily, he places his hands behind his head and smirks as I position him at my entrance and then sit down on him.

"Christ," he breathes out, his chest taking a deep breath.

I do the same because I'm not used to him yet and how deep he gets and how much he stretches me out. It's new and different and addictive, because no one has made me feel the way he does.

I place my hands on his chest and start to rotate my hips, over and over again, riding him in just the right way where he's connecting with a spot deep inside me no one has touched.

A spot that feels so damn good that I don't want to lose the feeling.

"Shit," I say, my head bowing and my stomach curving, getting the most out of the angle. "Oh God, Bennett."

"Mm, that's it, baby. Ride me. Ride me hard."

His hands fall to my hips and he helps me move up and down, swirling and thrusting over his cock.

"Jesus, I love your tits. They're so fucking sexy," he says as his hand palms one of my breasts and squeezes. "So perfect." His thumb rubs over my nipple and I moan, my pussy squeezing around him. "Fuck." He bucks up into me.

"Play with my tits," I say, squeezing them together as I continue to thrust over him.

He palms them, massaging them and playing with my nipples.

"I want to come on them," he says, staring in awe up at me. "I want to come all over you, mark you as mine."

"Do it," I say, the thought of him claiming me sending a thrill through me. "Come all over me."

He growls and thrusts up into me harder while squeezing my breasts.

"Yes. Again."

He repeats it, once, twice, three times...and on the fourth, I'm feral. I'm digging my fingertips into his chest and riding over him at a relentless pace, seeking out my own orgasm that's building until he thrusts one more time, hitting that spot that only he can reach.

"Oh my God! Bennett, fuck!" I scream right before my pussy contracts around him and I come all over his cock, my body shaking with euphoria.

"Goddamn it," he grunts as he flips me to my back, pulls out of me, and then straddles my body. His strong hand grips his cock and he furiously pumps himself over me, every muscle in his body straining, and it's the hottest thing I've ever seen. "Fuck," he grunts just as he starts coming, shooting himself all over my chest.

Pride surges through me as he slows down, the meaning behind this choice powerful, because now...I'm his.

He opens his eyes and stares down at me, a feral, hungry expression crossing his features as he takes his palm and spreads his cum over my chest while stating, "Mine."

His.

I'm all his.

No one else's.

"Fuck," I cry out as he spanks me again, the sound ringing out in the shower, water pelting around us as he has me bent over, pumping into me while his other hand is pressing against my clit, playing with it, bringing me to the edge once again.

"Squeeze my cock, all of it," he says, thrusting into me so hard that I have to put my hand against the tile to steady myself.

"Right there, Bennett, right there," I call out as he grinds into me and glides along my clit. "Fuck, so good." I bite down on my lip, my body buzzing, my legs numbing, my orgasm right on the edge. And with one last thrust, I'm flying over the edge, calling out his name as he pulls out of me, grunts, and then comes all over my ass and back.

"Jesus fuck," he groans.

I let out a deep breath and turn around to face him.

His face is pure joy as he presses his thumb under my chin, angling my head back so he can take my mouth with his.

We make out for a few moments, the water hitting the both of us as he claims my lips, my tongue, my body.

When we separate, he whispers, "Mine."

I smooth my hand up his rock-hard chest and say, "I'm all yours."

"Good." He kisses me one last time and then helps me wash up before wrapping us both in towels.

Towel wrapped around his waist, he rubs his hands up and down my arms as he stares down at me, a smile pulling at his lips.

"Why are you smiling?"

He chuckles. "Oh, I don't know, the girl that I've been crushing on for fucking years just admitted that she's mine. No big deal or anything."

My cheeks pinken. "So that crush you always talked about, it was me?"

"Yeah, I told you that. It was you the entire time. Always has been you." His thumb caresses my cheek. "No one has ever come close to comparing to you."

I think about all the times he mentioned his crush or I mentioned it, how he must have felt, knowing that it was me the entire time and he couldn't do anything about that. I can't imagine the agony he went through. It explains why he looked so desolate when I walked away from him, saying I wouldn't choose him. *God, I hate myself for that.* I never want to put that look on his face again.

"Why did you wait so long to say something?" I ask.

"You weren't ready," he says. "You didn't see me as the man I am. You saw me as Gabby's little brother. It wasn't until you moved here that I saw a chance to change that."

I slide my hand over his thick pec and marvel in how much he has changed. "You are quite different. And you're right, I never saw you in that light until I moved here. I was kind of caught off guard, honestly."

"Caught off guard by what?"

I look up into his eyes. "My attraction to you. I thought for a moment that I was broken. That I didn't know how to get aroused anymore, but then every time you came near me, or held my hand, or snuggled into me, a bout of electricity zapped through me. I tried to deny it, but that feeling only grew stronger." I rub my hand over his chest. "I'm sorry I left you in the hallway like that." I feel tears spring to my eyes from the expression he gave me when I bolted. "I was scared—"

"Shh," he says, placing his finger over my lips. "No need to apologize. We're here now, together, that's all that matters."

"I know, but I don't want you thinking I didn't want you, because I did. I was just struggling with admitting that."

"You don't need to explain."

"I do." I wet my lips. "You matter to me, Bennett. So much, more than

I ever expected, and I'm so sorry that for a moment I made you think you didn't matter."

He leans down and captures my mouth with a soft, thoughtful kiss. When he pulls away, his forehead connects with mine. "I've been in this headspace for years, where I accepted you as the person I was supposed to be with. You're just getting there. But you're here now, and that's all that matters."

I nod against him and then say, "I do think we need to talk."

"Yeah, I saw that coming. Want to talk in bed?"

"Sure," I answer.

We both finish drying off and then he hangs my towel, leaving me naked as he leads me back to his bed. I pause and ask, "Naked?"

"Going to tell you right now—from here on out, if you're in my bed, I expect you to be naked."

I chuckle and lift up on my toes, pressing a kiss to his jaw. "I think I can be okay with that."

We both slide into bed and face each other as his hand falls on my hip, pulling me in a few inches closer. When his eyes connect with mine, he slightly shakes his head, almost as if he's in awe.

"What?" I ask.

"I'm just struggling to comprehend that I'm not dreaming. That this is all real and I'm not going to wake up any moment and have it all taken away from me."

"It's real. It's so real that it's freaking me out."

"Because of Gabby?" he asks.

"Yeah." And damn it, I get emotional all over again. Tears spring to my eyes and I swear under my breath from not being able to control my feelings on this. "Sorry." I wipe at my eyes.

"Don't apologize. You're allowed to have these feelings. You and Gabby are practically sisters."

"We are. We've been through so much together that I don't want this to break us apart, and I know it will."

"Not if we don't let it," he says, so certain that it almost makes me mad.

"She's not going to talk to me, Bennett. She was adamant about me not getting involved with you. I'm *her* friend and I'm supposed to protect you, and God, we have fucked so many times."

He chuckles and I push at his chest.

"Not funny."

"It's kind of funny."

"It's not. I can't stop myself. I'm insatiable. I really think there is something wrong with me. I've never been like this with anyone else."

"Thanks, babe. Makes me feel special."

"Bennett," I groan, pushing at him again. "You're not supposed to make light of this."

"First of all, if we don't make light of it, then you're going to keep crying, and I won't stand for you crying when it comes to you and me. Second of all...is it my dick? Is that what has you all randy and ready to go?"

"Oh my God, I'm leaving." I start to turn over, but he laughs some more and pulls me in close, trapping me under his arms so I'm caged in.

"You're not going anywhere. And in all seriousness, we'll figure this out, okay? We don't have to tell her right away. We can keep this quiet and just between us. We can have dates here, in our apartments so no one can spot us together, and we can build up our relationship until you're ready to tell her."

"You wouldn't mind that?"

"Bower, I've waited so fucking long to be in this position with you that I don't care if I have to wait a year to go out in public with you. As long as I know you're mine, then I'm good."

I lift my hand to his cheek, rubbing the scruff with my thumb. "I want to tell her. I just have to figure out how."

"I know." He turns his head and kisses my palm.

"I'm not trying to hide you or anything. I don't want you to think I'm ashamed."

"Trust me, from the way you were screaming my name, I know for a fact you're not ashamed."

I'd roll my eyes, but he's right.

"Do you think your neighbors heard?"

"I think the entire apartment building heard."

"Bennett, seriously."

He smirks. "Seriously, Bower, you were fucking loud." I cover my face and he chuckles, nuzzling his nose into the side of my neck. "Hot as shit, though, and I can't wait to make you scream again."

"Given your stamina, I'd say it would be in the next couple of minutes."

"Don't tempt me," he says, as he starts to massage my breast.

I moan lightly and melt into the mattress. "Wait, before you go any further," I say, my hand to his chest, "can you promise me that you will let me tell Gabby?"

He kisses my neck, my cheek. "I promise. This is all on your schedule, when you're comfortable. But can you promise me one thing too?"

"Depends, what is it?"

He grows serious. "End things with Cougar. I can't fucking take the thought of you with him."

"I already ended it with him when I came back up here."

"Yeah?" he asks, looking so adorably excited.

"Yeah."

"So you're all mine?"

"Pretty sure you know the answer to that after you came all over my tits."

His smile grows. "Maybe I need to do it again just to make sure."

"I think I'd prefer it."

He growls and then moves down my body, spreads my legs, and buries his face between them.

God, he's so perfect.

CHAPTER 34
BENNETT

SHE'S BEAUTIFUL.

Stunning.

Fucking steals my breath every time she smiles at me.

And she's all mine.

I know it's real, I understand that, but fuck, it doesn't feel like it. It feels like I'm dreaming, like I'm about to wake up and Nolan is going to slap me across the face, telling me to get my ass in the dugout.

And yet, there she is, sitting at my dining room table, eating a raspberry Danish, wearing my T-shirt and looking thoroughly fucked, gazing at me with heart eyes.

Actual heart eyes.

And I know I'm looking at her the same way, especially after last night. We didn't get much sleep. The moment one of us woke up, or stirred, we were on top of each other. I've never been inside someone so much in my life, and yet, I couldn't get enough. If I didn't just bend her over the couch and fuck her until she screamed my name, I'd clear the table and take her here now, but I know I have to give her time to rest. Plus, she has work—even though she told Adalade that she'd be late today.

"You're staring," she says, her cheeks pinkening.

"Yeah, because I can stare now and not have you question me. Before, I was stealing glances; now I can look all I fucking want."

Her head tilts to the side. "You really felt that strongly about me?"

"Bower, you have no fucking clue." I chuckle. "Infatuated doesn't even begin to describe it, but out of fear that I might scare you away, I think I'll keep the obsession to myself."

"Obsession?" She sets her pastry down and leans her forearms on the table. "Ooo, I'm intrigued, tell me more. Did you have a shrine? Keep my hair in a box? Collect my trash and sniff it before you went to bed?"

Deadpanning, I say, "I stopped the trash thing when I hit twenty."

"Stop." She laughs, making me chuckle as well.

"Nah, I just...I don't know, I stole glances, I keep our pictures we've taken together in my favorites folder on my phone—"

"You do? Let me see."

"Are you going to make fun of me?"

"No, I'm sure it's going to make me fall for you even more."

"In that case..." I scoot my chair out from the table and pat my lap. She comes over to me, where she sits and then kisses my cheek, wrapping her arm around my neck. In fucking heaven, I pull up my favorites album in my phone and show her all the pictures I have saved in there. It's not many, but it's kept me satiated.

"Oh, I remember the welcome home event in Almond Bay. You so did not want to be there."

"Yeah, I don't love events that are solely focused on me. Not a fan."

"I could tell that day you were so not into it. But that was one of the first times I was caught off guard by how much you changed."

"Yeah?" My hand falls to her thigh. "You noticed my muscles?"

"Just a little," she says. "And then there was this picture that Gabby sent me, after visiting you, and I was shocked. You just changed so much. You weren't the boy I first met."

"So the truth comes out. You were obsessing too."

She scoffs. "I wouldn't say obsessing, but I would say I noticed things."

"Pervert."

"What?" she says in protest, making me laugh. "You're the one with pictures of me in your phone."

"You were the one lusting after a twenty-year-old."

"Bennett," she says, almost insulted as she starts to pull away. That makes me laugh some more. I hold her tight, not letting her get away.

"I'm kidding, babe."

"I think it would benefit you greatly if you don't mention the age difference. I'm already feeling like I'm a grandma here."

I set my phone down and kiss her neck, letting my hand wander up her shirt. "There is nothing grandma about you, beautiful."

She turns toward me, straddling my lap. "Better not be." Her arms rest on my shoulders as she asks, "Did I see that I'm your wallpaper on your phone?"

"You did. Manifesting."

She chuckles. "You really do like me, don't you?"

"If I have to tell you, then I clearly did not do a good enough job worshipping you last night."

"Oh, you did. You did such an excellent job."

My hands slide under her shirt and up her back. "I do have something I want to talk to you about, and I know if I don't mention it, it will eat away at me, and I want to be as transparent and honest with you as possible."

"I'd appreciate that."

"Okay, and this might be the jealous asshole coming out of me, but it's driving me nuts that Cougar helped you with your book truck."

Her expression frowns. "How do you know about that?"

"Gabby told me. She called me and raved about Cougar and how great he is and how he's been helping you. It fucking ate at me." I rub her sides, not wanting to sound like a jealous fool, but knowing that's how this will come off. "Why didn't you come to me? Gretchen has been asking about everything, and well, I feel like I could have been helpful."

Her fingers play with my hair, sending goose bumps over my arms. "It was nothing against you, Bennett. It was me trying to fixate on something, anything that wasn't you. Although, it made me think of you all the time. I was trying to put distance between my thoughts about you and just trying to focus on something, anything besides the feeling of letting my friend down because I was falling for her brother."

"But why ask him?"

"I didn't seek out his help," she says. "Not sure if that makes you feel better, but I was at the coffee house, just trying to get some work done, and he happened to run into me. A few times, and well, he's nosey and asked what I was doing, so I showed him. I will admit, he gave me some good advice." That makes me go still, anger pulsing through me, and she must feel it because she tries to soothe me by rubbing her thumbs over the back of my neck. "It was nothing too big, though, and if I wasn't trying to compartmentalize, then I would have asked you."

"You should have," I say, irritated by the conversation. I knew I would be. I've been so irritated by anything Cougar has had a part of in her life. If anyone should be helping her with the book truck, it's me.

"Bennett, don't get angry."

"I am. He's an idiot. He shouldn't be having a hand in your dreams."

"You're the one who set me up with him," she says, pulling away slightly.

"Yeah, because I wanted to set you up with an idiot to make me look better."

She blinks and then gets off my lap. "Are you serious right now?"

Shit, probably shouldn't have said that.

I reach for her hand, but she backs away, so I stand, not wanting her to take off. "Bower, it was self-preservation. I was desperate to get you to notice me—"

"So your plan was to set me up with someone who could have possibly hurt me?"

"No." I push my hand through my hair. "The intention was to make him seem like a douchebag so when you hung out with me, you saw me for who I am."

"And who is that?" She crosses her arms over her chest. "A conniving little punk?"

"No," I say, panic starting to surge through me. "I wanted you to see me for the man I am, not the boy I once was."

"Well, that was a very boyish thing to do, Bennett."

"I was desperate. What did you want from me? You were hanging all over me, asking me to set you up with someone."

"Yeah, and you could have asked me out instead."

I sarcastically laugh. "Please, Bower. If I asked you out when you were looking for me to set you up, there is no way you would have said yes. You would have booked it out of here so fucking fast. Don't act like you would have treated the situation any differently."

"What, so this entire thing was some sort of slow, drawn-out plan to get me into your bed?"

"No," I say, not quite understanding how we got here when moments ago she was on my lap.

"You're unbelievable, Bennett." She shakes her head and moves toward the entryway of my apartment.

I chase after her, not wanting her to leave like this.

I step in front of her, blocking the door. "It was not some plan to get you into my bed. It was to get you to fucking notice me, Bower. I had no goddamn chance at getting you to even look at me other than as a friend without a plan. If I came up to you and told you how I felt when you first moved here, you would have gone running. I had to take my time. I had to slowly help you realize that I'm the guy you deserve, and if I had to use someone else to do that, then I don't fucking care, because it means that I was able to bring you closer. I don't understand why that makes you so upset. I did what any hero in your romance books would have done, or any other man with a massive crush would have done."

She crosses her arms over her chest but doesn't respond, making me believe that I might be able to put out this fire.

Calmly, I walk up to her and place my hands on her hips. "I like you so fucking much, Bower. And I'm sorry I set you up with Cougar, sorry for more reasons than you could probably think. And if it's any consolation, the entire plan blew up in my face as I had to witness you going out with him, see pictures of you two together with dating rumors swirling around. It was fucking torture."

She looks away and says, "Well, you deserved it for doing something like that."

"And I took my punishment," I say, moving in closer and sliding my hands up her sides. "It just about killed me seeing you two together."

"I'm glad," she says, like a brat, but I fucking like it.

"Hey." Her eyes meet mine. "I'm sorry, Bower."

And just like that, her anger disappears as she pretends to maintain the same disposition. "Well, how do you suppose you make it up to me?"

"I have some thoughts." I grip her shirt and tug on it, pulling it up and over her head, leaving her naked in front of me.

"It better involve your face between my legs."

"Trust me, it does." I lift her up and carry her to the couch, where I lay her down, prop one leg up on the back and spread the other wide so it's hanging off the side. I look her in the eyes and say, "Really sorry, babe."

"Mm-hmm, show me."

And then she grips the back of my head and pushes me between her legs.

"Muffins for the table," OC says as he takes a seat and places a plate of a variety of muffins between us.

Graydon eyes me and I glance up at OC. "If you do anything disgusting with those, you're no longer a part of the Gladdy Daddies."

"My tonguing of muffins—in public—is done."

"Hate that he added *in public,*" Graydon says as he picks one up.

"Same. Make a note to never go to his place."

"Missing out. I have a pinball machine," OC says.

"You do?" Nolan asks, walking up in a pair of holey gray sweatpants with the pant legs pulled up, showing off his tube socks and slides. He paired the outfit with a Bombers shirt that he cut the hem off of so it shows off half an inch of his skin, and on top of his head is a cowboy hat.

If he was looking to go incognito, he failed.

"Nolan Hart, right?" OC asks, looking him up and down.

"Damn right." He lends out his hand and OC shakes it. "You're Oden O'Connor, right? Fucking fast as shit on skates, dude."

"Thanks. I do a lot of squats."

"It shows, my man." Then Nolan turns to Graydon and salutes him. "Graydon, I understand you don't like attention of any sort or people touching you."

"Correct," Graydon says.

"Nice to meet you then." Nolan picks up his chair, turns it around and takes a seat, resting his arms on the back of the chair. "Muffins, fuck yeah." He picks one up and then turns to OC. "What kind of pinball machine?"

OC seems to light up, clearly appreciating the addition to our threesome. "*Mandalorian.* Has the theme music and everything."

"Sick," Nolan says with a nod. "Invite me over. I want to bat around your balls."

"You can bat around my balls anytime you want," OC says, hearts in his eyes as I sit front and center to a new bromance forming right in front of me.

Graydon clears his throat and not so politely asks, "What the fuck is he doing here?"

Nolan just smirks at Graydon and bites into the muffin without taking the paper off.

"Is this a real cowboy hat?" OC asks, fingering the edge of it.

"No idea. I took it from one of my teammates. I only wear it away from the stadium. Fool is still looking for it."

"That's Adrian's?" I ask, knowing damn well if Adrian Banks knew that Nolan took his hat, Nolan would find his head five-feet deep in the dirt of the infield. He's been looking for it for months.

"Yeah. Don't tell him, you narc."

"I'm not a narc," I say, offended.

"You have the face of a narc," OC says.

"He does, doesn't he?" Nolan adds.

"The fuck I do."

"Can we fucking bring it back?" Graydon growls. "Why the fuck is he here?" He gestures toward Nolan.

"I don't care. I'm just happy about it," OC says, handing Nolan a napkin, and I can see the urge in him to pat the corner of Nolan's lips for him.

"I thought it would be good to gather all of you together and tell you that Bower and I are together."

"Wait, really?" OC asks.

"Shut the fuck up," Nolan says, pushing at my shoulder so hard that I nearly fall out of my chair. "You bagged her?"

I right myself, caught off guard that I was so easily pushed just now. "Don't fucking say *bagged her*."

"But did you?" he asks, wiggling his brows.

"I'm not going to talk about that shit, but we did spend the night together and I'll leave it at that."

"He fucking bagged her." Nolan slaps me on the back. "Congrats, man. Told you my plan was going to work."

"Your plan?" Graydon scoffs. "It set him back weeks. If he'd come to us at first, it wouldn't have turned into the mess it was."

"Big man is jealous."

Graydon's eyes narrow. I want to tell Nolan to back off, but I think he might have to learn the hard way when it comes to Graydon.

"I liked the plot twist of the second guy involved," OC says, "but it did cause unnecessary drama."

"Nah, it caused just enough chaos for everyone to figure out what they wanted. In a situation like the one we were presented with, there really was only one option: Get her to notice him, and how do you do that?"

"Make him take his shirt off in front of her," OC says.

Nolan shakes his head. "No, that's too easy. Our heroine wouldn't have fallen for it."

"Shirt off would have worked," Graydon says, folding his arms.

"Maybe if the scenario was they were just friends," Nolan says. "But we had an added twist in the plot here: the sister."

OC nods. "He's right. The sister adds an extra element."

"Shirt still would have worked."

"You're sticking to a failed plan. Let me ask you this"—Nolan turns toward me—"before you introduced her to Cougar, did she ever see you with your shirt off?"

"She did."

Nolan gestures toward me. "My point exactly. She was unaffected by his nakedness."

"Uh, she was affected a little. I caught her staring," I say, wanting to make that clear.

"Yeah, but not enough to tip the tides. Therefore, we needed to add the dramatics, enter Cougar." Nolan takes another bite of his muffin and looks around the table.

After a few seconds of silence, OC says, "I think we need to add him to the Gladdy Daddies."

"Fuck no," Graydon says, leaning back in his chair.

"What's the Gladdy Daddies?" Nolan lights up, looking interested.

"It's our man group. Kind of like how Ted Lasso had the Diamond Dogs, well, we have the Gladdy Daddies."

Nolan looks between us and says, "Is it because you're hot-as-fuck daddies who are glad to be together?"

Jesus.

Christ.

What have I done?

OC chokes up and whispers, "I think I might be in love."

"Well, consider me in." Nolan stares at Graydon. "Glad to be a daddy with you, big guy."

"Over my dead body."

OC: I want to formally thank Nolan for taking the oath of initiation into the Gladdy Daddies. We couldn't be happier to have you in the group.

Bennett: When did you take an oath?

Nolan: In the bathroom while I was taking a piss. He made me repeat that I wouldn't mention a single thing we talk about in this thread to anyone else. I shook my dick at the end to seal the deal.

OC: It was a sturdy shake.

Bennett: Don't say shit like that, man. Graydon is barely sticking around.

Graydon: I did not approve of this.

Nolan: Aw, you'll get used to me, big guy.

Graydon: No.

OC: Aren't his words like a warm hug?

Nolan: Or an ice pick up the urethra. Either way, I dig it.

Graydon: Bennett, you did this to us.

Bennett: I know and I'm sorry. I was just excited to tell you guys about me and Bower.

OC: Which is something we didn't spend enough time talking about.

Graydon: Because you two asshats were searching the internet to see if the cowboy hat was real.

Nolan: Worth a cool two thousand dollars. Glad to know I'm decorating the hat rack with gold.

Graydon: OC didn't have to order the same one.

OC: I ordered one for all of us. Fuck, I couldn't keep the secret. Next meeting, we can match.

Bennett: That's a no.

Graydon: No.

Nolan: Count me in, you dumb fuck.

OC: I should take offense to the nickname, but Jesus Christ, it gives me life.

CHAPTER 35
BOWER

Bennett: Gretchen wants to meet us today. You available tonight?

Bower: Yeah, just let me know the time and place.

Bennett: Got it. P.S. I can still taste you on my tongue.

Bower: Good. Maybe you can have another taste later.

Bennett: Count me fucking in. Miss you, beautiful.

Bower: Miss you. XOXO

"YOU HAD SEX WITH BENNETT, didn't you?" Adalade says from across the table, where she's looking through curtain swatches. She wants to redo her office, even though she doesn't ever do much in there.

"What?" I ask, surprised as I set my phone down on the table.

"Don't mess with me. I can tell from the look on your face. You had sex, didn't you?"

I bite the corner of my lip and Adalade's eyes widen.

"Goodness, you had a lot of it."

I bury my head in my hands and squeal, unable to hold back, causing her to laugh. "Ahhh, Adalade, I made a huge mistake, one that I made over and over and over again."

She chuckles and pushes the fabric swatches away. "I'm disappointed that you've been here for over two hours and you haven't said anything to me. That seems like it's grounds for being fired. Tell me why I should keep you around when you're withholding such information from me?"

"Because I'm still trying to comprehend all this and accept it myself."

She eyes me suspiciously. "I can understand that. I don't like it, but I can understand it. So, tell me what happened."

I let out a deep breath and recount what happened last night, Bennett showing up at my door, begging for me to be with him, going to his place, him not being there, only for him to show up later and take me in his bed.

"Wow." Adalade picks up a brochure from the table and fans it in front of her face. "He begged?"

I nod. "It broke me."

"I can see how that would break the strongest of women. And what happened to Cougar?"

"I let him down the best I could."

"Did he accept it?"

I nod, thinking back to how understanding he was. "He did. He was really nice about it, which of course made me feel more guilty. I kind of wish he was a jerk about it, you know? Would have made it easier."

"Yes, but at least you were honest with him."

"I was."

Adalade has a glint in her eye. "You know, I was researching him the other day out of pure boredom. And did you know his real name isn't Cougar?"

"It's not?" I ask, surprised.

"No. His real name is Logan."

"Logan?" I ask, my eyes widening. "Why on earth does he go by Cougar?"

"I watched an interview where he said his high school coach gave him the name for being a cougar on the field, and he thought it was fitting, so that's what he goes by."

"Goodness, someone needs to tell him Logan is better."

Adalade chuckles. "I don't know, I wouldn't mind a little Cougar in my life."

"Adalade." I laugh.

She casually adjusts the bracelets on her wrists, as if what she's saying is completely normal. "Consider me infatuated after my google search. Glad to hear he's on the market."

"Shall I make an introduction?"

"No, no, I'll put it into fate's hands." She winks and then folds her hands together. "I'm happy for you, though. It seems like you have a lightness about you, like perhaps this is what you should have been doing for a while now."

"That's what it kind of feels like," I say, admitting to the feelings I think I might have been harboring but not realizing it. "I'm still kind of sick and nauseous over the whole thing and what we're going to do when it comes to Gabby, but Bennett said we will work it out together."

"A good man." She picks up a plaid swatch and tests the material with her fingertips. "Now, when are we going to a game?"

"You want to go?"

She looks up at me. "I demand that we go."

"Then I guess I should look into tickets."

"Make it a suite," Adalade says. "I don't tend to mix with the general public."

I chuckle. "You got it."

"Bennett?" I call out when I walk into his apartment. I set down my bag and keys, not even bothering to go to my apartment.

"Baby," he calls out as he slides on his sock-covered feet from his bedroom right into the living room. When he stops, he runs right up to me, picks me up, and plasters me against the wall.

His mouth is on mine before I can even say hi, while his hands find their way up my shirt.

I chuckle against his kisses from his excitement, causing him to pull away and give me the cutest look ever. "Uh, I'm seducing you. You shouldn't be laughing."

"I'm sorry, you just did this whole Tom Cruise slide-in thing and then like a happy dog, excited to see their owner, just started attacking me. I wasn't expecting it."

"Excited dog, huh? Want me to lick you all over like a dog would?"

My brow furrows. "I feel like you might have thought that was something sexy to say, but I didn't like it."

He scratches the side of his face and says, "Yeah, didn't hit right. Either way, I want to lick you. Let's get you out of these pants—"

"Gretchen is coming over."

"Babe," he says, in a serious tone. "I can get you off in thirty seconds, and you know it."

"That's very cocky of you."

"It's true. Do we need to revisit how quick you got off this morning when I had you on the kitchen counter?"

"You were putting ice on your tongue and flicking my clit. I had no chance."

"So what you're saying is…you want a repeat? Not a problem. Just take these pants off."

I chuckle while stopping him. "She's going to be here any minute. Just wait until she's gone and then you can do whatever you want to me."

"Is that a promise?"

"As if you need a promise," I say, leaning into him. "The moment she's gone, I'll be shedding your pants off."

"That's what I like to hear." His lips find my neck and I sigh into him as his hands roam my body and he kisses all the way down my neck and starts tugging on my shirt again.

"Bennett." I laugh just as there's a knock at the door.

"Fuck," he mutters and then pulls away, planting a kiss on my lips and then going to answer the door.

Without a hello, Gretchen steps into the apartment and says, "I don't make house calls, so there better be a reason for this." She walks right past Bennett and straight to the dining room table, where she takes a seat, crossing one leg over the other. When she looks between us, her expression falls to irritation as she says, "I knew it."

She then reaches into her bag and pulls out a folder.

"Knew what?" I ask, joining her at the table, along with Bennett.

"Knew that you two were fucking."

Wow, way to be eloquent.

She pulls out a pen, slaps open the folder, and pushes a document toward me. "Fill this out and sign at the bottom."

"What is that?" Bennett asks, taking the form from me before I can even start reading it.

"It's an NDA. If you two are an item, she needs to fill it out. I make every person I work with who is dating someone, or in your case, fucking, fill it out."

"We're more than just fucking," Bennett says, insulted by the term, which I think is pretty cute.

"Call it what you want, but I need that signed and I won't be leaving until it is."

"It's fine," I say, grabbing the form.

"No, babe, you don't just sign something because someone tells you to."

"It's an NDA, as if I'd say anything about us to anyone else. Plus, I already signed one for the book stuff."

"That's why you don't have to sign it, because I trust you."

"That's cute," Gretchen says. "But unfortunately, trust doesn't get you anywhere in this business, especially when it comes to matters of the heart. She needs to sign it. It will protect you from any backlash if this relationship ever comes to an end."

"It's not going to end," Bennett practically growls at Gretchen.

"I'm sure it's not, but she still needs to sign it."

"It's fine," I say, trying to grab the form again.

"Just let me look through this for a second," he says, scanning through the pages.

And I let him, because it's cute that he wants to protect me. As he reads, I awkwardly smile at Gretchen and say, "I like your nails."

They're painted a matte black, very businesslike and dark...probably like her soul.

"You don't need to talk when he reads," she says in response, clearly fine with silences.

"What's this?" Bennett asks, pointing to a paragraph. "Bower would have to assume all blame for the breakup if it were to happen?"

"Typical protocol for a celebrity/peasant relationship."

"Peasant?" I ask, insulted.

"Yes, when one party is more valuable in the public's eye than the other, the less valuable party will take on the burden of the breakup to save the image of the higher-valued party."

"How the fuck is that fair?" Bennett asks.

"It's not, but that's business." She looks down at her watch and then up at us. "Please, I don't have all day."

"It's fine, Bennett," I say, not caring at all. I take the form from him, and before he can protest, I sign.

"Bower, I wasn't done reading it."

"Like I said, it's fine. I don't care. If something goes wrong between us, I have no problem taking on the blame."

"Nothing is going to go wrong."

"Aww, that's sweet," Gretchen says, sarcasm dripping from every word as she snatches the paper from me and stuffs it in an envelope. "Now, who knows about this relationship?"

"Um, well, it's kind of private," I answer. "We aren't really telling anyone, because his sister is my best friend, and if she found out, she'd be very angry, and we're trying to work that all out before we go public."

"Is that right?" Gretchen glances over at Bennett. "Then why does he have a guilty look on his face?"

I turn to look at him, too, and sure enough, he does look guilty.

"Who did you tell?" I ask.

He tugs on his hair in that cute, boyish way before saying, "Uh, I might have told—"

"Do not say OC," Gretchen says.

"OC," Bennett responds with a nod.

"For the love of God." Gretchen pinches the bridge of her nose.

"And Graydon," Bennett adds.

"Bennett," I say in surprise.

"And Nolan Hart," Bennett says on a wince.

"My God, Bennett, did you have a gossip session?" I ask, surprised he told so many people.

"I'm sorry. I was just so excited, and they were a part of the whole plan to get you to like me, and since it worked, I wanted to tell them how we succeeded."

"When you put it like that, it makes me look bad," I say, irritated all over again about this stupid plan he conducted.

"It doesn't make her look great. Sort of like she was played."

"Thank you," I say, gesturing to Gretchen.

"It wasn't like that," Bennett pleads. "Please, let's not go through this again. You know it was because I was desperate to get you to see me, nothing else."

He's right—his attempt at wooing me—that's how I will refer to it.

"Either way, you told them?" Gretchen confirms.

Bennett nods. "I did."

"Do they understand that what you told them is private information and that it's not to be repeated, and did you highlight that fact with OC?"

"They know whatever we talk about in the group stays in the group," Bennett says.

She eyes Bennett. "Do you want me to check with OC just in case?"

"No, I think he understands."

Gretchen purses her lips. "I'll check with him."

She whips out her phone and starts texting. When she's done, she turns back to us and says, "Now that that is settled—" She pauses when her phone buzzes. She looks down at her screen, reads a text that I'm sure is from OC, and then rolls her eyes, muttering, "He's such a fucking idiot." She quickly types away and then puts her phone in her bag.

"Is he good?" Bennett asks, looking concerned now. "Did he tell someone?"

"No. He's just...you know how he is in text messages."

"And in person," Bennett adds.

"Yes, you're right about that." Clearing her throat, she looks between us with the cold, hard stare of a woman on a mission. "So why am I here?"

"We want to talk about the book club," Bennett says. "From what you've said, there has been a lot of interest."

"A lot, to the point that I want to hire a social media manager for it because we have traction, but we're not capitalizing on it."

"I can do it," I say before I can stop myself.

"Really?" Bennett asks, surprised. "I don't want you to have to take on more work."

"I can handle it while I'm running errands in the car. Plus, I already have experience since I've been posting my own quick book reviews. It wouldn't be much different."

"Great, then that's settled," Gretchen says.

"Wait." Bennett turns to me. "Are you sure?"

"Positive," I say. "And when the time comes, I can start doing collab posts with The Whimsy Wagon."

"I'm glad you mentioned that," Gretchen says. "We were able to skirt by this month without a bookstore to work with, but to really get the community involved, we'll need to have it up and ready by next month, or we don't have a deal and will have to work with someone else."

"I'm not working with anyone else," Bennett says.

"Well, we can't wait that long either. What you need to understand about social media is that you have to capitalize when you start to trend, and right now, we're sitting ducks. We don't have any content, we don't have community involvement, we don't—"

"I can handle it," I say. "I can, uh...I can set up a small in-person, ticketed event with Bennett. We can find a venue and celebrate our first book club night. I can theme it out and have a lot of fun with it, and we can announce the partnership then as well." My mind starts to race with all the ideas. "We can make it baseball themed and intimate."

"We'll have to have security present," Gretchen says.

"Oh yeah, of course."

"And I'd say twenty people at the most, VIP bags, no drinks. We can't have fans getting rowdy, but we can serve mocktails. VIP bags should consist of the book—try to get signed copies from the author—a gift card to The Whimsy Wagon for next month's pick, maybe some NSFW art print, and one of Bennett's favorite things. Like a snack. We should try to find local small businesses to sponsor the event as well for the swag, reach out and we can use it as a promotional tactic—" She pauses and looks at me. "Why aren't you writing this down?"

"Oh, sorry," I say, pulling my phone out and taking notes, writing as fast as I can to keep up with her.

It takes about fifteen minutes of Gretchen rattling off a laundry list of things to do for the event as well as creating invitations, establishing the venue, and deadlines she needs to be met before she gathers her things and is out of Bennett's apartment.

When he shuts the door, he turns to me, concern in his eyes as I stand and grab my bag.

"Where are you going?" he asks.

"I need to get started on this. I need to figure out when the truck is going to be done at the wrap shop, and I need to start ordering books and swag. I have no time."

"Whoa, slow down," he says, gripping my shoulders. "Bower, this is so much work. Let me help you."

I shake my head. "No. I got it. You have other things you need to worry about." I head toward his front door, but he grabs me by the hand.

"Bower, seriously."

I turn to him and rest my hand on his chest, looking him in the eyes. How I didn't see the adoration in his eyes before now is beyond me. *He is one of the good ones. His concern is always for me.* "Let me just get a head start on this, okay? My mind is racing and I need to get organized. I have no doubt I can get it done, but I have shoddy notes and a million things rolling around in my head. I need some quiet time to mesh it all together."

He nods in understanding, thankfully.

"Can I bring you dinner?"

"Let me see how it goes." I grip his chin and pull him down for a kiss, his lips lingering for a moment before I move past him. "I'll text you."

And then I'm gone.

Okay...so I haven't texted him.

Not because I haven't wanted to, but I haven't had a moment to stop to think.

My phone buzzes again and I pick it up finally to see a few texts from Bennett.

Bennett: You hungry?

Bennett: Why don't you take a break for a second and we can grab something to eat?

Bennett: Babe, I know you're stressed, but it will help to just take a second to breathe.

Bennett: Bower…

I'm about to text him back when there's a knock at my door.

Guilt washes through me as I get up from my couch, pushing past my notebook and crumpled notes. When I open the door, Bennett is on the other side with a grocery bag of food in hand.

"I'm sorry," I say as I let him in.

He winks at me and leans in to kiss me before heading into the kitchen. "Don't worry about it. Do you mind if I cook you some dinner?"

"Mind? Are you kidding me? That sounds like a dream. Do you mind if I keep working?"

"Not as long as you work topless."

Crossing my arms and jutting my hip, I say, "Okay, but you have to cook topless."

"Already planned on it, babe," he says before pulling his shirt up and over his head and tossing it to the floor. My hungry eyes roam his chest, my mouth watering from the thought of dancing my fingers over every hard contour of his torso.

Even though I had more sex last night than I did in an entire year, I don't feel like I got my fill. I need more of him.

"Work isn't going to get done if you're staring." Then he motions a finger at me. "Off with the shirt, beautiful."

I guess a deal is a deal. I remove my shirt and toss it with his, leaving me in a lavender lace bra.

I turn from him, only for him to clear his throat.

"Can I help you?" I ask.

"Yeah, I said topless."

"And I took my shirt off. That's topless to me."

"That's not topless to me," he says. "Want to see those tits."

"These aren't for free," I say, motioning to my breasts. "You have to earn them."

"And the orgasms I gave you didn't earn them?"

"No," I say, turning away and going back to the couch.

"Wow, Bower. I always knew you had a saucy side to you, but to be just flat-out vindictive, I didn't see that coming."

"Show me what you can do in the kitchen, and then I'll show you what I can do in the bedroom."

"I know what you can do," he says.

"You've barely cracked the surface." I sit on the couch and purposefully lean slightly forward, exposing more of my breasts. From where I'm sitting, I hear him clear his throat, which makes me chuckle.

I'll be shocked if he gets through making dinner without touching me.

CHAPTER 36
BOWER

"THIS IS SUCH A GOOD video," I say as I sit on Bennett's lap, completely topless now because he cooked me one hell of a chicken dinner. "I'm getting turned on from you fingering chicken."

"Can you not say it like that?" he says.

"That's what you're doing. You butterflied the chicken breast and then slid your finger through the crack. God, it looks like you're fingering a woman. I wonder if Gretchen will approve."

"Given how she doesn't seem to care how we get views, as long as we get them, pretty sure she'll approve."

His hand climbs up my stomach so his thumb caresses the underside of my breast gently, his other hand slowly working over my other breast, his fingers toying with my nipple, making me feel dizzy with need.

"How is that going to coincide with the book club?"

I turn to look at him. "Are you serious? Bennett, it's a romance book club. This coincides perfectly. Just watch. I'll say something in the text like, 'Come join us for book club.' But then italicize the word 'come.' We have to be suggestive here."

"Yeah, well, I've been trying to be suggestive this entire time, and you still have your phone in your hand."

He pinches my nipple, making me yelp. "Bennett."

He chuckles and then whispers in my ear, "Did I hurt you?"

I shake my head and set my phone down before straddling his lap. "No, just surprised me."

He connects his forehead with mine. "Would you tell me if I ever did?"

"Of course, but I know you wouldn't."

"I'd like to think so, but I sometimes feel myself lose control when I'm around you. . . in you. I just want to make sure you're communicating with me, letting me know if I ever do hurt you."

"I'd tell you," I say.

"Good." He kisses me lightly and then lifts us both out of the chair, his strength so impressive, because he did that without even grunting.

I cling to him as he carries us into my bedroom and he stands me in front of the floor-length mirror propped against my wall.

Standing behind me, he says, "Ever since I saw this mirror in your bedroom, I've had visions of what I'd do to you in front of it." His fingers trail down my side, sending chills up my arm and making my nipples pebble.

"What do you have in mind?" I ask, my breath catching as he drags my pants down, along with my thong, leaving me in nothing.

"Getting you naked is job number one," he says and then walks over to my nightstand in nothing but a pair of sweatpants that barely cling to his hips, his erection swaying between his legs, enticing me to do all sorts of naughty things to him.

He opens my drawer and pulls out my vibrator.

"How did you know that was in there?"

"Assumed," he says and then switches it on, the vibrating sound ringing out in the room. "Ever since I heard you use this, I knew I needed to try it on you." He smirks. "But before I do that, you need to try it out on me first." He nods at me. "On your knees."

A thrill chases up my spine as I grip his hips and slowly lower in front of him. Kneeling, I take his pants and drag them down his thighs, revealing what I thought ever since he came into my apartment, that he's not wearing any boxer briefs. He steps out of his pants and I stare up at his massive erection as he lowers the vibrator down to me.

"Bring me to the edge, but don't make me come. If you do, I'll edge you all night without relief."

The thought of going all night, edging me until I cry almost feels like a fantastic way to spend the evening, but I also don't think I'd withstand the torture.

So I take the vibrator and turn it on and then run it lightly up the inside of his leg. He spreads a little wider for me, allowing me more access. I run the vibrator between his legs, right up against his balls for a moment before I drag it down his leg, causing him to moan.

I repeat the sensation, dragging up, just lightly grazing his sensitive flesh, and then all the way down, switching legs. I watch as his cock jolts every time I graze his scrotum. I marvel at the way the muscles in his chest ripple with every deep breath.

And I get lost in the blue of his eyes as he stares down at me with awe and hunger.

When I notice a drop of pre-cum on his tip, I bring the vibrator back up and then place it right at his perineum.

"Fuuuck," he drags out, his head falling back, his cock twitching. "That's it, beautiful."

He's so hot.

So fucking hot.

Just from the sight of him, I'm aroused, but mix in the tone of his voice when he's being pleasured, oh my God, I'm so wet and ready for him.

As I continue to pleasure him with the vibrator, hitting him in a sensitive spot, I take his length in my other hand and roll my tongue around the head, carefully swiping around and around and around until his hips lightly thrust, looking for some sort of pressure.

I shift the vibrator to be pressing against the underside of his balls just as I take him in my mouth, sucking just the head, but sucking hard, lightly using my teeth around the rim.

"Fuck," he shouts as his legs go weak for a moment. "Fuck, baby, yes."

Inwardly smiling, I continue to lightly tug on him, over and over again, watching as his control slips, his pleasure starts to heighten, and every muscle in his body tenses.

"Close...fuck, I'm so close, baby."

And I take that as my sign, letting him go and removing the vibrator, leaving his cock straining up his stomach, looking so fucking hot that I don't care about the edging. I want him coming on my tongue.

I go back to take him in my mouth, but he stops me. "I'll explode if you do that. And I want to come inside you. I want to fill you fucking up."

He nods for me to stand as he helps me up with his hand, and then he spins me around, so his cock nestles between my ass cheeks.

One hand falls to my stomach, while the other takes the vibrator and runs it across my nipples.

Whispering into my ear, he asks, "Are you turned on?"

"Yes," I say on a gasp when he kicks my legs wider apart.

"Show me."

I reach between my legs, swipe at my pussy, and then bring my wet fingers up to his mouth. I watch in the mirror as his lips wrap around my digits, only to gently suck them until they're out of his mouth.

Staring into the mirror, he says, "Fucking perfect."

And then his hand moves to my breasts, his fingers grazing over my nipples.

"You're so goddamn beautiful," he says as his other hand lowers the vibrator and gently presses it against my slit.

I melt into his touch.

"Eye contact," he snaps, forcing me to look at him in the mirror.

"Good girl," he whispers and then presses kisses along my neck, looking up at me in the mirror every other kiss.

"Could you feel me inside of you today?"

"Yes," I moan as he presses the vibrator harder against my clit.

"Could you taste me on your tongue?" He rolls my nipple and I let out a hiss of pleasure as I continue to look at him in the mirror.

"Yes."

"Did you crave me every fucking second of the day?"

"I wish I had the day off. I wanted...your...fuck," I groan as he continues to play with my nipple.

"What did you want, beautiful?"

"Your cock. Badly."

"Then fucking take it," he says before lifting my leg up on the ottoman next to us and then angling himself so he can slip inside me, the spread of my legs heightening the experience as he brings the vibrator back to my clit.

"Oh God, Bennett." My head falls back to his shoulder and he thrusts up into me, making my entire body jolt with his movement.

"Eyes on me," he snaps, causing me to lift my head and focus on him in the mirror. "That's it, baby. Fuck, I can already feel you squeezing me."

"Because...I'm...close." The vibration's right against my clit, sending me into a tailspin of pleasure.

Pleasure only Bennett has been able to give me.

The type of pleasure I always read about but wasn't sure actually existed. I'm here to say that it does exist.

"I want you coming hard." His hand grips my neck. "Drench my cock." He squeezes just enough to send a thrill of passion through me as he thrusts, the vibrations of the vibrator sending me all at the same time.

"Fuck, Bennett," I yell as pleasure rips through me, my clit spasming, my pussy clenching around him.

"Yes, baby, fuck. Squeeze me. Fucking good girl."

He holds the vibrator against my clit, not letting up as I continue to spiral over and over, his thrusts and slide almost too much for me as my pleasure doesn't stop, but keeps going.

"Jesus fuck," he shouts as he drops the vibrator, bends me over, and then pounds into me at an angle so deep that he's hitting me in a different spot, sending me over the edge once more, my moans uncontrollable, the pleasure so intense that I black out, vaguely noticing the sound of his groans before he spills into me, his body stilling and his chest rumbling with pleasure.

After a few seconds, he helps me back up to standing, turns me around, and holds me tight as I feel his cum start to drip down my leg.

And I love every single second of it.

He kisses the side of my head, both of us sweaty and spent.

"Christ," he whispers, his body slightly shaking. "I've never come as hard as I do when I'm with you."

"I didn't know sex could be like this," I admit. "Sure, I read about it, but that's fiction."

"There's nothing fictional about this," he says and then leads me toward the bathroom where he turns on the shower, keeping me close the entire time.

I wrap my arms around him, finding so much comfort being held by him, up against his chest, like nothing could ever harm me when I'm in his embrace.

I kiss his chest and say, "The way you pressed your hand to my throat, did you learn that from one of the books we've read?"

He chuckles and nods. "I did. That okay?"

"Are you kidding? Of course it was okay. It was so hot."

"You liked it?" he asks as he helps me into the shower and starts wetting us both down.

"A lot," I say.

"Does that mean you're interested in other things, like being tied up?"

I look up at him and feel my entire body light up with the idea. "Yes."

His eyes darken. "Looks like I need to get some silk ties."

"Looks like it."

He kisses my forehead and helps me clean up with soap before he lathers up his own body. Once we rinse and dry off, he helps me into my silk robe and then slips on his sweatpants.

Once we're on the couch, and he has me sit on his lap once again, I show him everything I've worked on so far.

"You know, I think I could see if we could get the clubhouse on the mezzanine level for the book club," he says.

"What's that?" I ask as his hand finds my thigh. He's never not touching me and I love it.

"An event space for corporate parties and whatnot. I could have Gretchen speak to the front office and see if it's a space we can reserve every month. Would make sense, too, because then it really is Books with Bombers since it's taking place in the stadium."

"That is actually a really clever idea, and any decor we use can just be stored there and we can reuse it."

"Yeah, that works."

I turn toward him, grip his chin, and kiss him right on the mouth. "You're so smart."

"Hell, if that's the kind of praise I get for a good idea, how else can I help?"

"You're so horny," I say with a shake of my head, going back to my notes.

"Because I've been waiting years to get you naked."

"Yes, but you've had your conquests in between."

"Yeah."

Curious, actually, I turn around and push him back on the couch as I straddle him again, my hand resting on his chest.

"Tell me about them."

"About the girls I fucked?" he asks, looking confused.

"Yeah, I want to know about them."

"Why?" he asks.

I shrug. "Would it be weird if I thought it was hot, thinking about you with other women?"

"Weird, no. But if it was the other way around, I'd rather cut my ears off than hear about you with other men."

"That's because you're possessive, and I'm more curious. So tell me, who was the last girl you fucked?"

He glides his hand over his jaw and thinks about it. "Uh…shit, I think it was in Houston. Earlier this summer."

"Houston, huh? What did she look like and where did you meet her?"

"You really want to know?"

I nod, fascinated and curious…and maybe turned on, all at the same time.

"Okay, uh…Nolan brought her up to me at the bar. I had a few drinks. I was horny as shit and well, she was hot."

"Yeah?" I ask, my robe falling over my shoulder, exposing it as I lightly move over his cock. "What did she look like?"

Getting into it now, he says, "She was a brunette, curvy hips, killer lips."

"Mm." His hands undo the tie of my robe so the sides open up. "What about her tits?"

"Average," he answers. "Everything about them were average. Just plump enough, nice nipples."

I start to rotate a little faster on his lap, picturing her in my head, him with her as he pushes my robe down so now it's sitting in the crooks of my elbows, my body fully exposed to him.

"How did you fuck her?"

He wets his lips, his eyes grazing over my body, his hands moving up to my breasts. "She had a great ass, so I bent her over the bed and fucked her from behind."

I can see it in my head. A curvy brunette, in a skirt, bent over the bed, and Bennett seeking out his own pleasure, just pounding into her relentlessly, his muscles flexing, his fingers imprinting into her skin…

God, I'm growing wet.

"Did you spank her?"

"Yeah," he says.

"Show me." I let the robe fall to the ground and then lean forward just enough for him to have a good angle.

"Fuck, baby," he whispers before his hand draws back and then connects with my flesh with a snap.

"Mmmmm," I moan into his ear. "Again."

He spanks me again, and then soothes his hand over the spot before going at it a third and fourth time, making me so wet and ready that I sit up, my breasts grazing his face before I stand up, tug on his pants until his cock springs free.

Then I turn around, straddle him so my back is to his chest, and I lift up, only to fall back down on his cock.

"Jesus," he says, his arm snagging around my waist and pulling me up against his chest. His hand slides up my stomach and right to my breast where he cups me, squeezing my flesh and playing with my nipple.

"What did she sound like? Was she loud?"

"Not like you," he says as I rock up and down over him.

"What did she feel like?"

"Tight," he says. "But not as tight as you."

"Did you make her come?"

"What the hell do you think?" he says with such a cocky attitude that it turns me on even more.

"Did you pull out or come inside of her?" I ask, grinding down on top of him as his other hand slides between my legs and plays with my clit.

"Pulled out, took my condom off, and came on her back."

"Fuck, that's so hot. Did you claim her like you claimed me?"

"No," he says, pinching my nipple, almost making me yelp. "She meant nothing to me, just a way to get off while I fucking thought of you the entire time."

"You did?" I ask, feeling breathless.

"All the fucking time. It's always been you in my head." His hand roams from my breast up to my neck, where he holds me tightly, his lips speaking directly into my ear. "Whenever I was with someone, or alone, it was you, right there, in my vision. You bent over the bed, me fucking you. You, in the shower, jerking me off…every scenario, it was you."

"Fuck," I whisper, so turned on by that. "How much did you want me?"

"Every goddamn day," he whispers, his lips caressing my cheek.

"And when you saw me…"

"Yearned, fucking burned for you. I was desperate, cherished every second while wishing that you would look my way, joke with me, touch me…"

"And when I did?" I ask, moving faster on top of him, his cock so big that I can practically feel him in my stomach.

"I'd think about it for days."

"Would you touch yourself at night?" I swivel my hips, trying to get the right position to push me over the edge as my orgasm builds at the base of my spine.

"Yeah, I would."

"Would you ever look at a picture of me and fuck yourself?"

"The picture of you in a bikini at the lake…"

"Oh my God, that's so hot." I turn my head to kiss him, and his hand climbs from my neck to my jaw, holding me in place as his tongue connects with mine.

His other hand moves up from between my thighs to my breast, where he plays with my tits, heightening the experience for both of us until I'm gasping and pulling away, my body falling forward so my hands are planted on the coffee table in front of me, my legs are tucked under, next to his, and I have the perfect angle and leverage to lift up and slam back down on him.

"Fuck," he groans as his fingers dig into my skin. "That's it, baby. Fuck me. Use me."

I bounce on top of him, the angle making him go deeper and hitting that special spot. My fingers curl into the coffee table as that fuzzy, dizzying feeling starts to overwhelm me, my orgasm right there…

"God, Bennett…you're so big. I love your cock." His hand slides up my spine, all the way to my hair, where he twists his fist into the strands and then lightly pulls my head back.

"Then fuck yourself with it," he says.

I scream his name as my orgasm tears into me, pulse after pulse of pleasure hitting me all at once as I feel feral with my hips, bouncing and grinding until I feel him stiffen under me, his cock swelling, and then he's groaning.

"Jesus fuck, baby." He thrusts up into me a few times, his orgasm the sexiest thing I've ever heard. He lets out a deep breath, lets go of my hair, and then pulls me back so I'm up against his chest again. He looks over my shoulder, his hand running like a feather over my stomach and my breasts, turning me on all over again.

"I will never get enough of you," he says as he plays with my pebbled nipples. "Never."

"Good," I say, squeezing his cock with my pussy, getting turned on all over again. "Because I can't give this up." I turn so I can kiss him on the lips. "I can't give you up."

"Not going anywhere, beautiful." His tongue runs across mine and I moan before leaning to the side until my back hits the couch. I place one leg up on the back of the couch and the other off the side. I wet my fingers with my tongue and then bring them down to my clit when I say, "I want your mouth now."

His eyes light up as he shifts on the couch, naked, ready to have a feast.

CHAPTER 37
BENNETT

"THIS IS A SAFE PLACE," Bower says as she places drinks in front of us as well as two quiches. I told her I'd grab the food, but she forced me to sit down. I didn't like it, but I also wasn't about to argue with her. "Public space, we look like friends sharing a meal."

She sits across from me as I stare back at her. "I spent fucking years trying to shake the title 'friend' when it came to me and you. Don't want to hear it again."

She smiles as she picks up her fork. "Ooo, a little sensitive, are we?"

"Yeah, I am. I swear that word haunts me."

"Should I call you my friend and add a hair tousle just for the hell of it?"

"Do it and see what happens when I spread your legs on this table and go down on you just to prove a different point."

She chuckles. "My, my, my, dare I say, I like this pissed-off side of you. Turns me on even more. And here I thought public was a safe place where my pussy wouldn't get destroyed by your monstrous cock."

"Monstrous cock?" I ask as I slice into my quiche with my fork.

"You know you have one. Don't go fishing for more compliments."

"I don't know, I think it's pretty average."

Her quiche falls off her fork as she says, "Bennett, you're kidding, right?"

Playing with her, I say, "No."

She leans forward and whispers, "There is nothing average about the freaking redwood between your legs."

I let out a wallop of a laugh, drawing the attention of a few people, but I ignore them as I say, "Redwood, huh?"

"Uh, yeah, redwood. Can be very intimidating at times. Honestly, when I first saw it, I didn't think my mouth could open wide enough."

"Ahh, you unhinged just fine, babe."

Her eyes narrow from the lightness in my tone. "Just fine?"

I chuckle. "More than fine. Best to ever suck my dick."

She picks up a piece of her quiche. "Why do I feel like you don't mean that?"

"How about this...I've never come in someone's mouth before you."

"Wait, really?" she asks, looking so adorably confused.

"Never." I shake my head.

"Why not? I sure as hell have come on other guys' tongues."

"Don't fucking like that," I growl.

"Where else am I supposed to come when they're down there? Their nose?"

"I prefer to believe you've never been with anyone else."

She laughs. "Okay, keep believing that." My eyes narrow, not happy, which only makes her laugh more. "Who knew that Bennett Brinkman was so possessive?"

"Only with you," I say.

"Just the way I like it, but seriously, why haven't you ever come in anyone else's mouth? That seems off given the way you like to shove your dick down my throat and lubricate it with your seed."

"Don't fucking call it *seed*."

She smirks at me. "Answer the question."

I just shrug, feeling stupid.

"Bennett." She toes my shin gently. "Tell me."

"No, you're going to think I'm some obsessed loser."

"I already think that, so it's fine." My expression falls flat, which makes her cackle. "I'm kidding. Seriously, just tell me. Does it have to do with how much you crushed on me?"

"Yeah," I answer.

"Okay, I find that hot. You know I thrive off the possession you demand of me. So just tell me."

I take a bite of my quiche and then wash it down with my drink. When I set the cup back on the table, I twirl it and stare over at Bower. After a few seconds, I say, "I never wanted anyone else to taste or feel my cum inside them. I only ever wanted you. I wanted you sucking it down and filling you up. That way, I could truly claim you as mine."

She sets her fork down and picks up her napkin. She dabs at her mouth and then lets out a deep breath while staring down at her quiche. "Good God," she mutters and then looks up at me. "Nope, this is not a safe space. I'm so turned on right now I'm about to climb over this table and hump your face."

I lean back in my chair and gesture to my lap. "Have at it, babe. Fucking have at it."

"What do you think?" I ask Gretchen as I show her around the clubhouse.

Bower wasn't able to come to look at the space because she had to help Adalade get ready for a dinner party she's hosting, that she just sprang out of nowhere, one that is about to take up a lot of Bower's time, something I'm concerned about. The moment she told me, I could see her stress level rise, and it made me nervous. With the book club, setting up her book truck, and now the book club event, I can see her calculating her time in a day, and I know she's going to have some late nights.

So I told her I'd walk Gretchen through the clubhouse and report back.

"It's not great," Gretchen says, taking in the space.

A bar's in the middle of the room, making it the center point of the space, which is quite gaudy and gives off more of a sports bar feel rather than an intimate book club space. The walls are white with pictures of past and present players hanging all around, and the high-tops and chairs fitted in the space have seen better days with their chipped and scratched-up wood that not even a black tablecloth can hide.

Yeah, I can admit it's not great either. For some reason, I thought it would be better than this.

"Fuck, what are we going to do?" I ask, dragging my hand over my face. "Bower doesn't have time to look for another venue."

"What do you mean she doesn't have time?" Gretchen asks, looking none too pleased. "I thought she said she could handle this."

"She can," I say in her defense. "But her boss just sprang a new event on her, so she has a lot going on." I look around the room, thinking about what the hell I can do. We have a game tonight that if we win, we win the wild card and go to the playoffs, so my mind is elsewhere.

"She said she could handle it."

I feel my mood shift from attempting to be helpful to downright angry. "And I told you a new project she's in charge of popped up. She's handling everything else. Help me the fuck out with the venue. You're the one pushing this. You're the one needing to help with public relations."

"To an extent," she says, looking just as tired as I feel.

"Well, what the hell am I supposed to do?" I gesture to the space. "Hold the event here? It looks like a shit pit. No one is going to want to come back. There's nothing intimate and cozy about this at all. And you're the one who said capitalize while you're trending. So fucking help out."

She folds her arms over her chest, staring me down, clearly not affected at all by my outburst. Then again, I'm not surprised. "I'm doing you a favor by allowing this side project, Bennett. We don't have to do it, and we can just up your time at the zoo since your season is almost over. I was trying to get you involved in another PR project to appease you."

"Jesus Christ," I say. "It seemed like you helped Graydon out a lot. Why not me?"

"Maple did all that work when it came to him, and so did he, on his own time. I just approved. If you can't handle—"

"We can handle it," I say, even though a small part of me worries that we can't.

"Are you sure about that?"

"Yes, we'll be fine," I answer as I start to move away.

"Okay, but do it right. Don't make me regret approving this. Do not harm the hard work and progress you've already made," she calls out as I move away from her and head to the elevator bank.

Yeah, wouldn't want to hurt the precious approval from the fans. Honestly, this PR bullshit is exactly that—bullshit—just made-up activities to make a human look good in the eyes of other humans.

Here's a novel idea: just be a good person and you won't need good PR to bolster your image.

But, unfortunately, that's not how the world works. Therefore, I have to resort to the next best thing. And trust me when I say I fucking hate this idea, but it's the only thing I have in my back pocket. So I pull my phone out and shoot a text to the Gladdy Daddies as I ride the elevator down to the locker room.

Bennett: I need help.

I keep my phone on hand, knowing OC will be the first to respond, and as I get off the elevator, sure enough, he's answering me. I head to the cafeteria to grab a protein shake as I read.

OC: What do you need? A kidney? I'm sure Graydon can give you one. He's got to have more than two in that huge body.

Graydon: You're a moron.

Nolan: Why would he come here, to a group chat, looking for a kidney? That's some dumbass thinking.

Graydon: You might be growing on me.

OC: Hey! I thought we were soul sisters, Nolan!

Nolan: Not if you're going to say dumb shit like that.

Graydon: This new addition might work out for me.

Bennett: Help, please!

Nolan: You have to tell us what you need help with, sweetheart.

OC: Yeah, look who's the dumbass now!

Graydon: Still you.

Bennett: Jesus. I need help finding a venue for the book club meeting. Long story short, Bower is struggling and I'm trying to help her out. We thought we could use the clubhouse at the stadium, but it's all worn out and not looking quaint. Nor does it give off book club vibes. She doesn't have time to find something else and I have no clue what the hell I'm doing.

Graydon: And you think we do?

Bennett: I don't know. Fuck!

OC: Do you want to hold it at my house?

Graydon: You really are a dumbass.

Nolan: Why don't you do one of those pop-up spaces? They're all over San Fran. Basically they're empty venues, small and intimate, and they can be rented out for different events.

Graydon: Shit, you're right. Maple's friend, Everly, actually works for the girl whose husband is in charge of them.

OC: That was tough to follow.

Nolan: They're huge right now. I see them all over social media. You could probably partner up with one.

Graydon: I can send you Everly's info.

Bennett: That would be amazing, thank you.

OC: Remember when Graydon didn't want Nolan in the group? Look at how helpful he is. I knew all along he was a great addition.

Graydon: Shut the fuck up, man.

Nolan: Have to go with him on this one. Shut the fuck up.

Bennett: Pointing out people's mistakes gets you nowhere.

OC: Oh yeah? I beg to differ. I told Graydon when he was being an idiot with Maple and he fixed it. I told you hooking Bower up with Gator was a huge mistake and you fixed that.

Bennett: His name is Cougar!

OC: Huh, why do I keep doing that?

Graydon: Because you're a dumbass.

The stadium is loud tonight. Really fucking loud.

The pressure to win almost feels overwhelming. We've had our ups and downs this season, some real highs and some fucking terrible lows. And this is the first time since I've been on this team that I've felt the fans are behind us after the cheating scandal.

I don't know whether that's because we're possibly in the playoffs or because some of the PR I've been doing has paid off, but the vibe feels different.

Very different.

Warm-ups are over, the field is being marked up and refined after we took our batting practice, and the stadium is filling up, fans filing into their seats. Up on the Jumbotron, they're playing highlights from the season, the crowd cheering over one of my home runs. I watch the clip, the casual way I trot the bases, no celebration, just a solid understanding that that's what's expected of me.

"I remember that hit," Asher Peppers says, shocking the shit out of me.

He's our snarly catcher that talks to no one. Don't think he's said more than five words to me since I came on the team.

So consider me confused that he's talking to me now. "Yeah?" I ask, unsure of what else to say.

He rests his head against the wall behind him as we both sit on the top part of the bench in the dugout. "Yeah, it was the first time I knew you were going to be a franchise player."

A franchise player? As in someone who represents the team their entire career? Like a Derek Jeter?

"That's a pretty heavy thing to say."

"I mean it," he says as I hold my breath, because I feel like if I make too much movement, I might scare him away. "You will do well here. The fans already love you."

"What about you?" I ask, feeling like I need to offer him a compliment. "The fans love you."

"Don't blow steam up my ass. They tolerate me."

That's a lie. They love him, even when he's a giant asshole in press conferences. I think that's when they like him the most.

"I've been tainted; you haven't," he says. "You're the new face of the club. Don't fucking blow it."

"You weren't part of the scandal, though," I say. Asher never took part in the cheating. You can look back at all the videos that proved that the Bombers were stealing signs, and he was never one of them, but he was here when it happened.

"Doesn't matter, guilty by association." He spits out a few sunflower seeds. No idea when he put those in his mouth. "It's my last year. Doesn't fucking matter either way."

"Wait, really?" I ask, wanting to turn toward him, but he's not facing me, so therefore, I feel like this is a conversation we're having that doesn't look like a conversation to those watching.

"Yeah."

"Does anyone know?"

"You."

"Why just me?" I ask.

"Because." He sighs and stares out at the field. "I love this team. I've given everything I have to it—my fucking blood, sweat, and tears. And even though I'm leaving, with my number stained with a scandal, it doesn't mean I don't love this team any less. I want to see it succeed, and it will best succeed with you at the helm."

"I have so much to learn," I say, thinking about the weight of that responsibility.

"You'll learn along the way. But if I were you, I'd keep your moral compass. I lost mine along the way and should have reported the cheating. But never did. That's on me. Don't make the same fucking mistake I did." Then he turns his head to the side and says, "Got it?"

"Yes," I answer, startled by the intensity of his stare.

And then with that, he hops off the bench and heads into the tunnel toward the locker room.

Jesus.

I stare out at the field, stunned and confused at the same time.

"What was that about?" Nolan asks, taking a seat next to me.

"Don't really know," I answer, not wanting to give away that conversation. Felt important and sacred.

"Guy is weird." Nolan unwraps some Dubble Bubble and shoves it in his mouth. "Your girl here tonight?"

"In one of the suites with her boss."

"Nervous?"

"Nah." I shake my head. "Fucking love it when she watches."

"Ahh, you like to show off?"

"Yup," I answer, feeling the buzz in my veins of knowing that Bower is here, wearing my number on her back. She sent me a picture when she arrived, looking all kinds of hot in cut-off denim shorts and her kid-sized shirt. I told her tonight that shirt and a thong are required—win or lose.

"Maybe when the season is over she can hook me up with one of her friends."

"Her friend is married."

"She only has one friend?" he asks incredulously.

"That I know of. She also has her boss that is in her sixties, and she's single."

"Right." He nods. "I could totally get into that. Don't mind having a mommy in my life."

"You're fucking sick," I say.

"Says the guy who has his very own mommy himself."

"She's not a mommy."

"Fine...an auntie."

"Get fucked," I say as I hop off the bench, his laughter trailing behind me.

CHAPTER 38
BOWER

"HOW DO YOU FEEL ABOUT all the women lusting after your man?" Adalade asks.

We're sitting in our suite together, just me and her. She has Cracker Jack in her hand, and I'm chowing down on some nachos.

"I like it," I say, taking in the sights and sounds of the stadium. Below us everyone is decorated in their Bombers gear, a high percentage of them with *Brinkman* on their backs, sprinkled in with some *Hart* and *Peppers* as well.

"Interesting. I'd assumed you'd be upset about it."

"Why would you assume that?" I ask, taking a big bite of one of my nachos.

"Because you seem like the type who would get jealous over someone trying to make a move on your man."

I shake my head. "Bennett would never even glance their way." I think about how much he likes me and how long he's been waiting to be with me and I love it. I love this feeling of reassurance, that he's all mine, no one else's and no one could even bother him to look the other way. "This might sound full of myself, but it's the truth. Bennett's obsessed with me, and I know for a fact that no woman will ever be able to turn his head. He only has eyes for me, so seeing all the women lust after him to get his attention, it almost turns me on in a weird way—" I say to my freaking boss. "Because I know I have something they'll never have."

"Mm, yes, I can see how that would make you feel. Valued and protected, so for you to look at a woman who is trying to get your man's attention, it's almost thrilling to see."

"Exactly, I like it."

"Well, isn't that a healthy new take on a relationship?"

"I guess so, but I will say this—he does not like it when I even speak another man's name. Ever. Very possessive."

"Now that is a turn of events. So he can talk about other women—"

"But he doesn't."

"But you can't talk about other men."

I shake my head. "Nope, it's not a two-way street where that's concerned, and call me weird, but I actually really like that that's our scenario."

"I can see the appeal. Do you ask him about other women?"

"I do. And he's honest with me. I find the whole thing fascinating, what and who turned him on, what he likes and doesn't like. I guess I'm at a point where I just want to know everything about him, especially when it comes to his sex life. I've never been like that with anyone else."

"Because you didn't care enough about them. Bennett is different."

"He is," I answer as the Bombers take the field and my eyes narrow in on Bennett at third. He adjusts his cap and waits for the ball to be thrown to him, tossing around a whole bunch of swagger with every step he takes.

God, he's so hot out there. And that ass, it's such a nice ass, but framed in those pants, even nicer. I can see why the women are all feral. Hell, so am I. I'm about to march down to the field and rub my whole body all over him like a cat in heat because I can.

"I knew you two would get together," Adalade says. "After I saw you two together at that dinner, I knew it would happen, sooner rather than later too. You both just looked...infatuated with each other."

"We are," I say, thinking about how much I can't stop thinking about him. "Enough about me. What about you? Whatever happened with Draco?"

She smirks as the game starts, the pitcher throwing the first ball.

"Well, you know the dinner party we're throwing? I'm putting it together in the hopes of getting Draco there."

"Wait...really?" I ask, turning to Adalade. "How come you didn't tell me that? I feel like that's a huge thing you need to tell me so I can make sure everything is perfect."

"I wasn't sure if it was in the realm of possibility to invite him, but I just got confirmation that he'd be open to an invite, so now everything has to be perfect. The styling of the table, the menu of the food, the drink pairings—it all has to be cohesive and flow because he is a food critic, and if I can put on a good show, he very well might consider going on a date with me."

"Don't you think he'd go on a date just because he wants to?"

"It's about building trust and a bond," she says. "Why do you think Bennett and you work so flawlessly together? Because you've built a base of friendship and understanding and you've worked up from there. That's what I plan on doing with Draco."

"I actually kind of love that."

"Thank you." She tosses some Cracker Jack in her mouth. "But that is why it's so important that we get everything right."

"Understood." I pull my phone out and open up the notes app. "Let's brainstorm on other things that we can make perfect for this dinner party."

"Don't you want to watch the game?"

"I'm good at multitasking," I say, just as a ball is hit to Bennett. I watch him cut across the diamond, catch the ball on what seems like some sort of insane hop off the ground in front of him, and then he chucks the ball, his arm flying across his body and shooting the ball straight into the first baseman's glove. I cup my mouth and let out a loud cheer, cheering for Bennett before I pull the phone back up and say, "See, multitasking."

"I guess so," she answers and then chuckles. "Also, next time you plan on cheering like a drunken man with nothing better to do with his life, can you give me a warning to prepare? Your yelping rattled my bones, and you know how fragile I am."

"Sorry." I chuckle as she adjusts herself in her chair.

"You may cheer, but it can be with a fancy clap."

"What's a fancy clap?"

She holds up her hands, and with her fingertips, she raps them on the palm of her hand, barely making any noise.

"He won't be able to hear me cheering for him with that," I say.

"As if he can hear you cheering against the rest of the crowd. Common sense, my girl."

"Oh, he can hear. He knows exactly what my screaming sounds like." I smirk just as Adalade slowly turns toward me.

"Well, that's an innuendo if I've ever heard one."

"Perhaps, and perhaps you're not the only one who has had their bones rattled recently."

She chuckles. "Oh, I know what you've been doing. I can see it all over your face. And all I have to say is...keep doing it."

Bower: Are you sure you don't want to celebrate with your team?

Bennett: There's only one person I want to celebrate with.

Bower: OC?

Bennett: LOL. No. You.

Bower: I'm finishing up some work things, kind of knee deep since I went to the game and Adalade and I made a list of things that have to get done. Trying to sort through all of that. So go out with the guys and when you're done, I can celebrate.

Bennett: You're serious?

Bower: Yeah. I'm sorry. I know you probably had plans, but I really want to make sure I get this right. Do you mind?

Bennett: I can just sit with you.

Bower: No, you will be bored and distracting. Seriously, go celebrate with Nolan and everyone else and then I'll catch you when you get home. I'll come to your place.

Bennett: Okay. Sure.

Bower: Are you mad?

Bennett: No, not mad. I get it, babe. Just want to see you is all.

Bower: I know, tonight, promise. I'll come to you.

Bennett: If you're coming, you're coming naked.

Bower: It's the only way I like to come. XOXO

Knock. Knock.

Startled, I lift my head up from where I'm lying on the couch, notebook and computer scattered next to me, a pen still in my hand.

What the hell…?

I glance around, trying to gain my bearings, and that's when I notice the sunlight pouring in through the windows and my front door opening, Bennett stepping through with two to-go cups of coffee in hand and a brown bag.

Fuck.

"Oh my God," I say, dragging my hand over my face as I sit up. "I fell asleep while working. Bennett, I'm so sorry."

He takes a seat next to me, sets our breakfast down, and then drags me up on his lap, where he cradles my cheek and presses a soft kiss to my lips.

"I missed you last night."

"I'm so sorry," I say, guilt consuming me in a way I've never felt before.

"It's okay."

I shake my head. "No, it's not. You won the wild card spot last night, and I wasn't there to celebrate. I just got caught up and, ugh, there's no excuse for the behavior. I'm sorry."

"Funny thing about relationships, it's all about give and take. There are going to be times where I'm really busy and will mess up, and there will be times where you do the same. The key isn't to try to make each other feel bad about it, but to have understanding and grace."

Where the hell did that mature response come from?

"That is...very mature," I say, shocked.

"I might be eight years younger, but I'm not a buffoon."

I laugh as he leans back on the couch, and I snuggle into him, missing his warm embrace. "You're not a buffoon at all; was just surprised."

"I have a lot of wisdom, you know."

"Do you? What other kind of wisdom do you have?"

"Well, let's see, I know where the G-spot is and how to make my girlfriend scream so the entire building hears her."

"Girlfriend," I say, slightly surprised by the title. I mean, yes, we're dating and we're exclusive, but it just feels so foreign to me. I haven't been called someone's girlfriend in a long time.

"Yeah, girlfriend," he says. "Is there a problem with that?"

"No, just surprised is all."

"Why are you surprised?" he asks, pulling away so I can look him in the eyes.

"Just haven't been called that in a long time. I'm not used to it, and I guess we never really had that conversation."

"What conversation is there to have?" he asks, looking truly insulted. "We are dating, we are exclusive to each other, my cock belongs to you... that qualifies you as my girlfriend."

I try to soothe the tension by leaning in and kissing his chest. "Yes, I'm sorry."

He studies me for a moment. I can see doubt in his eyes and I hate that. "Listen, Bower, if you're second-guessing—"

"I'm not," I say quickly, not wanting his mind to go there at all. "I'm not second-guessing anything."

"Okay, because it just seems..." He pauses and then shakes his head.

"What?" I ask, not wanting him to hide his feelings from me. "Talk to me. Tell me what you're thinking."

He scratches his cheek and then says, "Okay, it just seems that you're maybe making tiny moves to slowly separate from me."

"What are you talking about?" I ask.

"And if you're second-guessing, then please just fucking tell me, okay? I'm already in so deep that if this is not what you want, then, please, just tell me now."

"Bennett." I sit taller. "What are you talking about?"

His eyes bounce between mine, almost as if he's trying to read my thoughts.

"You know what? Never mind. Forget I said anything."

"No," I say, not wanting him to drop this. "What would make you think that I'd be slowly trying to separate from you?"

"Seriously, Bower, just forget it."

"No," I say more sternly, looking him in the eyes. "I want to know how I'm making you feel any less confident than you should be."

"No, you're not; you're perfect." He cups my cheek. "Fucking perfect. Just ignore me."

"I don't want to," I say, straddling his lap and pressing my forehead to his. "I don't want you thinking that I care about you any less or that you're the only one putting in the effort into this relationship. I want you to know that I value you and cherish you." I softly kiss his lips. "And I'm sorry if I made you feel any other way than that."

His hands rub along my thighs. "Thanks," he answers and then lightly kisses my cheek, but a part of me feels like he doesn't believe me.

Like there is something inside of him that's doubting my words.

"Bennett, I—"

"Hey, it's fine. Let's eat breakfast, okay?"

"Wait." I stop him from grabbing the food. "Are we okay?"

"Of course," he says, a pinch between his brows.

"Are you sure? Because it just seems like...like you're a little off."

"I just think I'm in a different place than you, and I think I'm figuring that out now, and it's okay, babe. I've been in a different frame of mind where you're concerned for a long time, and this is all still new to you."

"Yes, but that doesn't take away from the way I feel for you."

"I know," he says, his hands rubbing over my thighs.

"And...if this is about the girlfriend thing, I was just caught off guard—"

"It's not."

"But it is," I say. "And I'm...I'm honored to be that person for you."

"Be that person?" he asks. "Can you say it, Bower? Can you say you're my girlfriend?"

"Of course."

"Then say it," he challenges.

Chills spread up my arms as his eyes bore into mine, looking for that validation, and as I feel the words on the tip of my tongue, there is something in the back of my mind telling me to tread carefully, to make sure I know what I'm getting myself into.

And it must be too much of a pause, because Bennett nods and says, "It's okay, Bower. I get it." And then he shifts me off him before standing.

He pushes his hand through his hair, looks around, and then says, "Yeah, I think I might just take my stuff to go."

"Bennett, don't," I say as I stand. "You didn't give me a chance to answer."

"I did, Bower," he says, looking defeated. "And you're just not there. That's okay. I'm not going to drag you into a situation you're not ready for."

"But I am."

"You're not." He shakes his head. "You're not, Bower. I think you might want to think that you are, but when it comes down to acceptance, you're not there. But I want you to get there on your own time. I want to show you that I deserve the title of your boyfriend."

"But you do." I claw at his chest, but he takes a step back.

"Bower, babe, please don't say things just to say them. I'm really okay."

"No, you're not, you're leaving and I'm. . .I'm sorry."

"I'm giving you some space. I know you need it. That doesn't mean I'm upset with you or that things are rocky. I can understand when things might be going too fast for you and when to take a step back."

"I don't want a step back," I say, panic lacing my voice.

He sighs and grips my shoulders, looking me in the eyes. "How about this? Give me a second to collect myself, okay?"

"Why?" I ask, tears forming in my eyes. "I'm sorry, Bennett. Don't go. You're my boyfriend. I'm your girlfriend. Please just don't leave."

He lightly shakes his head. "Bower, don't say that just to keep me here. That's going to piss me off. Don't throw those words around just to throw them around. I want you to say them to me when you're fully ready."

"But I am."

"You're not." He shakes his head.

"I am," I say, growing angry. "Don't tell me how I feel."

He pauses, studying me, his jaw ticking. After a few seconds, he says, "I think it might be best if we just cool off."

"Yeah, I think you're right." Then I bend down and pack up my notebooks and computer. "I think I'm just going to go out and get some work done." I shove everything in a tote bag and then I head into my bathroom, where I flip the shower on and start undressing, my irritation getting the best of me. I take two fucking seconds to answer a question, and he takes that as I'm not ready to be with him.

I'm ready. I'm risking my longest-standing relationship to be with him. I could lose one of my favorite people in my life for him. So yeah, I paused for a fucking second. I should be allowed to do that. I slip into the shower and wet my hair as I hear him enter the bathroom.

I grab my shampoo just as the shower door opens and he steps in, naked. He takes the bottle from me and turns it upside down, squirting some in his hand. When I look up at him, a bout of tears hits me all at once, and I'd like to say that it's from the stress of everything happening and the unknown of what's to come, but what I think it really comes down to is that I'm falling fast and hard for this man and I don't know how to manage the emotions of it all. I'm just not ready to say it out loud yet.

Because it terrifies me.

"Shhh," he says as he massages the shampoo into my hair. "You're good, beautiful. We're good."

I wrap my arms around him and start to sob into his chest as he holds me, his arms encircling me tight, giving me that warmth and comfort I rely on when it comes to him.

He means so much to me...so much, and I just hope that I can convey that to him, even if it's hard using or finding the right words. Because as much as the truth scares me, I can't lose this.

I can't lose him.

CHAPTER 39
BENNETT

"HONOR TO MEET YOU, MAN," Brody, Maple's friend's husband—yeah, a mouthful, I know—says as he shakes my hand. "Congrats on the wild card. Huge for the team."

"Thank you," I say as we stand outside one of his pop-up storefronts.

"Although, I'm a Rebels fan, so I can't be rooting for you in the playoffs. Duty calls, you know."

"Rebels?" I ask, sticking my hands in my jeans pockets. "Fan of Jason Orson?"

Brody perks up. "I am. Do you know him?"

"I've shaken his hand."

"Which hand? Your right." His eyes go straight to my hand and I take a step back.

"Dude, you're being weird and I just met you."

"Right, sorry." He clears his throat and straightens out his suit coat. "Sorry, I just, umm, I get really excited about Jason Orson. Have you tried his potato salad recipe?"

I grip the back of my neck and say, "I really was just here to see the space."

"Right, sorry." He clears his throat again. "Right this way." He unlocks the door and opens it up to me while turning on the lights. "This is what we like to call our library space because it's double insulated, making it extremely quiet from the outside street noise. And because of that, we decided to lean into a more studious decor, with earth tones, multiple styled rugs, and a variety of furniture that you can choose from in the back that ranges from leather chairs to velvet couches. And it's one of our only spaces that has a working fireplace." He walks over to the fireplace that's inside an exposed brick wall and presses a button on the side, lighting up a fire.

I take in the space with its tall ceilings painted the same deep brown as the walls. The floors are old, worn wood that could probably be refurbished, but because of the vibe of the rest of the space, they've kept them to their original scuffs and I dig them.

"What do you think?" Brody asks.

"Hell," I say, smoothing my hand over my jaw. "It's kind of perfect. Can I see the furniture?"

"Sure." But before he takes me to the back, he says, "And these curtains will cover the whole window, so there will be privacy, and we're able to have security at the door as well, which I know was a concern."

"Yeah, if we held this at the stadium, security would have been easier to control, but in a more open space like this, I think we would need it. Just to make sure everyone feels safe."

"Agreed. Maggie has a company she works with that I can hook you up with, but if you have someone you work with already, that could work too."

"I'll ask Gretchen, my PR manager."

"Sure." He nods toward the back of the space and opens a door to an expansive closet that I was not expecting. It's almost as big as the space and stacked with furniture, including couches, chairs, and tables.

"Holy shit," I say, taking it all in, eyeing a few pieces that I think would work. "Wow, this space is almost bigger than the event space."

"Yeah, we wanted to make sure we kept it quaint up front with a lot of options for decor to make it unique and your own."

"Nice." I run my hand over a deep turquoise couch. "I think this would be perfect with a few of the brown leather chairs and then some of the wooden ones. Scatter some of the coffee tables around, and that should be perfect."

"That's what I was thinking as well."

"Can I take a picture to show my girl—" I pause, almost saying "girlfriend," but just leave it at "girl."

Brody nods. "Have at it."

I snap a few pictures for Bower, and then we go out to the front of the space and I take some pictures there as well. Brody makes me take a picture of myself in front of the fireplace, which is so stupid, but he insisted.

When I'm done, I pocket my phone and say, "I think this works perfectly. Could we rent it once a month?"

"Of course. I can get you the details of the rental space along with all the legal bullshit that goes with it, and we can get this set up for you pretty quickly."

"That's great. Thank you, man. I really appreciate it." I hold out my hand and he takes it, his eyes closing for a second, freaking me out. "Are you trying to feel Jason Orson's essence?" I ask.

Looking guilty, he says, "How long ago was it? Have you washed since then?"

"What the hell do you think?"

"I want to say no, but that's just a guess."

"Jesus." I shake my head and take off toward the door. "You're lucky that I'm just desperate enough to put up with that shit, or else I'd be looking for another space."

"Glad you reek of desperation, then."

"I'm sure you are."

"I'll be in touch."

"Yeah, thanks." I give him a nod, not wanting to go for another handshake, and then I hop into my car, my driver pulling away from the curb as I buckle up.

I take my phone out again and send the pictures to Bower.

Bennett: Hope this place works for you, because I confirmed with the guy that it would work for us.

I flip through my emails and see one from Gretchen, asking if I've found a space, so I send her an email with the pictures inside it. I sort of want to tell her off, but I know what little that will do. She's unaffected by that kind of shit.

Just as I press send on her email, Bower texts me back.

Bower: OH MY GOD! Bennett, are you serious right now? That's…that's perfect.

Smiling to myself because I know how happy this will make her, I type her back.

Bennett: And the fireplace works too. We could really have a cozy gathering.

I press send just as Gabby texts me.

I click on her message next.

Gabby: Ryland just surprised me with tickets to watch the wild card game! Ahhhh, I'm going to come see you play.

Smiling, I'm about to respond when Bower texts back. I read the preview message.

Bower: Thank you for finding this place. It means so much to me.

I press reply and type her back.

Bennett: I got you, beautiful. We're in this together.

Once I press send, I go back to Gabby's message, only to realize that I just texted her…

I texted her the response I was sending to Bower.

Fuck!

The immediate need to fucking throw up churns the pit of my stomach as a clammy sweat breaks out over my entire body.

Shit. Shit. Shit.

What do I do?

What the fuck do I do?

Doesn't really matter, though, when my phone buzzes and a reply from Gabby shows up.

Gabby: Umm…excuse me? Who is beautiful? And you're in this together with who?

FUCK!

I don't…I don't know what the hell to do or how to handle this. I can't tell her the truth. Bower would never forgive me, and from the convo I just had with her, she's not even close to being ready to tell Gabby.

My phone vibrates again, but this time, Gabby is calling.

"Fuck," I mutter under my breath as I answer the phone and close my eyes, bracing for impact. "Hello?"

"Bennett Brinkman," she practically squeals into the phone. "Who was that text meant for? Because I know it wasn't meant for me."

"What, uh…what are you talking about?" I ask, knowing there is no way she's going to buy it, but I'm just trying to gain a little more time to think about how I'm going to handle this.

"Do not mess around with me. You said, 'I got you, beautiful. We're in this together.' So who is *beautiful* and why are you in whatever you're in together?"

"Oh that, yeah, uh, that's awkward," I say. "That did go to the wrong person."

"Uh-huh, and who was it supposed to go to?"

"Great question, might be weird if I tell you, though, so—"

"Bennett, don't you dare. Who was it supposed to go to?"

A crazy idea hits the forefront of my mind, and because I really don't have any other way around this, I go with it.

"Yeah, that was actually meant for Nolan."

"Nolan?" I can hear the doubt already in her voice. "You call Nolan beautiful?"

"Yup," I say, with all the certainty I can muster. "Started, uh, a few weeks ago and we just carry it through. You know how superstitious we can be, especially during playoffs. Can't change anything, so yeah, he's beautiful and we're, uh, we're in this together."

There's silence on the other end of the phone, and honestly, I think that's a surprisingly good explanation. Believable, doesn't open it up to many questions.

I think she's going to buy it.

"You're lying to me."

Or maybe not.

"And I don't know why you're lying to me, but there has to be a reason, because you would never lie to me. We established from the very beginning that we would always be truthful with each other because we're all each other have."

Christ, she's going to go there? Over a misplaced text? That almost seems...cruel.

I can't even say that I'm lying to her because I can't muster it. So instead, I stay silent, hating that I can't tell her the truth, because honestly, if this was any other woman, I'd be gushing to fucking Gabby right about now. Tell her how I'm falling in love, how I know I've found the person I want to spend the rest of my life with, even talk to her about proposals and all that bullshit that I know she'd be hyper-fixated on.

But I can't do any of that, because it's Bower.

"You know what? It's fine," she says. "You don't have to tell me. I get it. Maybe it's new and you're still feeling it out, but will you promise me something?"

I'm hesitant to say yes, but then again I don't think I have much of an option.

"Sure," I say.

"Thank you. When you're ready, will you tell me all about her? Give me the scoop. Don't leave one droplet behind."

Hell...

"Promise me, Bennett. It's the least you can do for my little romantic heart."

"When did you develop a romantic heart?"

"Ever since I fell in love. I want everyone else to be in love, too, including you. Wait, oh my God, are you in love?"

Yes.

"Are you nervous you're going to jinx it, and that's why you haven't said anything to me?"

No.

I haven't said anything because it's your best friend.

"Uh, Gabby, I'm pulling up to the stadium," I say, even though that's a lie, which fucking sucks, but I can't handle the stress of this moment. "I have to go."

"Bennett, don't you dare hang up on me."

"I love you, sis," I say, guilt consuming me.

"Bennett Brinkman, at least tell me what her name starts with."

"Glad you got tickets. Text me the details. Love you," I say quickly and then hang up the phone.

I stare down at the screen, my heart racing a mile a minute while my skin prickles with fear.

What the fuck did I just do?

And how much is this going to hurt me?

CHAPTER 40
BOWER

"OKAY, WE CAN GO WITH the blue toile," I say, taking a napkin off one of the place settings I worked meticulously hard on putting together. "Or we can go with the red hand-painted flower with autumn accents."

Adalade stands back, observing each place setting, taking her time to study every angle. And yes, this is what my life is, agonizing on what place setting to pick for a dinner party.

"The blue toile is very much me," she says, running her finger over the patterned plate. "But the red floral is unexpected, and if you pair it with that olive-green table runner, stunning earthy florals with some soft set candles, I truly believe it will be a night for the ages."

"I agree," I say. And just as reassurance, I add, "I feel if you were to have this dinner party in the winter or the summer, the blue would have been stunning, but the red is calling out to me for this time of the year."

"Yes, it's quite fabulous." She picks up one of the plates and takes a look at the back. "Williams-Sonoma. Oh, I never would have guessed."

"Is that okay?" I ask, worried that it's not fancy enough china for her.

"Of course, just a surprise that such a beautiful design would come from a mass-produced store. I thought you said it was hand-painted."

Oh shit.

"The original design was," I say as she looks up at me, eyeing me with that "I don't believe you" look, but she drops it.

"Very well. Please order a setting for twelve. I'd like to have them by the end of the day so we can do a few test runs ahead of the event."

"Not a problem," I say, writing it down.

"Has the chef given you the menu ideas yet?"

"He said by tonight. He's just perfecting it to make sure it reflects your final decision on the plating. He wasn't sure if he should go more traditional or spring for the autumn harvest feel."

"Ah, I see. I'd request to see both, but I'm inclined to lean into autumn harvest."

"I think he is too," I say. "I heard something about butternut squash, so I'm pretty sure he has something wonderful up his sleeve."

"I should hope so." She yawns. "Oh, I feel like I might need to take a little nap. Do you mind finishing up here?"

"Not at all," I say.

"Right, then. Once you clean up, you can be on your way. Thank you, Bower."

"Of course. I'll make sure to check with Chef that your dinner is delivered on time along with the menu options so you can look over them while you eat."

"Lovely." She offers me a kind smile and then takes off for her bedroom.

Thank God she likes the red because that was what I was attempting to lean her into since I thought it was the better option as well.

Since she's taking a nap, I pop my headphones on and go to my music just as my phone starts to ring.

Gabby.

Ugh, I've been avoiding her, which I know I can't do for long, so I answer, promising myself to keep it light and airy.

"Hey, Gabby. How are you?"

"Oh my God, Bower, did you know Bennett is dating someone?"

I nearly drop the plate in my hand as my stomach falls out of my body and hits the floor. Are you freaking kidding me right now? My absolute worst fear is coming to life. How does she know?

"Wh-what?" I ask.

"Yeah, I just got off the phone with him because I was texting him and he texted me back, but he must have been texting with her as well, because he sent me the text that was meant for her."

Oh my God. Oh my God. Oh my God!

"What did he say?" I ask, shaking.

"Let me pull it up so I get the wording right. Oh, here it is. He said, 'I got you, beautiful. We're in this together.'"

Okay, okay, that's not bad, that doesn't really give away much. For all she knows, it could be some girl he met at a bar. This doesn't really have any implications on me, right?

"Huh, interesting," I say as I stack the plates away into their respective boxes.

"You didn't know about this girl?" she asks. "You two hang out. Have you not seen her around the apartment? You told me you would tell me everything."

Guilt immediately consumes me.

"Umm, hmm, I don't think I've seen Bennett with any women."

Not a lie, that's true. The only woman he's been around is me. And I don't look at him with a mirror…well, besides that one time when he was getting me off in front of a mirror, but that's neither here nor there.

"Really? Are you sure? Maybe he's being extra stealthy, but why?"

"Maybe it's new and he doesn't want people to know yet," I say, wishing we could change this subject immediately.

"Perhaps, but I don't think it's new."

"What makes you think that?" I ask.

"Well, when I was asking him about it and trying to probe, I asked if he loved her. And he fell silent. I feel like the natural response to that is outrage or denial because it's all happening too soon. But that's not what it was. He was just silent, like he wanted to confirm but didn't. It seemed like he loves her but he's not ready to admit it out loud."

Stunned, I slowly take a seat at the table, my heart pounding a mile a minute as I try to process what she's saying.

No, he doesn't…does he?

That feels outrageous. He can't possibly love me.

Then again, it's not like he's showed me any other kind of treatment other than love.

He's treated me like I'm the most precious and important person in his life.

He's fought for me, cherished me, encouraged me.

He's taken every small opportunity when around me to make me feel comforted and protected. He's made me laugh and he's made me feel joy. He's helped and he's challenged.

And he's waited. He's waited so long for his moment to be with me. He's waited years to call me his, to be able to express himself…

And not because he's my friend.

He wouldn't have done all of that if he was just my friend.

No, it has to be because…

Oh God, he loves me.

He does and that should…that should scare me, because it's so quick, it's so soon, it's so not what I should be accepting right now, but he does, he loves me.

So the question is: Do I love him back?

"Bower?"

"What?" I ask, snapping out of my thoughts.

"Do you think he's in love?"

My mouth goes dry.

My pulse hammers.

And the fight-or-flight feeling that would normally pump through me in a situation like this slowly starts to disappear as the thought of Bennett—the kind, sweet, thoughtful man that he is—could actually fall in love with the hot mess that I am almost feels…too good to be true.

It's also not something I can answer for him, nor do I want to.

I shake my head as if she can see me. "No, I don't think he's in love," I answer, letting out a deep breath.

"Oh, really? I don't know, I really got a different impression. Have you seen a change in his behavior?"

I'd say so…

"Uh, you know, I feel like this is not the conversation for me," I answer, just wanting to move past this, because I'm feeling a gauntlet of emotions that I was not expecting. "Actually, Adalade is flagging me down, so I have to go. Love you, Gabby."

And before she can even say bye, I hang up.

Fuck, this is…this is unbelievable. He loves me. He has to and I think…oh God, I think…

I'm about to say it out loud when Gabby's face pops into my mind, immediately reminding me why I'm a terrible person.

I bury my head in my hands as the feeling of betrayal, guilt, and disappointment in myself collide in the pit of my stomach, making me nauseous.

He loves me, but I don't think I can love him.

I don't think I'm allowed to.

Standing, I rush to the bathroom, where I shut the door and sit down on the floor next to the toilet. The stress of it all, the deception—it's almost too much for me.

Tears prick at my eyes as I lean over the toilet and my nerves get the best of me right before I throw up, tears streaming down my face and my nausea winning out.

Gabby: Hey, that was weird how you ended the call. I feel like things have been weird between us. Is everything okay?

Gabby: I know you're busy and I don't want to bother you, but I feel like we talked about you moving to Almond Bay and doing the book truck thing and if I pressured you too much, I'm sorry. I didn't mean to. You know I love you and I'm happy wherever you are.

Gabby: I just want to talk to my friend. I shouldn't have hounded you about Bennett. I know you don't really spend that much time with him, or maybe you do, I don't know. Maybe I was feeling jealous and I haven't heard from you much. We promised to always be honest with each other and it just seems like things are off, and ugh, I'm sorry I was just so curious. It seems like he's distanced himself as well.

Gabby: I miss you guys. Hopefully when I come down for the playoff game, I'll see you. Maybe you won't be too busy.

Gabby: Okay, you're probably busy, that's why you're not responding. Love you, Bower. Miss you. Text or call when you get a chance.

"Okay, that would be great. Thank you so much," I say before hanging up the phone.

I check the box on my never-ending to-do list that seems to continue to grow with every new thing from Adalade—she couldn't have chosen a worse time to throw a dinner party to impress Draco, who, if he doesn't show up, I will find out where he lives, drag him by the ear, and personally deliver him to Adalade myself.

Letting out a sigh, I sit back in my chair just as a pair of black sweatpants come into view.

"Nice seeing you here." I look up to find Cougar smiling down at me. "This seat taken?"

Surprised to see him, I shake my head as he sits, sets his cup of coffee down on the table, and then pulls out a protein bar from his pocket, placing that on the table as well.

"Lunch?" I ask.

He nods. "Nothing fuels the body more than some protein and coffee." He smirks and then unwraps his protein bar. "How's it going?" He takes in my disheveled notebooks and papers.

"Oh, you know, busy."

"Like always. How's the book truck coming along?"

I smile and say, "Just about done in the wrap shop."

"Yeah?" he asks, looking surprised.

"Yeah, they just sent me a picture of what one side looks like with the logo."

"Really? Well, fucking show me." He gestures to my phone, making me chuckle.

"You really want to see?"

"I wouldn't have asked if I didn't," he answers.

Grateful for the reprieve from work, I pull up the picture on my phone and flip the screen toward him.

"Shit," he says, taking my phone and looking at it carefully. "Bower, that looks really fucking good."

"I know, right? I almost couldn't believe it when I saw it."

"And look at the shelves. I like the wood feature. Gives that old-timey feel."

"That's what I thought too. And I know it's taken a little extra time to add the wood and stain it properly, but I think it was worth it."

"Agreed." He zooms in. "The logo is fire." Then he looks up at me with a wink. "The truck being the mascot was the right choice."

"Yeah, some guy told me to do it."

He hands me back my phone and says, "You can say it was me. It's okay."

"I don't need to when you know it was you."

"But validation is nice."

"Do you really need to be validated?"

"I don't know." He twists his cup on the table. "After you ditched me on our date, might be nice to have a little validation from you."

I know he's teasing, but it doesn't make me feel any less guilty. "I'm sorry about that," I say, even though I know I already apologized. "It was bad timing on my end and I didn't want to lead you on."

"You don't need to apologize, sweetheart," he says. "I get it, and I don't think it was until I met you that I actually got it."

"What do you mean?" I ask.

He nervously looks to the side before leaning forward, growing closer. Looking me in the eyes, he says, "I didn't really know what I wanted in life, was just kind of floating around, fucking whoever, and not necessarily getting to know anyone. But, uh, you sort of changed all of that." He cutely ruffles his hair. "You made me realize that I could actually have feelings for someone."

Oh God.

"Cougar—"

He places his hand on mine and says, "I'm not trying to get you to change your mind. I get it. You're into someone else, and that's something I'm cool with, because if that means you're happy, then I'm happy. But you changed my perspective, Bower. Made me realize that there's more to this dating world than one-night stands and that sounds so fucking dickish, but it's true. You made me want to try for more."

I don't even know what to say to that.

Is there anything I really can say?

Other than I'm sorry it didn't work out for us?

I'm sorry that I started to fall for someone else?

"Do you think, in an alternate reality, where the other guy didn't exist, we could have made things work?" he asks, his eyes so sincere, the guy I first met in the bar completely gone as his true self shines through.

This is not Cougar.

This is Logan.

This is the man off the field, not looking like a douchebag in the bar.

This is the man he needs to show everyone.

"Do you think it would help if I answered that question?" I ask.

"In all honesty, probably not," he says. "But because I'm a fucking curious, desperate bastard to know if I truly had a chance, I think it would."

I nod, knowing that he's looking for that kind of validation. After a few seconds, I say, "I think if we continued to go on dates and you showed me more of this side of you…the kind, caring, sweet, genuine side, yeah, I think there could have been a chance with us."

He nods and then leans back in his chair.

"It's the Logan side of you."

His eyes shoot to mine. "You know my name?"

I chuckle. "Come on, what parent would actually name their kid Cougar?"

"Fun parents with a passion for animals?" he asks cutely, making me laugh.

"Sure, but that's not your parents."

"No." He laughs. "My dad fucking hates it and refuses to acknowledge the use of Cougar."

I chuckle. "Maybe it's time for an overhaul."

"Professionally, no." He shakes his head. "I'll always be Cougar on the field, but maybe in my personal life, I can lean on the Logan side of me."

I nod. "I think that would be really great, because if I know anything about you, it's the Logan side that I was the most attracted to."

He softly smiles and gives me a curt nod. "Thanks, Bower. I really needed this." Then he stares at me for a moment and says, "Can I ask you something?"

"Sure."

“That guy you ditched me for, that you have feelings for, is he worth it?”

An image of Bennett comes to the forefront of my mind. His beautifully handsome face, captivating eyes, and gentle, sweet soul. The love I know he has for me, that he shows me every chance he gets.

“There’s a pause,” he says. “Leads me to believe he might not be.”

I look up at Cougar as realization rolls over me. I shake my head. “No, he is.”

Because even though I’m terrified about what would happen with Gabby, even though I know I’m risking so much, the thought of not being with him terrifies and hurts me more.

“I can’t…” My breath catches in my throat. “I can’t imagine a moment where he doesn’t see me and his face doesn’t light up. I can’t imagine a day without his nose nuzzling along my neck. I can’t imagine not hearing his deep, sultry voice calling me beautiful.” I nod, my mind letting him brand himself all over me. “He’s worth it. Everything about him is worth it.”

Cougar studies me for a moment, almost as if he’s calculating in his head that he believes me or even that he wants that same feeling.

Finally, he says, “Then he better not fuck it up.”

I shake my head. “I can’t imagine a scenario where he would.”

“Good.” He stands. “I should get out of here. Can I get a hug?”

“Yes, of course,” I say as I stand and wrap my arms around him.

He rubs my back and whispers, “I really hope everything works out with the other guy, but if it doesn’t, you have my number, sweetheart.”

I chuckle as I pull away. “Good luck with everything…*Logan*.”

He picks up his coffee and protein bar. “You too, Bower.”

As I sit back down, I stare at my blank computer screen, my mind racing while my nerves tangle up into a knot in the pit of my stomach.

My heart is there. I can feel it. Without Bennett, it would crack, not feel whole, bleed for the man who has claimed it.

But my mind…my mind is holding me back.

And my guilt? Ooof, that’s handcuffing me.

CHAPTER 41
BENNETT

"ANYONE ELSE SICK OF COMING to the zoo?" OC asks as he places an informational brochure with a picture of us on the front into a paper bag. "This shit could be done by assistants, and yet we're stuck here packing bags for an event they're having. Why is this something we have to do?"

I agree with him, but then again, I'm not going to complain about it. I'm just going to do it.

"Do you really think they have assistants that can do this work?" Graydon asks. "They're not raking in multimillion-dollar contracts like us."

Valid point, but I stay quiet as I work to just get this done.

When Gretchen said this is what we were doing today, I was fucking pissed. Even though we won the wild card, we have two games left before the playoff game, and I want to spend those spare moments in my day helping out Bower, not stuffing gift bags while a photographer takes pictures of us.

Things have been off with us. I can feel it. She worked late last night again and skipped dinner, but I made sure to go to her place so I could at least spend the night with her, which I did, but we just held each other all night.

She wasn't all over me like before, but rather just let me wrap my arms around her and pull her into my chest.

I'm fucking worried.

I know we had that awkward conversation about the boyfriend/girlfriend thing, and I've tried to pull back on that. I don't want to push her. I know she's going through a lot right now and trying to figure it all out—the pressure is mounting—but fuck...the pressure is mounting for me too.

If we can push through into the playoffs, it could be the kind of revitalization we need for the team, more than any zoo PR or book club could ever help with.

But things have to work out in our favor, and I'm just not fully confident in that. We have injuries plaguing the lineup, we're tired, overworked, and there's still a disconnect among all the players, between the old—who cheated—and the new, who are trying to reform the ball club.

There's a lot going on, and the pressure of losing Bower is weighing on me.

"I think I got all the pictures I needed," the photographer says to Gretchen, who is sitting in the corner, tapping away on her phone.

"Great, I'll walk you out." She points her well-manicured finger at us and says, "Keep working. We need all those bags filled." With that, she takes off with the photographer, leaving us alone.

"She's such a fucking beast," OC says, his eyes lingering. "I swear she makes us do this shit just to fuck with us because she can and she knows we're scared of her."

"I'm not scared," Graydon says.

"Me either," I add.

OC looks between the two of us. "You mean when you hear her heels clacking, your taint doesn't swallow your balls whole?"

Graydon looks to me and then says, "Shit like that is why you don't have friends."

"I have friends. I'm looking at them."

"Acquaintances," Graydon says.

"I've heard you have sex, so I think that counts as more than just acquaintances."

Graydon's jaw tightens and I fear if I allow them to keep talking to each other, it's going to go south. "I'm unsure how things are going with me and Bower."

Of course that draws OC's attention immediately. "What do you mean? I thought shit was good with you two."

"So did I," I say, plopping a bag to the side and picking up another. "But we had this awkward moment and I really don't know what to do with it. I feel her pulling away a bit, and, I don't know, the fear of her leaving is stressing me."

"What was the awkward moment?" OC asks.

"It's dumb," I say, feeling slightly embarrassed about it.

"Probably," Graydon says. "But just fucking say it. We don't have all day."

And that is his level of empathy.

At least it's something.

"I called her my girlfriend and she wasn't expecting it and then it got weird after that."

"What do you mean she wasn't expecting it?" OC asks. "I thought you two were a thing."

"So did I," I say. "And then she fell asleep on the couch after the wild card game night and she was supposed to celebrate with me. I know she was overworked, but fuck, I keep thinking that she's pulling away and I can't figure out how to stop it."

OC takes a seat at the table and thumbs through his phone. "You know, I thought that maybe this was old or something, but…do you think this has anything to do with it?"

He turns his phone to me and I see a picture of Bower and Cougar together, his hand on top of hers.

"What the fuck?" I whisper as I take the phone from him and scroll through the pictures. One of them laughing. One of him holding her hand. One of them hugging.

I scan over the picture, trying to figure out when this was taken, but I don't fucking know at this point.

"Is it old?"

"I don't know," I say as Graydon steps up behind me and looks at the pictures himself.

I can feel him tense next to me, but then he goes back to stuffing the bags.

"What?" I ask.

"Nothing," he says, keeping his eyes down.

"No, not nothing. Fucking tell me," I say.

He glances at OC quickly and then back at me. "Cougar just got that haircut. It's a new picture."

Every fucking piece of hope drains from my body as I stare down at the image of the two of them.

The joy in her eyes as she looks at him.

The way he's holding her hand, almost as if his thumb is rubbing over the back of her knuckles. Their hug, how it's their bodies pressing against each other rather than a friendly hug where pelvises stay as far away as possible.

Fuck. "Do you think…do you think they're seeing each other?"

"No," OC says with a headshake. "I don't. She seemed committed to you."

"Then what the fuck is this?" I ask, flashing them the screen again.

"I think that's a question you need to ask her," OC says. "Don't make assumptions. Talk it out, because the worst thing that could happen is you don't communicate those feelings and you wind up doing something stupid."

"He's right," Graydon says. "Talk to her."

I glance down at the time on OC's phone and say, "I have to be at the stadium in two hours."

"We can finish up—"

"OC," Gretchen snaps, coming into the event space again. "What are you doing?"

OC springs out of his seat and starts stuffing bags again, not paying any attention, just working as if that's what he's been doing this whole time.

Graydon whispers, "Just go."

I glance at him and he gives me a curt nod, so I grab my shit and head toward the door.

"Where are you going?" Gretchen asks.

"I have shit to do," I answer, moving past her as I hear Graydon say something to her in the background. I don't care what it is. I'm just on a mission to go talk to Bower. We said we were going to be open and honest with each other, so that's exactly what I'm going to do.

I rock on my heels, hands in my pockets as I stare at the stained-glass doors in front of me, nerves wreaking havoc on my stomach. The entire drive over here, I thought about what I was going to say, how I was going to approach this, and every scenario, it ended with me trying not to fucking beg her.

I'm not going to do it.

I'm fucking not.

She either wants to be with me or she doesn't, and I'm going to have to accept that. I've been in a position where I've liked her much longer than she's ever even thought about giving me a chance, and if she needs a break, to gather herself, then I'll give her a break. But it doesn't mean I'm fucking throwing in the towel. Just means that I will wait. I've waited as long as I have already, so what's longer?

The door opens and Bower stands on the other side, surprised, wearing high-waisted jeans, a button-up shirt with one side tucked in, and her hair loosely tied back, a few strands falling forward, framing her beautiful face.

Fuck, I love her.

So fucking much.

"Bennett," she says, surprised, before looking behind her. "What are you doing here?"

"Can we talk?"

She comes closer, closing off the open space between her and the door. "Bennett, I'm at work."

"I know, baby, and I'm sorry, but I really need to talk to you."

Concern draws her brow together. "Is everything okay?"

"Not really," I say.

"Okay, umm, give me a second—"

"Who is it?" Adalade calls out.

Bower winces and then says, "Umm, it's Bennett."

"Bennett? Well, what on earth are you doing? Bring him in."

"I'm sorry," I say, knowing this is crossing the fucking line, but Christ, I just need to figure this shit out before my game tonight.

"It's fine," she says and then to my surprise, takes my hand and pulls me into the old Victorian-style house.

Adalade walks up, decked out in a maroon silk blouse and matching silk skirt, her hair tidy in a bun at the nape of her neck, and delicate gold bracelets framing her wrists.

Posh and sophisticated, it's the only way to describe her.

"Bennett, it's so great to see you." She comes up to me and presses a kiss to each of my cheeks.

"Hi, Adalade, I'm really sorry that I'm barging in on you like this."

"Oh, it's fine, we're just trying on outfits for my dinner party." She steps back, showing off her skirt. "What do you think?"

I give her a loving smile. "I think you look great in anything you put on."

Adalade winks and then says to Bower, "He's a keeper."

"Do you mind if we step outside for a moment to talk?" Bower asks, her hand still clasping mine. *But for how long?*

"I do," Adalade says. *Fuck.* Again. "I don't want you outside, so please, use my office."

Oh…well, thank fuck for that.

"Thank you," Bower says. "I won't be long."

"Please, take all the time you need. I have to make a call to Greta anyway. She spoke of wearing maroon, and I believe I might claim the color for the evening. She's quite the talker, so I might be a while." Adalade heads toward the living room, while Bower takes me past the ornate staircase and wallpapered walls, past the kitchen, and to a den in the back where she shuts the door.

She brings me over to a green Victorian-style couch and sits us both down. "What's going on?" she asks, her eyes searching mine.

This is it. Communication.

"Babe," I say, feeling my throat grow tight.

Fuck.

This is embarrassing.

"I, uh…fuck, this is not the time to talk about this and now that I'm sitting here, in your place of work, I realize just how inappropriate it is to disrupt you, because I know this is not something you'd ever do to me."

"What's going on?" she asks, looking scared.

"I'm sorry," I say, wanting her to know that. "But I have a game tonight and it's stressing me and I just want to fucking know."

"Know what?"

"I, uh…I've been struggling with where things are going with us." She sits taller, her eyes looking concerned, but I keep moving forward. "I feel like you've been pulling away, and fuck, I like you, Bower, more than I think I can tell you at this point, and I know you're not there yet, but…"

"Bennett, you're worrying me," she says, her eyes searching mine.

"I need to know where you're at mentally with me, because if you're just not in the same place and want some space, that's okay. I can honor that and give you time, but I do…I do want to know, because the wondering is going to fucking kill me. And if you're seeing other guys, then just let me know because—"

"Bennett, where is this coming from?" she asks, looking so confused that I almost wish I never brought this up.

"It stems from the distance I've felt," I say. "The worry I have over your feelings for me. And the fact that there were pictures of you with Cougar at the coffee house again."

Her eyes search mine again before she says, "Let me see them."

Let her see them?

No denial?

No reassurance?

Just let her see them?

Stomach churning, I pull my phone out and look them up quickly, then turn my phone to her. She takes it and scrolls through the pictures, nodding for a moment before she hands me back my phone and stands up.

"Bower," I say, panic filling my chest. "If that's what you want, just tell me, it's not going to—"

She places her hand on my chest and pushes me back on the couch before straddling my lap. She grips my face and looks me dead in the eyes.

"I want you. That's it. No one else."

My hands fall to her hips as the smallest of weights is lifted off my chest.

"Those pictures, I can see how they might look. But it's not as it seems. And I do believe you deserve an explanation, because if I saw you with another woman, I probably wouldn't believe it, but I'd be extremely jealous."

Her fingers play with the hem of my shirt, my skin prickling with the nearness of her, the comfort of her touch.

"I was at the coffee house, trying to get everything checked off my to-do list, and he showed up. We frequent the same place, so it was bound to happen. He asked to sit with me and I let him, because I felt like I owed him that after the night of our date. I showed him the progress I made on The Whimsy Wagon and then I apologized to him for the way I ditched him. He understood and asked if there wasn't another guy, would he have possibly had a chance. I told him maybe, but that I was falling for someone else." She pauses, her eyes connected in all earnest with mine. "That's you, Bennett. I'm falling for you, and as you know, I can't stop that from happening."

Relief floods through me. *Thank fuck.*

"He did say if it didn't work out to give him a call."

My expression falls to annoyance, which makes her smile.

"It's always good to have a backup plan."

"Bower," I say, making her chuckle.

"But in all seriousness, I know those pictures look like something else happened, but I can promise you, it was a conversation where I let him down gently. He actually said that he wants to change his dating lifestyle too. And I'm sorry I didn't tell you. I've just been..."

"Avoiding me," I say, wanting to get that out of the way.

"Maybe," she says, with a shrug.

"Why?" I ask, my grip on her hips tightening, not wanting to let her go.

She sighs and looks off to the side, and I can see that there's a distinct reason but she is questioning whether or not she should tell me.

"Open communication," I say to her. "I came here, looking like a fucking jackass, asking why you were with another man. I think you should open up too. Don't you think?"

She nods. "You're right. You did come here looking like a jackass." We both chuckle and she sighs, her head tilting to the side. "A handsome jackass, though."

"At least I have that going for me," I answer.

"You have a lot going for you," she says, her fingers playing with the waistband of my jeans.

"So..." I encourage her.

"Right, umm." Her eyes dip down to my stomach. "Gabby called me…"

Probably should have fucking guessed that.

Whenever she pulls away, it's because she's reminded of the promise she made Gabby.

"What did she say?" I ask.

"Well, she asked if I knew about this secret girl you were dating, because apparently you accidentally sent her a text that I'm assuming was meant for me."

"Fuck," I say. I'd forgotten that my sister is nosey as shit and probably would have asked Bower about it. "I'm sorry I didn't tell you about it, because it wasn't anything where she'd suspect it was you I was texting. And I didn't want to cause more stress, but I should have known she would ask you about it."

"I know. She read it to me, but she was asking me a bunch of questions, and well, she said that it seemed like whoever you were texting, it seemed like you were in love with them."

Oh.

Fuck.

Her eyes connect with mine. "And she asked if I thought that was true. I, uh, I really didn't answer her."

"But it freaked you out," I say, knowing that the girlfriend thing nearly split us in two, but this…this could end us. I can feel it.

"It did," she answers honestly. "On many levels." Her eyes meet mine again. "I don't want to hurt you, disappoint you, or make you feel any less than you are."

"You don't," I say.

She nods. "I do. I know I do, or else you wouldn't be here, at my work. And then there's your sister. Every time I feel better about these feelings for you, she reminds me why I *shouldn't*. So then I pull away, because that feels like the most logical thing in my head. But…" Her hand connects with my cheek, her thumb playing with my scruff. "Then you come to see me, and I can't…I can't pull away, Bennett. Everything about you makes me feel better. You make me feel desired, needed, comforted. My life is so much better with you in it, in the capacity where I can call you my boyfriend."

My chest expands from that title, one that I will fucking hold on to.

"But I'm in turmoil all the time—"

"Don't you think that if we could face these feelings together and they continue to grow, that when we're ready and we do tell Gabby, she can't really be mad at us, because it's not like we're just fucking…right?"

"Maybe," she says, dragging her hand down my chest. "But I'm not ready."

"I know. And you know that I promised on your terms. When you're ready. There is no pressure on my end. I just want to make sure we're headed in the right direction, you and me. That there is nothing between us. That you're not holding back on sharing anything with me." I cup her cheek. "Because, babe, I'm in this for the long haul. You know that."

She nods. "I do." Her fingers play with the waistband of my jeans again. "I know how much of a long haul you've already gone through." Her fingers slip under my shirt and then right to the button of my jeans, where she undoes them.

"Babe," I say, my breath catching in my chest as she slides off my lap and between my legs. "Bower, what are you—"

She unzips my jeans and then tugs on them, pulling them down just enough to release me from my boxer briefs.

"Bower, baby."

Her tongue circles over my cock, swirling a few times to get me hard as a goddamn stone before her mouth descends over my shaft, taking me to the back of her throat.

"Fuck." I lean my head back, knowing this is not the fucking place for this, but to hell if I can stop her. Her mouth is sinful, and the moment it touches me, I have no control.

My hand falls to her cheek, where I cup it gently as I stare down at her, my heart beating a mile a fucking minute as she sucks hard, working all the way down to the root of my cock and then back up, not gagging once, just taking me all the way in. It's never been like this with anyone else. No one has loved on me, pleasured me, turned me on like her, and that's how I know my feelings for her are not just infatuation, but something so much more intense than that.

"Fuck, beautiful, you're so good," I say as she cups my balls and starts massaging them in her hand. "Yes, Jesus, babe."

Her head bobs up and down, her hand working along the seam of my sack, the pressure she's applying along with the light scrape of her teeth, it has me so goddamn close…

"Right there, babe. Right fucking there, so close…"

She pulls me in a few more times, swirling her tongue, playing with the head. My body tenses, my legs starting to grow numb as my orgasm builds at the base of my spine.

"That's it, about to…fucking…come," I say, my chest expanding with breath, my hand tensing in her hair.

Fuck…so close.

So goddamn close…

"Christ." I tense and then she's pulling her mouth off, her hand replacing it as she pushes my shirt up, exposing my stomach and chest. Her lips trail up my skin to my neck as she pumps hard on my shaft. Her tight grip getting me there, right fucking there.

Her lips move to my ear and just as her hand flies over my cock, giving me the best goddamn hand job of my life, she whispers, "I love you."

I still, my heart exploding as she squeezes my cock and pumps down, causing my dick to swell. My cum shoots out of me, all over my stomach, along with the most intoxicating pleasure ripping through me. I'm almost dizzy.

"Fuuuck," I moan, my head falling back as she continues to lightly pump me until I stop spilling all over my stomach. "Jesus, Bower." She leans in and kisses my lips, her hand releasing my cock just as she pulls away, and then with her finger, she swirls it around my cum, spelling something on my stomach.

When I look at her, feeling dazed and the most satisfied of my life, she whispers, "Mine." Then sticks her finger in her mouth, where she cleans it off before helping me back in my pants and pulling my shirt over the fucking beautiful mess all over my stomach.

I'm still catching my breath, watching her in a haze as she leans in and presses a kiss to the corner of my lips.

Then my mouth.

Then my cheek.

And back to my ear.

"So much," she whispers. "So freaking much."

I didn't know this kind of joy could ever be felt. I thought when she finally gave me a chance, that it was the epitome of joy I could feel, but this, this is on another level.

And I'm so stunned, so shocked, that I don't even know how to respond as she starts to move away from me. My brain gets it together for a moment and snags her hand before she can get too far away. I pull her to me, tugging her on my lap and cradling her in my arms.

She smiles sheepishly, cups my cheek and says, "I know."

"But I want you to hear it."

"I don't need to hear it. I've known for a while. Looking back, I could see all the ways you showed me just how much. So it's not new to me. I've experienced it without you ever having to say anything."

"I'm glad, baby, but please let me say it."

She leans in, presses the softest kiss to my lips, and says, "Say it."

Cupping her cheek and looking into her eyes, I say, "I love you, too, Bower."

Her smile stretches across her lips, the joy in her expression unmatched. "You're right, I needed to hear you say it too." She kisses me again. "Tonight, can we have a night of just you and me and nothing else?"

"I have a game, babe."

"I mean after the game. I can meet you at your place. And it just be us. No distractions, no pressure, no worries—just us."

"I want nothing more than that."

"Good." She kisses me one more time. "Then it's a date."

She stands from my lap and tugs on my hand, pulling me up from the couch, my shirt sticking to me in the worst fucking way. But I'll be honest, I love it. Because I know under my shirt, written across my skin, is her declaration.

Her hand in mine, she walks me out of the office and past the living room, where Adalade is on the phone. She offers me a wave and a smile before Bower walks me to the door. I turn toward her and place my hands on her hips as she leans into me for a hug.

I wrap my arms around her and kiss the top of her head.

"Thank you," I say to her, knowing she probably doesn't want it, but I want to say it to her anyway. "Thank you for not freaking out on me when I came here. Thank you for quelling my nerves and for understanding me." I tilt her chin up. "I've loved you for so fucking long, so thank you for not running away, but accepting me for who I am."

"How could I not?" she asks, her hands smoothing up my chest. "You're irresistible, Bennett. Everything I could have asked for. Everything I didn't know I was looking for." She kisses the underside of my jaw and whispers, "I love you so much. I'll be watching your game. Good luck."

"Thank you, beautiful."

I kiss the top of her head, feeling like the happiest motherfucker on the face of this earth as I say my goodbye and head out the door.

Bower loves me. And now I have forever to show her how precious she is to me.

CHAPTER 42
BOWER

I GLANCE AT THE TV. Bennett is stepping up to the plate, so I pause my work for a moment, sit back on my couch, and pull my knees into my chest.

I don't know how he does it.

People are yelling and screaming for him. There's the pressure of the game, of the team…and he's so calm. He looks like none of that is even playing in his mind as he adjusts his helmet, taps the plate with his bat, and then gets into his stance.

The announcers talk about how well he's been playing this season, especially in the fall, how he's leading the team in hits and RBIs and how they see him as a true leader on the field.

He swings and misses but doesn't seem upset as he steps out of the box and stares at his bat, composing himself. The camera zooms in on him like it always does, taking advantage of the mysterious shadow the brim of his helmet casts over his face. And sure, I know a different side to him, one that's not dangerous at all, but on the field…it's different.

And it's hot.

He's so freaking hot that all I can think about is tearing off his jersey and having a repeat of what I did to him this afternoon.

He steps back into the box and repeats his process before turning his head toward the pitcher.

The pitcher kicks his leg up and shoots the ball at Bennett, plunking him in the back and sending Bennett to the ground.

"Oh my God," I gasp as I cover my mouth with my hand.

But it's as if it's nothing, and Bennett stands up while his team's medical staff walks over to him.

They're asking him questions, but the entire time, Bennett is staring down the pitcher while taking off some guard on his elbow and removing his batter's gloves.

And it has to be the single hottest thing I've ever seen.

Bennett is ready to rip apart the man on the dirt hill, and I'm here for it.

He nods toward the medical staff and then with one more glare at the pitcher, he jogs to first, where he sticks his batting gloves in his back pocket and then stares down the pitcher again.

Well…I'm horny, and I know exactly what we'll be doing when Bennett gets home.

I fluff my hair one more time and check myself in the mirror.

Bennett should be home any moment. Some days it feels like he's home right away after a game, and others it feels like an eternity.

Tonight, though, tonight is for us.

I check out my shirt, smiling to myself at the idea.

I took the far-too-small Bombers shirt I have and cut it even shorter, so it hits me mid-stomach. Then I cut a deep V in it so my breasts are nearly spilling out of it. I chose not to wear a bra, because…why? And then I paired the outfit with a navy blue thong and matching fluffy socks. I curled my hair, leaving the ends straight but didn't bother with makeup because I plan on making out with my man the entire night.

The door to his apartment opens and then shuts right before I hear him say, "Babe, you here?"

Smiling to myself, I play with my nipples for a few seconds, making them hard so they poke against the shirt. "In your room."

I hear him set something down, probably his bag, and kick off his shoes before he heads back to the bedroom. I'm sitting on his bed, one leg over the other, hands propped behind me, waiting for him.

The moment he sees me, he stops as his eyes grow hungry. "Jesus Christ," he growls. He reaches behind his head and yanks his shirt off. My eyes fall to his chiseled chest, thick and carved in all the right places. "You look fucking hot."

He comes up to me and pushes me down on the bed, hovering over me with his hands on either side of my head.

"Congrats on the win," I say as my hand drags over his chest. "How's your back?"

"Fine." He lowers his mouth to my neck and starts dragging his tongue along my skin.

"Are you sure?"

"Beautiful." He takes my hand, placing it on his dick. "I'm hard as a fucking stone right now because my hot-as-shit girl is welcoming me home in the best way possible. I don't give a fuck about my back."

I chuckle as his mouth goes back to my neck and he plays with my breasts on the outside of my shirt.

While he makes me feel insane with his mouth, I push down his joggers, along with his boxer briefs, and he steps out of them before coming back to me.

"Fuck, baby," he says as he squeezes my breast and kisses my cleavage.

I reach between us and start pumping him, causing him to groan, the rumble of his pleasure turning me on even more.

"I want these tits." He squeezes them together, and then to my surprise, grabs each side of the V in the neckline and rips it open, tearing the shirt in the front so my breasts spring free and the shirt falls to the side. "Better," he says and then pulls my right nipple into his mouth.

Sucking.

Licking.

Nibbling.

"Fuck," I moan as my hand drops from his cock and glides up his back to his head, where I attempt to hold him in place, wanting so much more.

He moves to my other breast, continuing the same beautiful torture, making me so wet, so ready, that by the time he pulls away, I'm panting, needing any kind of pressure or friction.

I look him in the eyes, holding his head still, and say, "Fuck me, Bennett."

His eyes go wild as he lifts and then turns me over in a blink of an eye. My ass is thrust into the air, but he keeps my head firmly planted in the mattress.

The feel of his palm dragging over my back, where his name and number are, down my spine and all the way to my ass, where he spanks me with a flick of his hand.

"Oh fuck," I groan as he does it again and then presses the head of his cock over my clit, rubbing it up and down. "Yes, more."

He spanks me again and starts flicking the head of his cock over my clit, up and down, up and down, while spanking me at the same time, creating a sensory overload. My brain's unable to comprehend pain and pleasure, but I'm still enjoying it all.

He slips the head of his cock inside me for a second and then pulls it out before planting his hand on my ass.

"Oh my God," I cry. I can feel my pussy contract, looking for any sort of pressure from him. "Fuck me, Bennett. Fuck me."

"Jesus, beautiful," he says as he lines his cock up with my entrance again. "Feel this. Take my cock." He slams himself all the way into me, to the fucking hilt, stealing my breath from my lungs. "You make me so goddamn hard. Fuck." He groans and then digs his fingers into my ass as he starts thrusting—hard and fast, relentless.

Not giving me a moment to adjust.

Not taking his time.

No, I asked to be fucked and he's delivering.

I have to grip the comforter for balance as he slams into me, one thrust after the other, jostling my body and shaking my bones.

"Yes, yes, oh God, yes, Bennett. Fuck me. Fuck me harder."

He growls under his breath and holds one hand to my ass and the other on my shoulder, pinning me as he continues the onslaught of his thrusts, over and over and over again until I'm close.

"Right there, oh my God, right there. Don't stop."

But…he does.

He stops and then pulls all the way out.

"Bennett," I complain just as he flips me back over and I'm met with a very hungry, aroused man, chest rippling, eyes on me, ready to fuck me into the wall.

He spreads my legs and then guides himself inside me again, but this time, he's slower, deliberate as he takes my hands in his and pins them to the sides of my head, our palms touching, our fingers clasped together. As he thrusts, slowly, in and out of me, swiveling his hips, he lowers his mouth to mine and captures my lips.

A wave of pleasure ripples through me, not from his thrusts, but from the intensity of his touch, the love I feel in this moment…like I'm the most precious thing he's ever held.

His tongue swirls around mine.

His chest lightly grazing my hard nipples.

His cock pulsing at just the right pace. The friction is far more intense than when he had my ass up and he was pounding into me.

When he releases my mouth and moves to my neck, he whispers, "I love you, Bower. So fucking much."

I clench around him, loving those words, eating up the tenderness in his voice.

He makes me feel desired, needed.

Like he won't find his next breath unless I'm next to him.

And that's the difference between him and every other guy I've ever been with. I'm cherished, important, and one of a kind in his eyes.

His lips find my neck and he starts sucking, biting, nibbling, and then soothing with his tongue as he continues to drive into me, bringing me to a point that I don't think I can take much more.

"Bennett, please."

He lifts up and looks me in the eyes, our hands still connected, our bodies sweaty, our pleasure building. "Please what?" he asks.

And as I stare up into his sultry eyes, I know there is only one answer to his question. "Please make love to me."

"Fuck," he whispers before kissing me and picking up the pace of his hips while he makes out with me.

I moan into him.

I grip his fingers tighter.

And I spread my legs wider, giving him more room as he bottoms out, giving me so much pleasure with one thrust that I gasp and start tensing around him.

"Shit," he whispers as he lifts and does it again, caressing my G-spot in a way that is unlike anything I've ever experienced.

"Bennett," I gasp, my eyes falling shut as my stomach coils and my pussy starts to clench, throb…contract around his thick, hard cock. "Oh God, I'm right…"

He thrusts again and the breath is stolen from my lungs.

Again and my legs grow numb.

One more time and white-hot pleasure springs through me in a flash, tipping me over the edge.

"Oh my God!" I cry out in a moan as he continues to pump, giving me that friction I need so I can extend my orgasm, the feel of him stoking the fire while I clench around him.

"Fuck," he groans, his eyes growing tight right before he lets out a guttural groan, stills, and then spills inside of me with a roar. "Fucking hell."

His head falls forward, our noses almost touching as I continue to contract around him and his cock twitches inside me, both of us on cloud nine as we look into each other's eyes.

He releases my hand and then cups my face gently, his lips pressing a kiss to the tip of my nose. "Fuck, baby, I love you."

I smile up at him and whisper, "I love you, too."

I stir in bed, noting the sun peeking through the curtains of Bennett's room. *I'm probably going to be late for work.* But there is not a chance that I'm getting out of bed right now, not with Bennett wrapped around me, his dick pressed up against my back, hard as a stone.

Last night was...everything.

I always thought that someday I'd find the man of my dreams and that we'd get married and start a life somewhere. But as time's passed, there hasn't been anyone that's checked all the boxes, and I've found myself making compromises to fit someone into the requirements.

That's why I kept pushing to be with Cougar, because I saw the potential, even though there wasn't that deep connection.

But Bennett...I don't have to try with him. It's just there.

The friendship.

The desire.

The commonalities.

The love.

And it's all because I dropped my shield, just a moment, and allowed myself to feel the love he has for me. I allowed myself to see it, and when I went to put that shield back up, it wasn't there anymore and it left me exposed in the best way possible.

And last night just solidified how much I don't want or need that shield anymore.

"Morning," he grumbles behind me as he shifts, his hard cock moving against my back.

"Good morning." I grow wet from the thought of him taking me, right here, right now, him barely awake.

So I lift my top leg, propping it up and then reaching behind me and guiding him toward my entrance.

"Mmmm, fuck," he groans, his body so warm as he slips inside of me. "Baby, you're so wet."

"And turned on." His hand slips around to my front, pulling me against his chest, and then he squeezes my breast as he starts to pump inside of me.

"Fuck, you're so warm."

And already on the verge of coming for some reason.

"Jesus, baby. So tight."

He squeezes one of my breasts, his fingers playing with my nipple, his hips thrusting into me.

"God," I groan, resting my head against him and bringing my hand between my legs, where I start playing with my clit.

"Shit, I like that. Make yourself come all over my cock," he groans, his voice so deep from just waking up.

So I work my fingers faster, spurring on my pleasure, bringing me to the edge quicker than I probably would have wanted, but God, it feels so good. He feels so good, and before I can pause and let myself just relax, my fingers push me over the edge so I'm coming fast and hard, clamping around him as he pulses inside of me.

"Fucking hell," he calls out as he pumps a few more times and then stills, coming inside of me with a low groan.

We both relax, the tension easing as he kisses my bare shoulder and then whispers, "Was not expecting that."

"You woke up with a huge erection, and it turned me on."

"It's all your fault." He chuckles and squeezes my breast again. "You're so fucking hot and warm and—"

Knock. Knock.

He stills and then lifts up. "Was that the door?"

"Yeah, I think it was," I say.

He drags his hand over his face. "Oh right, I scheduled breakfast to be delivered for us."

"And that is why I love you," I say as he slips out of me and puts on a pair of joggers.

His eyes are barely open, his hair's a mess, and he looks so freaking delicious that it takes everything in me not to jump him right now.

"That's why you love me?"

I laugh and nod.

He points his finger at me. "You're going to regret that."

I pretend to shiver in bed. "I hope you don't punish me."

"You can bet that sweet, spankable ass of yours that I will."

I press my hand to my chest. "Oh, whatever will I do?"

He laughs and takes off down the hallway as I slip out of bed and into the bathroom just as I hear him answer the door.

I'm about to pee when I hear him say, "Gabby…what…what are you doing here?"

I still.

Oh my God.

CHAPTER 43
BENNETT

I CAN STILL FEEL HER perfect fucking pussy clenching around my cock.

I can still taste her on my tongue.

I can still smell her all over my goddamn body as I open the door, Bower on my mind…*and* my sister's face comes into view.

Smiling.

Excited.

Looking for a surprised reaction.

Well, she's fucking getting one… Because what the actual fuck?

"Gabby…what…what are you doing here?"

"Good to see you too," she says with a grin. "Surprise!"

Yeah, you can fucking say that.

"You could have waited for me," I hear Ryland say as he walks up to us in the hallway, luggage in hand.

Fuck.

FUCK!

"Hey, dude," Ryland says as he looks me up and down, taking me in. "Rough night?"

"Uhh…" I scratch my chest, trying to figure out a way around this, because they're going to want to come in, and I can't even remember what the apartment looks like at this point. Did Bower leave anything laying around?

"Oh my God." Gabby presses her hand to her mouth. "Is she here?"

My eyes widen, because…what?

"Is that girl you've been seeing here?" Gabby pokes her head around me, or attempts to, but I quickly stand in front of her, preventing her from seeing anything.

"Umm, no," I answer, not wanting her to think anyone is in there. "No one is in here, Gabby," I say a little louder, hoping that Bower can hear me. "Just, uh, just surprised is all." I scratch the top of my head, still not letting them in. "I thought you were coming in tomorrow."

"We were, but Hattie and Hayes said they would take Mac for a long weekend, so we came in early. Isn't that exciting?"

"Yeah," I say, realizing that I'm being so fucking awkward. At this point, I should have given her a hug, brought her into my place, and sat her down, but I smell like fucking Bower. I don't want Gabby anywhere near my apartment, and the last thing I want to do is sit down and chat.

But I have to get her out of here. I need to give Bower a second to remove herself from my apartment.

"Are you okay?" Gabby asks, sensing how fucking awkward I'm being.

"Yeah, sorry, your knock just woke me up, startled me. Now I'm, uh…I'm hungry," I say, an idea forming in my head. "Can we grab something to eat?"

"I'd love that."

"Great. Let me grab a shirt and some shoes and then we can get going. Be right back." I go to shut the door, but Ryland stops it and gives me a look.

"You really going to make your sister stand outside and wait for you?"

"Oh, no." I chuckle nervously. "Come in."

I turn around and do a quick scan of the living room, grateful that I don't see any of Bower's things, and then I rush to the bedroom, where I shut the door and whisper, "Bower?"

"Closet," I hear her whisper back.

I move toward my walk-in closet where she's huddled up, wearing one of my shirts, looking terrified.

"Does she know?" she asks, practically shaking.

I pull her into a hug and shake my head. "No. She doesn't have a clue. I'm going to take them out to breakfast to get them away so you can slip up to your place."

"What if she wants to have breakfast with me too?" Bower asks, looking so terrified that it actually hurts me to see her like this.

"I'll tell Gabby that I want it to be just her, me, and Ryland so we can catch up." I lift her chin and whisper, "I promise it will be okay. I have your back, beautiful."

"I know." A tear falls down her cheek.

"Please don't cry."

"I'm sorry, I just…I wasn't expecting this."

"Me either, but I have it handled, okay?"

She nods and then I lean down and press a kiss to her lips. "I have to go. Wait until we leave and then you can sneak out, okay?"

"Okay."

I give her one more kiss and then find a shirt, a hat, and some socks. I slip on my slides, throw on some deodorant, and then I head out of the bedroom, where Ryland and Gabby are waiting in the living room.

"Ready?" I ask.

"Do you have a place in mind?" Gabby asks, following me, Ryland trailing behind her.

"Yeah, there's a place around the block that's good." I guide them out of the apartment and shut the door. "Maybe like a two-minute walk. Serves pancakes and French toast, all that shit."

"Great." Gabby pulls me into a side hug and then says, "Oh, wait, I need to go to the bathroom."

Alarm bells ring. "Ah, just go at the restaurant."

"What?" She laughs. "No, don't be weird. I'll just go in your place."

And before I can stop her, she opens my door and barges in, only to stop flat in her pursuit. I know the minute Gabby sees her, because it's as if a knife of betrayal is stuck right into my sister's back...metaphorically held by Bower.

She's silent for a second and then she says, "Are you kidding me?"

"Gabby," I say, rushing into the apartment, where Bower is standing still in the middle of the living room and dining room—in just my T-shirt and nothing else—looking both freshly fucked and terrified at the same time.

Ryland follows me in, takes in the scene, and then whispers under his breath, "Fuck."

"Is this why you were trying to usher us away?" Gabby asks, pointing to Bower but looking at me.

"Listen," I say in a calm, mature voice, but it doesn't click as Gabby starts to get incredibly emotional.

"You promised me," she says to Bower. "You promised you wouldn't go there with him. You looked me in the eyes and said you would never. You lied."

"Gabby," Bower says, tears spilling down her face now. "It wasn't planned. I didn't...I wasn't..."

"I don't want to hear it." Gabby shakes her head. "I knew this was going to happen. I just knew it. We're supposed to be each other's person. Is that why you've been avoiding me, because you were fucking my brother and knew it was wrong?"

More tears from Bower as she nods.

"So you're not even going to deny it. You broke our relationship all for what? A quick fuck?"

"Hey," I snap, stepping in. "That's not what—"

"Yeah," Bower says. "That's what it was, Gabby. A quick fuck. Because that's all I'm ever good at, right? No relationships, just fucking? I ruined an almost-decade relationship for a quick fuck with your brother." She moves toward the entryway, blowing past me as my heart hammers in my chest.

Gabby lets out a sob and Ryland is by her side in an instant. "I begged you to watch over him, protect him."

Bower, looking stoic now, just shrugs and says, "Guess having him spread my legs was far more important than protecting him."

"Bower," I say as I go after her before she can leave. "What are you doing?"

"Leaving."

"Why are you saying that when you know it's not true?"

"Isn't it, though?" she asks, making me step back. "In her eyes, that's all she'll see."

"That's not true," I say, but when I turn to look at Gabby, Bower slips out of the apartment without another word, stealing my heart along with her.

There's no fucking way I'm letting this happen. I'm not going to let her walk away like that. But before I can go after her, there is one thing I have to fix.

I turn around and face my sister, who is looking at me as if I just betrayed her in the worst way I could imagine.

"Bennett, why?"

Wetting my lips and trying to not let my anger get the best of me, I say, "Because I love her. Because I've loved her for a long goddamn time. And when she finally saw me as more than her best friend's little brother, when she saw me as a man who would do anything for her, she let me into her heart. And I took advantage of it, because I refused to let the woman I love go." I point to my chest. "I took advantage of the situation, Gabby. Not her. I pushed her to be with me, to break your trust, because I'm a selfish prick who didn't care that she broke a promise with you, despite how much she agonized over it. I didn't fucking care, because I love her and I wanted her."

"You don't—"

"I do," I say with all the conviction I can muster. "I have from the moment I first met her."

Gabby rolls her eyes, actually rolls her eyes, and when I say that my sister is the sweetest, most protective human I've ever known, I mean that. But to see her like this, dismissing my feelings, it cracks and breaks me. I don't want to be the man she taught me to be.

"That's infatuation, Bennett. There's a difference."

Taking a step forward, anger brimming from every surface of my body, I say, "Do not fucking tell me what I feel for her is infatuation, because I know the goddamn difference. Infatuation is what you felt for Ryland when you two first started fucking."

"Watch it," Ryland growls, but he doesn't intimidate me.

"Love is what I feel for Bower. It's buried itself into the marrow of my bones, where I itch to see her, where I feel at ease when she's in my arms, where I'm content and satisfied knowing that I'm the one she's going to bed with and I'm the one she's waking up next to. This is not a fling. This is not a one-night fuck. This is real. This is love, and she feels the same way." Gabby's eyes widen. "And for you to insult her, to her fucking face, without giving her a goddamn second to explain..." I shake my head. "That's not the sister I grew up with. That's not the sister who raised me. You're better than that, Gabby, and I'm disappointed that you would treat someone you love in such a manner, angry or not. Broken promises and all. She deserved more than that."

I head toward the door, ready to chase after Bower just as she walks through the door, tears still streaming down her cheeks, but with some bravado in her face.

She walks right up to me and places her hands on my chest. Looking me in the eyes, she whispers, "I'm sorry. You know I love you. This isn't a quick fuck to me. You were never that to me. Ever." She cups my cheek. "I love you so much."

Fuck.

Talk about a way to make my heart nearly fly out of my chest.

She takes my hand in hers and leads me to Gabby, standing tall, chin held high. "This is not a fling for me," she says, standing up for me. "This is not some fantasy I'm trying to fulfill. This is real. Everything about it. I attempted to push him away every chance I got. I tried desperately to shut down my feelings. I agonized over what this would do to my relationship with you, and I tried to stuff it all away, but every day I felt pulled toward him. Like the universe was shoving me in his direction, not even giving me a chance to deny it. And so one day, I gave in. I allowed myself one moment with him, just to satisfy the feeling, but it only intensified it."

Gabby swipes at her eyes, looking between the two of us.

"And as that feeling intensified, the more I knew I couldn't stay away, as hard as I tried. And when...when you told me you thought Bennett was in love, I knew it was with me. I knew what you said was true, because I saw it in every little thing he did for me or said to me. And normally, I'd have run from finding out such a thing, because I wanted to protect us, Gabby. I wanted to protect our relationship, but I realized, as much as I love you...I love him more. And if you genuinely loved me the way you've said, then you would understand what I'm saying to you."

Bower draws closer, and the pride in my chest nearly bursts at the seams.

"I love Bennett. I see my future with him, so much so that the moment I walked out that apartment door, I realized that if I took any steps farther away, I'd be distancing myself from the life I want, the life I've been working toward. And I wouldn't allow myself to do that." Taking a deep breath, she continues, "I'm sorry that this is how you found out, and I wish we could have told you in a way that wasn't so shocking, but now that it's out in the open, I will not cower. I will not change because you're uncomfortable. I love you, Gabby, but this is my life, this is Bennett's life, and it's unfair for you to try to dictate how we live it."

Holy.

Shit.

Gabby asked Bower to protect me, and well...she just fucking did.

Gabby looks between the two of us, confusion in her eyes.

"As much as I'd love to talk about this with you, Gabby, sit down and work it out, I'm late for work and I can't call in sick." With that, she tugs me toward the door and leads me outside into the hallway. With the door shut, she stands on her toes, pushing me against the wall, and claims my mouth, her tongue swiping open my lips.

I groan into her as my hands fall to her hips, tempted to pick her up and pin her against the wall, but I hold back. Her eyes stare up at me dreamily. "I love you, and I'm sorry for a moment it seemed like I didn't."

I shake my head. "Don't apologize, beautiful, that was…fuck, thank you."

"Anything for you," she answers. "You're it for me. You're my number one, above anything and anyone else. That won't change."

And I hadn't known how much I needed to hear that, because this entire journey of getting to this place in our relationship has felt like an uphill battle of me convincing and begging her to give me a chance. At times I've felt numb, like whatever I did wasn't going to work. I've felt anxious, like at any minute she was going to slip through my fingers. I've felt nervous that I was coming on too strong.

But this…this reassurance, it feels like that final weight that has been resting on my chest has finally been lifted off and the girl I love is officially and forever mine.

"Thank you, baby," I say, leaning my forehead against hers. "I love you."

"I love you, too. I have to go, though. No game tonight, right?"

"No game."

"Okay. Then I'll see you tonight." She kisses me one more time and then takes off, in only my shirt, through the hall of our apartment building.

I watch her disappear up the stairs and then I head back into my apartment, ready to face my sister.

When I shut the door behind me, Gabby is still in the same place, looking stunned and speechless.

Ryland clears his throat. "I, uh…I'll just let you two talk it out."

"I ordered breakfast earlier," I say to him as he heads toward the door. "It should be delivered soon. You can eat it."

He just nods and then heads out of the apartment, leaving me alone with Gabby.

I tug on the brim of my hat and say, "Want to sit?"

She swallows and then after a few seconds, she nods.

We both head to the couch, and once we've sat down, she picks up a throw pillow and holds it as she crosses her legs. She looks out my window and I wonder if she's going to be the first one to talk when she says, "I don't know what to say, Bennett." Her eyes meet mine. "I truly…I think I'm still trying to comprehend everything."

"I get that," I say. "And like Bower said, I'm sorry you found out this way."

"Were you ever planning on telling me?" she asks.

"Of course," I answer, my voice softening. "Gabby, you matter so much to me and I want you to be a part of every aspect of my life—"

"Besides this one."

"No." I shake my head. "It was…it's been hard. Bower wasn't lying when she said she agonized over her feelings. It's been a fucking roller coaster, one that has put me through the wringer because she didn't want to hurt you. She didn't want to break your trust, and therefore, she was off and on with me until…well, she couldn't fight it anymore. It wasn't until recently that I've actually felt confident in our relationship, that I didn't think she was going to slip between my fingers. And with that confidence, I was going to come to you with the truth, but you beat us to it."

She bites down on the corner of her mouth. "How long?"

"When she moved here," I answer. "It took a bit, but I started making my move. She never hit on me. It was always me moving in on her."

"How long for you?" she asks.

"Like I said, ever since I met her. And sure, maybe when I was sixteen, that was infatuation. But as I got older and spent more time with her, that infatuation morphed into so much more. She became a best friend, and from there, so much more. And I'm sorry, Gabby, I really am. I know how much she means to you, but...I love her and I can't deny that anymore."

She slowly nods and stares out the window. "And she loves you?"

"She does." I reach over and force my sister to look me in the eyes when I say this, "You asked her to protect me, take care of me, right?"

"I did. I made her promise."

"Well, she just did, Gabby. She stood in front of you and stood up for me, for our love. Even though I know she was breaking inside knowing that she lost your trust. She did that because she didn't want to hurt me."

She stares at me for a moment and then slowly nods. "You're right, Bennett. She did."

"She could have walked off. She could have let me handle it, but instead, she didn't. She took it upon herself to talk to you and stand up for us. Protect us."

"She did."

"So, shouldn't that mean something?"

Gabby looks off to the side. I can see her trying to accept the idea of us.

"I know it might be weird and it might take some time to get used to, but I promise you, this isn't a fling. This isn't something that will break your relationship with her. I think it's only going to amplify it."

"How?" she asks, her eyes finding mine.

"Because I'm not letting her go," I say. "She's it for me, Gabby. And when the time is right, when she's ready, I will propose. I don't want anyone else. It's her and only her."

"Oh my God," Gabby says, sitting a little farther back. "You're serious."

"Dead serious, sis. She's it. She's the only person I've ever loved and the only person I ever want to love."

"Wow. I'm just…" She shakes her head and then takes a deep breath before looking at me. "Wow, Bennett, I'm…I'm so happy for you." Tears stream down her face before she leans in and hugs me. I wrap my arms around her and hold her tight. *This is the sister I've loved forever. This woman.* "All I want is for you to be happy. We've been through so much together, so fucking much, and I just want you to have the happily ever after you deserve."

When she pulls away, I smile at her. "Bower is that for me. She's my everything, and I never want to lose that. I love you, Gabby, so much, but I need you to accept this."

She nods. "I do."

"Really?" I ask.

"Yes. It might take me a second to adjust my mind when I see you two together, but you're right, she did what I asked, she protected you and…your happiness matters most, and if you're serious, if she's the one, then…I guess…" Tears threaten to fall over. "Tell me how I can help you propose."

I chuckle as her tears fall and I wipe them away for her. "I don't think she's there yet, even though I am. But when I think she's ready, I'm coming to you."

"You better."

And then she pulls me into a hug once more.

CHAPTER 44
BOWER

"ADALADE, I'M SO SORRY," I say as I shut her front door and move into her house. "It's been a morning." And that is an understatement. How I hated seeing Gabby's crestfallen expression of betrayal and disgust. That's so not her, and it hit me hard. But when I knew I had to turn around and go back, I'm so glad I got to hear Bennett's words.

"Love is what I feel for Bower. It's buried itself into the marrow of my bones, where I itch to see her, where I feel at ease when she's in my arms, where I'm content and satisfied knowing that I'm the one she's going to bed with and I'm the one she's waking up next to. This is not a fling. This is not a one-night fuck. This is real. This is love, and she feels the same way..."

They gave me courage...because the man I love also stood up for me, showing me *my* worth in his eyes. How did I get so lucky? *Even if I feel as though my heart has been shredded today.* And I'm hungry. And without coffee.

I walk into the dining room, where Adalade is sitting at the table, looking over a menu. "What can I get started on for you?"

She looks up from the menu and says, "Bower, I believe it's time I let you go."

All the color drains from my cheeks. "Wait, what?"

She carefully sets the menu down and crosses one leg over the other as she looks up at me. "I've noticed that you've been distracted lately, and that's when I came across this." She pulls a folder from the chair next to her and sets it down on the table.

It's my book truck folder. Shit, I must have left it here accidentally.

"I assumed this was something you wanted me to look through, but after I sorted through the papers, I realized it's a business venture you're currently pursuing."

"Adalade, I wasn't—"

She holds up her hand, silencing me as she stands. She takes a step forward and then takes my hand in hers. With a genuine expression of understanding, she says, "You can't have this job forever, Bower. As much as I'd want to keep you forever, you need to grow and blossom and do something that interests you, not take care of a spry, yet older lady."

"I love working with you," I say, desperation clawing at me.

"We do have our fun, but there is so much more you can offer. This is not a goodbye right now. This is the push you need to pursue other things. But I will require you to offer me thirty days' notice before you leave."

"But you're the one firing me," I say, so confused.

"Not firing, dear, encouraging you to move on."

"But—"

"You're scared?" she asks, calling me out.

"Yes," I say, my emotions starting to get the best of me, because this is not what I was expecting after the morning I had.

"It's good to be scared. Without the fear, you're never going to push yourself to work harder and accomplish your goals. I am where I am today because I lived in that fear for so long. It's time you do the same." She pats my hand and then walks over to the living room. I follow behind her. When she takes a seat on the couch, she pats the spot next to her, so I join. Is this some sort of nightmare? "You will land on your feet and succeed, I know you will."

"I don't understand. I thought I was doing a good job. I know I was late this morning, but Gabby showed up and it was a mess—"

"This has nothing to do with this morning or your work ethic. Frankly, you're the best assistant I've ever had. This has everything to do with you and that folder you left behind. It's a folder of ideas. I want it to be a folder of reality, and you can't make it a reality by working for me." She turns toward me. "I care about you enough to let you go."

I know what she's saying, and it's incredible to have a boss so thoughtful, but it doesn't make it any less scary.

"What if I fail? My dad failed spectacularly when we were young, so who's to say I won't?"

"If you fail…then you fail. And then you try something else. Just because you fail doesn't mean it's the end of the world. But you will never know unless you try. For all you know, you could be opening yourself to so much more, and the fear is holding you back. Either way, you won't be working for me, so you can either try achieving your dream, or you can go look for another job with a boss who isn't as fabulous as me."

I chuckle as I lean back on the couch, staring up at the ceiling. "Ugh… I'm not ready."

"No one is ever truly ready. You can prepare all you want, but that's all it will ever be—preparation. And you need action. And you're just about there. So, take action." She pats my leg. "You have thirty days."

I let out a deep breath. "How about sixty?"

She laughs. "Don't make it fifteen."

"Okay, okay." I sit up now and turn to Adalade. "Thank you," I say, knowing it's the right thing to offer her right now, even though I'm terrified.

"You know, I've always seen something in you, something special. It's why I hired you in the first place, and I couldn't quite put my finger on it. But this idea, this is that something special. I see you succeeding and succeeding *spectacularly*." She squeezes my hand. "Best of luck, and I better be on the list of guests for the grand opening."

I smile at her. "How could you not?"

"My thoughts exactly. Now tell me about Gabby. She came over this morning?"

I groan. "Adalade, she found out about me and Bennett."

She crosses one leg over the other and says, "Now this is the type of stuff I'm going to miss when you leave. Tell me everything."

Bower: I'm headed home. Where are you?

Bennett: At the stadium, getting a workout in. Are you okay? I've been texting all morning.

Bower: Rough day. Adalade fired me—well, gave me thirty days, and I'm still trying to wrap my head around that as well as the Gabby thing.

My phone rings in my hand and I don't have to look at the screen to know who it is.

"Hey," I say as Mark drives me back to my apartment building, a benefit I'll miss when I'm finished working with Adalade.

"Babe, what's going on? She fired you? Was it because you were late this morning?"

"No. She found my folder for the book truck, and well, she loves the idea, thinks I can succeed doing it, but knows that I won't put my full effort into it if I'm still working for her. So, she's letting me go."

"Shit," he says as I can hear weights being set down in the background. "Are you okay?"

"I think so. Still kind of in shock, trying to convince myself that everything will be okay."

"It will be," he says softly. "You have me, and I'll be there for you every step of the way."

"I know, and I love you for that," I answer, staring out the window. "How are things with Gabby? I know I just left you there with her, but I figured you two needed to hash things out."

"Things are good," he answers, giving me hope. "We talked through things, and I know she wants to talk to you tonight. She's at the apartment she's borrowing from Hayes right now, but she and Ryland are coming over later. Do you think you would be up for a chat?"

"Yes," I answer, not even having to think about it, because if anything, I need Bennett in my life, and if that means having an awkward conversation with my best friend, then so be it.

"You sure? I can reschedule, given everything that's happened."

"No. I want to talk to her. I want this to be out in the open and okay, because I don't want to have to hide anymore. You mean so much to me. I want to be able to celebrate that."

"I don't think you understand how happy that makes me, baby."

"Hopefully so happy that I can take advantage of that happiness tonight, when your sister leaves."

He chuckles, the sound so sweet and giving me comfort. "Yeah, I foresee you taking advantage multiple times."

"Words I love to hear."

"Is Mark driving you?" he asks.

"Yeah, should be home soon. When are you getting back?"

"I have about a half hour longer here and then I'll head home. Meet you at my place?"

"Yes, but no sex until after we speak to your sister. It was awkward talking to her this morning for many reasons, but one of the main ones was that I could still feel you inside of me."

He chuckles some more. "Nothing wrong with that, beautiful. Also, that position we did this morning, I don't think I've ever come that fast."

"Bennett Brinkman, is that how you're going to talk in public?"

"Sure as hell is."

I laugh, feeling lighter, knowing that even though everything is so up in the air, as long as I have Bennett by my side, everything is going to work out.

"Okay, I'll see you when you get home. Love you."

"Love you, too, baby."

"Do I look okay?" I ask, smoothing down the plain black shirt I chose to wear with my wide-leg jeans.

"No, you should wear the shirt you wore for me last night."

My brows draw together. "First of all, you ripped that to shreds. Second of all, I'd never wear something like that in front of your sister."

"Shame, I thought it really had 'meet the sister' vibes."

"You're not being funny like you think you are," I say as he loops his arm around my waist and pulls me into his chest.

"It's going to be fine, I promise." He kisses my neck, easing some of my tension. "And then when they leave, I can fuck you until the morning."

"Your wild card game is tomorrow. You are not fucking me until the morning. You can have one fuck and then a decent amount of sleep."

"No way. More than one fuck."

I shake my head. "No, just one orgasm for you tonight."

"That's fine. I can have one; you can have multiple."

"Bennett, one for both of us."

His face contorts into full-on displeasure, which is really cute. "Do you really think I'll be able to fuck you just once? With the way my dick reacts to you?"

"Fine. One fuck and then one morning fuck in the shower."

"Or like this morning. I want to wake up inside of you again. Fuck, it was so good." His hand creeps under my shirt and up my back.

"Stop that." I step away from him and hold up my hand. "Do not turn me on right before your sister gets here. I'm warning you."

Smiling a devilish smile, he takes a step toward me and grabs my hand, placing it right over his dick. "Already turned on, babe."

"Oh my God, you need help. This is why I shouldn't date someone younger than me. Your virility is unmatched."

"Don't really hear you complaining about that when I'm tongue deep in your pussy."

"Bennett, I swear to God—"

Knock. Knock.

I still and look over toward the door.

"Oh my God, my nipples are hard and your sister is here."

"They are?" He looks down at my breasts. "Shit, that's hot." Then he tugs on my shirt and I slap his hand away.

"What do you think you're doing?" I whisper.

"Playing with them."

"Bennett Brinkman," I hiss, causing him to laugh.

"Chill, baby, it will be good. Promise."

Then he kisses me on the lips and walks over to the door while I adjust my clothes and hair and will my nipples to calm down.

The door opens and I hear Bennett greet Gabby and Ryland before they walk into the apartment. When Gabby's eyes meet mine, I feel my stomach twist in knots, with a bout of nausea for fun too.

She pauses for a moment, taking a deep breath, and then to my utter freaking surprise, she walks up to me and pulls me into a hug.

Relief floods through me, tugging on my emotions and turning me into a sobbing wreck as I cling to my best friend.

In between sobs, I say, "I'm sorry. I didn't mean to. I didn't want to, but it just happened. I meant what I said, that I would always protect him. I just, I couldn't stop it. I…I love him, Gabby, and I need him."

"Shhh." She rubs my back. "I know," she says softly. "I know."

I bury my head into her shoulder, crying as I hold on to her, not wanting to let go. "I'm not going to hurt him, I promise. This isn't a fling."

"I know you won't." She cups the back of my head. "I know you will protect him. You already have by standing up to me. By standing up for him."

"Because I love him."

I feel her nod and then after a few seconds, she grips my shoulders, looking me in the eyes.

"I'm sorry," I say again. "I didn't want you to find out like that. I wanted to tell you, I was just trying to figure out the best way so I didn't hurt you either."

"I appreciate it," she says, her voice full of understanding. "And I'm sorry I freaked out. I should have trusted that you would have Bennett's best interest at heart. You always have."

"And I always will," I say. "It's just…it's just a little different now."

"Just a little." She smirks and then hugs me again before letting go.

Bennett comes up to my side and wraps his arm around me before kissing the top of my head. Gabby watches us, curious but also confused, which is quite funny, watching her try to process it all.

"So you two are really together?" she asks as Ryland goes to her side.

I look up at Bennett and say, "Yeah, we are."

Gabby slowly nods, still processing. "How did it happen?"

Bennett's hand curls around my waist, holding me tighter. "A lot of fucking patience and pursuing."

"But…didn't you set her up with Cougar?" Gabby asks.

Bennett drags his hand over his face. "Please, don't fucking remind me. That was a huge mistake that caused me far too much anguish."

"Why did you do it?" Gabby asks, utterly confused.

"Because Nolan Hart told me to set her up with someone douchey so I could swoop in when she got disappointed."

"Jesus." Ryland shakes his head. "I wouldn't take advice from a guy who wears crop tops during warm-ups and humps the water cooler for good luck."

"He humps the water cooler?" I ask, causing Bennett to roll his eyes.

"It's a new tradition that he gets fined for by the team, but he doesn't care, because we keep winning."

"I like it when he dick-bumps you guys," Gabby says with a smirk.

"Dick-bump?" I ask, thankful that the tension in the room's starting to fade.

"Yeah, instead of a chest bump, he bumps dicks."

"No one likes that," Bennett says, causing Gabby to laugh.

"I don't know. Seems like something I'd like," I say, smirking at Gabby.

"Perhaps we need more of it," Gabby says.

"I think we do."

Bennett looks between the two of us and then says, "I will not allow you two to gang up on me." Then he forces me to look him in the eyes and says, "Remember, I'm your number one Brinkman now."

"Ooo, I don't know." I glance at Gabby. "She's my girl."

"Yeah, well, can she make you come on her tongue like I can?"

"Bennett!" Gabby screeches, pushing at his shoulder, making him laugh. "Oh my God, don't say that stuff. I know I'm okay with this now, but boundaries."

"Says the girl who was telling me all about the sex she had with Ryland."

"Bower is my best friend," Gabby defends.

"Yeah, and Ryland was my coach."

The room falls silent and Ryland leans over and whispers, "He has you on that one, babe."

Bennett brings his attention back to me and puts me on the spot. "So...who is your number one again?" He wraps his arms around me and lifts my chin up.

Smiling, I reach behind him, my hand out to Gabby, and I hold it as I look him in the eyes and say, "You are." And then he kisses me while I squeeze her hand at the same time, Gabby squeezing it back.

"That's what I thought," he says as he pulls just far enough away to add, "I love you."

"I love you, too."

"This is great and all," Ryland interrupts, "but I'm fucking starving. Can we get some food?"

"Yes, we must feed my husband," Gabby adds. "How on earth will he be able to pleasure me with his tongue this evening if he's deprived of food?"

"Jesus…Christ," Ryland groans as Bennett pretends to throw up in his mouth.

Gabby and I share a smirk, one that's laced with all the understanding and appreciation we have for each other. This might have been a bump in the road, but I know…I know that we will be okay.

"I don't know. This whole dating-marriage scenario could be fun," Gabby says.

"You know two can play that game," Bennett replies, both of them looking at me curiously.

I glance between the two of them and shrug. "Don't look at me. I'm here just for the plot."

EPILOGUE
BENNETT

"CAN YOU HAND ME THAT candle?" Bower asks as she fidgets with her display.

"Baby, it looks amazing." I hand her the candle, even though it's not needed.

"Thank you." She takes a step back, checking out The Whimsy Wagon and her shop setup.

We were able to secure another property from Brody, an open courtyard with vines covering the bricks and a spot that fits the wagon as well as seating and extra shelves for extra merch. Bower has the spot for the next two weeks, which we thought would be smart—establish a solid location and following and then move around the city. She's thinking that she could always rent the spot again for events, maybe even book signings since there's an attached building that would hold about two hundred people.

"God, I'm sweating." She shakes her hands out and I quickly scoop her up and pull her off to the side, where I set her down on one of the high-top chairs and trap her with my arms.

"Don't be nervous. You worked so hard for this, the book club is already a success because of you, and this grand opening will be a success, too, because you put it together."

Her expression softens as she cups my cheek. "I couldn't have done it without you."

"Nah, you could have. You just would have been sexually frustrated."

She chuckles just as Everly, our event planner, who has been so helpful, calls out, "Bower, can I borrow you for a moment?"

She looks me in the eyes and says, "I have to go."

I give her a quick kiss and then help her down from her chair, watching as she walks away looking so fucking good in her deep teal dress and black heels. I have plans for her tonight, so many goddamn plans, because we can finally relax.

After Gabby and Ryland found out about me and Bower, we went out to dinner and had one of the best nights, all of us joking and enjoying each other's company as if nothing had happened. But I got to hold Bower's hand and kiss her whenever I fucking wanted, which only made Gabby kiss Ryland. Weird, maybe, but we laughed about it.

The next night, we wound up losing the wild card game. Our team just wasn't cohesive enough to make it work, which meant we were done for the season.

Honestly, it felt good to be done, given everything that was going on.

And I hate that mentality, but I know management is going to shake up the team for next year, get rid of some of the soured contracts and try to create a whole new image around the team, which I think will help... as well as the book club.

When I say that popularity in our female fans has picked up, it's an understatement. We're already planning a romance book night, and we're trying to invite some authors out for the event. Bower is assisting and having the time of her life with it.

We're both still reading, but now I'm starting to branch out and send her some of my romance recommendations. Bower found it incredibly hot that I was taking the initiative in our romance reading journey, and then proceeded to play with me, a vibrator up the ass, and well, let's just say the entire building could have guessed what she was doing to me by the moans coming out of my mouth.

Bower also started a tradition that once a week we read a passage from one of our books and we reenact it. Not that we needed any extra spice in our life, but fuck, do I look forward to those nights, because not only do we read it, we listen to it on audio as well.

I was telling Nolan about it the other day, and he's convinced that he has to start reading now, that maybe if he spends some time in bookstores, learning and educating himself on the romance community, he might be able to find someone as freaky as him.

I told him his chances would increase if he hung out in the romance section.

I think he's going for it.

Also...last week, Bower moved in with me. It was dumb, having her live one floor above me when she was already spending every night at my place, so she's subletting her apartment to Adalade's new assistant. I think her name is Marlowe, but I might be wrong on that. Either way, she's gotten to know Bower and they hang out every once in a while. Sometimes Bower lends a hand with helping Marlowe on Adalade's likes and dislikes.

And as for Adalade, well, Draco did show up to the dinner party, but it wasn't who Adalade had her eyes on the entire night. Nope, it was a man named Ramond, who brought her flowers and wooed her right off her feet.

They've been on four dates now, and it seems like Adalade might be smitten, at least that's what Bower has told me.

"I think we're ready," Bower says, coming back over to me. "Adalade and Ramond are handing out pamphlets. Gabby and Ryland are poised at the register, and Maple is ready to take pictures at the photo booth." She presses her hand to my chest. "I can't believe we have all these people willing to help."

"I can," I say, tipping her chin up. "You're the type of person people want to help." I lean down and kiss her. "I'm so proud of you, beautiful. So fucking proud."

"Thank you." Her eyes swim with tears.

"Don't cry. Enjoy this moment. It's the beginning of something so much more." I kiss her one more time and then send her on her way to greet all her patrons waiting to be let into the courtyard.

Ryland walks up to me and pats me on the back. "You ready for tonight?"

I stare off at Bower and smile. "I am. Do you have the ring?"

"Protecting it with my life."

"Does Gabby know?"

He chuckles. "No goddamn clue."

"Perfect."

My eyes track Bower's movements, knowing damn well by the end of the night, she will no longer be the girl I lusted after for years with no chance of having. Instead, she'll be my fiancée.

Mine.

For life.

DISCOVER MORE OF MEGHAN QUINN'S HILARIOUS ROM-COMS WITH A SNEAK PEEK AT

PROLOGUE
RENLEY

"WHAT ARE YOU DOING?" I ask the man who's joyfully down on one knee in front of me, a sparkle in his eye and hope in the upturn of his lips.

Dressed impeccably in a bespoke suit, holding out a monstrous engagement ring in a wooden box, is Theodore Williams, properly known as Theo.

British, posh, and delusional…an alarming combination in my opinion.

"What does it look like I'm doing?" he asks, his brown hair curling over his forehead while his clear blue eyes gaze up at me.

"It looks like you're proposing."

His curled smile lights up the front yard of my home where he's firmly planted himself for this momentous occasion. "That would be correct." Then to my horror, he clears his throat and says, "Riley—"

My expression falls flat, while his friend, Rupert, whispers, "It's Renley. Her name is Renley."

Theo's eyes widen. "Oh shit, you're right." Plastering on that charming smile again, he continues in that posh British accent of his. "Pardon me. Renley Henrietta—"

"My middle name is *not* Henrietta."

"It's not?"

"No. It's not."

Confusion laces his brow, his nose scrunching up in a cute way. "What is it?"

I fold my arms over my chest. "It's Lynn."

"Lynn?" He tests that out for a second. "Renley Lynn...Renley Lynn. Are you sure? Because Lynn doesn't sound right."

"I'm positive. It's Lynn."

"Well then, my mistake." Clearing his throat again, he continues. "Renley Lynn Gosling, will you do me the honor—"

"Gossage."

His face contorts in confusion. "Huh?"

"My last name is Gossage."

"Now you're fucking with me." He stands up. "It said on your profile that your last name is Gosling. Like Ryan Gosling."

"No, it didn't. It said Gossage, like Goose Gossage."

"Who the hell is Goose Gossage?" he asks.

"This is very romantic," Rupert says off to the side, looking like he's watching a tennis match, his head bouncing back and forth.

"Richard Michael Gossage, also known as Goose, was a pitcher for the Yankees."

"Oh." Theo shakes his head. "I don't do sports, sweetheart."

"Yeah, I could tell from the leather tassel on your loafer."

He glances down at his shoes. "These are Berlutis."

"That means nothing to me."

"Obviously. I could tell from the paint stains on your threadbare overalls."

Pardon me?

"Not the way to win her over," Rupert mutters from the side of his mouth.

"You're right." Theo takes a deep breath, shakes out his arms, and then gets back down on one knee.

You have got to be kidding me.

Note to self, never drink margaritas with Aunt Kitty, ever again.

Get Aunt Kitty a new tablet that is not cracked so we don't mistake the words *financier* and *fiancé*.

And never give your home address to strangers!

He opens the ring box again, holds it in front of me, and then smiles. "Renley...uh—"

"Lynn," Rupert assists.

"Yes, that's right. Renley Lynn Gossage, will you do me the greatest honor of my life and be my wife?"

"Nice rhyme," Rupert says.

"Thanks, mate," Theo replies, and I swear, that smile of his, reaching from ear to ear, it's gleaming. Actually sparkling.

I have known him for less than a day—yes, *a day*—and I already hate him.

Despise.

Desperately want to take him to my backyard and shove his face into a patch of poison ivy because he's a thorn in my side, a massive disappointment, and everything I hate about a drunken mistake.

"So?" he asks. "Will you be my wife?"

"Absolutely...not."

His expression flattens and he stands tall, snapping the ring box shut. "Why did you have to say it like that? With the pause? That was spiteful. I thought you were saying yes for a moment."

"I told you I didn't want to marry you from the beginning."

"That's not what your profile said."

"Stop bringing up the profile."

"Why would I stop bringing it up when that's the reason I flew across the Atlantic Ocean to be here with you?"

"That was your choice, not mine."

"Uh, it was *your* choice, when you selected 'match.'"

"That's not what I thought I was matching for, and you know it."

He tosses the ring box to Rupert, who catches it, and sheds his suit jacket, throwing it to his friend as well. He undoes the buttons of his shirt and untucks it too.

"What on earth are you doing? If you think getting naked will convince me to marry you, then you have no idea what kind of woman I am."

He scoffs loudly. "I have a lot more respect for myself than to flash you the goods to get you to marry me. It's a bloody heat box in this town and I dressed up for you. I'm not going to stay dressed up if you're going to turn me down."

He sheds his button-up shirt and then exhales loudly before flopping back on the grass of my front yard.

For a moment, and I mean a very small moment, I allow my gaze to travel over the well-defined contours of his chest and the delicious ripple of his abs. Good for him, being able to obtain such an impressive physique. Must be nice to have that amount of time on your hands.

Not that I want to pay him any sort of compliment.

"Rupert, I'm going to need a lemonade instead of tea this afternoon."

"Uh…I'm unaware of when I became a butler?"

Theo lifts up and blocks the sun from his eyes as he says, "Mate, my fiancée just turned down my marriage proposal. I'm hurting. Lemonade is my only cure."

"Oh my God," I say with a giant eye roll. "Can you wallow somewhere else? Your limbs are creeping over onto my neighbor's lawn and I don't want them thinking that I have strange, half-naked British men just lazing about my yard."

"Don't worry, they won't be mad."

"Pretty sure they will be."

"No, they won't." He casts his hands over his face again, blocking out the sun as he looks up at me. "I'm renting their place for the summer. I'm your new neighbor, love."

Wait…what? He's going to be here all summer?

I turned him down, he's "hurting," he should be finding a flight back home.

"And this fiancé is not quite finished with you yet," he adds.

Ohhh, hold on a freaking second.

"What the hell does that mean?"

"It means by the end of the summer, mark my words, you'll be wearing my ring. I'm incredibly persuasive."

Rupert leans in and says, "He is. He once convinced me to run a half-marathon in my mum's best Sunday dress...and heels."

Jesus, these two.

I don't care if he hypnotizes me, there is no way I'm going to marry this man.

No chance.

"Dream all you want, but it's not going to happen. Now, if you'll excuse me, unlike you, I have actual work to do."

As I walk away, Theo calls out from the grass, "Gossy, the British are coming and you have no idea what's about to hit you."

I glance over my shoulder to see him smiling once again. "You're delusional." Then I slip into my house and shut the door, leaning against it as I take a few deep breaths.

Dear God in heaven, where is that tablet? I need to know as much about this man as possible...and I need to order Aunt Kitty a new one.

ABOUT THE AUTHOR

New York Times, #1 Amazon, and *USA Today* bestselling author, wife, adoptive mother, and peanut butter lover. Author of romantic comedies and contemporary romance, Meghan Quinn brings readers the perfect combination of heart, humor, and heat in every book.

Website: authormeghanquinn.com
Facebook: meghanquinnauthor
Instagram: @meghanquinnbooks